Harry Cole was born and brought up in Bermondsey, south London. He left school when he was fourteen, during the war, and became a cricket-bat maker, soldier, stone-mason and, in 1952, a policeman. For thirty years, until his retirement in 1983, he served at the same police station in London.

He is a qualified FA coach, a referee and a keen cricketer. The author of the popular *Policeman* books about life on the beat ('Harry Cole is the police's James Herriot' *Sunday Express*), he has also written two volumes of autobiography.

In 1978 Harry Cole was awarded the British Empire Medal for voluntary work. Since leaving the force, in addition to writing, he has taken up after-dinner speaking.

Queenie

Harry Cole

HEADLINE

Copyright © 1994 Harry Cole

The right of Harry Cole to be identified as the Author of the Work has been asserted by him in accordance with the Copyright, Designs and Patents Act 1988.

First published in 1994
by HEADLINE BOOK PUBLISHING

First published in paperback in 1995
by HEADLINE BOOK PUBLISHING

10 9 8 7 6 5 4 3 2 1

All rights reserved. No part of this publication may be reproduced, stored in a retrieval system, or transmitted, in any form or by any means, without the prior written permission of the publisher, nor be otherwise circulated in any form of binding or cover other than that in which it is published and without a similar condition being imposed on the subsequent purchaser.

All characters in this publication are fictitious and any resemblance to real persons, living or dead, is purely coincidental.

ISBN 0 7472 4727 7

Typeset by Keyboard Services, Luton, Beds

Printed and bound in Great Britain by
Cox & Wyman Ltd, Reading, Berks

HEADLINE BOOK PUBLISHING
A division of Hodder Headline PLC
338 Euston Road
London NW1 3BH

To brother Stan

I would like to thank the following for their invaluable assistance in the completion of this book:

Mary Boast (Southwark historian),
Dave Brooks (naval research and advice),
Mary Clucas and staff of the Scotland Yard Library,
Barbara Garrett of Scotland Yard (for her help and constructive advice),
Robin Gillis and Ken Stone (Metropolitan Police Museum),
Fred Start (for his invaluable knowledge of Queen's Buildings).

Chapter 1

Harry Bartlett announced that the jagged slate he had hurled had gone clean through the seat of the corduroy trousers that hung from the communal washing-line. Charlie Diamond claimed it had missed. A simple enough premise to be sure but Harry was twelve years old, big for his age and aggressive, Charlie was ten, slightly built and thoughtful. Sadly for Charlie, size was not his only problem – he was also wrong. The chance of a large lad repenting when in error is remote, but when he is right, it is nil.

Charlie sighed deeply and took a moment to weigh up the facts. After all, four glass marbles were at stake – not a wager to be taken lightly. The trousers, now hanging sorrowfully from the line, were brother Sam's only pair. True, they'd originally sported a small hole in the seat. Unfortunately, as a result of Harry's unaccustomed accuracy, they now had a rather larger one. All in all, the Diamonds had not done too well over this rash bet. There was the tragic loss of four glass marbles for starters. Then there would be Harry Bartlett's insufferable smugness to contend with. Finally, and by no means least, there was the delicate problem of the trousers. Charlie would grudgingly concede that Sam was as good a brother as a boy could wish for but he also knew he would be unnecessarily touchy about his stupid trousers, especially when they were his only pair. Perhaps the best ploy to adopt would be 'family pride'. He could then thump Harry and indignantly question his honesty. In this way, the undecided amongst their little group might instinctively side with the underdog. He thought it worth a try.

'Bartlett,' he announced, with patently false bravado, 'you're a bleedin' cheat!'

Within seconds, and to the approval of the rest of the gang, they were locked in an arm-flailing embrace. Over and over they tumbled in the noxious grey mud that lay permanently beneath the old backyard tree.

The Diamond washing-line was not the only one attached to the oak; its gnarled trunk radiated them like spokes from a hub. They ran to ground-floor kitchens and third-floor attics; to drain pipes, gas-pipes and sheds. One even snaked its way down to a deep basement scullery. Forty-two families, at the end of two back-to-back streets, hung every pinafore, vest and liberty-bodice from a criss-cross mesh of half-inch sash-cord. This was not, however, the tree's only function. Generations of children had climbed its uppermost branches, having served their apprenticeship by swinging on its lower ones. Arrows, hearts and initials were carved into its tough old bark, most swearing undying love or perhaps just swearing. No one knew how long the old oak had been there, over a century some claimed but it was only a guess. Whatever its age, Inkerman Place, a rambling hotch-potch of assorted dwellings built in a state of post-Crimean euphoria, had grown up around it. By 1907, fifty-three years after the Light Brigade's charge, that euphoria had long vanished. The very name 'Inkerman' was only acknowledged by the sign at either end of the street. Locally it was more appropriately known as 'Gally Ally', an abbreviation of 'Gallows Alley' which had been the even less salubrious structure that had previously dominated the site.

It would have been scant consolation to the fighting Charlie to have known that, though he was receiving the worst of his fight, a couple of miles away on Brixton Hill,

Sam, his idolised older brother and owner of the controversial corduroys, was getting the better of his.

Samuel Obadiah Diamond, who was wearing his father's old trousers, had finally decided he had heard enough jokes about them for one day. He arrived at this conclusion moments before his workmate Jim Forsythe, for the third time, tugged playfully at their ample seat. 'Jim, I'm warning you,' Sam announced. 'You sod me about once more and I'll wallop you!'

This was talk no self-respecting paviour could ignore. Jim reached out and gave the garment another slow deliberate pull. 'Right, you bugger!' snapped Sam. 'You've asked for it!'

The rest of the eight-man paving team turned expectantly towards the sparring duo. 'They're at it again!' came the shout. A scrap between the two was by no means unusual, hardly a day passed without one scuffle or another. Though the best of friends the pair could scrap like sworn enemies. Archie Surridge the foreman usually allowed them to spar for a few minutes before ordering them back into line. After all, because of the repaving work the pavement was already roped off and most passers-by seemed to enjoy watching their brief but intense little bouts. Sam had thrown two quick jabs before Jim settled into his usual easy relaxed style. Though Sam was the stronger, Jim was easily the better boxer. Yet this skill did not always stand him in good stead, particularly if Sam slipped in close and used his much greater strength. It was because of the fight that no one noticed the horse-drawn cab ease slowly into the roped kerbside.

'Oy! You lot!' called down the cabbie. ''Ow abaht clearin' some of this bleedin' junk orf the pavement so a lidy can git 'ome?'

The 'junk' consisted of four huge mallets, an assortment of chisels, hammers, two piles of paving stones and scattered heaps of sand. The 'lidy' consisted of five feet ten inches of magnificent, over-attired, fair-haired womanhood and was poised, as delicately as her statuesque frame would allow, on the footplate of the carriage. The interest of the young paving team was instantly transferred from the verbal encouragement of the fighters to a silent, open-mouthed admiration of the new arrival. Even the combatants dropped their fists and joined the worshipping group. The silence was finally broken by Archie Surridge. 'It's Billie,' he breathed reverently.

'Bill who?' whispered an adolescent voice.

'B-i-l-l-i-e, you idiot,' emphasised Archie, 'Billie Bardell to be exact, she's appearing at the South London Palace this week. She's bloody wonderful and I love every inch!'

Though half of the team had heard of Miss Bardell, only Archie had previously seen her. The whole gang appeared to be making up for this neglect by staring in mute fascination. A further request from the cabbie was drowned by the rattle of a passing tram, yet not even the proximity of this noisy monster could break the spell. Resigned to their inaction, the new arrival finally stepped down from the footplate and on to the granite kerbstone.

Sam was first to shout a warning but it was already too late. The stone had been laid simply as a guide line and not secured in any way. Immediately the soft leather, elegantly buttoned boot touched the kerbstone, it rolled almost leisurely over. Before anyone could move, the woman pitched forward and she fell first on to the stretched rope, then, rolling off a pile of paving stones, came to rest face down in a pile of wet sand. 'Bloody hell!' exploded Archie, moving towards the prostrate female. But he was too late. Sam had preceded him by a full second.

Slipping a hand beneath the woman's left shoulder, he rolled her on to her back. Other than a graze to her knuckles, a smudge on her face and the ruination of her dignity, she appeared unharmed but her battered hat and confused expression made Sam want to burst out laughing. He hid his amusement with difficulty then realised she was still quite dazed and not fully aware of what had happened. Her showy feather-adorned hat now covered her eyes and yellow sand caked the rest of her face. As she opened her mouth, even more sand could be seen on her tongue, between her lips and all around her large white teeth.

'Are you all . . .' began the youth. Further inquiries to her welfare were interrupted by an explosion of spluttering as she sprayed him with a fine shower of best builder's sand. Suddenly Sam realised that this woman spitting sand all over him was not just a star of the music hall but was unquestionably the most glorious creature he had ever seen. The image of a goddess flooded into his mind. He remembered it from a book he had once seen at school. The goddess had been tall, fair and stately with a frilly white dress and a perfect complexion. Billie may have been a mite more buxom and a few years older but the similarity was obvious. Yes, that was it – a goddess. Anyone that beautiful could only be a goddess, or at least a goddess's big sister. Cradling her head protectively to his chest, he withdrew a large red spotted handkerchief from his pocket and made to wipe away the worst of the sand from her face. Blinking it from her eyes, the goddess gave one last great ten-second splutter and angrily knocked away the handkerchief.

'Get orf me, you bleedin' oaf!' she ordered, pounding his chest. 'Not satisfied with pushing me on me face, now you dump me on me arse and try to stuff that rotten rag in me mouth. Pull me up, you sod! Pull me up at once, d'you hear?'

Sam froze. Goddess she may be, lady she wasn't. Instead of pulling her to her feet he removed his arm quickly from beneath her, causing her to fall back once more on to the sand. She let out a frustrated squeal and furiously kicked her feet. Jim Forsythe had begun to find his friend's discomfort amusing, whilst the rest of the team remained in silent awe. Archie was the first to gather his wits. Apart from seeing his idol pushed off her pedestal, he could see his own dismissal looming very large.

'Er, here, Miss Bardell,' he faltered nervously as he stretched out a helping hand. 'Allow me.'

After four determined attempts, she finally retrieved a solid lump of sand from somewhere in the region of her adenoids. This she expelled vengefully over the grovelling foreman. 'Are you in charge of this bleedin' lot by some mischance?'

'Er, yes, Miss Bardell, I'm afraid I am.'

'Oh "afraid", are you?' she asked sarcastically. 'Well, I don't wonder you're afraid. Who wouldn't be? If I was in charge of *this* soddin' lot, I'd be scared to soddin' death!'

The woman had almost struggled to her feet when she gave a loud cry and, with lips pursed in pain, drew in a sharp breath whilst clutching dramatically at her left hip. 'Blimey, that hurt!'

'What can I do, Miss Bardell?' begged Archie almost tearfully. 'Just tell me where you live and I'll have the boys carry you indoors.'

'No bleedin' fear!' she snapped, 'I'm not havin' your lot clumping about all over my place – I'm not that heavy. One of 'em will do. Get him, that silly bugger who buried me in the sand. He's big enough to carry me on his own.' She nodded towards a flight of steps just beyond the pavement. 'Anyway, I only live there, number 200. Least, that's where I live at the moment but if your lot's goin' to be working here much longer, I shall probably bugger off to Hampstead.'

Archie Surridge decided it was time to assert his authority. 'Diamond!' he called curtly. 'Carry this lady up those steps immediately.'

'No,' answered Sam curtly.

'Diamond, do as you're told . . . please?' Archie's voice

had softened noticeably. 'Now come on, Sam, be a good lad. After all, if you hadn't been fighting in the first place, none of this would have happened, would it?'

'Don't worry, Arch, leave her to me, I'll have her indoors in no time,' offered Jim Forsythe. He turned to the still smouldering music hall star and bowed with mock gallantry, 'It'll be a pleasure, ma'am.'

'No you won't!' growled Sam, still smarting from his friend's insolent attitude towards the communal Diamond trousers. '*I'll* do it.'

'Well I sincerely 'opes one of you buggers does it, and quick!' called down the cabbie. ''Cos I ain't bin paid yet.'

'Oh Gawd, I forgot you!' exclaimed the woman as she rummaged around in her purse. 'Here,' she said, thrusting a half-crown piece into the foreman's hand. 'Give him this.'

'How much change d'you want, Miss Bardell?' asked the impressed Archie, whose most expensive journey in his whole forty years had been a two-shilling return on a Wapping paddle steamer.

'That's all right, he can keep it,' she replied with an air of casual indifference. If Archie Surridge had been impressed before he was almost laid low by this gesture of magnanimity. His later recounting of it was to bore his family for weeks.

Miss Billie Bardell, voluptuous ageless star of many of London's finest music halls, graciously lifted her left arm at the approach of the powerful young paviour. She assumed he was going to drape her child-like across his arms and carry her up the front steps. In fact, Sam reached for the proffered arm, then, tugging it towards him, bent swiftly forward. He straightened instantly and with the fair Billie slung sack-like over his right shoulder, began to pace the few yards towards the front steps of number 200.

'You've got some sauce you have, lady,' he called over his unencumbered shoulder. '"I'm not *that* heavy,"' he mimicked in a falsetto voice. 'Not much you ain't! You weigh more than our paving department's mare.'

Quickly realising struggle was futile, the woman changed her ploy. With both hands she seized the ample seat of the Diamond trousers, by then almost in front of her face, and tore at them frantically. 'You reckon *I've* got some cheek!' she echoed. 'How about this then? Anyone who wears trousers like this must *be* the bleedin' mare!'

Ignoring her struggles, Sam began the climb of the half dozen or so spotless white steps that led up to a wide portico. As he reached the final step, the large, white-painted, brass-trimmed door swung open. A fair and petite uniformed maid stood wide-eyed in the entrance. Sam's first thought was that she was the prettiest girl he'd ever laid eyes on. He couldn't believe the last few moments. Females hadn't bothered him unduly before, yet within the space of five minutes he had been almost knocked sideways by two of them – and from the same house!

Before he could speak the girl rushed forward and pulled down the ruffled hem of Billie's full-length dress to conceal some six inches of white-stockinged calf. 'Oh, Miss Bardell.' she cried anxiously. 'Whatever's the matter?'

Tearing his eyes from the maid, Sam glanced quickly around for a suitable spot to deposit his burden. He saw it in the large red plush armchair that stood invitingly at the foot of a picture-lined staircase. Leaning forward, he gave a slight heave with his shoulder and dumped the woman neatly in the chair. 'Here y'are, miss,' he announced to the maid. 'Clean her up and she's all yours – and welcome y'are to her. Oh, and while you're at it, wash her mouth out with carbolic, will you? She definitely ain't the lady she looks.'

He was almost at the door before Billie spoke again. When she did it was in a voice he had not heard her use before. Her accent had all but disappeared. Until that moment her dialogue had been one with which he was all too familiar. It had been that of a confident, quick-witted, cockney street girl. Now her tone was much more authoritative, almost commanding. It gave the young man a strange feeling of unease, 'Wait!' she ordered. 'Come back here. I wish to speak with you.'

If her tone caused him to stop, his pride prevented him from turning. For a moment he stood with hand outstretched towards the door. 'Come back here,' she repeated. 'I said, I wish to speak with you.'

He turned and walked the short distance back to her chair where, feet astride and hands on hips, he stood defiantly before her. But it was a pose and they both knew it.

'There's something I must ask you. Something personal. Do you mind?'

Sam suddenly felt uneasy. No one had ever spoken to him quite like this.

'I'll send Queenie upstairs for a minute if you wish?' She gave the maid a hint of a glance and the girl turned dutifully towards the staircase.

'No, let her stay,' replied Sam with embarrassing haste. 'I ain't afraid of no "personal" questions.'

'Sure?'

'O' course I'm sure.' In fact he was anything *but* sure, yet could see no way out of the trap he had stupidly walked into.

'Very well.' She nodded. 'There's something that puzzles me about you . . . puzzles me very much in fact. You *seem* a bright enough young man and you are certainly quick enough on the uptake. On a dark foggy night and at a fair distance, you could even pass for good-looking.' She turned to the girl, 'Wouldn't you say so, Queenie?'

The maid smiled. 'It would have to be a *particularly* foggy night, Miss Bardell, and *quite* a fair distance though,' she teased.

'Yet . . .' The woman paused as if she had neither asked a question nor heard the reply, but it was a contrived pause and Sam was as aware of that as she had been of his pose, though this did not stop him from blushing. 'Sam, tell me . . .' she leaned forward intimately and stared intently into his face '. . . why do you wear those bleedin' awful trousers?'

Sam knew by the maid's suppressed chuckle and the woman's shout of laughter that he had just been made to pay for the indignity he had inflicted upon her. Whatever his reply he knew he must not lose his temper. Being aware of that fact was easy, acting upon it was a totally different matter. At least, it was for Sam.

'I wear these trousers, Miss High-and-bloody-mighty, because while mine are being washed I don't have any others. There are eleven of us in my family and only me and one of my sisters are working. My dad has TB so I'm wearing his old railway trousers . . . he's not got long, so he won't need them again, you see. We're not all like you, you know.' He waved one arm. 'Pictures on the wall, carpets and a maid. D'you know what all the kids in my family are doing at the moment, have been doing all day and will be doing till midnight? Well, do you?'

The woman lay back in the chair and stared at him with bored indifference. She gave the slightest shake of her head. 'They'll all be clustered round the kitchen table making paper windmills to sell to a stall-holder at the Blackheath Whitsun Fair next Monday. There, now ain't that something?'

'I thought perhaps they might have been at school,' she reproved quietly.

'They will be, they will be! I'm talking about *after* they come home from school, you selfish know-nothing cow!' he exploded.

'Well, well, now. Aren't you the unfortunate one then?' she mocked. 'And just where d'you think this lot came from?' She gestured around her. 'D'you think it fell out of the sky? Or perhaps you think some toff gave it me?' Her eyes narrowed as she shook her head angrily and pointed a finger directly at him.

'Don't you *dare* give me your bloody hard luck stories, lad. I was born and raised in Seven Dials and that's the shithouse of the world! I made my mind up very early I would drag myself out of it. All I'm suggesting is that you get yourself a different pair of trousers. I don't want to hear about your sad little life. I'm not interested, mate. Look . . .' She paused and sighed, her voice changing tone yet again. 'I don't want to row with you, Sam. All I'm trying to do is to get over to you that you should have a little pride in yourself. I'm sure that deep down you do have it – it's just that the way you dress, it doesn't look like it. After all, you can't expect people to take you seriously, not with the arse of your trousers swinging around like a bag of your own bleedin' sand, now can you, eh?'

At first it looked certain that the young man would go straight for her throat but suddenly his anger evaporated. His left hand dropped to his backside where he found himself tugging self-consciously at the slack material. 'Anyway,' he muttered, 'it's only for a little while. My mum's washing and patching my own trousers today. Providing it stays sunny, they'll be as good as new tomorrow, you'll see.'

'*Patching* did you say?' she asked in horror. 'Are you telling me that at your age . . . how old are you?'

'Twenty.'

'That at twenty years of age, you only have one pair of trousers and they're *patched*! Is that what you're telling me?'

He nodded.

'Good God, no wonder you're such a touchy bugger! Listen, can you stay for a cup of tea?'

'No, I must get back to work, they'll be wondering what's happened to me.'

'Oh, don't worry about them! If your foreman says

anything, refer him to me. I'll threaten to sue for negligence, that'll keep him quiet.' She looked up at the maid who had remained interested though impassive throughout the verbal exchanges. 'Stick the kettle on, Queenie, we'll have our tea in the parlour.' The girl smiled and gave the slightest of nods before disappearing through an oak-panelled door at the rear of the staircase.

'Come on, you,' said Billie cheerily. 'Come into the parlour – but take those bleedin' boots off first!' Placing both hands on the arms of the chair, she eased herself painfully to her feet. 'Christ, but my hip hurts. I think I will sue that fool of a foreman, whether he calls here or not.'

'Can I help you at all?' asked Sam, for the first time showing genuine concern.

She raised her left arm. 'Well, you can give me a hand into the parlour – and no bloody wrestling tricks this time, mind.'

'I'm sorry, miss, really I am,' stammered Sam. 'I didn't realise . . .' His voice trailed away and he shrugged helplessly.

As she slipped her arm over his grimy, collarless shirt, he eased his around her well-corseted waist. The clean, perfumed smell of her suddenly made him tremble. 'Here, don't you fall over,' she chided. 'I'm relying on you. You're the one whose going to get me on the stage tonight.'

'On stage!'

They had reached a red leather-covered day-bed close by the large bay window. Sam eased her gently down. On the footway outside he could see his workmates industriously making up the time he had lost them.

'Oh, don't worry,' she assured him, 'I'm just pulling your leg. But the fact is that I'm on stage in two different halls tonight and this hip's going to be a hell of a problem if it doesn't improve.'

'I don't understand, how can you possibly be in two halls in one evening?'

'Bless you, lad, I've been in *three* before now, especially when they've been close together. Tonight I shall be closing the first half at the South London Palace near the Elephant and Castle. I shall have a cab standing by and then go straight to the Canterbury in Westminster Bridge Road, where I'm the last act before Harry Champion's finale – that's a good billing, I can tell you,' she said proudly. 'How would you like to come with me? I shall need a big lad like you to carry me to and fro.'

For the second time in five minutes Sam felt his face turn crimson. 'No . . . I don't think so, thank you very much.'

'Why?'

'Well, because—' His voice faltering, he made two more attempts to explain before shrugging his shoulders.

'Wouldn't be that you have no suitable clothes by any chance?'

'No, it's not that at all,' he lied sharply. 'It's just something I can't see myself doing.'

'You're like bleedin' Cinderella you are, only happy when you're in rags and cinders. Oh, well, suit yourself, but you're not a very good liar, are you, Sam?'

'Look, I really must get back to work,' he answered, pointedly ignoring the question.

'You are staying for tea surely? Queenie's almost made it now.'

'No, really, I can't. I must go. The supervisor is due soon,' he lied. 'It wouldn't be fair on Mister Surridge. In any case, can't your maid help you? She looks a competent enough girl.'

'Oh, she's competent right enough, none better,' agreed Billie. 'But she ain't very big and it'd do nothing for my image. I don't want no slim young girls helping me in public – I want big men.' The woman lowered her voice and winked provocatively. 'And you *are* a big man, aren't you, Sam?'

He made no reply but once more felt himself redden.

'In any case, Queenie is doing her own "turn" tonight. She's quite a little mystery girl is that one. You must get her to tell you about it sometime.'

'Whatever is it?' asked the puzzled Sam.

'It's not something I approve of, I can tell you. But then, it's her business . . .' Billie gave an exaggerated shrug. 'So there you are. Sure I can't persuade you to change your mind about this evening? I'd pay you well and I think you'd really enjoy it.'

'It's very kind of you, but no.'

She gave a long sigh 'It's your loss, me old son, but will you just pass me that handbag afore you go?' She pointed to a small white bag that lay on top of a writing bureau. Sam stared at it but hesitated for a moment. 'It's quite all right,' she assured him. 'I'm not going to insult you by offering money if that's what's bothering you. I've already learnt better than that.'

He passed the bag and she rummaged for a few seconds before producing four small calling cards.

'Here, take these.'

'What are they?' he asked suspiciously.

'What do they look like, for Gawd's sake?' she asked irritably. 'They're my calling cards, of course. Why are you always so bloody suspicious? If you produce them at the South London Palace box office just before the show tonight, they'll give you four complimentary seats.' She glanced up at the rosewood wall clock. 'Right, if you won't drink my tea or massage me bruise then hop it, because I'm going to have my customary two hours nap before the show. That's if I manage to get any sleep with this hip you've broken.'

Sam took the cards but still appeared doubtful. 'It's all right,' she insisted, 'if it makes you feel any better you can buy your own programme. Now clear off and give me a good round of applause tonight. Queenie will see you out.

QUEENIE!' she called. 'Show Galahad to the door . . . and don't molest him, mind, 'cos he's shy.'

Sam, unfamiliar with the name of Galahad, knew yet again that she was mocking him. He turned angrily towards her but her smile had returned and she tipped him the sauciest of winks. 'See you tonight, Sam. Oh, by the way, you'll change those trousers, I hope?'

'How did you get on, Sam?' 'What did she say to you?' 'Is it really posh in there?' 'Whose that little sweetheart who saw you to the door?'

The questions flew thick and fast as the young man rejoined his workmates on the footway.

'Well, it's all right, I s'pose,' he sniffed with a pathetically false air of indifference, 'I've seen better. Now, which of you would like to come to the South London Palace tonight? And you don't have to worry 'cos the treat's on me!'

Chapter 2

The tram rattled swiftly along Blackfriars Road – but not swiftly enough for the impatient young paviour. Still fifty yards from the official stop, he dutifully dropped his ticket in the collecting box and, to a chorus of abuse from the carters behind, leapt wide from the crowded platform. Twisting and turning between streams of laden vehicles, he avoided injury by the dexterity of his footwork though, fast as this was, it still wasn't enough for him to avoid the lightning lash of an old carter's whip. Bobbing and weaving, with a hand on his now scorching ear, he disappeared quickly down a sunless alley.

Number 14 Inkerman Place was a tiny two-up, two-down dwelling that backed on to a rectangle of four streets, each of identical dimensions. Sam had approached via the narrow alley that criss-crossed every back yard. As he passed, he glanced up at the old tree. There were six youngsters playing in its branches but not a Diamond amongst them. Entering the house through the kitchen door, he soon saw the reason. Huddled around the bare scrubbed table were seven Diamonds of varying ages, earnestly engaged in glueing, cutting and shaping.

'Sam's home, Mum!' the cry went up. Each greeted him eagerly, their reason not so much friendly as self-interested. Since he had become the senior breadwinner, mealtimes had revolved around his presence rather than that of any other member of the family including their father, John.

'I'm in, Ma!' he called. The announcement was the signal for little Maisie, duty toaster for the day, to take up position in front of the old kitchen range with a long, copper-wired fork. 'Don't burn the crusts, Maisie, d'you hear?' came the routine call of Mrs Nellie Diamond from the scullery.

According to the unwritten rule of the household, those in work received a 'knife-and-fork' tea. This could be kippers, a sheep's head or a pair of pig's trotters. Those not in gainful employment would have what Nell Diamond chose to call 'a relish'. This could be jam, dripping, or as a real treat a herring roe. As head of the household, John Diamond was immune from these strict rules and on at least three evenings a week would ritually dissect a plump pair of best Yarmouth bloaters. Nell, on the other hand, would stay with her relish which, on Monday, was always dripping toast. Jane, third in the pecking order and the second highest wage-earner, worked as a machinist at Spenser's, the local printers, and had arrived home just minutes before Sam. A place at Spenser's was much sought after. The work, though tedious, was well paid and more than one Inkerman Place household knew the dubious advantages of a skilled daughter earning more than her labouring father.

With everyone finally in place the meal was served. 'Bloaters tonight, Sam, all right?' asked Nell Diamond anxiously. He nodded a gracious assent. After Billie Bardell and Queenie, bloaters sounded terribly mundane. He was anxious for everyone to sit down so he could recite the story. Toast was still being scraped when he began. 'Guess who I saw today, Dad?' The question may have been courteously addressed to his father but was for general interest. The old man gave a shrug of feigned indifference.

'Who, Sam? Who did yer see?' asked Maisie eagerly.

'Don't speak with your mouth full and the word is "you", not "yer",' cut in Nell. 'Even so, Sam, who was it?'

'Billie Bardell,' he announced proudly. 'And she invited me in for tea . . . just me, mind, no one else.'

It was immediately obvious that only his parents and possibly the two eldest girls had the faintest idea who he was talking about. 'She's a famous music hall star,' added Sam huffily, conveniently forgetting his own earlier ignorance. 'You *must* know her surely?'

At this insistence from an idolised elder brother, the youngsters tactfully decided they knew the famous Billie after all. 'Of course! We remember her now,' agreed Kate on behalf of the formerly uninitiated.

'Anyway, what did she want with the likes of you?' asked old John with surly interest.

'I carried her home after she'd hurt herself and she gave me four tickets for her show tonight at the South London Palace. Me and Jim Forsythe are going and we're taking our foreman Archie because he's . . .' Sam paused and raised an eyebrow. 'Well, he's quite barmy over her. I've got one ticket left if you'd care to come, Dad?'

'No, thank you,' snapped the old man curtly. 'And if you take my advice, you won't go either.'

'Well, I'm only going to see the show,' protested the young man defensively. 'I'm not eloping with her. Anyway, what's she supposed to have done?'

'What's she done?' echoed his father bitterly. 'She's betrayed her class, that's what she's done. Strutting around on a stage half-dressed . . . she's nothing but a tart. It's degrading to decent working-class womanhood, that's what it is!'

'What?'

'The way she performs.'

'You've seen her then?'

'Don't you *dare* try to trap me with words, boy!' thundered the old man as he pounded the table and kicked back his chair. 'No, *I haven't* seen her, and what's more, I wouldn't be seen in the same street as her, let alone pay good money for the privilege. And, if you've got any sense at all, neither will you!'

'I take it all that means you won't be coming?' said Sam acidly. 'How about you, Ma?'

Nell shook her head vehemently. 'Wouldn't be right, Sam, wouldn't be right.' She turned to her husband. 'The boy's still young, John, he didn't mean no harm. Come on,' she soothed. 'Sit yourself down, you know you mustn't get upset.' Reaching out, she placed a gentle, restraining hand on his wrist. Breathing rapidly, he allowed her to ease him back into his chair. The frail truce was immediately shattered by an eager Kate's begging: 'Please take me, Sam. Oh, go on, please! I've always wanted to go to a music hall.'

He shrugged. 'Well, if Mum and Dad won't come . . .'

The offer was interrupted as the old man jumped once more to his feet. 'She's not going to no music hall, especially one featuring that painted whore, so get that into your head, will you?'

'But, Dad—' began Sam.

'Don't you "but Dad" me. Kate's starting a new job tomorrow morning at the market. She starts at five o'clock so she's certainly not going to a music hall tonight and that's final!'

'Oh, please, Dad. Please!' begged the girl. 'I'd get up in time, I promise.'

'Oh, you'd get up all right, young lady, I'd see to that. The question is, what state would you be in when you did? You'd never be able to hold down a job if you arrive half asleep on your first morning. The matter's closed, we'll hear no more of it.'

'I'll get her back early, Dad, I promise,' pledged Sam.

'You promise! You promise!' echoed the old man furiously. 'It's not down to you to promise anything! I'm her father and as long as she's under my roof she'll obey my rules. I may not be fetching any money into this house but I'm still the head of it and don't you forget it. If you must take someone, take Jane, she's a wage-earner, she has a right to go.' He crashed his fist down on to the table. 'Now that's an end of it, I say, we'll have no more talk at this table.'

A heavy silence hung over the remainder of the meal, with the first words nervously spoken by Jane. 'Please, Dad, may we all leave the table?'

The old man grunted his assent and the chairs all slid back in unison. It was as Nell and Jane piled the plates in the scullery sink that panic suddenly struck Sam. His trousers! What if they had not been repaired? 'Are my cords patched, Mum? I'll need them tonight.'

'No, Sam,' came the dreaded reply. 'I'm afraid they're not. The kids threw stones at them this afternoon and I had to wash them again. They're still wet.'

'But, Mum, they *have* to be ready! I've only got Dad's old trousers to my name! Look at the bloody things, will you?' he tugged angrily at the seat. 'They're not even fit for paviouring, never mind the music hall. Oh, come on,' he pleaded. 'Can't you just iron them or something?'

'Sam, I tell you, they're wringing wet. They won't even be dry by the morning. There's absolutely no way you can wear them tonight.'

'Nell!' Old John's hoarse voice suddenly rang round the house. 'Nell, I'm going to The Feathers. I shall be back soon after ten o'clock, and when I am, I shall expect to see everyone except those fetching in a wage, working on the windmills. Have you got that?' Without waiting for a reply, he slammed the door and was gone.

'Can't you have a word with him, Ma?' appealed Sam.

'He's getting worse. Jane is nineteen, for God's sake! He can't keep ruling her life like this.'

'I know Sam, I know,' she soothed. 'But you must bear with him. Your father is a very worried man. He is also very ill. But, listen, I don't want to talk about that for the moment. Has he definitely gone?'

'He slammed the door loud enough.'

'Good. Wait here a moment, I have an idea.'

Leaving a puzzled Sam and Jane, Nell hurried down the passage and up the stairs. Within minutes she had returned with a large brown paper bag that smelt strongly of mothballs. 'Let's see what they look like against you.' She removed from the bag a pair of neatly folded pin-stripe trousers. Sam recognised them instantly. 'That's part of Dad's best suit!' he whispered. 'What are you doing with it?'

'Just stand up straight and mind your own business.' She held them to his waist for a moment before turning thoughtfully to Jane. 'If I put a quick tuck in the waist he could wear them tonight at the Palace. What d'you think?'

'What!' exclaimed a horror-stricken Sam. 'I wouldn't dare! Supposin' he was to find out? He'd skin me . . . you too!'

'He *won't* find out,' cut in Nell. 'He only wears them when he goes out posh, and he's not done that since he's been ill. He's hardly likely to put his best suit on when he comes home from the pub tonight, now is he?'

'That's right,' agreed Jane excitedly. 'In fact, Sam may as well use the whole suit if it fits. After all, if Dad won't be needing the trousers, he won't be needing the rest of it either.'

'But I can't wear Dad's best suit,' protested Sam. 'I'm not that brave, if he found out he'd kill me.'

'That's the very point,' explained Nell, now revelling in the whole conspiracy, 'he won't find out. All you have to do is leave your old trousers and jacket under the stairs. Then, when you return tonight, change into them and leave your father's clothes in their place. I can put them back upstairs tomorrow morning when he's shaving . . . here, you don't fancy using his bowler hat as well, do you?'

Sam's arrival outside the South London Palace, wearing his father's suit and his attractive sister on his arm, caused his two friends to gape in astonishment. He enjoyed the effect immensely.

'Sam!' exclaimed Archie. 'I never knew you were such a dandy. You're as smart as . . .' He paused and racked his brains frantically for a smart person. 'You're smart as Clem Botwright the undertaker! Yes, that's it, you're as smart as old Clem.'

Even Jim Forsythe grudgingly approved. 'Not bad, Sam boy, though that bowler hat don't do you no favours. Perhaps you ought'a left it on the corpse. Still, credit where it's due. If Archie thinks you look like an undertaker, I'll go along with that.'

Sam blushed at the words. Dubious praise it may have been but it was an accolade compared to what had passed before. 'But then, if you look a toff,' Jim added, 'Jane looks a lady. Absolutely every inch a lady – and much too pretty to be your sister.' The girl dutifully dropped her gaze but made little attempt to hide the glow of pleasure flooding her face.

Introductions over, Sam presented the cards at the box office and the four made their way eagerly to their seats. Row A seats 1, 2, 3 and 4 proved as good as they sounded. They were situated at the extreme left side of the gallery. The seating narrowed at this point to just a single row. The curvature of this placed the quartet almost immediately above the orchestra pit and barely inches away from the first of the two boxes. With twenty minutes to curtain up, they eagerly watched the comings and goings beneath them in the stalls and pit.

'Who else is on the bill?' asked Jim, glancing across at Archie's programme.

'There's Victoria Monks for starters . . . she's great.'

'What does she do?'

'Sings mainly: "Bill Bailey", "Call Round Any Old Time", songs like that.'

'Who else?'

'Harry Weldon, he's a comic. Oh, and there's one 'specially for you, Sam – Billy Williams.'

'Why me?' asked the puzzled Sam.

'Well, it's the title of his speciality song. You'll never guess what it's called.'

Sam's eyes narrowed suspiciously. 'Go on?' he murmured.

Archie smiled nervously. 'It's called, "Go and Put Your Trousers On, John!"'

'You really enjoyed that, didn't you?' asked Sam wryly. 'Anyway, is there anyone else we should know, besides Billie of course.'

'Yeh, this should be interesting.' Archie read in silence for some seconds. 'There's a bloke called Eugene Sandow. It says here he's the strongest man in the world. I wonder what he does?'

'Perhaps he only smells strong?' suggested Sam.

'We're in trouble if he does,' pointed out Jim. 'We couldn't be much closer to the stage!'

Further conversation was interrupted by a flat rasping voice behind them. 'Which o' you lot is Sam Diamond?'

Sam turned to face a tall, powerfully built, heavily moustached man with small fierce eyes, little or no neck and a distinctive hooked nose that made him resemble an enormous kestrel. Sam's first reaction was one of instant dislike.

'Who wants to know?' he asked curtly.

'Speakin' personally,' snarled the kestrel, 'I don't give a shovel of 'orse shit. But Miss Bardell's asked me if I'd bring 'im to 'er dressin' room for a few minutes a'fore curtain up.' The messenger stared Sam straight in the eye and gave a slight nod. 'You 'im?'

Sam responded with an even slighter nod.

'Then don't sod me about, son, I ain't got all night. You comin' or ain't yer?'

Resentment oozed from the young paviour. 'Go on, Sam,' urged Jim. 'If you don't go, I will.' Aware this approach would be more likely to motivate his friend than any other, he continued, 'I think she fancies me anyway.'

The ploy worked perfectly. Sam sprang quickly to his feet.

'Follow me an' look lively,' snapped the newcomer. 'It's curtain up in ten minutes.'

Sam found the back-stage confusion a startling contrast to the comparative orderliness of the auditorium. There the audience had meandered sedately to their seats, either in pairs or small groups, but behind the heavy red curtain pandemonium reigned. Everyone appeared to be running in different directions. 'This way,' ordered the rasping voice as the man descended a tiny staircase. There was a thud as Sam's forehead struck a low lintel. 'Oh, yeah, mind yer 'ead.'

The staircase led into a corridor that turned towards a door with flaking grey paint. The man knocked and opened it in one fluent movement. 'I've got 'is nibs outside, Billie luv, what d'you want done with 'im?'

'Thanks, Frank. Show him in, will you, please.'

'Okay, sweet. Anything else you want?' Sam noticed how the man's whole demeanour changed the instant he spoke to Billie.

'No thanks,' she said. 'In any case, it's time you were changing for your own act.'

'Anything for you, my lovely, y'know that. Shall I see you later for a drink?'

'Not this week, I'm afraid, Frank. I'm doing a second stint at the Canterbury. Some other time perhaps.'

'Okay, sweetheart.' He turned to the young man who still stood motionless in the open door. 'In 'ere, you,' he commanded, propelling Sam into the room by his lapel. 'And behave yerself with the lady, understand?' Without waiting for a reply he departed, slamming the door behind him.

The dressing room was much smaller than Sam had imagined and was incredibly untidy. He found this surprising, contrasting as it did with the calm order of Billie's own home. Perhaps there was no little Queenie to pander to the star's whim here. He glanced quickly around. There was no sign of Billie.

'Sit yourself down, Sam lad, there's some gin on the table if you fancy a quick 'un.' He turned towards the voice and realised in that gloomy room, he had not noticed a small set of screens, painted the same drab grey as the walls. 'You'll have to forgive me for receiving you like this but Frank does have a maddening habit of knocking and entering at the same time.'

'Can't you lock the door?'

She laughed loudly, 'There's not a lock in the place, luv. In any case, the room isn't just mine, you know, there are two other turns. Fortunately they're both doing the first half at the Canterbury. Anyway, how do you like your seats?' she asked, emerging from behind the screens. 'I chose them 'specially, they're the closest gallery seats to the stage.'

Sam gaped. Because she had been concealed behind the screen, he had assumed she would emerge dressed. But, other than the time he had called on Jim Forsythe unexpectedly and stumbled on both Jim's sisters strip-washing in the scullery, he had never before seen so much female flesh. Eye-opening though the previous occasion had been, he had to admit that two Forsythe girls did not make a single Bardell woman.

'Close your mouth, Sam, or you'll collect flies,' chided the half-naked Billie as she strode quickly across the room towards him.

The young man felt the colour flood to his cheeks as he looked quickly away from the corseted, high-heeled, stocking-clad woman. 'And don't you start going all shy on me, Sam Diamond, 'cos I've gotta use for you. Here, pull this tight.' She turned her back on him, then, taking and holding an enormous deep breath, squared her plump bare shoulders. The criss-cross cords of the black satin corselet swung loosely down from the small of her back. Sam took both cords nervously, gently pulling on each of them. His effort was so weak that she rapidly expelled most of the breath that had been stored in her powerful lungs.

'Bloody hell, Sam! Give it a tug, for Chrissake! You won't hurt me, you know, I'm a big girl. Right, when I say NOW – really pull the bloody thing. Ready?' She took another great gulp of air. 'NOW!'

There were no half measures in the young man's second attempt and he salvaged at least an extra three inches of cord from the lace holes as the garment bit deep into cool pink flesh. 'Phew! Can you tie a neat bow?' she gasped over her perfumed shoulder.

'I s'pose so.'

'Good. Make it as neat as you can, but for Gawd's sake make it *secure*. I don't want me tits popping out when I lean over the footlights, or the Lord Chamberlain will have a bleedin' fit.'

'You don't go on stage dressed like this, do you?' asked the still embarrassed Sam.

'O' course not! I wear a dress, you idiot.' She pointed to the back of the door where a low-cut, heavily fringed red dress hung from a large wooden hanger. 'Now . . . join me in a drink? I want a quick word with you, m'lad.' She poured herself out a measure of gin that would have laid him low for a week.

He shook his head. 'No thanks, I don't like gin. So what is it you want?'

'Look, I'm afraid I'm going to have to talk whilst I'm dressing, okay?' Without waiting for an answer she continued, 'We have a bloke on the bill this week called Eugene Sandow, The World's Strongest Man. He's been playing the halls for years and Frank Cootes, who you've just met, is his assistant. Anyway, during the interval they run a competition. It's sponsored by Sandow's the herbalists. Anyone who wins on the night receives a thumping good meal at the eel and pie shop opposite. They also go through to the grand final at the end of the week with a chance of winning five gold sovereigns. How about that, Sam?'

'How about what?'

'The competition, you fool! Why d'you think I'm telling you?'

'I'm not entering. In the first place I wouldn't win, and in the second, I couldn't go on the stage to save my life.'

'Sam, you would win, I'm sure of it. I've seen many of these competitions and most of the competitors are pissy-arsed drunks. If nothing else you'd be in with a good chance.'

Bending towards him, she momentarily disappeared as she tugged the dress over her head. Emerging, her exertions had caused her corselet to slip and she had all but popped out of the bodice. Firmly gripping the top of the garment, she pulled it away from her breasts and, with a series of flesh-quivering ripples, eased her torso back down into its rightful place. 'Bloody hell!' she panted. 'The room's going round. I've either got to get a bigger bleedin' corselet or lay off the gin. It gets more difficult every week.'

Recovering both breath and composure, she stepped within a pace of him and, placing her hands on her hips, feet firmly astride, squared up at him. 'Well, Sam, do I pass muster?'

The young man was transfixed. This woman was like nothing he had ever experienced before. Even within the short time he had known her, she had shown herself a mistress of many guises. Common she most certainly could be, fat she practically was, young she certainly wasn't, yet, as he stared at her full round face, her room-brightening smile and proud voluptuous bearing, he suddenly thought her the most magnificent creature he had ever seen. As he stared in silent worship her expression suddenly changed. Her eyes and mouth opened wide. 'Sam!' she exploded. 'Oh, Sam, I've only just noticed – don't you look a toff! You look a right little stage-door Johnny. Where did you get the clobber from?'

Before he could answer, the distant sound of the orchestra could be heard tuning up in the pit. 'Look, Sam, I don't have much time. I must go through a couple of things with the conductor. Will you enter the competition or not?'

'No!'

She gave an irritable shrug. 'Suit yourself, you miserable sod. I thought you might be able to do with the money. Who knows? You might have been able to buy yourself another good suit. Anyway, I'm the last act before the interval. Watch out for me and I'll give you all a wave. Ta-ta.'

He moved towards the door and had almost reached it when she called, 'Oh, Sam! Before you go there's something I *must* show you. After all, it was your doing.' He glanced back to see her smiling provocatively. Raising her skirt high above her waist, she turned and saucily tilted her left hip towards him. Then, tugging up the bottom of the corselet, she arched it up over her hip to reveal an enormous black bruise set colourfully in an ample pink buttock. 'That, my lad, was caused by your bleedin' paving stones.' She gave a long slow wink. 'Now, a proper stage-door Johnny would offer to kiss it better for a poor young lady . . .'

Sam fled from the room. Even after he had slammed the door, her peals of laughter pursued him the length of the staircase.

The others looked expectantly as Sam eased himself back into his seat. 'Well, come on then?' whispered Jane excitedly. 'Tell us all about it.'

'Nothing to tell really. All she said was . . .' Further conversation was cut short as the lights dimmed and the hubbub faded. The familiar opening bars of 'By the Side of the Zuider Zee' rose from the orchestra pit then softened for a few moments to allow the chairman to announce: 'It gives me great pleasure to introduce to you a young lady making her debut at the South London Palace. Here, direct from engagements all over Europe, that delightful, desirable, delicious, delectable debutante, Miss . . . Fanny . . . FIELDS!'

The curtain parted to reveal a nervous toothy young girl with her hair in bunches and her feet in clogs. As the song progressed her confidence visibly increased and soon the vast majority of the audience was singing with her. She finished to roars and stamps of approval.

'Oo, this is real smashing, Sam!' exclaimed Jane as she squeezed her brother's arm in gratitude.

Act followed act until the chairman finally announced, 'And now, ladies and gentlemen, to top the first half of our show is the lady you have all been waiting for, a real favourite of the South London Palace, who will sing first for you "Are We to Part Like This, Bill?" I give you that bright-eyed, beautiful, brilliant, bonny, blooming, buxom belle, Miss . . . Billie . . . B . . . A . . . R . . . D . . . E . . . L . . . L!'

Though only Archie had visited a music hall before, the

rest instantly appreciated the talent of the singer. Her voice not only had real power but also seemed to indicate the same strength when half-used. As the song progressed so the potency increased until she finished in a style that sent every note crashing against the far wall of the auditorium. The audience erupted.

Billie sang four songs, each better than the one before. After the fourth, she moved to the edge of the stage and, after shooting a quick glance into both wings, bent forward over the footlights as if to take the audience into her confidence. Her deepening cleavage caused great whistles of approval to go up from the gallery. 'I'm particularly happy tonight,' she announced. 'And can you guess why?'

'NO!' came back a unified chorus.

'I'm in love,' she said with mocking demureness. She turned side on to the audience and, lowering her chin to her shoulder, fluttered her long eyelashes with exaggerated coyness. 'And he's here tonight, at this very establishment.'

'Where, Billie, where? Tell us where he is,' called a female voice from somewhere near the front.

Billie gave a deep sigh and, clasping her hands together, she tilted her head to one side. 'I shouldn't really tell you because he's ever so shy. But if you promise to keep it as our secret, well . . .' This was obviously a rehearsed cue to the orchestra leader because as he raised his hands the faint introduction of a familiar tune could be heard and Billie started to sway gently. This movement was greeted by another roar but, as she raised both hands for silence, the cheers quickly faded. Of the quartet only Archie even faintly suspected what was afoot. The others leaned further over the brass rail to obtain an even closer view of this artiste who held the whole theatre spellbound.

Billie began by singing the first line softly, almost

conversationally. 'The boy I love . . . is up in the gallery.' By the second line her dialogue had escalated into song. 'The boy I love . . . is looking down at me.' At the start of the third line poor Sam thought he had gone blind as a powerful spotlight struck him square between the eyes. At that exact moment Billie threw back her head and, dramatically thrusting up her right arm, pointed straight at him. '*There* he is . . . can't you see? Sitting in the g-a-l-l-e-r-y, happy as a robin . . . that sits upon a tree.'

For a moment, Sam was unable to grasp what was happening. When he did, he groaned with embarrassment The last notes finally faded but the applause was too great for the singer to leave the stage. Billie nodded almost imperceptibly to the conductor and the orchestra again repeated the introduction. This time there was no gentle preamble into the verse but an all out attack from the very first note. The audience was ecstatic and the cheering only curtailed by the lowering of the interval safety curtain. As many of the crowd began to ease their way to the bars, the crashing of the chairman's gavel stopped them en route.

'L-a-d-i-e-s and G-e-n-t-l-e-m-e-n! Tonight, as an additional attraction, and sponsored by Sandow's the herbalist's, the management is proud to present to you, Eugene Sandow, The World's Strongest Man. And, straight from South America, his more than able assistant, The Bolivian Bull, Franco De Costa!'

The chairman raised his hand to cut short a more than generous round of applause. 'These two gentlemen will, in addition to appearing on the second half of our bill, organise a competition during the interval to discover the strongest man in South London. The prize for the winner is an excellent meal for two in Wood's Eel and Pie Shop, plus a golden guinea piece. In addition, the successful participant will have the opportunity to return here on Saturday night and compete against our other five nightly winners. The overall champion will receive no less than

FIVE golden guinea pieces! That's right, ladies and gentlemen, you heard me correctly, I repeat, FIVE golden guinea pieces! Right, now, who's going to be first?'

As he spoke, the safety curtain rose to reveal two powerful-looking men, half clad in leopard skins, who stood flexing their enormous muscles centre stage. Behind them was a variety of weights, barbells and parallel bars. Within seconds, two inebriates attempted to negotiate the few steps to the stage.

'Go on, Sam,' urged Archie. 'This is right up your street.' Sam shook his head and buried himself deep into his seat.

'He's right,' agreed Jim. 'I'd be up there like a shot if it was for boxing. But this is just for brute strength and bloody ignorance – it's absolutely made for you.'

'Oh, come on, Sam,' pleaded Jane. 'You know you like pie-and-mash. Perhaps we'll all get some,' she added optimistically.

'L-a-d-i-e-s and g-e-n-t-l-e-m-e-n,' called the chairman, 'I understand from Miss Bardell that the "boy in the gallery" would also like to take part, so can we have a big hand for him, if you please?' The chairman led the applause with Jane, Archie and Jim only marginally behind. The volume was so great that Sam found it more of an embarrassment to remain in his seat than to venture down on stage. As a result, he soon found himself joining a dozen or so other competitors at the top of the stage steps. Of these rivals, six were sober, three were drunk and the remainder in an indeterminate state.

Sam found the tests undemanding and, fifteen minutes later, had accomplished more pull-ups and press-ups, and lifted more weights than any of his competitors. All in all, the competition had been easy, too easy for most of the audience who had, in the main, drifted away to the bars. He not only received his golden guinea but, on promising to return for the Saturday night final, also a free supper for himself and his three companions.

It was close to midnight as the quartet pushed away their empty plates. 'Sam, that was a really great evening,' said Archie, wiping his mouth on the cuff of his jacket. 'So I'd like to do something for you in return.'

'Yeah?' questioned the suspicious Sam.

'Yeah,' echoed his grateful foreman. 'Instead of reporting to the depot at seven o'clock tomorrow morning, you can go straight to site. I shan't be looking for you until eight o'clock. Suit you?'

'Arch',' exclaimed the delighted young man. 'That's the second best present I've had all night. An extra hour in bed! Archie Surridge, that's really handsome of you!'

'That go for me too, Arch?' asked Jim optimistically. The briefest look at the foreman's face told him the answer. 'Oh, well,' he sighed, 'no harm in asking.'

'Sam,' whispered Jane, 'a friend of yours has just arrived.' She nodded towards the door where Billie Bardell had just made a regal entrance, closely followed by Queenie.

'Two bowls of stewed eels, Lew,' Billie called to the hovering proprietor. Strolling over to the foursome, she took a seat alongside Sam and waved her hands casually towards the empty plates. 'I take it you won then?' He made no attempt to answer but stared at her angrily. 'Well, did you?' she persisted.

'Why did you arrange for that spotlight to be shone on me, and why did you say I wanted to take part in that bloody awful competition?'

Billy glanced thoughtfully at the three intrigued, though silent, listeners. It was obvious she would have been happier if they had not been present. For once her customary bounce seemed to have deserted her. 'Sam,' she began, as she fiddled with a large opal dress-ring, 'I once knew someone so very much like you. Someone equally as obstinate and pig-headed. So just let's say I feel an allegiance – an attraction if you like – because you remind me of a good friend I once had. I don't think any purpose would be served by telling you any more, so will you please accept that as an explanation, at least for the time being?'

He shifted in his seat. He had not expected such a truthful reply. Insults and teasing he could deal with, but honest emotions were something new and he had little or no idea how to cope. Defensively he sought refuge in changing tack. 'I thought you said Queenie couldn't be with you tonight?' He nodded towards the girl.

'Nor was she. I've just picked her up from a little performance of her own, ain't I, gel?' The maid nodded. 'Go on, tell him where you've been and what you've done. Don't be shy.'

'I doubt if Mr Diamond is a person who'd understand,' said the girl quietly.

'Well, he won't unless you ask him, now will he?' Billie turned once more towards Sam. 'P'haps *I'll* tell him. My little maid – who looks as if butter wouldn't melt in her mouth – has been out smashing windows . . . amongst other things.'

'Smashin' windows?' began the puzzled Sam. 'Why, is she a crook?'

'Well, she don't think she is. In fact, she thinks she's quite the reverse.'

The girl gave a deep sigh. 'What Miss Bardell is trying to tell you, Sam, is that I'm a suffragette. Unfortunately Miss Bardell doesn't hold with suffragettes, which is a great pity because, as I tell her regularly, she would make a great one.'

'And I tell *her* regularly that I don't need to smash windows or bite coppers to get *my* way, dear. I can do it by much subtler means. So we just agree to differ, don't we, gel?'

The maid nodded ruefully. Although the two women still seemed quite friendly, an embarrassed silence hung over the remainder of the group. Jane was the first to break it.

'Well, I for one would like to thank you, Miss Bardell,' she said gratefully. 'I've loved this evening and, whatever Sam may say, it would never have taken place without you.' She turned to her brother. 'You will come back Saturday, Sam, won't you?'

'Oh, yes, I'll be back right enough, but not because of her. I'll come back because of those five guineas. That's nearly three weeks wages for me.'

'You'll need to win it first,' pointed out Jane cautiously.

'I'll win it all right,' murmured Sam. 'I need five guineas so badly I could lift the whole bloody theatre for it. So don't bother yourself about Miss bloody Bardell's little schemes. I shall be there because I *want* to be there and no other reason.' He glanced up at the old brown wall clock. 'But now it's almost midnight. Time to go home. Don't forget Cinderella has to change back into his rags . . . come on, Jane.'

Indifferently he stood by whilst the trio took their farewell of Billie and her maid. Then, much to their general disapproval, he declined Billie's offer of a lift from the carriage-and-pair that stood patiently outside the pie-shop. Having said their goodnights to Jim and Archie, the brother and sister threaded their way through the back alleys. When they reached their house, the whole of Inkerman Place was dark, except for a solitary yellow lamp flickering in their kitchen. Peeping through the curtains, they saw the reason for this late illumination. With the exception of Kate and their father, every member of the family was bent over the scrubbed white table busily cutting and glueing. Sam eased open the door and, faint though the breeze was, it tricked the gas-light into a nervous dance.

'Where's Dad?' he whispered, anxiously, looking about him.

'It's all right,' his mother assured him. 'He wasn't well and has gone to bed so you can take your time changing. Did you both have a nice time?'

'Yes, but what the hell are you all doing up at this time of night? It's ha' past twelve, for God's sake! Why aren't the kids in bed?'

'Sam,' said Nell softly, 'we still have a hundred or so of the windmills to make and the fair is next weekend. Besides, no one wanted to go to bed until they'd heard all your news.'

'But, Mum, the kids are out on their feet, look at them!'

'You think I don't know? You think I like doing this? If we can finish the last hundred by Saturday afternoon, old Dawkins will collect them on Saturday evening and we'll be eight pounds better off – *eight pounds*! Sam, I can rig out seven kids for eight pounds. We don't have a choice, son.'

'So after Saturday they'll get a break?'

'After Saturday they'll get a break, Sam,' she agreed. 'Leastways till August.'

'Sam-won-a-golden-guinea-and-a-pie-and-mash-supper-for-four-and-we-met-a-suffragette-Mum!' blurted out Jane proudly. The tired group listened rapturously to her tale whilst Sam made his Cinderella-like transformation from Stage-door Johnny to paviour.

'I wouldn't mention suffragettes or winning the competition to your father if I were you, son,' advised Nell. 'Women voters and the stage are not amongst his favourite things. Oh, by the way, what are you doing about a suit for Saturday?'

'Could I risk Dad's once more, Ma? I'll be able to buy a new one out of my winnings.'

'Sam, you haven't won yet!'

'I will, Ma, I will. Don't worry.'

Nell gave a long sigh. 'Well, providing he goes down to The Feathers at a reasonable time, it should be all right. We'll just have to keep our fingers crossed and pray.'

Maisie and Charlie were much too tired to pray, though they did manage to keep their fingers crossed until they fell exhausted on to their bed.

Chapter 3

'Mrs Diamond,' announced the trilby-hatted little man, graciously laying eight one-pound notes on the kitchen table, 'you don't know how refreshing it is to find at least *one* of our workers who has actually met our schedule. It shows integrity and dedication and does your family great credit.' He gave a deep sigh and shook his head. 'Integrity and dedication, Mrs Diamond, the two things sadly missing from society nowadays.'

Sam glanced up from the open scullery door where he sat polishing his boots. 'Integrity?' he queried. 'It's not *integrity*, Mr Dawkins, it's *necessity*. And it's not *dedication*, it's sweated bloody labour. We don't shove kids up chimneys any more, Mr Dawkins, we shove 'em around kitchen tables so they can sit up half the night for a pittance making your bloody windmills!'

'SAM!' cut in Nell Diamond sharply as she turned towards the amazed Dawkins. 'Take no notice of him, sir, he doesn't mean it. Do you, Sam?'

'No, Mum,' he said, oozing insincerity. 'Just a joke, Mr Dawkins, just a little joke. Come again in August.'

The children had barely carried the last of the windmills out to Mr Dawkins' pony cart before Nellie Diamond rounded on her eldest. 'Your big problem, Sam, is that you're always right! Well, you've not learnt it *all* yet, boy, no, not by a long chalk you haven't. We need that money badly. If you can think of another way of earning it, we'll listen. Until then, mind your tongue.'

Sam lapsed into silence. He rarely gave anyone the last word but had always had the greatest respect for his mother's ability to keep the family united, in spite of regular aggravation from his father – and sometimes, of course, her children.

'Now, Sam,' whispered his mother softly, as if the friction had never happened, 'what time d'you need Dad's suit?'

It was the very question of 'Dad's suit' that had bothered him all week. It was the only part of the big evening that he felt was out of his control. With his father more curmudgeonly each passing day, anything could happen. 'I'll get ready, Mum, so all I'll have to do is change quickly the instant he leaves for the pub. Though, knowing him, he'll be cantankerous enough not to go!'

By seven-thirty, the younger ones had long been packed into their beds, though the running conspiracy over their father's suit ensured not one of them slept. Jim Forsythe had called and, with Sam and the two older girls, was going through the motions of playing cribbage in the kitchen. Old John lay back in the sole fireside armchair with the evening paper hanging limply from his grasp, peacefully dozing. Every few minutes, on some pretended task, Nell would scuttle in from the scullery to assess the situation but though the minutes raced by, nothing changed.

'Do something,' mouthed Jane anxiously to her brother but Sam could only shrug in despair.

'We need to wake him ... but how?' whispered the almost tearful Kate as she willed the clock's hands to slow. Suddenly Nell tip-toed in and carefully stepped over the legs of the sleeping patriarch. Jane's intake of breath as her mother all but slipped on the newspaper caused the woman to turn in sharp, silent reproof. Gingerly she eased the fire-tongs into her hands and, agonisingly slowly, picked up a piece of glowing coal from the front of the fire. She froze for a second as the remainder of the coals threatened to slip but, once reassured, eased the smouldering piece carefully on to the edge of the old man's newspaper which opened wide on to the hearth-side. Then, taking a backward pace, she stood poised with tongs at the ready for the instant he opened his eyes. A few seconds of smoke gave way to a dancing flame which was her cue.

'John! John! Look at you, luv, you're practically on fire!'

The old man's bewilderment rapidly turned to anger. 'There are four of you layabouts in here and it takes your mother to see it from the scullery! I could have burnt to bloody death for all you lot care!' He slid back his chair from the now fading flames and allowed Nell to tidy up the fire-grate.

'You've had a good sleep though, John, haven't you?' she marvelled. 'Must'a been at least an hour or so. Still, it'll do you good to stay in for an evening, I shouldn't wonder.'

To the watching foursome her approach was screamingly obvious but would the old man see through it? He slipped his hand into a waistcoat pocket and eased out a large silver-plated pocket-watch. 'Huh!' he grunted. 'I'm well late. Get my coat, scarf and hat, Nell, they're under the stairs.'

Within five seconds of John Diamond's closing the back door, playing cards were stacked, chairs slid back and the girls raced upstairs in their quest for their father's suit. Within five minutes the threesome were sprinting towards the Blackfriars Road in search of a 68 tram with Kate and Nell's best wishes echoing behind them.

Archie Surridge anxiously paced the front of the music hall. The distant sounds of the overture were suddenly masked by the groaning brakes of the approaching tram-car. Before its wheels had ceased rolling, half a dozen latecomers had jumped dangerously from its crowded platform. To Archie's relief, John Diamond's best bowler hat figured prominently amongst the forerunners.

'I thought you were never coming,' he reproached. 'They

wouldn't give me the tickets without you being there. But guess what?' Without giving them a chance to do just that, he continued excitedly, 'Because it's the night of the finals, Billie Bardell has told them to give us a BOX! Imagine that! Us in a box!'

'It's easy to see what *his* conversation is going to be for the next few weeks,' murmured Jim as Jane squeezed his hand in excited anticipation.

The attendant, whilst showing all due respect to the occupiers of a box, also felt it was his duty to point out that a little silence would not come amiss as they raced eagerly along the carpeted corridor. Holding back the box-curtain, he whispered to Sam, 'The young lady is already there, sir.'

'The young lady? What young—'

His question was answered on seeing the slim figure of Queenie – tense and white-faced, he noticed – in the darkest corner of the box.

'You look surprised,' she said through a tight smile. 'You don't mind, do you?'

'No . . . no . . . not at all,' stammered Sam who, apart from not actually liking surprises, felt himself becoming more and more tongue-tied in her presence. She was certainly the perfect antidote to Billie. Towards Queenie he felt protective, whereas whatever responses Billie aroused, protectiveness was not one of them.

'Have you come straight from home?' she asked. He nodded.

'All of you?'

'All except Archie, we met him outside. What's this all about?'

'Miss Bardell said I should trust you. Can I?'

All Sam's instincts were to say no. He could scarce believe it was his voice he heard utter, 'Of course.'

'All you have to do, if anybody should ask, is say I called for you about sixish and have been with you ever since. Nothing more.'

'Can I ask a question?'

'I'd sooner you didn't but you certainly have the right to. Go ahead.'

'This "anybody", is it the police?'

She nodded. 'It *is* the police but I assure you I have not hurt anyone, it's not in me to do that. You do believe me?' She placed her hand upon his forearm.

'I'm not sure I'd go *that* far,' replied Sam curtly, though without moving his arm an inch. 'And I'm not happy that Miss Bardell is still trying to make decisions for me – she seems too bloody fond of doing that – but, yes, I'll go along with your wishes. If anyone wants to know, you've been with me since six.' He shrugged. 'Though the rest must speak for themselves.'

The 'rest' only really included Jim and Jane. Archie Surridge was in such a state of euphoria that at that moment he would have been reluctant to blow the whistle on Jack the Ripper. Sam gave a questioning glance towards the two youngsters. The half nods they gave him sufficed.

If they had enjoyed Monday evening, they were rendered ecstatic by the Saturday show. Firstly, the house was packed to the rafters, secondly, the atmosphere was even livelier, and thirdly, as if in response to their worshipping audience, each artiste pulled out every trick in their repertoire. They were five acts into the first half when the curtain-door at the rear of the box was hurled open. 'You comin', yer pansy, or are yer goin' ter 'ide up here behind Miss Bardell's skirts all evening?'

Sam did not need to turn to recognise the grating voice and maddening demeanour of Frank Cootes. The mere presence of the man made Sam bristle and he knew the feeling was mutual. Sam stared down at the stage, without really seeing it, the rage within him racing to the boil. 'No!' commanded Queenie as she placed both slender hands upon his thick right wrist. 'Wait, Sam.' She looked up at Cootes. 'What is it you want, Mr De Costa?'

'Personally I want nothin', sweetheart, not from you nor from 'im. You're not my type an' all I want with 'im is to tell 'im I'm goin' to break his neck in the interval. It's an announcement, I s'pose you'd call it. Miss Billie's on next an' when she finishes it's interval time. That means it's your little pansy's big moment. I've come to tell 'im ter make the most of it. He'll never git another.'

A chair slid back and Jim's voice cut sharply in. 'It's not your box, Mr Cootes. Nobody invited you here. You're not welcome. Please leave.'

'Oooh, 'ark at 'im!' whooped Frank. 'So they all talk, do they?'

'Mr De Costa . . . Mr De Costa!' called the timely voice of an attendant from the corridor. 'Stage manager wants to know your arrangements for the competition.'

'Duty calls, me old darlin's,' sang Frank. 'But don't worry, I'll sort yer out later.'

Sam's fury and Jim's anger were partially assuaged as the chairman announced the imminent appearance of Billie.

The heavy red curtains parted to reveal her standing centre-stage, clad in long white gloves, a wide-brimmed white hat trimmed with light blue ribbon, and a matching blue off-the-shoulder dress with a neckline that strained every notion of Edwardian decency. With head slightly tilted, mouth slightly parted, and saucy defiant eyes sweeping every corner of the auditorium, the entire audience would have agreed that 'magnificent' was the only way to describe her appearance. Archie had buried his chin deep in his hands in order to keep his gaze riveted unblinkingly on her. An explosion of applause rose from an audience who had yet to hear a note. As this slowly faded, the orchestra began a few familiar bars and Billie gave just a hint of a bow to the boxes on either side of the stage. 'I think I must be in heaven,' murmured Archie. 'I tell yer, if God had given me a big box of bits and said, "Go on, Arch', make one yerself," I'd a made *her*. E . . . v . . . e . . . r . . . y bloomin' inch of her!'

Having learnt his lesson five days previously, Sam made his exit from the box just before Billie had reached 'The Boy I Love . . .' and made his way down towards the wings. There he stood passively, with four other nervously chattering contestants, whilst her finale of 'Come Home, Bill Bailey' came to a rapturous end. As the curtains swung to, Billie left the stage and caused a large gin to vanish easier than 'Great Count Comiski! World Famous Illusionist', the fourth act on the bill.

'Sam!' exclaimed the star as she suddenly clapped eyes on the waiting contestants. 'How smart you are! I looked for you before the show, where were you? Getting togged out, I'll bet,' she chided, smoothing down his lapels.

'Something like that.' He firmly removed her perfumed hands from his borrowed suit. The other four competitors simply gazed on in reverential silence.

'I'll see you in Woods's after the show again, all right?'

'No, I can't make it tonight, sorry.'

'Sam, you're not *still* angry surely? Look, if you win tonight, we'll make a new start, what d'you say?'

'I've got nothing against you, Miss Bardell, but just don't keep pushing me. I think between you and your maid, you're trying to manipulate me and I don't like it one bit.'

'She told you then?'

'She told me nothing! Except some guff about you saying she could trust me.'

'Get her to tell you about it, Sam, you might be surprised. She's a bloody deep one, that Queenie. Oh, and I'll tell you something else – she don't half fancy you!'

So saying, Billie threw back her head and, hands on hips, roared with laughter. Sam was about to answer but lost his train of thought on hearing the opening strains of Arabian music from the orchestra pit as the manager introduced

'The World Famous Sandow Trial Of Strength'. Bert Brewster from Clapham, alias Eugene Sandow, The World's Strongest Man, and Frank Cootes from Battersea, alias Franco De Costa, The Bolivian Bull, strode purposefully on to the stage in their baggy leopard-skin leotards.

'Why are they playing Arab music?' asked one of the puzzled competitors.

' 'Cos that's as close as that band can get to Bolivia,' Billie informed him. 'Look, Sam,' she added, 'I must go, I'm at the Canterbury in a few minutes and I haven't time to worry about your sulks. But there's something you must remember. If you *do* win the competition, Frank Cootes will challenge you double or quits in such a way that the audience will think you a fool not to accept. Don't take it. The man is a professional thug and trickster and he's also quite ruthless. So be warned . . . Quick kiss?'

Without waiting for a reply, she threw her arms around his neck and gave him the first passionate kiss he had received in his life.

The competitors were invited to shed their hats, coats and waistcoats and wait in the wings. Being 'Grand Finals' night, audience interest was greater than on Monday. Brewster and Cootes quickly went into an unexciting routine in which they tossed daunting-looking dumbbells to each other. Then, with much quivering of forearms, they alternated in holding each other head-high. This was followed by a few press-ups with a large bench across their backs, on which two pretty young lady volunteers from the audience nervously squatted. This daring feat was, of course, prior to the statutory invitation to feel the oiled biceps of the performing pair whilst sustaining a farewell kiss. All that remained before the competition proper was for the centre-stage to be cleared of all props. There was much 'alley-ooping' and rolling of drums as Brewster tossed each dumbbell and weight across to Cootes whose task it was to stack them neatly. All appeared well until the last 112lb weight. Frank Cootes appeared to catch it comfortably enough but then an agonised groan from The Bull suddenly implied all was not well. Sam had the fleeting impression that the whole thing had been contrived but, in truth, thought little more about it.

Franco De Costa bravely exited stage-left with a pained expression and a stiff right shoulder which he clutched tightly, as if he were in fear of it falling off. Eugene Sandow demanded – and got – a sympathetic round of applause for his unfortunate assistant. Yet another roll of drums announced the five competitors who stood dutifully in line. Five volunteers from the audience were then invited on to the stage to see fair play and to pile up the weights in front of their opposite number. The competition was going to be assessed by points. One point per press-up, ten points for one dumbbell, thirty points for two, but fifty points for two dumbbells if they could be raised above the head from a squatting position. Tuesday and Thursday's winners could barely lift the first weight and soon left the stage together with their two minders. Wednesday's lasted a little longer but it was obviously going to be a two-man race between Sam and leading-stoker McGrain, a powerful bearded sailor who had won his golden guinea on Friday and appeared to have half the navy spread around the gallery in support.

When the event appeared to have reached stalemate, a tie-breaker was introduced with each of the two young men allowed to nominate a task. The sailor nominated five lifting squats, which each of them achieved only with enormous difficulty. 'Still neck and neck, ladies and gentlemen,' boomed the excited Sandow. 'And now it's Sam's choice!'

The exertion of the five squats, coming after the previous tasks, had virtually turned Sam's shoulder muscles to jelly. He quickly calculated, fitness aside, that his occupation as a paviour would be an advantage providing all other matters were even. He took a chance and nominated thirty press-ups. On the fourth, the sailor stiffened momentarily before groaning and crashing face down exhausted on the floor. Only Sam knew how close he had been to defeat. All he needed was five good press-ups to win. Having completed them, he knew he could have done no more. The stoker was generous in his congratulations and grinned ruefully when in response to his, 'I could na ha dune thirty press-ups ta ha' seved mae life,' Sam replied, 'And I could na ha dune sax!'

'What a winner, ladies and gentlemen! What a winner! Have you ever seen such a contest?' Sandow raised his hands. 'Now could we have your appreciation for a gallant loser – Stoker James McGrain – who, in addition to his golden guinea last Friday, has won another two guineas and a whole month's supply of Sandow's Health and Strength Elixir.' Eugene led the sympathetic applause as the bearded matelot, guineas in one hand and Sandow's Elixir in the other, made his way to the steps leading down to the front of the stalls.

'And now, ladies and gentlemen, for the final drama of this action-packed evening, we have "The Challenge". This is the point where we offer our winner a chance to double-or-quits his five golden guineas to ten. Yes, ladies and gentlemen, you heard right – TEN!'

Billie's words came instantly to Sam's mind . . . but ten guineas? That was really a prize worth having. He could get himself a suit for three pounds ten shillings and still have more than six pounds left over! If he had any doubts about accepting the challenge, the rest of the announcement cleared these up. 'We invite our winner to take part in a wrestling match with my brave assistant, Franco De Costa. They will wrestle until the first submission, which will mark the end of the contest. Now you may think Franco is a professional and *should* win, but, as you know, he has sustained a debilitating injury and it is only his courage and dedication that enables me to make this offer. What do you say, ladies and gentlemen, should our bold contestant accept the offer?'

A great roar of 'YES!' erupted from the auditorium, to be followed by two solitary girlish cries of: 'No, Sam, no!' from the direction of his box.

'*Do* you accept this most generous offer, Sam?' He nodded. 'Okay then,' continued Sandow. 'Let's have the ring up.'

A flurry of attendants scuttled on to the stage and within a minute a makeshift ring was in place. 'And now, ladies and gentlemen, a big hand for the courageous Bolivian Bull, Franco De Costa!' Turning to the wing, Sandow raised his arm in welcome to a woefully over-acting Cootes.

Jim Forsythe rose from his seat and bent forward over the rail of the box. Cupping his hands to his mouth, he bellowed, 'What's he limping for? I thought he hurt his shoulder!' At that, Cootes ceased limping but again clutched at his shoulder – his *left* shoulder.

'It's a fix,' snapped Queenie. 'There's nothing wrong with him. Tell Sam that – Cootes will kill him otherwise. I've seen him in action before. He's a monster!'

'SAM, NO!' shrieked Jane. 'NO! NO!' But such protests were of no avail. The possibility of ten guineas, a suit of his own and a chance to thump Frank Cootes rendered Sam deaf to anything other than the matter in hand.

The mere act of ducking into the ring seemed to cure whatever ailed the courageous Bull and he promptly went through a brief though elaborate routine of exercises. 'Okay, lads,' boomed Eugene, sweeping his arms up dramatically. 'Now shake hands and . . . WRESTLE!' Turning his head to the glowering Frank, he whispered, 'But don't prolong it too much, Frank, the stage-manager's making hurry up signs.'

It was doubtful if Sam had any idea what was happening

to him. One moment he was shaking hands, the next he was somersaulting over Cootes' shoulder and crashing in a heap several feet away. Before he could clear his head, Cootes was on him again. The pain as his arm was pushed high up his back was unbearable and he knew he would have to submit. Yet suddenly, and to his great surprise, Cootes released him.

'It's not goin' ter be that easy, me ole mate,' he hissed as he seized Sam's left knee into a pain-wracked hold. If the agony from his arm had been bad, the pain from his leg was like an amputation. But once more the limb was released. He had only been fighting for a minute and twice during that time could screamingly have conceded defeat. He suddenly realised Cootes was playing a sadistic game. His ploy was obviously to inflict as much pain as possible before delivering some neat and tidy coup-de-grâce.

Cootes stepped back confidently as Sam struggled wearily to his feet. The cheers, counter-cheers and whistles merged into one roaring cacophony, yet through it Sam could just hear Jim Forsythe's voice: 'Your strength, Sam! Your strength! Use your strength!'

Jim was right! When it came to wrestling against Cootes, Sam was totally out of his depth. What he had to do was blunt Cootes' attacks by sheer strength, then somehow use that strength to fight back. He slowly began to sway, as if ready to faint. Cootes' concern was immediate. Fainting would not do at all. For an opponent to slump quietly to the floor was definitely not in the act. Whatever the finish, it had to be dramatic. He would sooner the victim drop dead than faint!

Sam slumped slightly forward and did a quarter-turn to his left. With hair hanging down and eyes half closed, he made a pathetic picture. Without the necessity for speed, Cootes could now pick his final hold for maximum pain and humiliation. Taking a pace forward, he bent slowly towards his antagonist's unprotected groin. It was the very move the young paviour had hope for. Pushing off with his left foot and pivoting on his right, Sam put all his strength into a forearm smash that, as far as The Bolivian Bull was concerned, came up through the floorboards. But if Frank did not know whence it started, he had no doubt at all where it finished. It struck the side of his neck like a catapulted rhino. Sam's own pain vanished as both revenge and ten golden guineas loomed large in his reckoning. His plan was to leap on the prostrate Cootes and inflict a little damage. This was foiled by the intervention of Eugene Sandow. The fair-minded Eugene said he felt compelled to point out that, as Frank was now unconscious, it would be considered unsporting to tie his limbs in a knot and jump on him. Gracious in victory, Sam reluctantly agreed and, to the great delight of the audience and the total irritation of the band, settled for dumping the vanquished wrestler upside down into the orchestra pit.

For the next two acts and corresponding twenty-five minutes, Sam's attention was all on his father's trousers. His own efforts were not altogether successful. A Walworth Road fifty-shilling suit, though reliable and serviceable, did not readily lend itself to stage wrestling. At least having the box allowed him to bend over a chair with his four friends taking turns to sponge and brush the suit's more battered sections.

The grande finale for the evening – the much-loved comedian George Robey – finally attracted their attention and even Sam and the somewhat subdued Queenie forgot their problems and joined in the laughter. The orchestra members had begun to reach for their instruments, indicating Mr Robey's act was reaching its conclusion, when the door behind them opened and a breathless Billie Bardell entered the box. 'Running late?' she whispered to Queenie. 'I thought you'd be finished by now.'

'Shush!' mouthed the girl, fingers to her lips. 'Drama at interval. I'll tell you after.'

'Okay, but are *you* all right?' Billie persisted anxiously.

Through a wan and unconvincing smile, the maid implied she was. Billie, with a half-shake of her head, indicated her doubts before reluctantly turning her attention to Robey's final monologue. The old performer then took his bow and gave a wink of acknowledgement to his fellow artiste. There followed a few token bars of the National Anthem before hissing gas-lamps took their cue and lit up the auditorium.

With Queenie whispering in her ear, Billie soon caught up on the evening's events. 'So you've got yourself ten and a half quid, Sam? Well done you! At this rate you'll soon be able to take me to Monte Carlo for a dirty weekend.' She quickly raised her hands. 'Okay, I'm sorry, I'm sorry,' she conceded. 'But why, when things have gone so well, do you always have to look so bleedin' miserable? Even you must admit that this evening merits a celebration, yes?'

'It's our dad's suit,' explained Jane. 'Sam thinks the trousers are stained.'

'Your dad's suit?' echoed Billie. 'You don't mean to say that's not even *your* suit? Good God, Sam, what *are* we goin' to do with you?'

Slumped in his chair, he was finally beyond argument. The combination of the evening's events had finally taken their emotional toll. Queenie slipped her arm around his bent shoulders. 'Came on, luv, look on the bright side. Miss Bardell's right, y'know. You *have* had a good evening and they don't come along too often.'

He nodded. 'I know, but with those ten guineas I could have done *so* much and now, when Dad finds out, he'll make me mum's life an absolute misery.'

'Look at you!' she chided. 'An hour or so ago you were like Samson, now you're more like Tinkerbell! C'mon, go to Wood's, you can finish the evening off in style. Then tomorrow you can be as miserable as you like. What d'you say?'

The young man stared at her for a moment. 'Will *you* come with us then, Queenie?'

She glanced quickly at Billie who nodded even quicker in return, both movements so swift and slight that Sam saw neither. 'Sure, I'll be pleased to come.'

'And I won't be expected to give you an alibi should anyone ask?'

'Not even that, Sam,' she replied.

'Six bowls of stewed eels, Lew.' Billie glanced around her. 'Any of you hungry lot want a pie as well? I thought as much! And three pies-and-mash. And don't forget the specials.'

'All a'taken a'care of, Missa Bardell,' replied the smiling old Italian.

'I've been coming to this shop since I was a kid,' said Billie as they sat at the reserved table. 'An' during that time that man hasn't changed a scrap. Neither has his accent.'

'What's the "specials", Miss Bardell?' asked Jane.

'Here they come now,' said Billie, nodding to the kitchen door. Ricardo, Lew's son, emerged holding high a tray with six glasses and three bottles of champagne.

'You must have planned this all along,' exclaimed Sam. 'Lew doesn't keep champagne. He doesn't even have a licence to sell beer!'

'Well, we've just changed all that. Cheers!'

'A bit ostentatious, though, champagne and stewed eels?' he persisted.

'Not a bit of it,' she said. 'Champagne's only ostentatious if you're skint. Don't forget you've just won ten guineas, mate. You're almost a bleedin' millionaire!'

Panic appeared on Sam's face. 'D'you mean—'

'Don't worry, your money's safe. Lew's treating us because I've given this place a mention every night in my stint at the Canterbury.'

It was during the second glass that Archie decided to

sing. Jim's and Sam's misgivings were dispelled, however, when a foursome at the next table, who had shrewdly conjured up glasses from somewhere, had the good sense to join in the champagne as well as the singing and happily turned out to be quite good.

'Can we do all this again next week, Sam?' asked an inebriated Archie as Lew diplomatically announced departure time by dimming lights and placing chairs on tables.

As midnight struck, Sam had mellowed enough to accept a ride home from Billie's carriage-and-pair. With Archie living close by Wood's, the remaining trio squeezed in together with the star and her maid as the grey horses set off sedately towards Blackfriars Road. 'Are you *really* worried about your father, Sam?' asked Queenie, cuddling next to Sam.

'It's not really *him* we're worried about, is it, Jane?' he called across to his sister, who shook her head in response. 'It's Mum. She's at his every beck and call and he treats her like dirt. If he discovers she's lent me his suit, he'll either have apoplexy or kill her. One thing's for sure, he'll never let her forget it.'

'Perhaps it's time you left the nest?' suggested Billie.

'Oh, I've known that for some time,' agreed Sam. 'But Mum needs the money.'

'Well, it's a decision only you can take,' said Billie. 'But if you do need to bed down anywhere in an emergency, don't be afraid to knock on our door. If I'm working out of town, Queenie will take care of you ... won't you, Queenie?' By way of a reply the girl snuggled closer to him. The little flap in the roof lifted and a gruff voice called down: 'Inkerman Place . . . you sure this is where you want, Miss Bardell?'

'No, mate, most definitely not,' she agreed. 'In fact, *I* wouldn't have it as a bleedin' gift but there are some poor sods here who don't have that choice.'

Jane suddenly leaned forward and clutched Billie's

hands. 'I know I keep saying this, Miss Bardell, but I have just spent the two happiest evenings of my life because of you, and I want to thank you very much.'

'Don't think about it,' replied Billie in a strangely embarrassed tone. 'Here, you . . . Jim? . . . whatever your name is. You want to look after her, you've got a right little treasure there.'

Sam suddenly felt unsure. It was time to take his leave of Queenie and he had no idea how to go about it. Shaking her hand would be silly and yet he couldn't just kiss her. Supposing she objected? It would be just too embarrassing. His worries turned out to be groundless when she made the decision for him. For the second time that day he received a kiss full on the lips. The thing that bothered him was, if they were both in the same place, why did they feel so different?

Amid much waving and many 'G'nights' the carriage moved away and Sam thoughtfully averted his gaze whilst his friend and his sister said their farewells.

'What we want now, sis',' he murmured as they finally made their way beneath the old tree, 'is a nice dark house. That'll mean everyone's asleep.'

'Mum won't be asleep, she'll be aching to know how the evening went. You know what she's like. I bet she's been staring out of that window ever since Dad went to bed.'

As they emerged from beneath the tree there was one solitary light shining from the whole of Inkerman Place, illuminating one solitary head.

'See!' exclaimed Jane, happily waving. 'What did I tell—'

Her arms fell motionless to her sides as the furious twisted features of old John Diamond pressed themselves to the glass.

Chapter 4

The pleasant stillness of the early evening had slowly given way to a rising breeze which, by the time the carriage reached the foot of Brixton Hill, had itself given way to steady rain. The horses shortened their stride as they began the slight but long climb. 'Well, do you want to tell me about it?' began Billie.

'Nothing to tell really,' shrugged Queenie. 'He's just a nice lad.'

'That's not what I'm asking and you know it. It's not *him* I'm referring to but *you*. And please don't insult my intelligence by telling me there's nothing wrong. Your face was as white as a sheet when I first arrived at the theatre tonight.'

The carriage stopped and the roof flap lifted. For the second time that evening, the driver pushed his face to its portal. 'Number 200, yer say, Miss Bardell?'

'That's right, mate,' she answered, irritated by the interruption. 'But we're not there yet and it's on the other side of the road anyway.'

'I knows that, ma'am, but I didn't knows if yer wanted ter go right up ter the front door. Leastways, not in view of that lot.'

'What lot?' snapped Billie as she pressed her face to the cab window and tried peering through the trickling raindrops.

'All those coppers, ma'am. There's a good half dozen of 'em shining their lamps all over yer 'ouse.'

Billie spun round on her maid. 'For Gawd's sake! What was it tonight then? No wonder you looked white-faced, you stupid cow!' Seizing the girl by her shoulder, she shook her violently. 'Are you going to stop this insanity or are you going to let it kill you?' She lifted her face sharply to the flap. 'As close as you can get to the front door, driver, if you please . . . and will you come down and help us out?'

The tall detective ceased knocking at the front of the house as his attention was drawn to the arriving carriage. 'Hemmings,' he ordered, 'see if that's someone we should be talking to.'

Hemmings and a colleague advanced towards the carriage just as the door was thrown open and Billie stood poised theatrically with one foot on the step.

'Ah, my man!' she greeted him. 'You're just the help I'm looking for. Give me a hand to get her inside the house, will you?' She gestured irritably to the unconscious girl slumped in the corner of the cab.

Jane Diamond pulled the key on its cord through the small hole in the back door of 14 Inkerman Place. The champagne glow had rapidly given way to a feeling of nausea. Sam restrained her in order to enter the kitchen first. 'So!' exclaimed John. 'The prodigal son returns!' He turned to the trembling Jane. 'Not the prodigal son of the Bible though – oh, no! This one is the *thieving* prodigal son. A prodigal son who steals from his own father, would you believe! A prodigal son who drags his whole family into a web of deceit to connive and deceive for him. In other words, a prodigal son who is a liar and a cheat and has no place in this God-fearing house!'

Sam had been rapidly rehearsing his apology since the second he had realised just whose face it was at the window but he had not been prepared for such a vitriolic reception. In the gloom of the unlit staircase he could just make out a line of little white faces spaced down the stairs, peering between the banisters. With his mother sitting bruised and tearful at the kitchen table, the old man's audience was captive and complete. 'So what is it?' demanded his father. 'You think because you're at work and I'm not, you can walk all over me, is that it?'

'I borrowed your suit and I'm sorry but . . .' the young man shook his head in frustration '. . . I'm twenty years old, Dad, and I've worked since my thirteenth birthday. And I don't even have a suit of clothes to my name!'

'So you stole mine!'

'Dad, I'll pay you for it, look.' He fumbled in a pocket and pulled out the ten golden guineas, scattering them over the table. 'I can buy you another suit, and one for me, and if I'm careful, probably a coat and shawl for Mum.'

The old man rose from his chair and moved ominously towards him. 'Where did you get that money from, boy?' he hissed.

'I won it, Dad ... I won it fair and square in the competition.'

'WHAT competition?'

Sam realised all was lost in his relationship with his father; perhaps it was time to see what he could salvage in order to help his mother. 'Look, I borrowed your suit entirely of my own accord, Mum had nothing to do with it. Be fair, Dad, I couldn't go on stage in my working clothes, now could I?'

'WHAT competition?' repeated the old man as if his son had never spoken.

'Sandow's competition at the music hall. Didn't I tell you? Tonight was the final . . . and I won.' Sam heard just the beginnings of a murmur of appreciation from the onlookers on the staircase before a blow to his chin momentarily blacked out the whole room.

'John! John, don't! He's your own flesh and blood, for God's sake!' screamed Nell.

Throughout the screams, shouts and pandemonium, Sam's first conscious thought was of the irony of surviving the crippling onslaught of The Bolivian Bull only to be laid out by a sick old man dying of consumption. His mother fussed over him as she eased his cut and grazed head from the empty grate. 'Sam, are you all right, boy?'

'MUM!' screamed Jane. 'Look at him!'

Nell glanced quickly over her shoulder to see her husband slipping slowly to the floor with blood-flecked foam rolling slowly from his mouth.

'I'm all right, Mum,' Sam assured her, struggling to his feet. 'Look after Dad.'

A space in front of the fireplace was quickly cleared as Nell and the older girls laid the old man on the worn rug. 'Get the young ones back upstairs, Kate,' ordered Nell. 'And get a pillow and a blanket for your dad whilst you're there.'

'I can carry him upstairs, Mum,' offered Sam. 'He needs to be in bed anyway.'

'You'll . . . do . . . nothing . . . for . . . me . . . boy,' panted the old man as he struggled to raise himself. 'Except . . . get . . . out'a . . . this . . . house.' Jane cradled her father's head and wiped his mouth before holding a cup of water to his stained lips. 'Shush, be quiet, Dad, and drink this.' He fell back open-mouthed and exhausted.

Sam drew his mother to one side. 'He must go upstairs, Mum, and the only way that's happening is if I take him. Agreed?' She nodded. 'Okay, so the best way is to do it quickly. You, Kate and Jane keep the doors open and clear the way and I'll carry him up. But listen.' He raised a finger and emphasised each point. 'Don't give in to him, Mum, don't listen to his protests, just let me put him straight to bed, understand?' Again a nodded reply.

Sliding his hands beneath his father's body, Sam picked him up in one quick movement. They were halfway up the stairs before the old man was aware what was happening.

Ignoring the protests, Sam laid him gently on the bed, leaving Nell to fuss over him.

Thirty minutes later she tip-toed down the stairs and into the kitchen where Sam sat staring at the long dead fire. 'Sam!' she exclaimed. 'You've changed your clothes. Aren't you going to bed, son?'

'How is he, Mum?'

She shrugged. 'Worse than he was yesterday – and not as bad as he'll be tomorrow.' She glanced down at the floor which was still damp from where Kate and Jane had scrubbed it. 'Least there wasn't so much blood this time. But how about you?'

Sam rubbed his head ruefully. 'The old sod can still pack a punch – *and* I never saw it coming!'

'But why have you got your old clothes on at two o'clock in the morning?'

Sam rose from the chair and put his arms around his mother, an action he had probably not performed more than twice in his whole twenty years. 'Mum, how long does the doctor at the Blackfriars Mission say Dad has?'

'Two to three months.'

'Well, if tonight is any guide, within two to three months you could be in an asylum! For some reason he's venting all his anger on me, isn't he?'

'Yes. But he never used to be that way,' she added hastily. 'It's only since he's been really ill. No woman could have wished for better till then.'

Sam made little attempt to hide his scepticism. 'If that's what you wish to believe, fine, but I'm only making matters worse by staying here. If I can't keep him from dying, at least I can make his living – to say nothing of everyone else's – a little easier by not being here.'

'But you can't leave!' she protested. 'We can get by. You're out working most of the time anyway.'

'So how about the kids, Mum? What sort of life is it for them? Our kitchen has just looked like the public bar of a dockside pub.' He shook his head. 'No, it's time to go and we all know it. I'll get some money to you every Friday and perhaps pop round to see you when he's at The Feathers. I won't be far away.'

'Where will you be?'

'Probably with Jim. Since his two brothers joined the navy, he reckons he's got a room to himself now.'

'At *this* time of night?'

'I can tap on Jim's window easy enough and it's Sunday tomorrow anyway. I've got a few bits and pieces in a bag here and I'll be in touch soon . . . now don't worry.' He kissed his mother and both tearful sisters and was gone.

Within a few minutes he had reached the darkened terraced house of the Forsythes. Whilst trying to visualise the exact location of Jim's room, Billie Bardell's parting words came back to him. 'Don't be afraid to knock on our door,' she had said. 'Queenie will take care of you.' Suddenly sharing a room with his lifelong friend lost any attraction it might once have had. He shouldered his bag and, bending into the heavy rain, turned himself and his destiny south towards Brixton.

After thirty minutes' brisk walk he was halfway to his destination, and drenched. St Mark's church clock at Kennington Oval appeared to have been waiting for him as it gleefully reminded the first traveller for an hour that it was a quarter to three. Though the rain fell steadily and continuously, every few minutes its volume increased dramatically. For Sam, wet was wet and there was nothing to be done about it.

The next fifteen-minute chime was from an anonymous distant clock but it reminded him, if any reminder was needed, that he was verging on his last lap. The earlier champagne was beginning to make its presence felt and he knew he must stop for a pee. He glanced quickly around but there was no one about and, with the exception of a lone hackney carriage at the Elephant and Castle, nor had there been since he left Blackfriars Road. He moved to the edge of the pavement and made to unbutton his trousers. As he did, he felt suddenly embarrassed. He had not peed in the kerbside since a child and, even though the rain was rushing through the gutters in a torrent, it still seemed wrong. Almost angry with himself, he turned in search of concealment. Five yards away loomed the deep dark doorway of a shopping arcade. With buttons still undone, he moved under cover and searched for a corner. Search completed, he shuffled his feet comfortably astride and breathed a contented sigh.

'I 'opes yer not 'onking yer plonker in that letter-box, boy!' boomed a deep West Country voice. ''Cos if you pisses on their letters they're gonna 'ave the right 'ump with you come Monday marnin'.'

Sam spun around, mouth and flies open. 'Who the hell are . . .' he began as a burly black-clad pipe-smoking figure rolled slowly out of the deepest corner of the blackness.

'Yer shouldn't be a'goin' around pissin' in letter-boxes, not when the whole bloody street looks like Niagara, yer shouldn't.'

'I'm sorry,' stuttered Sam, shorn of all dignity. 'I got taken short I'm afraid, officer, and it seemed wrong somehow to pee at the kerb.'

'So yer thought yer'd pee in a letter-box?'

'No, no, honest. It was so dark I didn't realise it was a letter-box.'

A booming laugh came out of the gloom. 'Thass orl'right, I was a'watchin' yer all the time, lad. Though I did wonder fust of all why yer were a'runnin' round wi' yer dick in yer 'and.' The policeman shook his head knowingly. 'I allus thinks a man lacks elegance wi' 'is dick in 'is 'and.'

'Er – I've never thought about it but I'm sure you're right,' said Sam as he scuttled back towards his original spot at the kerbside. 'Is here okay?'

'Aye, as good a place as any, I s'pose,' agreed his

companion, lifting up his heavy glazed cape. 'Fact is, all this talk about peein' and all this rain 'as made me think I ought ter be a'joinin' yer.' There was a full minute's silence, broken only by the downpour, as the two men stood on the granite kerbstones and peed out into the puddled roadway.

'Anyway,' said the fat policeman as he buttoned up and returned to his pipe in the doorway, 'what yer a'doin' out 'ere this time o'night?'

Sam briefly recounted the story of the evening and left the old policeman suitably impressed. 'So yer belted that bloody vagabond Cootes, did yer? Good on yer! I've seen some o' 'is 'andywork. Nice ter think that sometimes these bastards get their due. So what yer propose ter do wi' yerself now?'

When he heard the vagueness of Sam's plan, the old copper shook his head. 'Yer knows what'll suit yer?' Without waiting for a reply he continued, 'This'll suit yer, this job. In fact, I think this job'll suit yer better 'an anyone I knows.'

'Be a copper!' exclaimed Sam. 'It never entered my head. Still, it's something to think about. In fact, I'll think about anything that offers me bed and board.'

'Well afore yer goes, take this.' Rummaging deep in his clothing he pulled out a small sheet of paper. Scrawling quickly upon it he passed it to Sam. 'Remember, if yer goes fer a police interview, show 'em that.'

'What is it?' asked the intrigued young man, peering through the damp darkness.

'It's me,' announced his companion proudly. 'It's me name, number and division. Baden Benjamin Bates, PC 515L. If they accepts yer inta the force, I gits a thirty-shilling bounty. Worth a piss wiv anyone, wouldn't yer say?' As he stepped back into the cosy darkness of the arcade, he chuckled. 'Look after yerself, son. I've got an interest in yer welfare. Wiv luck I could be thirty bob better orf.'

Sam soon covered the last mile to the top of the hill and

was surprised to see lights still shining from the downstairs windows. Climbing the wide white steps he paused instinctively to smooth down his soaking clothes before pulling at the bell. Brisk footsteps and angry mutters preceded the opening of the door.

'What now?' began the white-robed Billie. 'Sam! What on earth . . . Look at you! You're bleedin' soaked.'

'I'm sorry if I woke you,' he began.

'Don't worry, we weren't actually in bed. Come in and get those rags off before you catch your death. Queenie! Queenie!' she called over her shoulder. 'Look who's here. We got any hot water left in that boiler?' A distant reply indicated chances were good. 'Great! We're goin' to shove this bugger in a bath before he touches anything other than the door-knob in this house.' She turned to Sam. 'And you – don't you even *think* about arguing till you smell sweeter. It's too bloody late and I'm not in the mood, so get your clothes off.'

Sam needed no one to tell him that he wasn't the smartest man about town. After all, what passed as common-place from an Edwardian paviour was not likely to intrigue the two most fascinating females he had met in his life. 'Here, have a gin while Queenie runs your bath,' Billie offered.

'I'm not sure I like gin,' he muttered apologetically.

'Then have a bloody scotch! Do have something, for Gawd's sake. I don't want you passing out on me as well.'

He sipped the scotch as Billie's questions flew thick and fast and a tired-looking Queenie soon entered to announce his bath was ready. 'Er . . .' he faltered. 'What room?'

'What room?' asked the puzzled girl. 'What d'you mean, "What room?" The bathroom, of course. Where else?'

'Sam,' said Billie quietly, 'it's a proper bathroom, not something in front of the fire. It's quite easy. You just get in and then pull out the plug when you finish. Nothing to it – show him, Queenie.'

The girl smiled wearily and led him up the red-carpeted stairs. 'Everything you need should be there. Throw out those clothes as soon as you can and I've hung a previous guest's robe behind the door – it should practically fit you,' she added.

Twenty minutes later a clean, if rather self-conscious young man, wearing an ill-fitting robe, emerged from the bathroom and picked his way gingerly out on to the landing. Of the five doors he could see, not one was open.

'Hallo!' he called repeatedly. The third 'hallo' was acknowledged by a quiet female response from behind one door that did eventually open. 'Sam,' whispered Billie, 'it's four o'clock and I've sent Queenie to bed. We all have lots to talk about but let's leave it till breakfast, agreed?'

'Agreed.' He nodded towards the staircase. 'Shall I kip downstairs on the settee?'

'No, Sam, that wouldn't be at all suitable. Unfortunately Queenie never had time to make up a room, so you're in here tonight.' She gestured behind her to where a sprawling white unruffled bed appeared almost to beckon. 'With me.' Childlike, he allowed himself to be led into the room as she eased the door closed behind her.

Billie turned down the gaslight to the faintest of glimmers and slipped out of her robe. The impact of her white silk nightgown was as pleasing to the young man as her stage-dress had been earlier. To someone from Sam's background, bed attire was strictly functional. If it wasn't warm or hard-wearing it had no use. Whatever description could be made of Billie's apparel, 'warm and hard-wearing' would not rate a mention. 'Sam,' she laughed, 'it's time to take off that ridiculous robe.' She tugged at the cord and in one experienced movement stripped it from his shoulders. Taking his hands, she fell back on to the bed and pulled him down on to her. Sliding her arms around his neck, she began kissing his mouth, face and chest in a flurry of soft warm lips.

'Touch me, Sam, touch me,' she pleaded as she relinquished her hold and let her arms fall back wide above her head. Sam found her silken covering as erotic as her silken skin as he caressed, kissed, and explored. As he tugged at the hem of her gown, she sat upright with arms raised high and allowed him to lift it from her voluptuous body. Once naked, she bore into him with such a fury that mere hands felt inadequate for such a curvaceous woman. Twisting on to her back, she sidled her left leg wide beneath him until he finally found himself slipping between her plump welcoming thighs. Yet, strangely, though his kisses had lost none of their intensity, his body had not stirred. 'Sam, is everything all right?' she whispered. He made no reply. 'Sam, speak to me,' she persisted. 'Is everything all right?'

Raising himself on his elbows, he stared down into the dark shadows between their two bodies. 'I . . . I don't know.'

'What do you mean, you don't know?'

'Well . . . nothing's happening . . . and I don't know what to do about it.'

In an instant all the fire seemed to leave her. She sagged back lifelessly on to the sheet. 'Oh, Sam, my poor Sam.' She kissed him lightly on the forehead as he slipped off her. 'This is your first time, isn't it?' He stared at her without reply. 'It *is*, isn't it?' she repeated.

'Yes,' he confessed mournfully. 'In fact, until you and Queenie kissed me goodbye early on, I can't remember a girl kissing me before.'

'So a girl kisses you this evening – and a woman drags you to bed tonight! I s'pose you're entitled to be a bit overwhelmed.' She gave a short ironic chuckle. 'Shame on me at my age.'

'Oh, yes, I'm pleased you mention that,' he said, brightening up. 'How old *are* you?'

'SAM DIAMOND!' she yelled, pushing hard and angrily at

his chest. 'You do not lay on top of a highly aroused, naked woman and ask her her bloody age! Particularly in view of what's just happened, or in this case what's NOT happened!'

Sam's first instinct was to respond angrily. Yet, for the first time in his verbal confrontations with this woman, he actually saw her point of view. But more than that, he knew that in spite of everything, he enjoyed her sheer sensual presence. He may not have consummated their relationship but just the thought of being in this woman's bed delighted him. 'I'm sorry, Billie,' he muttered. 'I should have known better.'

'Well, isn't *that* a win-double?' She smiled. 'That's the first time you've called me by my name *and* the first time you've given me an apology! I bet you don't chuck many of them about.' She turned towards him and lifted one arm. 'Truce?'

'Truce,' he agreed as he rested his head against her full breasts. She slid one arm about him as he responded with both of his. 'At the moment, Sam,' she whispered, 'you're a lousy lover – we'll just have to see what we can do about that – but you're certainly a lovely cuddle. Oh, well, I s'pose a girl can't have everything. G'night, luv.' Within minutes her breathing announced she was asleep.

Sam felt far from sleep as the thoughts raced through his mind. It seemed years since he had sat in the kitchen at 14 Inkerman Place to wait for his father to go to the pub. In reality it was less than ten hours. If he had stuck with his plan to knock at Jim Forsythe's window, he would be curled up in the corner of Jim's cold sparse bedroom instead of here. But then how long would he be here? Seeing as he had failed her so badly, how long would she be prepared to put up with him? How old was she really? God, but she felt and smelt good! He kissed her shoulder lightly and drifted slowly into sleep.

The glare of a bright June morning filtered through Sam's

closed lids. When working six days each week, some built-in clock will always tell a worker that it's Sunday. Good, he didn't have to open his eyes. Someone was moving around on the bed. Being Sunday it was certainly the kids. Best way was to pretend sleep. With any luck Mum would call them. 'Let Sam sleep,' she'd say. 'Sunday's the only chance he gets.' Yes, bless her, she'd probably ensure he'd be good for another two hours yet . . . Was that a tram? What was a tram doing in Inkerman Place? More importantly, why was this bed so spacious and comfortable? It was no use, there were just too many things that couldn't be explained. Jane would know. Good old Jane, she always knew. It was no use, he'd have to find out. 'JANE!'

'So you're finally awake?'

Sam squinted at the sun and tried to place the slightly familiar voice. It was certainly not Jane's . . . Oh God! Of course! He sat bolt upright as the trim figure of Queenie parted the last of the curtains. 'I'm sorry,' he faltered. 'For the moment I couldn't think where I was. I was calling my sister. What's the time, please?'

A downstairs clock began to chime the hours. 'You won't get better service than that,' replied the maid aloofly. 'As you heard, it's noon.'

He looked around the room. 'Where's – er—'

'Miss Bardell?'

'Er, yes. Look,' he said uncomfortably, 'it's not at all like it seems, y'know. Nothing took place.' He suddenly realised just how stupid that sounded, particularly coming from someone who was naked at midday in another woman's bed. In any case, it was *exactly* like it seemed, or at least he thought it was.

'Mr Diamond,' said the girl with icy politeness, 'Miss Bardell is the mistress of this house. I am the maid. Miss Bardell tells me what she requires me to do and I do it. I don't question it, I don't consider it, I do it. Miss Bardell has asked me to tidy the room and wake you for breakfast.

That is precisely what I have done. No more, no less. And if it is of any help to you in future, when I am working for Miss Bardell, "seems" is not a word in my vocabulary so please don't let it worry you. Breakfast will be in ten minutes and the bathroom is exactly where you left it last night.'

'Er – excuse me,' he bleated, 'but I haven't got any clothes.'

'You have the robe.' She lifted it from the side of the bed. 'I understand Miss Bardell is going to discuss that problem with you over breakfast.'

Sam entered the hall, where the smell of bacon reminded him he was ravenous and the mirror reminded him he looked ridiculous.

'Morning, Sam,' greeted Billie a few minutes later. 'We've been waiting for you so we could all have breakfast. Sleep well?' Much to his relief, she spoke as if nothing had happened between them. It could hardly have been for Queenie's benefit seeing as she had sent the girl to wake him.

'What am I going to do about my clothes?' he asked, rather ungraciously.

'You're going to have breakfast.'

'I can't *wear* breakfast!'

'Oh, I don't know,' she answered thoughtfully. 'It might look better on you than that robe.'

'Then give me my old clothes back and I'll go this very minute.'

'Tut, tut, Sam. Tantrums aren't allowed at breakfast in this establishment. Queenie's under strict instructions that those with tantrums are to have no breakfast. So be good and sit down, we have a lot to discuss.'

Sam was hardly conversant with the world of domestic service but he was still surprised when Queenie, after serving breakfast, joined them for her own meal. Not only did she join them but she had obviously overcome her earlier detachment. 'Now, Sam, first things first,' said

Billie, buttering her toast. 'This is a very serious discussion so you are not to move around the room in that robe, otherwise Queenie and I will wet our knickers and forget what we're talking about.'

'If you're going to do nothing but insult me . . .'

'I'm sorry, I'm sorry,' she soothed, 'I couldn't resist it. But you're right. Joke's over, now down to the main item of the day – your clothes. How much of that ten guineas have you got left?'

'All of it.'

'ALL of it!' she echoed. 'You mean to say, you walked here from Inkerman Place at two in the morning, in the pouring rain, with ten guineas in your pocket, and you didn't get a cab?'

'I wasn't ill,' he protested. 'I wouldn't dream of getting a cab unless I was ill.'

'Well, you looked nigh on dead when you got here! But never mind, we've got to get on. Write down your measurements and give them to Queenie and she'll take them to Melvyn Silverman. He lives over his shop in Brixton. He'll come back with her with a collection of suits, shirts and shoes and fix you up. Once we've done that, you and I will go to Brixton police station and find out about you joining the police. All right so far?'

'There's a problem.'

'Then let's hear it.'

'I don't know my measurements. I'm six foot two inches tall, take size ten shoes, and I weigh about twelve and half stone but as for the rest . . .' He shrugged.

'Well, most of it's in the right place, I can tell you that,' she said, almost silently. 'Queenie, get a tape measure and measure him. Back, front, top and bottom. Whatever bit of him that's covered by a suit, stick the bloody measure over it. Better too much detail than not enough. Old Silverman may owe me a favour but I don't want to push my luck.' She turned to Sam. 'Right you, up on a chair. No, on second thoughts stay on the ground. I don't want you up on a chair in that robe, leastways not when I've just had breakfast. You know what they say. What the eye don't see, and so forth.'

'I'll do any measuring that needs doing, thank you very much,' he said firmly.

The maid was already advancing on him, tape-measure at the ready. For the first time he saw on her face a real smile. 'Sam,' she said gently, 'please, no false modesty, eh? And, anyway, how can you possibly measure yourself ? For the first time in your life you have a chance to wear something that not only fits but belongs to you. Take it.'

Sam stood up and wearily closed his eyes. 'At least I don't have to look.'

In little over an hour Melvyn Silverman had done him proud. Eight suits of different cuts and colours were laid on the dining-room table before the unanimous vote made it a plain grey three-piece. Sam had to swallow when it came to price. He discovered that tailors who come to houses do not come cheap. Four pounds fifteen shillings was at least twenty-five shillings more than he had intended to pay but Queenie's declaration that he looked 'a real sport' settled the choice. After that, fifteen shillings for a pair of black brogues and ten shillings for two shirts did not seem the least expensive. Once he had the clothes on, he was reluctant to take them off, so it was with great pleasure, following Billie's suggestion, that he went out to search for a cab. He did point out to her, albeit none too strenuously, that the police station was barely five minutes journey on a tram.

'Bloody tram? I've not been on a tram since I was a virgin,' responded Billie, though carefully failing to clarify either date.

Returning with the cab, Sam was surprised to see Billie emerge from the house alone. True to form, she looked as majestic as ever. Whenever Sam saw her unexpectedly, she never failed to impress him. Did I really sleep the night with this woman? he thought.

'As we're calling at the police station, I thought I'd leave Queenie at home to make up your room for tonight.'

'You're very kind but I can't impose on you again,' he said. 'It wouldn't be fair.'

She placed a hand on his arm. 'Once we've been to the constabulary, we're going to discuss your immediate future. But remember, unless you're staying with me, you don't even have an address to give. Let's not argue.'

Sam shrugged and within a few minutes the cab rolled to a halt in the rutted road outside the police station.

Eyebrows were certainly raised when a well-dressed young man left a beautiful woman waiting in a cab while he made inquires on joining the force as a street constable.

'Not quite our usual applicant,' muttered the old station sergeant, stroking his chin after Sam's departure. 'Lives in the big white house near the top of the Hill. Don't know what the job's coming to nowadays.'

'One thing's for sure,' said Billie as she studied the handful of recruiting forms scattered out on the seat of the carriage, 'you won't die a rich man. One pound, six shillings and sixpence a week. That's . . . let me see. That's about the cost of one leg and two arms of the suit you've just bought. I'd pay you more than that to clean my windows.'

Leaving the cab they climbed the steps to her door. There was no answer to Billie's double ring. 'She's gone! She's gone!' she repeated. 'The daft cow has done it again. Help me, Sam, please! We've got to do something about her, we must!'

Chapter 5

'Just what is going on with that girl?' asked Sam as Billie slumped down on to a settee.

'The "girl", as you call her, is my niece. My brother-in-law was a docker and was killed at work before she was born. My sister died in childbirth. My mother looked after her until I began to make money and Queenie's been with me since. She was away at school until a year or so ago but she was never happy there. Now she's back with me.' Billie paused and shook her head as if she did not really wish to tell him more. Which was probably true. 'Anyway, in her last year at school, she fell in with a group that called themselves The Women's Social and Political Union. Nowadays they call them Suffragettes.'

Sam looked hard at her. 'Is that why you asked me to cover up for her last night at the music hall?'

'Mostly, but there's more to it than that. Suffragettes don't mind being arrested. In fact, they mostly welcome it, it's part of their policy. They claim they hurt no one but will not hesitate to damage property, cause commotion and seek publicity. If they are sentenced to prison, they will frequently go on hunger strike.'

'Are you one?' asked Sam.

'Bless you, no,' Billie chuckled. 'I don't usually need a vote to get my way. Especially with men. But, anyway, that's her choice. The big problem with Queenie is that if she does go to prison, even once, it could well be the end of her.'

'But why?'

'Because she is also a severe epileptic. Any form of stress can bring it on. I don't know if you've ever seen Holloway prison but personally I would have a fit just passing by in a cab. The organisation have told her she can help by doing administration work and such like, which would at least keep her off the streets, but she won't agree. She's a stubborn bitch at times, gets it from my side of the family, I s'pose. She says that as long as she's a Suffragette then she'll do all the things that Suffragettes are expected to do. That is except one. That "one" is, of course, be arrested. Yet even though she's terrified, still she goes out with those bloody lunatics. And, what makes me even madder, they let her! Personally I think they're looking for martyrs and you won't find many better martyrs than a young epileptic orphaned girl. She'd be such a perfect tear-jerker, they'd think she was a gift from heaven.'

'But haven't you told them?'

'Haven't I told them!' she echoed. 'At times I feel I do bugger all else! But they're fanatics! Nothing matters to them except their soddin' "cause". Trouble is, the police are getting closer and closer. They were here last night when we arrived home. The only thing that put them off the scent was she had a fit in the cab. When you see her in that state, you just can't believe she can go around smashin' windows, wrecking elections and slinging eggs at prime ministers. Blimey! That's a thought, Sam! What happens if you became a copper? I reckon you'd have to nick her.' She poured herself out a gin. 'Join me?' The young man shook his head. 'You know the answer, Sam, don't you?'

'I don't, but my dad always reckons most problems are caused because kids didn't have their backsides smacked as children.'

'Thoughtful man, your dad, but he's only half right.'

'What d'you mean?'

'Well, there's no fun havin' your arse spanked when you're a kid. But with the right bloke, it can be a lot more interesting when you're a big girl!'

He stared at her with a bewildered frown. 'You know, there are times when I haven't the faintest idea what you're talking about – and this is one of them.'

She took a long sip from the glass. 'As we discovered last night, Sam, you've quite a bit to learn but, to put it bluntly, I'm saying this girl needs a good man. If nothing else it'd give her another interest. Trouble is, she doesn't agree.'

'And I'm s'posed to be the answer?'

'Oh, c'mon, Sam, you can't fool me. You like my Queenie a great deal, it's written all over you. You would have been far more relaxed in bed with her last night than ever you were with me. I'm pretty sure you're a man who has to be in charge of his relationships and, for that reason, you found me too intimidating.' She shrugged. 'And you're probably right, I *am* intimidating, both in and out of bed. In fact, Queenie reckons I'm a scalp hunter. But then my Queenie's like an iceberg – seven-eighths of her are concealed and a man would need to work on her to melt her. But with me, what you see is what you get. By the way, you were very lucky last night because I intended to devour you . . .' she shook her head in slow disbelief '. . . instead I finished up mothering you. And believe you me, Billie Bardell is *not* the mothering sort. So don't worry, there'll be no heavy seduction again.'

Further conversation was interrupted by the doorbell. On opening the door, Sam was faced by an elderly cab-man who respectfully touched his hat. The man's face was annoyingly familiar. 'Could I speak ter the lidy of the 'ouse, sir? Miss Bardell, I fink she is, sir.'

Billie was there almost before the man had finished. 'Yes, George?'

'Ma'am, I drops orf four o' them Suffragette ladies for a demonstration they wuz all 'aving in Battersea Park this arter'noon and, as I does, I fort I'd go dahn the riverside ter eat me san'widges, it bein' a nice day an' all that. As I does, I sees a young gel on a bench. She didn't look yer usual type that kips on park benches an' I'm fair sure it's your young lidy. I couldn't git too close, y'understand, her bein' a young gel an' me 'aving me badge ter consider.'

'Where? Where, George? Take us there now!'

'O' course, ma'am.'

For the third time in twelve hours Sam found himself travelling through the centre of Brixton. He sheepishly glanced at the arcade entrance but still could not see a letter-box, though it suddenly came to him where he had previously seen the cab driver. On their last meeting the man had been anything but respectful.

'Here !' he exclaimed to Billie. 'I know him ! He was your cabbie when you fell over our kerbstone. He might be nice and respectful now but he was a miserable old sod then, and he called me a bugger!'

'Just goes to show the difference a good suit makes for you,' she replied.

'I s'pose so,' murmured the young man, staring down at his cuffs.

'That's where she was, ma'am, the bench nearest the river . . . though she ain't there nah!' he added needlessly.

'Stop the cab, George,' said Billie. 'There are some bushes behind that bench, we'll have a search around.'

'Has she a yellow scarf?' asked Sam.

'Yes,' said Billie. 'With little green patterns on the corners.'

'There!' pointed Sam. Entwined in some tired late-season wallflowers was the scarf in question. He ran to the spot and pointed to scuff marks leading from the bench, over a short section of pavement, through the flower-bed and into the bushes.

'My God! She must have been dragged!' exclaimed Billie.

Sam tore through and over the bushes. Crashing through the last of them, he was in time to discover two men kneeling beside the prostrate girl. One was crouched by her waist and, with her handbag stuffed in the top of his coat, was busy tearing the rings from her fingers. The other had ripped open her blouse and was obviously trying to disentangle a delicate crucifix from her neck. Blood seeping from her ear-lobes indicated some success had already been achieved with her earrings. To make matters worse, the girl was barely conscious and obviously terrified.

Sam's first blow was with his brand new right shoe. This all but lifted the necklace thief from the ground. The second man unwisely concentrated on one last pull on a ring, rather than the first quick steps of an escape. Crouching, with an unprotected head, was never going to be the best way to avoid a punch from an angry Sam Diamond. Frank Cootes would have sympathised. The necklace thief, minus his entire front teeth, was at least sitting up but when the young girl's first scream was emitted, he wished he'd feigned death.

'Shush, my baby, shush!' cried Billie as she rocked and cradled the now hysterical and bleeding Queenie tearfully to her breast. 'Kill 'em! Kill the bastards, Sam! Drown the fuckin' scum!' she screamed as she nodded her head towards the head-high river wall a few yards distant. If Sam had any charitable notions as to the immediate future of the two footpads, the sight of the weeping Billie and terror-stricken Queenie erased them. After the recovery of all the loot, first one thief, then the other was rolled unceremoniously over the thick granite wall and into the river. Turning back to the two women, Sam barely noticed the splash.

The girl had grown quiet but Sam found her pale haunted face even more distressing than her screams. Billie gritted her teeth and snarled, 'Before you threw them over that wall, Sam Diamond, I should have cut the balls off 'em! At least I'd sleep better at nights.'

'Nah, ma'am, nah,' said the old cabbie, suddenly appearing with an equally ancient park-keeper in tow. 'You've got it all wrong, you 'ave, ain't she, Bert? I fink you wus too upset ter see proper. Wouldn't yer say so, Bert?'

Bert said he thought the nice lady was too upset and had not quite understood what had happened. Anyone looking at the poor lass lying on the ground could easily see how anyone *would* be upset in the circumstances, it was enough to upset a saint. The two felons had obviously been frightened by the young rescuer and had tried to escape by running along the river wall. Very dangerous practice, Bert said, running along river walls. People fall in, he said, happens all the time. In any case, he added rather sadly, they didn't appeared to have drowned because he could hear them shouting. The three men went to the wall and looked over. The thieves certainly had not drowned, the river was barely eighteen inches deep at low tide. On the other hand, the debris in the water had hardly cushioned their fall and neither of them appeared to be moving very much. Bert said he thought it would be a good idea if Sam and Billie took the young lass home and sometime or other he would see if he could find a policeman and tell him how the two men had been silly enough to run along the river wall and fall in. In the absence of boiling oil to pour down on them, Billie accepted.

Cuddling and soothing the girl for most of the journey home, she asked Sam to carry her into the house. 'Shall I put her in her room?' he asked.

'No, put her on the day-bed in the parlour. She's come round quite a bit now. Perhaps it may be a good time to talk.' Adding under her breath, 'Whilst she's still terrified.'

'Sam, can you give us a few minutes while I clean her up and bathe her cuts and grazes? Perhaps you could make some tea or something? Take your time, I'll call when we're ready.'

He picked his way round the kitchen like a fusilier in a

minefield. In Inkerman Place almost everything was in the kitchen. It needed to be because the kitchen *was* everything. Workshop, bathroom, dining-room, store-room, social club and, in some households, bedroom. Here, a kitchen was four times the size with a twentieth of the function. In Inkerman Place each kitchen contained a hundred tiny items and all could be found. Here there were barely a dozen and Sam could find nothing. After twenty minutes of prodding and prying, a weak-looking Queenie entered. 'Miss Bardell said you'd be unable to manage,' she said with a wan smile. 'And she was right.' She came straight up to him and kissed him on the cheek. 'I've also heard what happened . . . thank you.'

She made to move away but he seized her around the waist and held her tight. 'You frightened me today as I've never been frightened in my life. Don't you ever do that again.'

'I can't help it. I don't do it to order, you know.'

'You went to Battersea Park by order though.'

'Oh, that.' She shrugged. 'That's got nothing to do with it.'

He gave a frustrated sigh. 'I would have thought it had everything to do with it. Anyway, how are you now?'

'I'm recovering very well, thanks to you. I've got my bag and jewellery back plus a couple of sore ears, but I'll live. You'd better let me make this tea or we'll get it in time for breakfast.'

Queenie allowed Sam to carry the tea tray into the parlour and for the first time in his experience, there seemed to be a relaxed atmosphere about the place. 'Talk to her, Sam,' said Billie softly. 'I'm bloody near giving up. Tell her she'll kill herself at this rate.'

Sam, whose own streak of obstinacy rarely lent itself to reasoned argument, did his best. 'But why on earth do you keep doing this? Surely now this has happened you'll think twice?'

'Sam, you're a real smashin' fellow and it's possible I even owe you my life but not even you can make my decisions for me. I am a grown-up woman. I live in a twentieth-century, allegedly civilised country. I'm not in the least ambitious, Sam. One day I want to marry and perhaps have children and that's about the sum total of what I really expect of life. Just to love and be loved if you like. But those two monsters who you threw – sorry, who fell – over that wall this afternoon, have the vote. AND I DON'T! That infuriates me, Sam, can you not see?'

'I don't know what the fuss is about,' sighed Billie. 'Half the buggers who can vote never do. So what's so bloody important about the privilege of voting?'

Queenie shook her head in despair. 'But don't you see? If I was allowed to vote but didn't, it's not even important. The fact is, I must have the *right* to vote. Not privilege – RIGHT!'

'But *that's* what I don't understand!' exclaimed Billie triumphantly. 'How can you say it wouldn't be important if you didn't vote? If I went through what you've been through these last few months, I wouldn't want just to vote for those buggers in Parliament, I'd want to be elected! And not simply for Parliament but for every bloody council south of Wigan!'

'Can I make a suggestion?' asked Sam. Both women stared at him by way of assent. 'You would agree you've had two near escapes in the last couple of days?' Queenie nodded. 'Okay, then let's have a cease-fire, at least until you're a bit more stable. It's now June. How about no more suffragetting till . . . shall we say . . . Christmas?'

'September?' offered the girl.

'November!' cut in Billie. 'And the thirtieth at that!'

'November,' agreed the girl. 'But the fifth – Guy Fawkes Day – would be more appropriate, don't you think?'

'No. But if you want to be "appropriate",' sniffed Billie, 'try April the first.'

The discussion was terminated by a ring at the doorbell. The maid's instinctive move was forestalled by Sam's restraining hand. 'I'll go,' he said. Glancing quickly at Billie, he received a brief nod of assent.

Sam returned within seconds, closely followed by a slightly built uniformed police inspector. 'Evening, ladies,' the newcomer greeted them. 'I'm Inspector Beck from Brixton police station. I've called on you regarding a telephone message we've received from Battersea police.' A look of anxiety instantly clouded the girl's face.

'Don't be alarmed, m'dears,' the inspector continued. 'I've just called to see if you can help on a matter that took place in Battersea Park this afternoon. Apparently Battersea police were called by a park-keeper, Mr Herbert Horace Hancock – though they tell me that's not quite how he pronounces it – and as a result apprehended a couple of right villains. Though "*they* apprehended" may not be the correct phrase. They apparently found them stuck waist deep in the incoming tide. One of them has sustained a broken jaw and half his teeth are missing; the other has a broken leg and collar-bone. Besides which they have an interesting motley of cuts and bruises. According to Mr Hancock, it would appear that these two characters slipped whilst running along the river wall and sustained these injuries on the debris laying in the shallows below the wall.'

Closing his notebook he ran his gaze around the trio. 'I understand from witnesses, Miss Bardell, that you were in the park at the time. It is just possible that these men could have either been seen by you, or may even have made some attempt to rob you. After all, robbery is their game. Could they perhaps have been making their escape? I must emphasise there is nothing for you to worry about. This pair have so much outstanding against them that we are delighted to have them in custody.'

'Have they not told you what they were doing?' asked Billie.

'Lord bless you, ma'am!' exclaimed the inspector. 'These two wouldn't give anyone the time of day, never mind recite their nefarious activities.'

'So what will happen to them?' asked Queenie quietly.

'With the form they've got, plus the offences already outstanding against them, I reckon they'd be looking at . . .' he scratched his chin thoughtfully '. . . at least seven years, with luck perhaps nine.'

'Seems a very long time,' murmured the girl almost sadly to herself.

'Well, I certainly didn't see anything, did either of you two?' queried Billie. Her companions shook their heads.

'That's what I guessed, ma'am,' replied the inspector folding his book, 'but you understand we have to pursue all these inquiries? I mean,' he said pointedly, 'we wouldn't like you to appear in a week or so's time and tell us you've been robbed when we could easily have cleared it up tonight, now would we, ma'am?'

'Certainly not, Inspector,' agreed Billie. 'Can I offer you a gin before you leave?'

'That's very kind of you, ma'am. Providing your good self will partake, I'd be delighted. Can I also say how much I have enjoyed your performances whenever I have seen you on the halls.'

'That's gracious of you, kind sir.'

'Whilst I am here, ma'am, and with your permission, I wonder if I might kill two birds with one stone – if you'll pardon the expression, ma'am?'

'And that is?'

'It concerns this young man here. I take it you *are* Samuel Diamond who has recently shown interest in joining the Metropolitan Police?'

'I am,' he replied, somewhat uncertain.

'Good. I am the Inspector for the Brixton area who has

to verify these applications. It would save me a great deal of time and also cut your waiting period if I may do it now. If it's convenient, o' course, ma'am?'

'Anything if it saves time, Inspector.'

'Excellent. Do you reside permanently at this address, Mr Diamond?'

Before the young man could answer, Billie cut in, 'He's my live-in footman-cum-handyman. He is staying here together with his fiancée who is also my maid and niece, Miss Queenie Cotterill. Separate quarters, of course!' she added hastily.

'Oh, of course, ma'am, of course,' agreed the inspector. 'But this fiancée business could present something of a problem. The constabulary frowns on it a bit, I'm afraid.'

'Whatever for?' exclaimed Billie.

'Well, recruits aren't allowed to marry until they have two years' service. Gives 'em a chance to establish themselves and such like. We find that young girls like to feel their man is settled when they marry.'

Sam felt the conversation was leaving him behind before he had even taken part in it. It was already too late to do anything about the address, the die had already been cast, but to be afflicted with an intended bride, delightful though she may be, was really too much. 'We have only *just* become engaged, sir,' he explained. 'So a two-year engagement would be ideal. It would take us that long to see if we were suited and to save for some furniture.'

'So you see no problems in that field?'

'None at all, sir, though I take it a man is permitted to change his mind?'

'In what respect?' the inspector asked testily.

'In his engagement, sir.'

'His engagement?' the inspector repeated. 'His engagement? Good God, man, a fiancée is not *obligatory*! In fact, to some gels I have seen, it's not even advisable!' Turning swiftly to the by now quietly seething Queenie, he quickly added, 'Present company excepted, of course, Miss Cotterill.'

'It's nice to hear it, Inspector,' she replied through tight lips.

'If you have no more questions, I'll thank you for your hospitality and take my leave of you all. Who knows? Perhaps I'll see you, Mr Diamond, some time during your service. Though you do realise the informality of this pleasant evening will not necessarily be carried over into duty matters?'

'I understand fully, sir.'

'Very well, Mr Diamond. I'm going to send you an appointment for a physical in a few weeks' time. D'you feel ready for it?'

'Well, I don't really know what "it" is, sir.'

'You will need to be able to write, spell, and know the first four rules of arithmetic. You will need to be of a strong constitution, free from bodily complaint and without debts. All right so far?'

'I think so, sir. Anything else?'

'Well, there'll be a medical but I should think you'll have no worries on that score. But after that, you will attend Wellington Barracks for three weeks where you'll learn first aid, drill, take the oath and be kitted out. You'll then go to a police station where you will learn the job via a twenty-six-page book and a series of attachments and lessons. D'you have any other questions you wish to ask me about the force?'

'Just one about days off, sir. I work a six-day week in my present employment. Will it be any different in the police force?'

'Oh, yes, Mr Diamond, it is indeed different. At the moment you will not be getting any days off at all. But nil desperandum, because we have heard on the grapevine that we may well be allowed a day's leave each week from next year. Yes,' he smiled knowingly, 'I thought that might please you.' He turned to the faintly amused Billie. 'And now I really must take my leave of you and your charming house, Miss Bardell. And have no fears about the two rogues in Battersea Park.' He placed a finger to his lips. 'There is no doubt in my mind you were nowhere near the scene of their unfortunate accident and I'll inform Battersea police to that effect.' Bowing low before her, he bade her goodnight again and followed Sam to the front door.

'What an insufferable prig!' exploded Queenie at the sound of the front door closing. 'He was talking about me as if I wasn't here!'

'And what's all this clap-trap about me being engaged?' added Sam who had just entered the room.

'Listen, you two,' instructed Billie. 'You, young lady, are very lucky that it wasn't some clever dick copper arriving with a warrant to swift you off to Holloway, or even the sodding Tower of bloody London! Whether you admit it or not, you most definitely have had a good result this evening. He thinks you're some demure little miss who's starry-eyed about marrying one of his thirty bob a week coppers. Little does he know that given half a chance you'd cover the Prince of Wales in horse shit!' She then turned to Sam. 'And as for you, what chance of getting in the force d'you think you'd have, if he knew that less than twenty-four hours ago you had nowhere to live and were clad in rags that, at the moment, are contaminating my dustbin? You know what I suggest you two do?' She glanced quickly from one to the other. 'No? Well, I'll tell you both. You should take this chance and start afresh. You –' she pointed an angry finger at the maid '– stop breaking windows, my heart, and being a complete bloody nuisance. And you –' she wheeled on Sam '– stop feeling so bloody sorry for yourself, take what's offered to you with good grace, and for Gawd's sake, Sam, laugh for once in a while!'

'It's all right for you to say that but . . .' he began.

'No, it's *not* sodding all right for me to say any such thing! In fact it's anything BUT all right. I shouldn't really have to say it at all! I'm offering you a job and accommodation here, either permanently or until you enter the police force. I'm prepared to pay you two bob more than you're going to get in the force but for that you are going to have to work. Maybe not as hard as you did on the pavements but bloody hard nevertheless. This is a big house, there's plenty to do, and you'll escort me to and from every show be it a matinee or a royal command performance. One of your first jobs will be to keep that bloody animal Cootes out of my changing room. Now I'm losing my temper with you, Sam Diamond, so take it or leave it.'

'Take it, Sam! Take it!' pleaded the maid, as she ran to kneel at his feet. 'It's just got to be the way for you, you must see that surely?'

He fondly ruffled her hair then looked across at the waiting Billie. 'So, when do I start?'

'You've already started, Sam. You started at three-thirty this morning when you first rang my bell. What say we all have a gin, eh?' The girl rose from her kneeling position. 'No,' said Billie, raising her hand. 'New start . . . my treat. I'll pour this one for you both, though I assure you it won't become a habit. And then – well, who's for an early night? I feel like I've been up since Wednesday.'

Soon they had all said their goodnights and, as the two women occupied the two bathrooms, Sam began the first of his official duties by making the final check of the house. The evening was warm and pleasant and he stood at the open front door idly watching the cab-horses plod their weary way up the hill. He wondered how his family were and what would happen when he failed to arrive for work next morning. He smiled to himself as he imagined Archie's reaction should the foreman ever discover that he had slept with Billie. The fact that 'sleep' with her was all he had done, would have made no difference to poor

Archie's fantasies. He would never have stopped asking questions. There was no doubt about it, even though it had been the most embarrassing moment of Sam's life, she was still a stunning woman. As he reminisced about her, he thought he could once again smell her perfume. He suddenly froze. It *was* the smell of her perfume.

'Don't worry, Sam,' she whispered softly from behind him. 'Your virginity is safe with me. I've just popped down to say that I'm delighted you're staying with me and Queenie. You know where your room is. And don't worry, you don't have to lock the door.'

He turned slowly to her and again felt the same thrill as he had last night. The white satin robe sat perfectly about her, no doubt covering the white silk gown that had so excited him before. She stood on tip-toe to kiss his cheek and, wishing him goodnight, began to glide away.

'Billie,' he called.

She stopped and turned. 'Yes?'

'In that outfit you certainly would be elected.' He shook his head in wonderment and recited: '"Not-just-for-parliament-but-for-every-bloody-council-south-of-Wigan!"'

She threw back her head and gave the widest of smiles. 'Not a joke, Sam Diamond, surely? There's no doubt about it, lover . . . we're getting there!'

Chapter 6

Distant chimes told the waking Nell Diamond it was fifteen minutes to some hour or other but she neither knew nor cared what that hour was. Slowly her thoughts settled. What day was it? God, Monday! Oh, well, at least it was still dark. Better check the clock though, Kate needed to be called at four. Tiredness lay on her like a stifling giant. Following Sam's departure the previous night, she felt she had not closed her eyes for an eternity. It was true old John had not been well but he had also been an absolute pig. She found herself envying Sam and wondering exactly where in the Forsythe household he would be sleeping. Very nice family the Forsythes, she'd always had a soft spot for Jim and secretly hoped Jane did, too. He'd make a lovely son-in-law one day, would Jim.

Peering at the double-belled alarm clock, it did appear to be verging near four o'clock. She must look, she dare not let the girl be late. Her discreet movements towards the clock were geared to avoid disturbing the old man. At least when he was asleep he wasn't complaining, threatening, or coughing up his lungs. She was marginally aware of a strange imbalance in the room. Something was missing but what? Of course, John's laboured breathing! She turned quickly but the other side of the bed was empty. The clothes were thrown back but of John there was no sign. She could not believe she could have failed to hear him leave, she *always* heard him leave. But then the sheer exhaustion of the last few days must have taken its toll on her. Yes, that was it.

Released from the immediate fear of disturbing him, she turned with the clock until the hands were clearly in focus. Five minutes to go! A whole five minute lie-in. Bliss! She curled up and closed her eyes in anticipation of the luxury. Suddenly she froze, almost before the thought had struck her. What *had* actually woken her and why was he not back? Never in all their married life had he used the chamber-pot. Rain or shine, hot or cold, impaired or untroubled, he would *always* insist on struggling down to the outside privy. God only knows how he had managed it at times, particularly these last few months, nevertheless he had always done so and always she had heard him ascend those creaking steps. Funny that, they never made a sound on the way down but almost every one of them creaked and groaned on the return. It was as if they did not want him back. She felt the spot he had slept on; there was no hint of body-warmth.

Sliding into her old felt slippers, she gathered her shawl about her voluminous flannelette nightgown and made quickly for the staircase. Her eyes, now accustomed to the gloom, told her the back door was open. It was open because it could not be closed. It could not be closed because a body lay sprawled over the step.

Sam opened the front door and bent to collect the milk and newspaper. It may have been his first day as a – what was it Billie had said – 'live-in-footman-cum-handyman' but already he found himself liking the hours. Normally he would have been at work for at least an hour before this time. As he straightened he watched the flurry of passing traffic. From six in the morning until near midnight, the rattle of the trams seemed non-stop. The smell of bacon was again pervading the air as Queenie busied herself in the kitchen. Sam spread the *News Chronicle* over the table and turned to the cricket page.

'Er – Sam,' began Queenie, 'if you are going to stay here any length of time, there are two things of which you should be aware at this time of the morning.'

'They are?' he asked, without lifting his gaze.

'Unless she has had a sleeping companion, Miss Bardell is not particularly chatty at breakfast time. And, though that improves if she has had, shall we say, a *happy* night, what does not improve is her aversion to anyone reading her paper before she does.' She raised her hands instantly. 'Yes, I know you think it's illogical, but when it's her house and she pays the wages then she can make the rules.'

'Does she have many of these – happy nights – as you call them?'

'How many she has is none of my business. I am just advising you of the house rules, that's all.'

'Well, as far as I'm concerned,' said Sam churlishly, 'she can sleep with the bloody household cavalry if she wants. I'm sure it's nothing to me either.'

'*Should* I ever contemplate sleeping with the household cavalry, Sam,' came Billie's voice from behind him, 'I shall request I sleep mainly with the band. That way they can wake you with a nice tune. What would you like – Post Horn Gallop perhaps?' Sam's intended response was interrupted. 'No, don't answer that. As my maid has just pointed out to you, if I've not had a *happy* night I'm not particularly chatty. Well . . . let's just say I've not had a happy night, shall we?'

The strained silence over breakfast was eventually broken by the doorbell.

'I'll go,' volunteered Sam, eager for any excuse to leave the stifling atmosphere. On opening the door he was surprised to be faced with Jim Forsythe. 'What on earth are you doing here?' asked Sam.

'I'm not being made welcome, if that's what you're asking.'

'Oh, come on, Jim, you know what I mean. How did you know I was here?'

'Well, you weren't at home with your mum, you weren't with me and you didn't turn up for work this morning. In addition to that, I was there when Miss Bardell offered you a place to stay. I didn't have to be a genius to work it out. Anyway, I have some bad news. Leastways, I think it's bad news – your father died this morning.'

Sam stared at him for several moments. 'Yes,' he murmured slowly, 'it *is* bad news. I suppose I can't say we were ever friends but things were different before he became ill.'

'But he used to knock your mum about even then,' said Jim undiplomatically.

Sam shrugged. 'I s'pose it's a way of life in a cess-pit like Inkerman Place.'

'If that's who I think it is, fetch him in,' came Billie's distant voice. Sam led the way and the two lads entered the room. After politely greeting the women Jim soon acquainted his audience with the details of John Diamond's death.

'Hardly a dignified ending,' said Queenie softly. 'How is Mrs Diamond taking it?'

'Pretty much how she takes everything else,' said Jim. 'She lives for her kids and seems unmoved by everything else.'

'But that's a front, we all know that,' said Sam, turning to Billie. 'I'm sorry but I must go home.'

'Of course you must,' she replied. 'Remember, though, my offer of a place here still stands. And don't forget that you'll need this address until your application for the police force is approved.' At those words Jim glanced quickly at Sam but said nothing.

The tramcar swayed alarmingly as it negotiated the tight bends at the Elephant and Castle. Jim sat enthralled as Sam recounted the events since their last meeting. 'But what's all this about the police?' he queried.

'I felt it was time I made a new start, that's all.'

'What sort of a new start is that going to be?' persisted Jim. 'You're going to get less money than being a paviour! Couple more new starts like that and you'll be in the doss-house.'

'Jim,' said Sam suddenly, 'why don't you join me? We get on together, we've known each other all our lives, I'm sure we could do it. If you get an application in soon enough, we may even be accepted at the same time.'

'You and me, coppers?' laughed Jim. 'I know what Archie would say. He'd reckon Billie Bardell had affected your brain.'

'And I'm not so sure he wouldn't be right,' agreed Sam ruefully, as the conductor rang the bell for Blackfriars Road.

Monday washday was obviously in full swing as the friends passed under the dripping garments hanging from the lines tied to the old tree. Clem Botwright the undertaker was just taking his farewell from Nell at the doorway of number 14.

'Oh Sam, Sam!' cried Nell as she threw her arms about her son's neck and, for the first time since her bereavement, sobbed pitifully.

'I'll leave you now—' began Jim.

'No. No, please, Jim, don't go,' she pleaded as she slipped her arms from round her son's neck. 'I've always thought of you as one of my own. Please stay, son.'

'O' course, Mrs Diamond, of course,' he replied with a thickening voice as he kissed her cheek.

'Is Dad still here or have they taken him away?' asked Sam.

'He's still upstairs. I've just paid Mr Botwright a deposit

and he's gone to get his cart. I can't have him lying upstairs until the funeral, not with all the children in the house.'

The friends and the new widow climbed the creaking stairs to the bedroom. The clay-faced corpse lay night-attired in the centre of the bed. Sam stared and shook his head slowly. 'The old chap seemed to have been ill for years,' he said. 'In fact, I can barely remember when he was well. How long has it been, Mum?'

'Five years, though it seems like fifty. By the way, Sam, you always seem to have referred to him as "the old man". How old do you think he really was?'

'I honestly don't know,' answered Sam. 'I suppose he always seemed to be old to me. What was he then . . . sixty . . . sixty-five?'

She gave a sad smile. 'I can't blame your guesswork, son, lousy though it is,' she said. 'But your father died four days before his forty-second birthday and your mother is two months out of her thirties. D'you know what that means, Sam?'

He shook his head. 'Then I'll ask you that same question, Jim Forsythe, d'*you* know what that means?' Again a shaken head. 'It means that whatever else you two boys do, you should get as far away from Inkerman Place as possible. Because in the end, it'll do for you just as easily as it did my John.'

Sam stayed at Inkerman Place until the funeral, then, more on his mother's insistence than from his own choice, he returned to Brixton Hill. For three weeks he settled into a routine of scheduling Billie's transport from one music hall engagement to another. Her trust in him deepened daily as she relied on him more and more.

After lunch on Sunday of the third week, Billie was studying her dressing-room accommodation details for the following day. Her customary double booking was going to be particularly tight. She was scheduled to close the first half of the show at the Gattis in Westminster Bridge Road, then she was to dash quickly down the Old Kent Road and across two boroughs to the New Cross Empire for her act before the great Harry Lauder's finale. This was complicated by the limited dressing-room space in the second theatre. Not only did she have to share once more, but the interval act was again to be Eugene Sandow and The Bolivian Bull.

'Luckily I've got my own dressing-screens, Sam, but get this straight – I want you in that dressing room from the moment I enter to the moment I leave. Frank Cootes is getting creepier by the minute.'

'You're not sharing the dressing room with those two?' asked Queenie in horror.

'No, they're in another room. I'm sharing with . . .' she studied a neatly written letter '. . . let me see. Oh, here it is! Elkela Sorensen – The Finnish Nightingale. I know her, she's all right. Her real name is Ada Brinks and she comes from Hackney. The other act is Nicoli Tominski with Serena and Sirdani. I haven't the faintest idea what they do, jugglers most probably. Have a look, Sam, please. There's a handbill on the hall-stand.'

Sam glanced quickly down until the name Tominski caught his eye. 'D'you say you've got screens?' he asked. 'You sure they're not nets?'

'O' course I'm sure! What the bleedin' hell would I want nets for?' she asked.

'You *might* need them to catch Serena and Sirdani – they're performing seals!'

'SEALS!' she screamed. 'Bloody seals! I'm not sharing a room with seals for any bugger and that's that!'

'It's all right,' assured Sam, desperately trying to keep a straight face, 'they're PERFORMING seals.'

'PERFORMING?' she echoed. 'PERFORMING! Look, I don't care if they sing and play bag-pipes, I am not sharing a dressing room with *any* animal, least of all soddin' seals. Deptford Creek's not far away, let them shove 'em in a boat. Can you imagine the stink and the noise? When they're not clapping their hands for kippers they're farting or belching. SEALS ARE OUT! OUT, d'you hear me? And if that prat of a stage-manager thinks otherwise, I'll have *him* doing tricks with a ball on his nose.'

Queenie, who could normally ride most outbursts by her mistress with ease, suddenly dissolved. Her uncontrolled laughter set Sam off in turn. The two of them fell on to the settee and the sight of their hilarity finally reduced Billie's absolute fury to a rueful smile. 'I'm sorry, Miss Bardell,' said the maid, wiping a tear from her eye, 'but just the thought of you – of all people – sharing with a pair of seals, well . . .'

Billie watched the pair until their laughter finally faded. 'Sam,' she said thoughtfully, 'you seem to be very happy here, wouldn't you say?' He agreed he was. 'In that case, why don't you make the stay permanent? I know your plans are to join the police but surely this can be a better life for you? I'll give you a raise and you can help your family any time it's needed. I'm sure you'll be happy here.'

'I'm sure I would,' agreed the young man. He stared out of the window for some moments. 'Let me think it over, please?'

'Okay, I agree. No more about it for now. Right.' She stood up smartly and rubbed her hands briskly together. 'That's the talk taken care of. You, Sam Diamond, get yourself out of here and get a cab down to New Cross and tell that idiot at the Empire if I so much as smell a seal in my dressing room on Monday evening, it'll be rammed up his arse before Tuesday morning. NO BLOODY SEALS! UNDERSTAND?'

He saluted mockingly. 'No bloody seals! Understood, ma'am!' Then, turning swiftly on his heel, he departed.

On the journey to New Cross, Sam reflected to himself how much he had enjoyed the routine of his few Sundays at Billie's. He would take a tram in the morning to see his family and slip his mother a few shillings. He would follow that with a quick pint with Jim Forsythe, who would update him on the news of his old workmates. Then, each week, the pair of them would concoct increasingly lurid tales concerning Billie for Archie Surridge to drool over for the next six days. Sam would return for an excellent lunch cooked by Queenie and, in the afternoon, Billie would usually hire an open carriage and the three of them would take a trip to one of London's many parks. Today, having received a grovelling apology from the Empire's manager, he was able to announce to Billie on his return that not only were seals out of the room but so was their trainer.

'In that case,' she said chirpily, 'what say we pack a bottle of bubbly and go to Richmond Park for the afternoon? Don't worry, Queenie,' she added, 'I'll pay out of household accounts.'

It had truly been a good day, as Sam later recounted to himself whilst checking the front door at midnight. He was surprised how easily he had taken to the life. Just to be near Queenie was more pleasing as each day passed. Both women had gone to bed an hour or so earlier but the sticky June evening caused him to sit on top of the outside steps and muse over the changes that had overtaken him. If he had had to make a decision at that moment, it would not have been difficult.

The last of the traffic had gone as he finally rose to his feet and closed the door. He was not the lightest on his feet and the total darkness of the house reminded him how long it had been since his companions had gone to bed. He took off his shoes and tip-toed to his room. Sam rarely drew his curtains, relying on the outside street lamp to give sufficient light for his needs. In any case, by now he knew the position of every piece of furniture in the room. He undressed and stood by the window, marvelling at the clarity of the midsummer night sky. He had slipped his right leg into the sheets before he realised he was not to be the bed's only occupant.

'Of course, you're not going to believe this, Sam Diamond, but bed is the only place where I think I can break down your defences.' He moved his hand instinctively across her body but this time there was no touch of silk, just woman. 'Listen to me, Sam. I'm offering you something dreams are made of. I think you already know that you and my Queenie are just about to topple in love. So why don't you finally decide to stay? This cosy threesome can't and won't last, and that's right and proper. But you can stay here for a year or so and let matters take their course. If by then you two see your future together then that's fine by me. Apart from anything else, you may be able to stop me prowling like some alley cat for a year.' She took his hand and began to slide it over her body.

'And what will Queenie have to say about that?' he whispered as, in spite of himself, he began to respond to her.

'If I know Queenie, she'll be bloody furious! But it's not a new situation to her. There have been men before, too many. But none of them has been of interest to her, or dare I say in love with her. Now *me* she can take in her stride, but whether she'll want to knife *you* is your problem. The situation would most certainly suit me – and, I suspect, you.'

As he began to kiss her he whispered, 'You are a hell of a selfish cow.'

'Oh, I know, I know, and I promise I'll be full of remorse. But, Sam–' she wriggled into a more yielding position '–let's leave the remorse for a nice chatty breakfast, eh? Meantime I've one or two things to teach you . . .'

Sam picked up the milk, letters and newspaper and, kicking

the front door shut behind him, strolled preoccupied to the kitchen, pausing only to drop several letters on the hall-stand. 'Mornin',' he called to Queenie who was already busy at the stove. Any reply the girl may have made was cut short by Billie's quiet humming as she descended the wide stairs. 'Mornin', Queenie. Mornin', Sam,' she greeted them gaily. 'One of the letters was for you, Sam. Not quite with it this morning, are we? I wonder why?'

Queenie shot an inquiring glance at Sam who blushed instantly. 'M-Me?' he stammered. 'Who's written to me? I don't know anyone who is likely to write to me.'

'How about the constabulary?' said Queenie. Although she addressed the remark to Sam, her stare never moved from Billie. 'Not only do they know you're here, they are under the impression you're a permanent fixture.'

Sam scanned the short note. 'You're right! It says I have an interview at Scotland Yard on Thursday afternoon.'

'Remember, my offer of a job still stands, Sam,' reminded Billie.

'Yes, I haven't forgotten. If you don't mind giving me till the end of the week, I'll let you know then.'

'Fine. In the meantime, your number one priority is to keep my dressing room free from Cootes. It's a bleedin' toss up who smells worse, Frank or the seals.'

The show at the Gattis had gone particularly well and Sam thought he had never seen Billie perform better. The ride to New Cross was not without its moments, though. They were still two miles from the theatre when Billie complained she could already smell seals. Sam wearily pointed to the stagnant black waters of the Grand Union Canal which bisected the Old Kent Road. This explanation pacified her until the cab finally rolled to a halt outside the stage door, whereupon a large photograph of Tominski rekindled the phobia. Sam left Billie speaking to the management and musicians whilst he sought out the dressing room. Deciding to put the time to good use, he explored every corner of the room, sniffing deeply. If there had been any seals he certainly couldn't smell them. 'Sam, what *are* you doing?' came a familiar male voice from the open door.

'Checking for seals,' he replied slowly, as if he was explaining a simple matter to a half-wit. 'Anyway,' he said looking up, 'what are *you* doing here?'

Jim Forsythe pulled a long white envelope from an inside pocket. 'I thought this is where I'd find you. Y'got one of these?'

'Uh huh.'

'Well, I got to thinking about your suggestion and I called into Stones End police station after I left you. Some senior copper ask me a few questions and this is the result. I've got an interview next Thursday afternoon.'

'Jim! How are you?' greeted Billie warmly as she strode purposefully into the room. 'Can you smell seals?'

A puzzled expression passed over the young man's face as he looked rapidly around the room. 'No, should I?'

'Jim's also got a letter from the police recruiting office,' cut in Sam, frantically trying to steer Billie away from seals. 'We're going together.'

'That's nice for you,' she replied unconvincingly. 'Perhaps you'd care to talk about it whilst I get changed.'

'Oh, I'm sorry,' apologised Jim. 'I didn't mean to intrude. It's just that—'

'Stop bleating, boy, for Gawd's sake!' chided Billie, unbuttoning her bolero. 'You're worse 'n him.'

Jim shot an anxious glance at Sam who returned a slow shrug of indifference. To Jim's relief, Billie soon disappeared behind the screens whilst the two lads began to discuss their interview. It was fortunate for Jim they had completed this task before Billie emerged, seeking her now customary assistance from Sam with her corselet. It was in the middle of this entertainment that a sharp knock was instantly followed by the door opening as Frank Cootes strode confidently into the room. It was too much for Billie. 'Would you kindly mind waiting for once, Frank?' she demanded. 'My dressing room is not some bloody ten-bob knocking shop where you can breeze in as you like, y'know. In future, if you knock, WAIT!'

'I see,' replied Frank acidly as he slipped both hands into his pockets. 'Come down to boys now, have we? My, my! Two at a time as well. I suppose that explains why you've never wanted anything to do with real men.'

Sam let go the strings and was halfway to Frank before they had fallen to Billie's back. 'Now, now!' admonished Frank raising a large forefinger with one hand and a wicked-looking knife with the other. Billie screamed but Frank continued, 'You and I haven't finished, Diamond, not by a long chalk we haven't, but it wouldn't be very convenient to gut you here. You cheated me last time but you won't do it again.' He prodded Sam's throat with the blade. 'Don't you ever think you can better me.' He dragged the blade slightly across the side of Sam's throat, causing the faintest trickle of blood. 'Just take that as a down-payment, I'll collect the balance in my own good time.'

He turned his attention to Billie. 'And *you*, Queen of the Kids, when you realise what a mistake you've made, knock on my door. You'll think you're in heaven.' He took a few backward paces towards the corridor and was gone.

Jim ran to Sam to examine his neck but the wound was only superficial. 'It don't look too bad but I think we should go for the police.'

'No!' snapped Billie. 'That's the last thing we want. Think about it, for Gawd's sake. Two young men in my dressing room . . . me partly dressed . . . a jealous admirer

. . . a knifing. I'd either wind up being the greatest attraction since public hangings or no one would employ me! Anyway, I'm not taking the chance. Then there's you two.' She gestured towards them. 'If you've got an interview for the force on Thursday, the last thing you need is a sordid little sort out with a music hall queen and a cut throat on Monday.'

'She's right, Jim,' pointed out Sam, staring ruefully at a bloodied handkerchief. 'But it'll not be forgotten.'

'Are you going to help me get this soddin' corselet on or not? I'm on stage in a few minutes.'

'I think Sam should wash that cut first,' said Jim opportunistically. 'I'll help you if you wish, Miss Bardell.'

'That's extremely gallant of you, Master Forsythe. Though I'm usually worried about "volunteers", I think you're right in this instance. Whilst you're helping me dress, my "pressed man" should certainly wash that cut. Anything to do with Frank Cootes is bound to be septic. Ugh!' She gave a false shudder. 'You'll be lucky if your bleedin' head don't fall off.'

Later, as the two young men stood in the wings and watched Billie handling a Monday night audience, Jim shook his head pensively. 'All that in one woman.' He sighed slowly. 'And you want to join the police! Silly bugger!'

Handing in their letters at the desk, the two young men joined thirty or so others in the billiard room which seemed to double up for most things. Privacy was practically non-existent and, as they removed their clothing, both lads were amazed at the poor physical state of many of their fellow applicants. Traces of childhood rickets showed in several, together with skin complaints and lice on others. Neither lad had ever experienced a medical before and Sam was particularly put out by the diligent quest for haemorrhoids. After thirty minutes they were ushered into a room with a desk where a short rounded man with an enormous grey moustache asked them questions about simple arithmetic, fractions, decimals and English, plus a short test on spelling.

They were then invited to take a thirty-minute walk by the Thames before returning to hear the results of their endeavours.

'How d'you think we made out?' asked Sam apprehensively of his friend as they dangled their legs over the parapet of Victoria Embankment.

'I'm quite confident we passed,' replied Jim casually, dropping an old match box into the river.

'You should never tempt fate like that,' reproved Sam. 'Why so confident?'

'You and me may not be the brightest in the world, Sam, but we ain't daft. And when it comes to the physical side, there weren't no one in that group to touch us. We'll not only pass, they'll probably make us both guv'nors, you'll see.'

It was a thought that had not entered Sam's head and he cheered up immensely. Eventually the group reassembled to hear ten names called to add to the twelve who had passed the morning interviews. It was not clear whether the names were in order of merit or just at random but Jim's name was first and Sam was last.

The unsuccessful were commiserated and thanked for their interest, whilst the remainder were ushered into an adjacent room where a gruff beer-bellied chief inspector stared at them disapprovingly for some moments.

'You'll report to Wellington Barracks on Monday week at 8 a.m. for three weeks' drill and training. If you pass that, you'll go out to your division three weeks later for attachments. Any questions?'

The speed with which 'any questions' had been asked was obviously an indication that questions were neither welcome nor expected. That is, it was obvious to all except Sam who, more due to niggling indecision than in search of knowledge, raised an arm.

The chief inspector glowered. 'Yes, you there. Firstly, what's your full name, and secondly, what do you want?'

'Is that the only training we have, sir, three weeks? Don't seem very long to me.'

'Did you hear what I said?' thundered the chief inspector. 'I'll say it again, just for you. What's your full name, boy!'

This was not an attitude to which Sam responded gladly. 'Calm down, Sam, take it easy,' whispered Jim soothingly from the side of his mouth. He was later to swear he heard the gears that drove Sam's temper to grind into angry reverse.

'Diamond, sir, Samuel Obadiah Diamond.'

'Well, Samuel Obadiah Diamond, the Metropolitan Police will no doubt be very distressed to know you don't approve of the length of their training. I'll make a note of it and perhaps you'll be invited to expound your theories when you report Monday week.'

'It was only a query, sir,' mumbled Sam defensively.

'AND it was accepted as such, lad! But don't forget–' he stared fiercely around the room for some seconds '–the Metropolitan Police have gained and maintained a reputation for skill and integrity which, owing to the apparent absence of training methods, must have been entirely due to the high standard of leadership set by senior officers.'

At those words, the uniformed sergeant by the door contrived a sniff that spoke volumes. There were, perhaps understandably, no further questions and the two friends adjourned for a quick pint before seeking their separate paths home.

'Thought you were very courageous asking old bluster-guts a question,' said Jim.

'Nothing courageous about it,' replied Sam smugly. 'He *invited* us to ask questions. You shouldn't invite people to ask questions if you don't want to answer them. Didn't you have a question you wanted to ask?'

'I did, as a matter of fact.'

'There you are! Well, you should have asked it. I always say, if you don't ask, you don't know.'

'That's true, I s'pose,' said Jim, nodding his head thoughtfully. 'Can I ask it now then?'

'Now?' echoed Sam, puzzled. 'I don't see what good it'll do *now* but go ahead if you think I can help.'

'Thanks, Sam, that's champion of you. What I want to know is, who disliked you enough to give you the name Obadiah? They must have really hated you, that's for sure.'

Big Ben struck five o'clock as Sam waved in farewell to his friend and ran for the 33 tram-car that was gathering speed at the slight incline of Westminster Bridge. If he was to have a meal and accompany Billie, the tram had to make good time. Good time was indeed made until the traffic pointsman at the foot of Brixton Hill seemed to hold them up for an eternity. Looking impatiently from the top deck, Sam saw the cause of his frustration was none other than Baden Benjamin Bates 515L. Eventually, as the tram eased past the sweating copper, Sam called down, 'Batesy! I've just been accepted – in the force, I mean.'

'Accepted?' muttered the puzzled Bates until he suddenly remembered his companion from the stormy night. 'Oh, *that* accepted! Hey!' he yelled as the tram gathered momentum. 'Did yer give the board me name an' number, boy?'

Sam instinctively clapped his hand to his mouth as if to wipe out the words he had just uttered. He did not need to tell the fat copper the bad news. 'You dozy letter-box-pissin' sod! You owe me thirty bob, boy!' yelled the policeman over and above the roar of traffic. 'Thirty bloody bob . . . an' don' you forget it.'

Sam's impatient ringing of the doorbell of 200 Brixton Hill was eventually answered by Queenie. It was on the occasions when he came on her suddenly that she seemed her most beautiful. 'Sorry for the delay,' she smiled, 'but I'm cooking while Miss Bardell is bathing. She was getting quite concerned about your absence. You'd better make your apologies double quick.'

Running two at a time up the stairs, he knocked lightly on the bathroom door.

'Er – it's me, Sam.'

'Not locked, come in,' came the curt response. As he entered, she was sitting waist-deep in the bath facing him, wearing just a white silk scarf tied loosely around her hair. Everything else above the rippling line of creamy water was bare and glistening wet. 'Right, tell me how your interview went and make yourself useful while you're here.' She handed him a large bar of Pears soap and turned her back towards him. 'And you don't have to be gentle on either count.'

As he soaped her shoulders, he suddenly realised she was two separate people. Though *he* was excited by his task, it was obviously nothing at all to her. It was almost clinical. She was on stage and he was an audience. Then he realised the same applied to her lack of embarrassment in her dressing room. In that place, as in the bath, he was just a sexless employee, rather like a princess and a eunuch. The big problem was he did not feel like a eunuch.

'Okay, that'll do, Sam, hand me that towel, the large one by the window.' He barely heard her words as she emerged naked from the water and he reached towards her with the towel. Yet at night, in her bed, she was a different woman. Here she was detached, there she was demanding. So which one was the real Billie Bardell? Two minutes earlier he had seen Queenie and thought she was beautiful. Now he was staring at this woman who, whilst never beautiful, was probably the most stunning creature he would ever see in his life.

'Well, Sam Diamond, have you made your decision?' She stood hands on hips, feet astride and gleaming wet. 'What's it to be? London's hard streets . . . or my soft bed?'

Chapter 7

Though Wellington Barracks was little more than a brisk twenty-minute walk from the Casbah-like Inkerman Place, it was worlds apart in every other respect. The broad, tree-lined Birdcage Walk, the adjacent gardens bursting with summer plants and roses, St James's Park lake shimmering in the early-morning sunshine, to say nothing of the people who were already strolling through the dappled shade and whose clothing alone would have kept most families south of the river for a week – all were to be seen and enjoyed.

Jim Forsythe had also enjoyed his stroll over Westminster Bridge. Though he had passed Big Ben many times in his young life, today seemed different. In Inkerman Place, he had lived beyond the pale. True he had been free physically to cross the class barrier that separated his abode from that of the privileged, but today he felt he had been invited in. True the invitation was for two shillings a week less than he'd earnt as a Brixton paviour but Jim told himself that this morning was to be just the start. Inkerman Place was an existence that was dead. This new life was beginning.

With twenty minutes to spare before he reported in, he lit his pipe and sat on a park bench gazing down the road towards Parliament Square. If Sam did decide to forsake the soft life, it was from that direction he would appear. Jim was a little ambivalent over his attitude to his friend. Selfishly he would have loved nothing better than for Sam to accompany him, particularly in such a new venture. In addition there was Jane. Never a bad move to stay friends with the brother of the girl you hope to marry. As a brother-in-law, Sam would take a great deal of bettering. On the other hand, he had already made the very move that Jim himself ached to make. Sam had left the stagnant creek and was now swimming in the main stream. Of course he had no idea exactly where he was going, but then that was by no means unusual for Sam. Then there was Billie. Always there seemed to have been Billie! She had been around for just a few weeks but he knew there were times when Sam had difficulty in remembering life before her. If Jim was honest with himself, he knew that if he had been Sam, then at that precise moment he would be picking up the milk and papers at 200 Brixton Hill and not jumping off the platform of a 33 tram-car on Westminster Bridge – and Miss Bardell would have been the sole reason. Strange that, he conceded, any long-term planner like himself would have known instinctively that Billie was a short-term commitment and should therefore be avoided like the plague, yet he would not have liked to have faced poor Sam's dilemma.

As the minute hand of Big Ben edged the hour, he made a final search of the few dozen pedestrians walking the pavement. Even at a distance Sam would have been easy to spot and he was certainly not amongst the walkers. Jim gave a disappointed sigh and, tapping out his pipe on the bench, rose to cross to the barracks. Thirty yards west of him and crossing from a point slightly behind him was a familiar tall figure.

'Sam!' he exclaimed warmly. 'Where'd you come from?'

Sam pointed in the other direction, towards the palace. 'Oh, I've just been for a stroll. I couldn't sleep and as it was such a nice day, I decided to come early and enjoy the park.'

'And you've left her?'

'And I've left her.'

'Hmmm, I'm not sure if I could have done it.'

'It was easy in the end. If I'd stayed there I wouldn't have been much more than a ponce. In addition, there's Queenie to think of.'

'Oh, Queenie, eh?' said Jim with an exaggerated wink. 'Serious?'

'Sometimes I think it is. But then . . .'

'Billie?'

Sam nodded. 'Billie,' he agreed. 'But to be fair to her, though, she was furious at first, when I finally mentioned Queenie she went quiet and wished me good luck and said I'd be welcome back at any time.'

'Are you two men per'lice recruits?' snapped a police sergeant at the gateway.

'Eh?' began Jim. 'Yeah, I s'pose we are.'

'Then git over there in a line wiv that lot . . . AT THE DOUBLE. AND BE QUIET!'

As the distant chimes of Big Ben announced the eighth hour, so the sergeant began a count. '. . . nineteen, twenty, twenty-one . . . Twenty-one?' he yelled to no one in particular. 'Who's missing? Should be twenty-two! There's only twenty-one! WHO'S MISSING?' The absentee appeared unknown by anyone present as each looked vacantly at the man standing next to him. 'Right! Pay atten-shun, you lot.' The sergeant strode slowly up the single line of young men. 'Me name is Sergeant Hart an' I'm yer instructer fer the next 'free weeks. Fust of all a reprimand – *all* of yer were late on parade this mornin'.'

Sam instantly shot an indignant glance at the speaker. 'Excuse me, sergeant, but—'

WILL YER BE QUIET, MAN! Yer on parade an' there's no talkin' on parade, NONE, e'cept fer me, y'unnerstand?' Obviously not expecting a reply he continued, 'Durin' yer time in the metropolitan per-lice – and by lookin' at most of yer I fink it's gonna be short – you will allus parade fifteen minutes afore the hour.' He stopped in front of a tall ginger youth. 'What's yer name, boy?'

'Dennington, sir – sergeant.'

'Well, Dennington, sir – sergeant,' boomed the instructor, 'I said fifteen minutes afore the hour. D'yer knows wot that means in the King's English . . . DO YER?'

'Fifteen minutes early, s-sergeant?'

'Very good indeed, Dennington, sir – sergeant. Yer obviously h'officer material. I shall now allus remember yer an tell me grandchildren 'ow I forecast yer meteoric career on yer fust mornin' in the job.' He retraced his steps down the line and stopped in front of Sam. 'And you, lad, you wiv' verbal diarrhoea, d'you now unnerstand? 8 a.m. does not mean 8 a.m. at all, it means 7.45 a.m. Geddit?'

Sam nodded.

'DON'T NOD, BOY! GOOD GAWD! Yer go from the ser'blime ter the bloody ridicul'us! Say, "Yes, sergeant"!'

'Yes, sergeant!' echoed Sam.

'Good!' sang out the sergeant with a beaming smile. 'Nah, carn't yer see an amazin' improvement? You've only bin 'ere ten minutes an' already yer answerin' wiv' intelligence.' Further dialogue was interrupted by the appearance of a rather rotund youth carrying a travelling case. 'An wot can I do fer you, young sah?' he asked menacingly.

'I've come to join the police force, sergeant,' said the well-spoken youngster.

'Not ter'day yer ain't, sah! I would fink it's probably two weeks' time yer talkin' abhat, sah, that's when the next intake assembles.'

'No!' persisted the young man, pulling out a long white envelope from his pocket. 'It's today, look – Monday 21st June at 8 a.m. Couldn't be much plainer, sergeant.'

'Deed not, sah! 8 a.m. it is fer sure an' the time nah is . . .' he pulled out a pocket-watch '. . . eight-twelve, sah, an' you 'ave sadly missed this intake, sah, and must wait fer the next one. Just like a train as yer might say, sah.' He turned to the recruits. 'Right, form yerselves inter two lines. We've lots ter do an' precious little time ter do it in.'

For the next three weeks the twenty-one young men were marched, drilled and kitted out before finally taking the oath of allegiance. Each evening they would remove their helmet badges, numerals and whistles and march the two long miles to the section house in Carter Street where they lodged in an old police barracks. After cooking themselves an evening meal, they would be required to study a twenty-six-page instruction book that consisted mainly of the discipline code and their expected attitude towards the public. On the Saturday of the third week, the group were assembled in the billiard room for their final briefing. 'I have three double postings,' said a clerk with a clipboard. 'If there are any of you here who would care to be posted to a station with a friend, put up your hands.' Four hands were raised and the clerk returned to his clipboard for a few moments before announcing the postings.

'Stones End police station?' queried Jim. 'Bloody hell, I'm almost back where I started! I was hoping for something salubrious like Hampstead or Hyde Park.'

'I'm only grateful it's not Brixton,' breathed the relieved Sam.

'Why? D'you think Billie Bardell would keep tipping your helmet over your eyes whilst she was taking advantage of you?' teased Jim.

'Never crossed my mind,' shrugged Sam. 'No, what terrified me was the thought of meeting "Baden Benjamin Bates PC 515L" who's after thirty bob or blood in lieu – mine on both counts!'

'ATTEN-SHUN!' came the now familiar call of Sergeant Hart. 'Right, you've bin 'ere for 'free weeks an' all yer can really do is march and drill, an' some of yer are bleedin' rotten at that. Agreed, Dennington, sir – sergeant?'

'Agreed, sergeant,' came the dutiful response.

'Nah, because o' that, I don't want'cha ter go around finkin' that yer all proper coppers an' doin' somefink dramatic this weekend, 'cos you ain't proper coppers.' He sniffed and looked at each man for a brief moment. 'In fact, some of yer won't be proper coppers as long as yer 'ave 'oles in yer arses. So unless it's a Fenian blowin' up the pub, or a anarchist jumpin' on yer muvver, let 'im go. There'll be plenty o' time in the future fer all that palaver. Right, yer can all take yer tearful farewells of each other 'cos you'll be leaving 'ere in a few minutes fer yer section 'ouse at Carter Street. A few of you'll be stopping there, the rest will be posted ter section 'ouses nearer their stations. Each of yer is ter report to yer stations on Monday mornin' at 9 a.m. And what time is Monday mornin' at 9 a.m., PC Diamond?'

'8.45 a.m., sergeant!'

'Ver' good, Diamond, you'll go far – at least ter Carter Street. Okay, lads, orf yer go nah, an' remember wot I said – no brave an' startlin' arrests this weekend. Fall out and ta-ta.'

An hour later at the section house Sam eased out of his sweaty serge tunic and dropped it gratefully on his bed. In keeping with most single men's section houses, Carter Street was built over a police station. This was to ensure that in an emergency the greatest number of police officers was available at a moment's notice. The building was primitive in design, closely resembling an Indian Army barrack room. The bed spaces were partitioned off by plywood screens with a twelve-inch gap between the bottom and the floor. There was just enough room for a hard single bed and a heavy, chest-high wooden locker. By the side of this was a small shelf with a couple of hooks which sufficed as a wardrobe. Down a draughty corridor were the communal wash-rooms and ablutions. A police horse dung heap steamed cheerfully in the corner of the yard and a four-track railway ran regularly overhead. These little tribulations outside the building were matched by the dozen persistent mice who played inside. Summing up, Carter Street Section House was a noisy, smelly, unhygienic dump. BUT in comparison to Inkerman Place it was a palace.

'Sam,' called Jim from over the partition, 'what you say we go round to see your mum tonight? You haven't seen her since we started training and—'

'—and you can see my sister, is that it?'

'Well, something like that,' agreed Jim bashfully. 'We can get a tram and be there in half an hour.'

It had been barely a month since Sam had last seen Inkerman Place, but as they ducked beneath the mass of washing-lines it appeared to be worse even than he had remembered. 'I couldn't come back now, Jim,' he whispered as they stepped over an open drain. 'Yet I feel a traitor. Mum and the kids are still here and look like being so for good.'

'That's no excuse for not getting out. You'd solve no one's problems by staying, Sam, and you know it.'

The friends parted at the corner, each to go to their respective family, with a plan to meet later at The Feathers. As Sam approached, he could hear Nell Diamond cursing a neighbourhood cat as she washed down the outside doorstep.

'Hullo, Mum,' he said quietly. Spinning around, still clutching the wet cloth, she hurled herself at her son and locked her arms around his neck. With her damp apron at his front and her wet cloth at his rear, Sam knew he was finally home.

'Oh, Sam, Sam! It's so wonderful to see you again! Here, let me look at you!'

'Mum, I've only been gone a month! How is everyone? Kids well?'

'Everyone's fine, Sam. Oh, by the way, we have a visitor. Friend of yours, I believe, she's called to see Jane. Go on in, I'll just make some tea and then join you.'

'Friend of mine?' he began as he hastened into the kitchen. He had not seen a carriage and certainly couldn't imagine Billie Bardell paying a social visit to Inkerman Place on a Saturday afternoon. So who . . . ? He found himself trembling in hope. 'Queenie!' he greeted, racing across the scrubbed floorboards and pulling the somewhat startled girl to her feet. Then, lifting and swamping her in a crushing embrace, he spun her around.

'Well! Well!' marvelled Jane. 'Just what have they been feeding you in that police force?'

Realising that he had gone too far, Sam let her go and started to falter, 'I'm sorry. I . . . er . . .'

The girl blushed but smiled. 'That's all right, Sam, I think it was quite sweet. If this is what happens when you go away, perhaps you should leave home more often.'

'*What* home is that?' asked the young man poignantly, thereby killing the moment instantly.

'How's Jim?' cut in Jane quickly, thinking it was as good a moment as she was likely to get.

'Jim's fine,' Sam assured her. 'I think he's going to take to this policing lark like a duck to water. He's just popped home to see his family and we've arranged to meet later in The Feathers.' As he said the words, he suddenly saw another chance to repair the damage. 'Queenie, you'll come, won't you?' he blurted. 'We could make a foursome. I'll make sure you get home in time for Billie's return from the theatre.'

She reached for his hand. 'Miss Bardell's not at the theatre. That is, not at any theatre that you'll know about. She's in Glasgow for two weeks at the Empire. It's a tremendous boost and I'm really thrilled for her.' She tip-toed forward and planted the softest of kisses on his cheek. 'So I'd love to come to The Feathers with you any time you wish.'

'You coming, Ma?' called out the now jubilant Sam.

'No, thanks all the same, son,' replied Nell, carrying in a

huge enamelled teapot. 'The four of you go and enjoy yourselves while you can. It don't last long, you know.'

The evening proved particularly close and humid and every door and window of The Feathers was propped wide open with an empty crate. By the sound of the piano, it would seem that Norman was enthroned at the ivories. You could always tell if was Norman. On most nights the pub would be comfortably full but on Norman's nights folks were practically hanging out of the windows. Norman – no one ever did discover his surname – was something of a simpleton whose condition was not helped by drink. He was unreliable, none too clean, always the worse for wear and would fall asleep at a moment's notice. But when Norman sat at a piano stool, he was a genius. He could be said to live in the nearby Salvation Army Hostel, but then again he didn't. He would disappear for days at a time and no one ever knew where he went or when he would return. If there had been a way to solve his vanishing walkabouts then landlord Jake Wantage would have found it years before. Any pianist playing for a pittance and doubling the pub profits is worth his weight in gold and deserves a great deal of thought. The problem with Norman was that 'great deals of thought' did not work. Norman was Norman. He was over-ripe, illogical, unpredictable – and greatly treasured!

The four friends were fortunate to find a recently vacated table just outside the saloon bar window. Slowly the atmosphere in the pub spread itself to those outside and, as twilight gave way to darkness, singing could be heard more than two streets away. By ten o'clock, the crowd had long spilled out from the oven-like interior and stood in groups swaying to Norman's infectious rhythms and melodies. Sam and Jim had long given up their seats to a couple of elderly neighbours and stood to one side of their table, chatting to a series of old acquaintances. Suddenly a powerfully built young man pushed his way through the crowd and made a direct line to Queenie. Without uttering a word, he pulled her to her feet. 'It's your lucky day, gel, I'm going to dance with you,' he then announced.

Though uneasy, Sam at first gave no reaction. He thought the youth looked vaguely familiar and supposed that Queenie knew him from somewhere or other and it was probably a poor joke. The sudden alarm on the girl's face soon told him a different story however. 'Just a minute, just a minute,' he began, 'I don't think this young lady *wants* to dance with you . . . please let her go – now!'

'O' course the young lady – if that's what you wants to call her – wants to dance with me. Not many get the chance, you know. She's very lucky and she knows it, don't you, girl?' She suddenly wrested her hand free and Sam's right arm was already back to throw a punch when the intruder bent forward and squinted through the poor light. 'Hang on! It's old Obadiah, ain't it? Old Obadiah . . . from Mr Shelly's class at Webber Row School? 'Tis, ain't it?'

Sam peered likewise. 'Maxie Roff? Look who this is, Jim.' He dropped his voice so the girls would not hear. 'It's "show-off Roff", d'you remember him now? Always the flashiest git in the school. If you had one, he had two; you had nine, he had ten. You might have got bigger, Max, but you ain't got no prettier – nor more sensible. That young girl is with us, or if you like with me, and she's a bit refined and definitely not used to the likes of you, so sod off, Show-off!'

Max looked quickly from one to the other as if he was assessing his chances; whatever conclusions he made he kept to himself. 'No, no, Sam.' He raised his hands. 'No offence. How was I to know you'd be capable o' pulling the best-looking tart in Blackfriars? Be fair, Sam. Tell you what, t' show no offence, let's all have a drink on me. What d'you say, eh?'

Before Sam could reply, Jim cut diplomatically into the conversation. 'That's bloody sporting of you, Max, but then that always was your best side. Port-and-lemon for the girls, a bitter for Sam and a brown-and-mild for me.'

As Max fought his way through the crowd Jim laid his hand on Sam's shoulder. 'Remember what Sergeant Hart said. Fenians blowin' up pubs and anarchists jumpin' on yer muvver are both okay, but anything else, let them go. No brave an' startlin' arrests are wanted this weekend.'

'But did you hear what he said?' protested Sam. 'He called Queenie a tart!'

'Sam, I don't *care* what he said. Your way, we'd probably be in the cells for a weekend and out of work on Monday. My way, the girls have their port-and-lemons and we've got a couple of pints. Now I know it's going to come hard to you but when he returns, be gracious and thank him nicely.'

'Jim,' murmured Jane as she leaned forward to plant a kiss on his cheek, 'I'm his sister and I love him dearly but, bless you, *grace* is not one of his gifts.' She turned to her brother. 'What he's actually trying to say, Sam, is for heaven's sake, shut up!' She turned to face Jim, 'Agreed?'

'Couldn't have put it better, luv.'

Sam obviously took Jane's advice to heart because for the rest of the evening both chat and reminiscences flowed as smoothly and freely as Jake's beer and Norman's tunes.

'So what're you doing with yourselves these days?' asked Max. Sam felt a little embarrassed to say they were policemen, basically because they were not, not yet anyway. On the other hand, if they were not policemen, what were they? Jim had no such inhibitions and was already recounting a tale of derring-do that was second or third hand when he had heard it two weeks earlier at Wellington Barracks. It seemed to impress Max.

'And you, Max, what do you do now?' asked Jane.

'Well, amongst other things, I inspects buildings and such but really I s'pose you'd say I was in to somethin' like insurance,' replied Max. 'Though it's a bit difficult to describe in words.'

'Insurance, eh?' nodded Jane, suitably impressed. Mr Bryant who called regularly at most houses in Inkerman Place, rain or shine, to collect a penny per week death insurance, always wore a smart bowler hat and a nice clean raincoat. She studied Max for some moments but somehow he did not seem the bowler hat type.

'Sam,' whispered Jim with some urgency as the first call went up for closing time, 'I've just had a thought. Did you read the note pinned up in your bed-space?'

'I didn't even see a note.'

'I hate to tell you this but we've got a curfew. As recruits who are not yet officially recognised, we have to be in by midnight. P'haps we change into pumpkins or something if we're late?'

'But how do I take Queenie home? I can't possibly get her to Brixton Hill and myself back to the section house by midnight!'

'Perhaps your mum can squeeze her in her house somewhere?'

'Look at her, Jim, for God's sake! Does she *look* like a girl who can be squeezed in anywhere in Inkerman Place?'

'Then we'll have to put her on a tram in Blackfriars Road. That's not too bad, Sam, she'll only have a few yards' walk at the other end.'

'I can't do that,' he said firmly. 'I can't possibly send any girl home alone after midnight on a Saturday – and neither could you.'

'I think I've got the gist of that,' said Queenie, looking up from her seat. 'Don't worry, Jane and I already have the answer.'

'And that is?' queried Sam.

'Jane is staying with me for the night, so if we walk to Waterloo station, we can get a hackney cab and drop you two boys off at the section house, then we girls can carry on to Brixton Hill. Don't worry!' she added hastily. 'I have more than enough for the fare.'

Sam was obviously about to protest but Queenie quickly put her fingers to her own lips then transferred them immediately to his and added, 'If you agree. And by way of a bribe, you can both come for breakfast in the morning. Not too early, mind.'

'Sam,' murmured Jim, 'we are never going to get a better offer than that. Let's say good night to Max and take it before she changes her mind.'

The sound of the piano finally faded in the distance as the quartet made their way happily through the twisting alleys and lanes that led the short distance to Waterloo station. As they climbed the ramp to the cab-stand, Sam, with Queenie on his arm, imagined for a moment that they were about to board a train for Cornwall or some other exotic part but reality reclaimed him sharply when he remembered the cash in his pocket would barely get him the three short stops to Clapham Junction.

The unusual, even unethical, request for the girls to stay on long after the men had alighted bothered the cabbie at first, but he appeared happy once he realised the men were actually to reside at the police station and not to be incarcerated there. He had no doubt they were a couple of kept men – coppers too! He had heard about people like that, lucky sods. The way each couple sat entwined throughout the journey did precious little to counter his theory, neither did their passionate farewells by the police station steps.

Both young men were by nature heavy sleepers but they also knew that Sunday might well be their last free day for some time. Not only that, but the day could start for them whenever they wanted it to start! The trick was not to sleep late so precious minutes would not be wasted. The girls would later say that whatever else was wasted that day it was certainly not precious minutes. How could it have been when their doorbell rang at 6.55 a.m.?

As the door was opened, there was one heart-stopping moment for Sam before he realised that Queenie had obviously loaned Jane a very familiar white satin robe. That shock over, he was delighted to hear Jim ask the one question that had been bothering him since they'd caught the first tram out of Camberwell garage half an hour earlier. 'How long do we have?'

'Do you still have a midnight curfew tonight, boys?' asked Queenie provocatively.

Jim glanced at Sam who shrugged by way of a reply. 'Yes, tonight and every night, we would guess.'

'Then that's exactly how long you have.'

'How about my sister's job? She'll never wake up in the morning.'

'Sam!' exploded Jane. 'You're sounding like Dad! Mum knows where I am and she also knows I'm going straight to the factory in the morning.'

'I want to make a short formal announcement,' said Queenie. 'Place your orders for breakfast now, but I warn you, it's the only meal I'm cooking today. The mistress of the house is away so it's the maid's day off.'

It was by general agreement an excellent breakfast and as they flopped into their respective armchairs afterwards the sun streamed brightly through the windows. 'So what are we going to do with the rest of this day?' asked Queenie.

Jim rose from his chair and, walking to the back of Jane's, gently tilted her head up to kiss her lips. 'I know how I'd like to spend it.'

'How?' persisted the maid.

'Cuddling up to the girl I love,' he said simply.

'And you, Sam?' she asked. 'How would you like to spend the day?' He shuffled his feet with a hint of embarrassment, basically because he had still not adjusted to being present when his sister was kissed so passionately. 'Er – yes, I s'pose I would certainly like to be with you . . .'

'Are you saying you would also like to "cuddle up" to the girl you love, Sam?'

'Er . . . yes.'

'And is she *here*, this girl you love?'

Sam jumped from his chair and seized his tormentor roughly in his arms. 'You know bloody well she's here, don't you?'

Queenie laughed. 'Yes, I do now, but I also think I know what's really bothering you.' She put her arms around his neck and her lips to his ear and whispered, 'You want us to be on our own, right?' He nodded. 'I guessed as much.' She took Sam's hand and looked across to the armchair where Jane was now sitting on Jim's lap. 'Listen, you two, if anyone feels like making a cup of tea around four o'clock this afternoon, then give us a call. We'll be in the first room up the stairs and I don't take sugar.'

Sam followed Queenie into the bedroom and closed the door behind him but even though the curtains were still drawn, the room was shadowy bright as the early sun infiltrated. Queenie had walked to the bedside then turned to him, arms extended. Even with his inexperience he spotted the difference between the sexually demanding kisses of Billie and the soft loving warmth of the girl. She made no protest as he removed her robe. They stood in an embrace for some minutes before he laid her gently back on the wide ruffled bed. Her nightdress was obviously one for summer, leaving bare as it did her satin smooth shoulders. As he undressed he stared down at her almost perfect form outlined through the crumpled silk. His initial move was towards the hem of the nightdress which he intended to raise over her head. He faltered. That was how Billie stripped for him, brazen and uninhibited. Here's my body, revel in it, seemed to be her philosophy. If he was to strip this girl naked, and he desperately needed to, it had to be in a way as different as possible. It had to be a loving offer, rather than a sexual assault. He lay down naked beside her and, as he kissed her shoulders then her breasts, slowly inched down the nightdress until it lay across her hips, revealing the gentle downward curve of her belly. With a final kiss of that belly she was naked.

'Oh, I love you so much, Sam,' she whispered.

In spite of his excitement he was still puzzled. When he had shared the older woman's bed, each exotic charm seemed to be better than the one before; the incentive therefore was to keep searching. But now, here in this girl's bed, it was the reverse. He had almost reluctantly left her lips for her shoulders; her shoulders for her breasts; her breasts for her belly; and her belly for her thighs. Every move was as beautiful as the move before, neither more nor less. He eased over on top of the girl and, as she felt him prepare to enter her, without drama she gently whispered, 'Please, darling, no.' He made no apparent move in response to her request but continued with his love play, yet slowly she was aware he had withdrawn from her thighs. 'Sam, listen . . .'

'You don't have to say anything, it's okay,' he whispered.

'But I *do* have to say something, Sam. Listen to me. I'll do anything you want of me except that. It's not because I don't love you. It's just that I daren't risk a . . . well . . . an accident, shall we say? I've got a good job here, Sam, but can you imagine where I would be without it – no job, no family *and* with a baby? You and Jim are struggling to get out of Inkerman Place, I'd be digging a tunnel to get in. I'm terrified, Sam, it's as simple as that.'

'But you will have a family, my darling. You'll have me! I want to marry you. I think I've known it since you were robbed in the park. I couldn't believe what had happened to you, I wanted to kill the men who did it.'

'You almost did.' She smiled, cradling his head to her breasts. 'But are you sure I'm what you want? I'm different from Miss Bardell, you know.'

'I'm sure you're what I want. *Will* you marry me?'

'Of course.'

'Great!' Sam leapt to his feet. 'Let's tell the others!'

'Good God, Sam, no! I mean . . . well, they might be doing anything for all we know. Let's leave it and surprise them later, eh?' She reached for his arm and pulled it around her. 'Cuddle me, Sam.' She snuggled against him as he held her firmly and closed his eyes. Within a minute they had both slipped irretrievably down the path of sleep. In fact, they were just a fraction too far gone to hear Billie Bardell's key turning in the front door.

Chapter 8

No matter from which angle it was studied, the image was wrong. The limousine was fine, it was the occupant, or rather the passenger, that offended the eye. The driver certainly looked the part, with his peaked cap, tunic jacket and stiff, shiny knee-high gaiters. He was as perfect an accessory as the cased-in spare wheel or the radiator mascot. No, it was definitely the passenger that ruined the presentation. A thousand weekend courses could not have hidden his origins. The car looked what it was – class. The owner also looked what he was – a stone-faced thug. Reginald 'Slicer' Simmons was ugly, not just ordinarily ugly but overpoweringly so. His huge bulk appeared to have attempted to reshape itself at one time or another, then, realising matters had only become worse, given up. Reginald Simmons had bits where no bits should be. There was an additional problem, though Reg was totally unaware of this. As far as he was concerned, the car and driver completed his image. He had money, he had power, he had the most violent gang in South London, and he was beautiful.

In different circumstances, his delusions would have been mocked but all mockery had ceased when, an hour earlier, three of Boris Rayner's toes had been removed. Boris had always been fond of a joke; in retrospect perhaps a little too fond. Reg heard that Boris had convulsed the public bar of The Crown with an impression of Reg's distinctive walk. He therefore, rather poetically he thought, decided to give Boris a distinctive walk of his own. It had not been a decision that had been taken lightly. Oh, no. Reg had put it to his committee, consisting of Long Tom Williams, Buster Slingsby, Sid and Nathan Green, and Frank Cootes. There were other fringe members but they had no say in company decisions. The committee came to the conclusion that dignity was everything. A small-time shit like Boris Rayner must never be allowed to get away with such a thing, especially in a public house that paid protection money to them.

'I think,' Reg had said, when the muse had first struck him, 'whatever the punishment, it should be reflected in 'is walk.'

'Agreed!' Frank Cootes had responded enthusiastically. 'I'll break one of his legs if you like?'

It had never been part of Reg's function to concern himself as to means, he considered he had shown sufficient qualities of leadership by suggesting that Boris be fixed with a suitable limp. *How* it was done had been a decision for his minions. He had looked around the table for the expected support. 'Frank to break the little shit's leg then, agreed?'

'I'm not sure,' Nathan Green had murmured thoughtfully. 'See, *anyone* can break a leg *anyhow*. I mean, you could fall downstairs; trip up a kerb; play football. A person can break a leg in a hundred different ways, can't they?'

'So what yer sayin'?' Reg had snapped irritably. He hated any discussion he did not immediately follow, there was always the suspicion the idea was getting away from him.

'Well,' Nathan had said, sensing Reg's awakening displeasure, 'I'm sure you're right. Making sure the bastard has a limp does have a nice ring to it. But medical science being what it is nowadays, who's to say that in six months – six weeks even – Boris may not be back to normal?'

'So what're saying?' Frank had growled. 'We should do nothing because some fuckin' quack can make him all better? At that rate we may as well give up this game and join the Salvation Army!'

'O' course I'm not saying that! What I'm saying is give him something a little more permanent, something he can remember.'

'Like what?' hissed Reg.

'Oh, I don't know . . .' said Nathan thoughtfully. 'P'haps minus him a few toes?'

At that moment Reg had confirmed his own quality of true leadership by his sheer ability to use a good idea, even one he had not thought of himself. Not only that, terms like 'medical science' always impressed him.

'Na-fan,' he had said admiringly. 'That's inspired, Na-fan! That's really fuckin' inspired. Go git 'im, Frank. Fetch 'im back 'ere and I'll give 'im a limp that no poxy doctor'll cure in a lifetime.'

So an hour or so earlier, Frank had fetched Boris 'back 'ere' and now, at this very moment, Frank was explaining to a doctor at Guy's Hospital how his unfortunate ashen-faced companion had lost three toes on his left foot whilst chopping fire-wood with an axe for a poor elderly blind neighbour. The incredulous young doctor pointed out that domestic axes are not widely recognised for their razor-like sharpness nor their ability to slice neatly through tendons and toes, particularly axes that belong to the poor, elderly and blind. 'How true, how true,' Frank had agreed. But, as he pointed out, only minutes before the accident, poor Boris had been so fed up with its inability to chop even the frailest of wood that he had unwisely put an edge on it that it could have shaved grapes. 'Wasn't that sad?' Frank had asked. Even Boris had tearfully to agree that, as far as he was concerned, matters were about as sad as they could get.

Reg first realised his plan had gone slightly awry when

Frank told him that the doctor decided to keep Boris in hospital for the next two nights. Shame that, there was to have been an award ceremony at The Crown in which Boris's three toes were to be returned to him just before he was invited to do another amusing walk. That idea was definitely out now. The toes had not looked too wholesome half an hour ago. In two days' time, in this heat, they would be toddling away on their own. Never mind, he would treat the boys to a drink just to celebrate a good job well done. 'Sling those toes in the dustbin, Buster, they're beginning to ripen. Now, before we celebrate, let's go upstairs to the club room and finish our last meetin', shall we? We were so fired up about Boris we forgot all about "Any other business".' He glanced at Nathan who was usually charged with keeping the firm's records, in his head of course, because semi-literate Reg never quite trusted paper.

'Well, does anyone know the latest on Maxie Roff?' asked Nathan. 'The last time we discussed this we held it over for a month or so to see if there was any improvement. Tom?' he queried.

Long Tom Williams was not at his happiest speaking in public and tended to be brief, too brief. 'Ain't much better.'

'Whad'ya mean, "ain't much better"?' interrupted Reg. 'How much is "ain't much"? What I want to know is if this bastard is workin' a scheme of his own when he's s'posed to be workin' for me.'

'I told 'im to watch it,' offered Tom.

'Oh, well, you should 'ave mentioned it, Tom,' said Reg sarcastically. 'I mean, that should be good enough for anyone, shouldn't it? Robbing yer bleedin' employer blind and then bein' told ter watch it. Blimey, I bet that really terrified 'im!' He stared angrily around the room. 'Don't anyone else know anythin'?'

Sid Green glanced thoughtfully at his fingers for a moment.

'I do, Reg. But you're not going to like it.'

'Try me?' he snarled.

'I've checked and double checked and there is no doubt he's well at it. We've got discrepancies all over the place. I think he's trying to build up his own little empire. I think in the long term he sees himself as a rival.'

Reg rose solemnly to his feet. 'This, gentlemen,' he announced, 'is serious. You can laugh at Dopey Boris as much as you like but Maxie Roff is *serious*!'

'You're right,' agreed Frank Cootes. 'If he thinks he can git away with that little game, he'll try anything. D'you want him brought upstairs for a trial?'

Reg nodded. 'Yeah, Frank, I think I do. Take Buster and Long Tom and let's have the thievin' git in here for my birthday, 4th August.'

'Fourth of—' began the surprised Nathan. 'Why so long?'

'Well, the first reason's a particularly subtle one, Nafan. We're goin' to give 'im enough rope to 'ang 'is bleedin' self. And the second one's artistic. Y'see, I do like gettin' a bit of revenge and what better present could I have than getting my hands on some double-dyed bastard on my birthday? It's all right, lads, yer don't have to buy me a card.'

Billie Bardell was not in her best mood. It had been a very tiring weekend and it had not finished yet, not by a long chalk. Directly she had closed the first half of the Saturday night show at the Glasgow Empire, she had gone straight to Central Station to catch an overnight sleeper for Euston. There was a contract to be signed in London with a representative of Florenz Ziegfeld, the American impresario. The result was an overnight dash down to London, to be followed by an equally exhausting dash back twelve hours later to Glasgow. She had toyed with the idea of not going back home to Brixton at all. After all, Queenie was going to use the chance to visit a few old friends and so the house would be empty. On the other hand, it would give her an opportunity to change and freshen up before meeting His Nibs for lunch at the Savoy.

Strange, Queenie's curtains being closed. The girl was usually an early riser and meticulous in her routine. If she had gone away she would have parted them before she left. The milk and papers were also on the step. Queenie would never have gone away without cancelling them. Perhaps she was ill? Oh God, not another fit! Supposing she'd had a fit and suffocated face down in her pillows or such like. Dear God, don't let it be that! She fumbled with the key before throwing open the front door and rushing up the stairs to the girl's room. Her intention to call Queenie's name was forestalled by having to catch her breath as she reached the top of the stairs.

Her initial reaction to the scene of the naked entwined lovers was one of awe at its classic beauty. That lasted a tenth of a second. It was possible that when Sam had gone to sleep he had thought he was in heaven. If that was the case, then he was under no illusion as to where he had woken up.

'YOU BITCH!! YOU FUCKING WHORE! There I am breaking my heart because I think you're dead, and here you are being turked by this sanctimonious bastard!' She then turned her attention to Sam. 'What an actor you are! Giving me all that shy-boy-holier-than-thou-shit and all the time you're fucking the maid – or should I say "Madam"? GET UP! GET UP!' She pounded her clenched fists on his chest. 'Oh I bet you laughed, didn't you, when you crept out of my bed to slide into this slut's. You've got two minutes to get out of my house, both of you! D'you hear me, BOTH OF YOU!'

Slamming the door, she loudly lavished on them the traditional olde English afterthought: 'AND A POX ON THE PAIR OF YOU!' as she stormed down the staircase. Sam closed his eyes in agonised anticipation of what was coming next; it was an accurate surmise. Within seconds came the second explosion as she obviously discovered Jim and his sister, probably in the parlour. Sam hoped for their sakes it had been a more dignified discovery, though by the sound of the slamming doors and screams it would appear that wasn't the case. He sat on the bed and eased the sobbing Queenie on to his lap whilst soothing away her tears if not her despair.

Minutes later, together with their two accomplices, they assembled in the downstairs hall. Billie stood halfway up the staircase, staring down impassively with arms folded and a face like stone. Sam kept glancing at her, wondering what had happened to that stunning creature who had emerged from the bath just weeks ago. When she had left the water she had looked like Aphrodite; now she looked like a gorgon. 'Where shall we go?' sobbed Queenie.

'Don't worry, you can come home with us,' assured Jane. She gestured about her. 'Our place may not be like this but Mum will willingly take you in.'

Stifling her sobs, Queenie turned to face Billie. 'I can understand how you feel and I'm truly sorry we put you through it.' She paused to swallow and compose herself. 'But . . . we do love each other . . . and we are going to marry. I would certainly have loved to have done that with your blessing but if that's not to be . . .' Her voice trailed away for a moment. When it came back she added, 'As you can see, I can't take all my things. I have no idea where I'm—' She turned and buried her face in Jane's shoulder.

'It was my fault,' said Sam, walking up the first few stairs, though stopping well short of Billie. 'And I offer no excuse except to repeat that what Queenie said is true. We are in love and we do intend to marry. If you cut yourself off from her it will be your loss, but I don't think you need me to tell you that.' He paused but his words had no visible effect on the woman who continued to stare silently. 'I would give ten years of my life for this not to have happened but it *has* happened, and if I remember rightly, you forecast something similar. Except in your version it was Queenie who did the knifing.'

She finally spoke. 'I got it right then, Sam, didn't I? The only thing was, I forecast she'd knife *you*. In effect, she's knifed me.' She gave a contrived little laugh. 'Don't worry though, Sam. It's a deep wound but it ain't fatal. I'm a tough old bird, I've survived worse.'

The young man made to speak again but she quickly raised her hand. 'No, Sam, no. There is absolutely nothing you could possibly say to me now. Take your friends and go. I don't think you two should marry but if you do . . .' she shrugged her shoulders, '. . . then I genuinely wish you every happiness. But, please, just go *now*. Go out of my house and out of my life.'

The tram ride down Brixton Hill was in sad contrast to the ride up it and barely a word was spoken until the vehicle rocked its way down Blackfriars Road. Sam knew that with a great deal of shuffling there was certainly room to squeeze in another body in number 14, especially bearing in mind his own departure and his father's recent death. But he also knew that if anything could possibly ruin his romance with Queenie, it was her taking lodgings in Inkerman Place. Yet there was no way around it. A few minutes later the foursome sat in Mrs Diamond's kitchen and, with a few delicate evasions, recounted the whole story. 'No problem at all,' assured Nell. 'We'll squeeze you in somewhere, dear. Though I can see one snag.'

'Only one, Ma?' said Sam ironically. 'Well, let's hear it.'

'What's she going to do about a job?'

'It's okay, Mrs Diamond,' said the girl. 'I'll go to the domestic agency in the morning. I'm good at my job and, with luck, I'll get a living-in position somewhere and won't have to put you to all this trouble.'

'But they'll want references and you've worked for Miss Bardell for how long?'

'Three years.'

'So how are you going to explain a lack of recent references, dear?'

Jane, as ever the first to see Queenie's despair, quickly interrupted, 'Look, mum, we're all tired. Let Queenie and me sort out our sleeping arrangements, the boys can go back to their section house and we'll take the whole world on afresh tomorrow.'

'PCs Diamond and Forsythe, sir, the two new recruits,' announced the sergeant as he ushered the two young men in.

'At ease,' muttered the chief inspector without once looking up from his papers. The sergeant closed the door and the two young men stood silent for what seemed an eternity. Seated, the inspector cut a very imposing figure. He was enormously broad with a spotless uniform and thick dark wavy hair. Finally he raised his head. A large and heavy moustache ranged wide across his face yet still failed to hide completely a deep old scar that ran a good inch-and-a-half away from his lip. Jim found himself with an almost overriding urge to ask how he had got it. 'You two men are extremely lucky,' he boomed. 'At this station you'll learn more in a month than you would in most stations in a year. And that's what you'll need to do – *learn*! You'll spend a week at court, a week on each of the three shifts, and you'll be a general dogsbody for the first few months. Now,' he leaned back in his chair and smoothed his moustache with the back of his forefinger, 'the biggest curse of this job is strong ale. It may be that you will find yourself in situations where everyone around you is drinking. If so, think about it, lads. Spend a few moments looking at the discipline lists and see just how many fall foul of drink.' He stared down at two sheets of neatly written paper on the desk in front of him. 'I've got your records here. I see you were a paviour, Forsythe. Good honest occupation paviour, I'd say. Probably set you up quite well for the hurly-burly of this job.' There was another pause whilst he raced through Sam's notes. 'Hmmn,' he sniffed and smoothed his moustache yet again. 'Says here you worked for a theatrical person. Is that right, Diamond?'

Remembering how impressed his interviewer had been with Jim's occupation, Sam decided to recount his own experience. 'Yes, sir, but I was also a paviour. You see, what happened was—'

'I know, I know, Diamond. It has it all down here, you understand. But you stopped being a paviour to work for a theatrical person. Now did you or did you not?'

'I did, sir.'

'Good, we've resolved that then. Now what I want to know is—' again a sniff, again a quick wipe '—are you a pansy?'

'SIR?'

'You know, pansy. I ask because you aren't allowed in the force if you are. Not only that, you'd have the devil's job trying to police this manor.'

'No, sir!' Sam protested. 'In fact, I've just proposed to my fiancée today!' His protest and amplification seemed to satisfy his interrogator, if only temporarily.

'Proposed, you say? Hmmm.' By way of variation he sniffed and wiped the moustache with a different finger. 'Bit of an obstacle there as well. Recruits aren't supposed to marry until they've been in the force two years. Still . . .' His frown was wiped away by a nod and a relieved smile. 'Much better than being a pansy . . . much, much better! Okay, lads, off you go and see Sergeant Hawkins in the outer office, and please don't forget what I told you about strong ale.'

'This way, lads,' called the sergeant. 'Sit down there and we'll give you some numerals, truncheons, and a few other-bits an' pieces. By the way, payday's Wednesday afternoon.' Both men slipped off their tunics and spent a few raw-fingered minutes inserting the numerals into the heavy blue serge. 'Are either of you conversant with this manor?'

'Both of us, sergeant,' answered Jim. 'We come from Inkerman Place.'

The sergeant raised his eyebrows. 'Don't get many recruits from that part of the world, boys. I suppose according to the book, posting you here is really a mite too close to home. Still,' he paused thoughtfully, 'it's nice to have someone who's got a feel for the manor instead of these bloody Brummies and Jocks we seem to be getting. Not only that, the border of our manor stops just short of Inkerman. On balance, I think we'll let it go. But if you find you're becoming compromised at all, come and see me and perhaps I'll be able to move you to Kennington. Meantime, off you go now to Tower Bridge Court and report to the court inspector at 9 a.m. each morning this week.'

'How do we get there, sarge?' asked Sam. 'We don't have enough money for fares.'

'How did you get here this morning?'

'We walked.'

'And that's exactly how you get to Tower Bridge.'

Their main problem in walking to Tower Bridge was not the distance, which was no more than a mile, but the fact that for the first time in their brief careers, they would be in a densely populated area, in full uniform, with no training other than PT and a warning about strong ale.

Most of their route to the court took them through Long Lane, which was a carriers' route to the docks. At most times of a working day the road would be packed with horse-drawn carts, wagons and wheel-barrows. They had emerged unscathed until they reached Tower Bridge Road when they walked into a collision between two wagons. It was hardly a serious impact but the side of an empty wagon had been lifted on to the rim of its laden counterpart and was wedged tight some eighteen inches off the ground. The situation would probably never have happened in the first place if both drivers had not been so obstinate. Damage was negligible but injured pride was rife.

''Ere's a couple o' coppers!' came the dreaded cry as both drivers eagerly recounted a totally different version of events. After a superficial inspection, Jim assessed the damage as practically nil but that still did not solve the problem of the locked wagons.

'What the hell do we do now?' asked the worried Sam.

'Lift it off,' said Jim. 'If we do it carefully, we can restrict the damage to a few scratches.'

'But it must weigh over a ton!' protested Sam.

'Well, look on the bright side,' suggested Jim. 'We haven't got to lift the bloody horse as well, so that's a result. If we put our shoulders under that ridge and pad it with a sack, then, providing someone holds the horse, we just ease it up an inch or so and the job's done.'

'Yeah,' muttered Sam reluctantly, 'it's the bloody horse that's worrying me. If that wheel goes over my foot I'm going to make sure it also goes over your head.'

In the end, the task proved easy. The difficult part was calming down the warring wagoners who both felt they had emerged the victor. Having brushed each other down, they were set to resume their journey when they realised someone was trying to attract their attention from the gloom of an open pub door on the opposite corner of the junction. At first they pretended not to notice but curiosity soon got the better and they made their way across the street. 'Oy! You two, in here quick!' Peering into the public bar Sam saw a very tall, slim policeman. 'Come in out of the doorway, you silly pair of sods!' the man ordered urgently.

Feeling it was part of some masterly police undercover operation, the silly pair of sods did exactly that. 'What is it?' whispered Sam. 'We're only recruits and don't know much, I'm afraid.'

'You've just saved my bacon,' the policeman said gratefully. 'I was supposed to have been on that traffic point and, because those juggin-heads crashed into each other, I was trapped in here. If I'd been out there it wouldn't have happened.'

'But what were you doing in here?' asked Sam naively. 'Were you called by the landlord?'

'Called by the . . . blimey, you're right, you *don't* know much, do you? Look, son, I simply slipped in for a quick pint and I'm so pleased with what you done, I've ordered you both one as well. Here it is, cheers!'

Jim raised his glass to peer at its texture. It was thick and black. 'Cheers,' he responded. 'What is it I'm drinking?'

'Home-brew,' replied their new colleague proudly. 'Landlord makes it on the premises, calls it "Black Pudden". You won't get many like this, I'll tell yer. Best strong ale in Bermondsey!'

'Yeah,' said Sam philosophically. 'I thought it might be. Cheers!'

Whatever the gravity content of the ale, it did its utmost to send the young pair to sleep as they sat at the back of the court and mutely listened to the droning procession of cases. First one would nod off, then the other. Finally, as business was finished for the day, the usher rudely disturbed them with a loud: 'COURT, RISE!' After slowly gathering their wits, they had started to drift out of the building. Suddenly the court inspector caught Sam's arm. 'If I were you, son, I'd get a good sleep tonight, because from tomorrow you'll be sitting in the front row and if there's one thing Mr Cluer, the magistrate, don't like, it's dossers in his court. If you blink more'n twice you might find you've been deported.' Giving an exaggerated confidential wink, he let go Sam's arm and bade them both goodnight.

Having no money until payday was going to make it a tiring walk back to the station, then to the section house to change, then to Inkerman Place to see how Queenie was getting on, before returning in time to build up sufficient sleep before appearing fresh and alert before the dreaded Mr Cluer next morning. As the weary pair turned the corner of Carter Street, a familiar figure could be seen sitting on the station steps. 'It's your Queenie!' Jim exclaimed. 'What on earth is she doing here?'

Sam broke into a sprint before Jim restrained him by tugging hard his sleeve. 'You're in bloody uniform, you idiot, you'll have the whole station turning out if you run!' In fact if anyone from the station had bothered to glance out of the window, they would have been more alerted by Sam's peculiar leaping walk than ever they would by his sprint. The gallumping footsteps caused the girl's gaze to lift from the pavement.

'Oh, Sam, Sam darling!' she cried, scrambling to her feet. 'I'm so pleased to see you.'

'What's happened?' he demanded.

'It's just that I've got a job, with accommodation. I move in first thing tomorrow. Jane said she didn't think you boys had much money left, so I decided to wait here. The sergeant said you should be back sometime about six o'clock. Sam!' she suddenly cried, throwing her arms about his neck. 'This is the first time I've seen you in uniform, don't you look handsome!'

'What's the drama?' asked Jim.

'She thinks I'm handsome.'

'Well, mark the calendar, you're never likely to be told again.'

'So where's the new job?' asked Sam.

'St John's Wood, next to the cricket ground. The family seem very nice.'

'But how did you get a job so quickly without references?'

'I *had* a reference.' She stared at him for a moment. 'Late last night, a cabbie knocked on the door. He said he had taken Miss Bardell to Euston and, as he dropped her off, she had given him a letter to be delivered to me at Inkerman Place. It contained a glowing reference, a month's salary and nothing else, not so much as a word.'

'She's a strange woman,' murmured Jim. 'She's a mass of contradictions. One moment she acts like a bitch and the next . . .'

'Miss Bardell has never been other than kind to me,' said the girl. 'I'm sorry you both had to hear what was said yesterday.'

She shrugged. 'They were only words, you can't bleed from words.'

'I can,' said Sam.

'Not forever you can't, Sam darling, not even you.'

'Listen,' said Jim, 'we can't stand here chatting away in uniform. Give us a minute to change and . . .' he stopped in sudden embarrassment.

Queenie laughed. 'I think I know what you were about to say. Would it have been something like, "And we'll pop into The Beehive for a drink"? Listen, you two, I haven't got the time and you haven't got the money. As soon as I'm straight I'll write to you, darling. In the meantime . . . no false pride now . . . why don't I let you have ten shillings each because . . . well, because I love you both?'

'I've a better idea,' replied Sam. 'Why don't you *lend* us five shillings each because we love you?'

'You two men!' came the call from the open window of he station. 'Idling and gossiping is a discipline offence. If you plan to stand around gassing to attractive females all night, get bloody changed!'

'You can't say fairer than that,' said the girl quietly slipping a ten-bob note into Sam's tunic pocket. 'I'll write soon. Take care. Bye, darling!'

The days at court proved a tedious chore but at least with sufficient money for tram fare, the friends were spared the brain-deadening perils of Black Pudden Ale and slowly the week passed. Letters from Queenie came with great regularity and, most days and some nights, they patrolled with an older policeman who, if truth be told, had not the least desire for their company. It was their fourth week at the station when they were ordered to see Sergeant Hawkins.

'We have an outing to Sandown Races next week. I understand you two are not going. Is that right?'

The pair shuffled their feet in some embarrassment. 'Well, sarge . . .' began Jim.

'Goodness gracious!' said Hawkins. 'Don't apologise! If you're like every other recruit in this force, it's all you can do to feed yourself, never mind handing money over to bookmakers. No, what I want to know is, do you feel confident enough to make your first solo patrol on next week's night duty? We're going to be a bit short of men and the guv'nor is not keen on asking a neighbouring station for help for a social event, so how'd you feel?'

'Great!' they chorused.

'Very well then, report for night duty in the parade room 9.45 p.m. Monday evening.'

The big advantage of their first stint of night duty meant having the best part of the preceeding day to themselves. As the force never officially had a weekly leave day, such chances of free time were precious. After a lengthy lie-in, because it would be Tuesday morning before they slept again, they took the opportunity to call on their respective mothers in the hope of cadging a decent meal as opposed to the dubious creations they often cooked themselves in the single men's mess.

They had no idea as to the success of the station outing but recently the marvellous summer weather had broken and the day was already gathering a soaking momentum. The two recruits had been posted on adjoining beats and, having yet to acquire the slow rhythmic plod of an old time copper, had met several times before one o'clock as they sped around their rain-drenched streets.

'I can't go on like this,' called Jim wearily. 'I'm getting dizzy, I definitely need a smoke. Is there a decent doorway on your side of the road?'

'There's a derelict warehouse on the corner of Clink Street,' responded Sam as he pointed to premises some fifty yards away. 'And the front door's broken. Any use?'

'Sounds like a palace to me!' replied his tired friend. 'Lead the way.'

Gaining entrance was more difficult than it first appeared. Although the door was insecure, it seemed to be wedged from inside. 'Probably vagrants sleeping here,' pointed out Jim. 'We won't disturb them but I must sit down for a smoke.'

There was an abundance of boxes so the two friends pulled up a couple of stout tea-chests and sat down. 'What we've got to learn,' said Jim, lighting his pipe, 'is to walk bloody slower. At the rate we're going—'

'Shush!' interrupted Sam. 'D'you hear that?'

'No, can't say I—'

'Shush! There it is again! Be quiet and listen for a moment.'

The pair sat in silence but all that could be heard was the rain bursting through the broken guttering and the holes in the roof.

'I did hear something that time, Sam.' Jim squinted at the floor. 'It's coming from there, I'm sure of it.' He crouched down with his ear almost touching the rough boards. 'My God, Sam! There's someone under here!'

With the aid of their old bull's-eye oil lamps, they soon found a variety of junk that could be used for a jemmy and within minutes had wrenched up three boards. There, lying between the joists, was a bound and gagged figure! Wrenching the gag from his face, Sam paused in amazement. 'Jim! It's Show-off-Roff!'

'Well,' said Jim, as he pulled and tugged at the bindings, 'I could think of better places to show off, Maxie boy, no one can see you there. What on earth are you doing?'

The figure struggled and gasped several times for breath before panting, 'Dying, Jim. I'm fuckin' dying!'

Chapter 9

As the two men tore at Max's bindings, they became more and more aware of his injuries. Yet, considering how near he had been to death, none of these were life-threatening. There were bruises and cuts in abundance, all in keeping with someone who had held no particular desire to be buried alive and had done their best to stress the point. Within a few minutes all bonds had been removed except those binding his legs. Max suddenly sat up, gave a great groan and, twisting rapidly on to his side, vomited the remnants of a small brewery. As Sam slipped the last of the bindings he looked up and noticed the colour already flooding back into Max's face.

'You certainly look better than you did a few moments ago,' he said. 'But then, unless you were dead, you were bound to.' He assisted Max to put a little sitting distance between himself and the former contents of his stomach. 'You want to tell us about it, mate?'

'I was a trustin' fool,' muttered Max. 'An absolute bloody trustin' fool. But I'll tell you this, I *owe* you two . . . owe you two a lot. I won't forget it.'

'So what is this then?' persisted Sam. 'Woman trouble?'

'Women?' Max almost shouted. 'Bloody women? It's somethin' more important than women, I'll tell you that much!'

'No,' ordered Jim firmly. 'You'll tell us a great deal more than "that much". Look, Max, if we hadn't dug you out of there, you'd be dead. I would guess whoever put you there either intended to come back for you before you died, in which case they intended simply to put the frighteners on you, or they intended for you to die in just about as unpleasant a way as they could think of – in which case they must have had the right hump with you! You are quite a big lad, Max, and they would have known you weren't going to lie down an' co-operate, so therefore they had to be mob-handed or you had to be drunk – or probably both.'

'I can see why you joined the force, James,' panted Max. 'No bad, not bad at all!'

'Listen, you two,' interrupted Sam. 'Before you do your Sherlock Holmes bit, we'd better take a look at his leg, there's a lot of blood running into his shoe.'

Sam ripped open the left side of Max's trousers to reveal a ferocious laceration running from mid-thigh to his knee. 'It's hospital for you, Max, otherwise you'll bleed to death.'

Max looked down anxiously. 'D'you know, my legs were so numb I didn't feel that! I can only feel it slightly, even now.'

'One of us has got to go for an ambulance right away,' said Sam, already making towards the door. 'You finish your pipe, I'll go to the fire station in Southwark Bridge Road, they're bound to have a telephone.'

'I don't want anyone knowin' about this!' called Max in vain to the vanishing Sam.

'Okay, Max,' murmured Jim. 'Now let's have the truth. The fairies didn't put you there, so who did – and how?'

'I'll tell you this much, Jim, I misjudged a certain meetin' that I went to and I got a bit pissed. The bastards would never 'a' got me in that pit if I'd been sober. As it was, it took four of them to give me a right poundin' before they could manage it.'

'So who were they?'

'Listen, Jim, as far as the rest of the world's concerned, I had a little stag party to celebrate my engagement. The lads thought it'd be an amusin' idea to leave me under the floorboards till mornin', me being the worse for drink and all that, then lo an' behold, who should turn up but two coppers! Well, bugger me, I thought, that's sodded up their plan good an' proper, ain't it?'

'So they took half your leg away just to make you fit nice and tight, eh?'

'You shouldn't have mentioned that, Jim boy, you've reminded me it hurts. No, they never did that, mate, *you* did. You and old Sam did it when you dragged me out. If you don't believe me, have a look at that jagged metal in the edge of that hole.'

Max's story was ludicrous and Jim knew it but he obviously was not going to name the perpetrators. Even allowing for the inexperience of the two policemen, by their very acquaintance and Max's gratitude, they would almost certainly get more information out of him than any detective ever could.

'Let's see your leg,' said Jim. 'I'll see if I can do anything about that bleeding. This "engagement" of yours, when's the wedding?'

'Oh Jim, Jim lad.' Max shook his head in disbelief. 'You don't think she'd have anythin' to do with me now, do you? Not after the way my friends misbehaved themselves?' He gave a long sigh. 'I'm afraid she's gone out of my life forever. Shame, she was a nice gel and all, we'd 'a' been ever so happy. Sad, isn't it?'

A few minutes later, the sound of wheels announced the arrival of some sort of help. Soon, under the directions of a dark-cloaked, huge-hipped nurse, who announced her name was Gladys something or other, the two recruits carried Max out through the maze of obstacles and holes and placed him carefully in the rear of the ambulance. 'I've never been in an ambulance before!' exclaimed Jim, looking around in childlike wonder. 'It's impressive.'

'Neither have I,' responded Sam.

'Well, one of you had better come, and double quick,'

retorted the nurse. 'We can't have a patient bleeding to death whilst two police officers sort out personal preferences for a ride!' Max pulled a sour face behind her.

'Nurse is right, you go,' Sam urged. 'I think one of us should go anyway.' He dropped his tone. 'Because if he does a runner at the hospital, we're going to look pretty stupid. You accompany him and I'll go back to the station and report what's happened.' He closed the door and banged on the side panelling. 'Okay, driver, take it away!' There was the roar of an engine followed by a loud clunk as the gear was engaged. The ambulance then lurched forward in a series of short sharp jumps before slowly gathering an even momentum and rolling away into the teeming night.

Station Sergeant Dale was always happy to see really lousy weather when he was on night duty; it kept most of the nutters off the streets and gave him a great opportunity to catch up on his paperwork. Without an endless procession of charges and complaints at the station counter, he reckoned he might just be able to put up his feet for the last two hours.

His papers suddenly rustled in the draught as the front door swung open to reveal the large, drenched recruit who, according to his posting, should be somewhere at the back of Great Suffolk Street. 'All proving too much for yer, boy, is it? Don't know wotcha goin' to do when it snows.' The last remark had been mouthed in perfect unison by Taff Jenkins, the communications operator who had heard the same words uttered to every wet recruit who had entered the station for the last five years. Dale glanced up at the old brown wooden clock that hung slightly askew above the fireplace. 'You're not due back here for your break for another . . . let me see . . . hour an' twenty minutes.'

'We found someone under some floorboards, sarge, and—'

'We?' echoed the sergeant. 'What d'you mean, *we*, you were supposed to be patrolling on your own!'

'D'you think we ought to hear his story first, sarge?' asked Taff Jenkins in what he hoped was a helpful tone. 'Sounds a bit serious.'

'Very well, this someone under the floorboards. Dead, I take it?'

Sam told the story, tactfully omitting Jim's search for a pipe-smoking refuge. Station Sergeant Dale was beginning to see his quiet peaceful night disappearing fast. 'So where are they now?' he asked irritably.

Sam looked puzzled. 'Hospital, sarge.'

'I know they're in a damned hospital, you've already told me that! I want to know WHAT bloody hospital! Where, boy, bloody where!'

'I forgot to ask, sergeant. I'm sorry,' apologised Sam. 'All I know is some big-hipped nurse, who said her name was Gladys something-or-other, simply took him away in an ambulance.'

'Oh, that should make the search ever so much easier,' replied the sergeant acidly. 'ALL we need to look for is a big-arsed nurse called Gladys. Find her and you've not only found a missing constable, you've found a half-dead crook. Brilliant!'

'Sarge,' cut in the still helpful Jenkins, 'I could telephone the local hospitals. I should think they've been quiet tonight, there's been no bugger about.'

'Yes,' agreed the sergeant tersely. 'And once you've found them you'd better tell the night-duty CID. That's providing they're not laying dead drunk in some ditch at Sandown Races. You know what a pissy-arsed lot they are!'

Within a few minutes, via the good offices of Taff Jenkins, the injured party was traced with some ease to Guy's Hospital and the night-duty CID was traced with some difficulty to the floor above the very room where

Station Sergeant Dale was sitting. There is nothing like a night-long downpour to ensure a bit of speedy attention in the early hours of the morning at any large hospital. Other than one dead-on-arrival from the Thames, no outsider had set foot in Guy's casualty for two and half hours when Jim, Max and the big-arsed nurse burst dramatically through the front door. Soon a scrawny Scottish doctor was pulling, twisting, raising, pressing and fingering various parts of Max's anatomy before eventually listing: one slightly torn ear; one developing black eye; a sprained right ankle; twenty-two bruises; four lacerations, the worst of which – a thirty-one stitch job – was allegedly sustained in his rescue; and finally, an upset stomach. 'That,' said the whisky-reeking detective later to Jim, 'is classic GBH. Therefore, all I want from our friend in the cubicle are the names of the perpetrators and we're home and dry.'

'You don't mind if I sit this one out do you, sarge?' asked Jim of the detective. 'Only I've heard it before and it's such a moving story I'm not sure I could take it again.'

'What're you saying?' asked the detective suspiciously.

'I'm saying Maxie Roff wouldn't give police the drippings from his nose. He's never going to tell you the truth. He claims it was done by friends at his stag night. That is, except for that bloody great gash in his leg. He reckons me and Sam inflicted that on him before getting him out of the hole.'

'P'haps you ought'a left the bastard where he was?' said the detective in disgust.

'Well, if I'd known how it was going to turn out, I might have been tempted,' replied Jim ruefully.

The detective rubbed his chin in thought for a moment then said, 'I'll have a private word with him but if he don't co-operate I'll swift him down to the nick for a statement. I'll inconvenience the bugger if nothing else, and it'll serve him right for getting me out from that CID office fireside on a night like this.'

It was during this period of Max's 'inconvenience' that matters began to go a little wrong for the young recruits. It was probably motivated by Station Sergeant Dale, who had seen his planned siesta vanish without trace. After all, if the two recruits had not been creeping around off their patrol, none of this would have taken place. If they had left well alone, all that would have happened was that the world would have been minus one small-time villain who would not have been discovered until the area was rebuilt, and who would shed tears over that? Meantime the night-duty station officer could have snatched a well-earned nap. There was definitely something about those two young constables that was not quite right. Suddenly it came to him. He went into the interview room where the detective was taking a statement from the unhappy Max.

'Just the man!' he exclaimed. 'Did you know either of the two constables who found you, before tonight I mean?'

'Never seen them in my life,' answered Max. 'Total strangers.'

'That's a lie and you must know that I know it.'

'Never seen them in my life,' repeated Max as if he had not spoken the first time. 'Total strangers.'

The station sergeant looked meaningfully at the detective who shrugged as if to say don't-tell-me-mate-I've-problems-of-my-own. Having drawn a blank there, he went into the tiny room that led off the front office where Taff Jenkins usually sat at either his switchboard or his teleprinter. As he thought, Jenkins was guiding the young constables through their pocket book reports concerning the incident. 'Ah, just the people I wish to see. Did either of you two know the prisoner Roff before you found him tonight?'

Both lads answered at once. Unfortunately Jim said 'No' and Sam said 'Yes'. 'Make your minds up. Did you or didn't you?'

Sam was in first. 'I knew him, PC Forsythe didn't. He

used to go to my old school but that was before Jim – I mean PC Forsythe – transferred there.'

The die being cast, Jim felt he had no choice but to continue. 'Er – yes, that's right, but of course we have our backgrounds in common so to speak, it's just that we never met.'

'Quite,' said Dale. 'But *you*, Diamond, you did meet him – yes?'

'Is that important, sarge?' asked Jim.

'It could be, it could be,' murmured the station sergeant thoughtfully. 'PC Diamond may find himself, well . . . shall we say compromised, if, in his professional capacity, he is likely to meet animals like Roff whom he knew as a civilian. I'll need to draw it to the attention of the chief inspector. After all, it's no good being wise after the event now, is it?'

'So what does all that mean, sarge?' asked Sam worriedly.

The station sergeant gestured indifferently. 'Could mean a transfer, could mean nothing at all, who knows?'

Jim was poised to speak but the tiniest shake of the head from Taff Jenkins stifled his words. 'Anyway, as soon as you two have completed your reports I want you back out on to the streets, all right?'

'Sergeant!' acknowledged the two lads in unison.

As his footsteps faded away, a cheery voice could be heard at the counter. 'It's old George Hemmingway,' explained Taff. 'He's a *Times* printer and drops a copy of the newspaper in on the way home every morning about 5 a.m. You won't get much more out of Dale now until he scans the main stories. But listen . . .' he gave a quick glance across the main office. 'There's absolutely no point in you, Jim, admitting you also knew Max Roff. It's not Sam's fault the situation has arisen but nevertheless it has. It's a fait accompli and you're stuck with it. Even if you do admit it and they decide a transfer's needed, there's no guarantee you would both be transferred to the same nick again.

You're two single men, they could put you anywhere in London.'

'So what're you saying?' said Jim.

'I'm saying Dale is a vindictive old bastard, so keep your head down, say nothing and see what happens. It may have all blown over by the end of the week. On the other hand, who knows?' He shrugged.

Later, as the two friends waited for the number 48 tram home, Jim said, 'I'm not at all happy about this, Sam. If it wasn't for me wanting a smoke it would never have happened.'

'And Max would be dead,' Sam reminded him. 'I know he's a bit of a bastard but surely not even Max should die like that? No one should. Listen, I've been giving this some thought. You want to go as far in this job as possible, don't you?'

Jim nodded. 'I thought I did, now I'm not so sure.'

'Shut up and listen. Now one of the problems Taff pointed out to me is that *if* a person is transferred, there's always the feeling of "no smoke without fire". No matter how innocent he may be, there's always a whisper somewhere. Can you imagine what it would be like to be transferred after your first night out on your own? Bloody hell, they'd think you were Jack the Ripper or some such. So be quiet, shut up and do as you're told.'

'Thanks, Sam, but in spite of all the drama I've just learnt one very important basic thing about police duty.'

'That is?'

'We walk too bloody fast! Tonight we'll do it half the pace, I'm knackered.'

Jim's fear concerning the pace of their walk moderated as each day and night passed. They had joined the night duty shift two weeks into its three-week stint so a week later both recruits were back on day duty, or to be more precise, late turn. Sam had heard nothing further about Max and had understandably thought the matter had died a death.

Both recruits widened their experience at every opportunity and acquired the reputation of being dependable and handy to have around when things went wrong – and Stones End was the type of manor where things *did* go wrong at fairly regular intervals.

Queenie meanwhile had settled into her new job and appeared very happy except that it had become extremely difficult for her and Sam to arrange shared off-duty times.

Early turn duty was easily the best for Sam. Being free by early afternoon the couple would sometimes meet at a mutual distance in Hyde Park and, during the later stages of the summer and on particularly hot days, would occasionally row on the Serpentine lake. Sam in particular enjoyed these outings. When he was alone in the boat with his beloved Queenie he felt, and indeed was, an eternity away from the Stones End's squalor. For many nights after such a trip he would walk the filthy streets of north Southwark and picture Queenie in her spotless white dress and straw boater. 'I adore you in that boater, girl,' he would repeat almost every time they rowed. 'You should always wear it!'

'It would look a little out of place when I'm black-leading the fire grates.'

'Fire grates?' he echoed, as he reached out to study her fingers. 'Surely you have scullery maids to do that job?'

'Sam, don't be such a snob!' she chided. 'I work for a charming, elderly and not too well-off couple, not the Sultan of Mahahraja. There are just two of us domestics in the household so we muck in and help each other.'

'I'm not sure I approve,' said the frowning young man. 'It's demeaning for you.'

'How many times did you tell your mother she shouldn't do demeaning tasks, Sam? And what do you think she would have said if you *had*?'

'That's different,' he sulked.

'Is it? And when we are married, Sam, who's going to

black lead our fire grate, whiten our front step and empty the chamber-pots . . . *our* maid?'

Sam, with the slightest hint of huffiness, gave the oars an extra tug. As a result his rhythm broke and the oar skimmed the surface, showering Queenie from hem to boater. He instantly dropped the oars and scrambled towards her, causing her far more alarm at the heaving of the boat than the wet transparency of her dress. 'Sam! Careful, the boat'll go over!'

By now one oar had floated away and as Sam steadied the boat Queenie was able to assess the state of her dress. It was better than she had feared but still quite wet in patches. The boat had drifted in towards the small island on the north side of the lake and fortunately so had the oar, though a yard or so out of reach. 'Can we pull in to the bank, Sam, so I can straighten myself up?' The overhanging branches caused some inconvenience but were handy for pulling in close to the shore. Slipping off his shoes and socks, Sam tested the depth which, to his great relief, was barely up to his knees. Striding ashore, he gave the boat an extra tug and lifted Queenie out over the rowlocks.

'I've got to rescue that oar else we'll be rowing round in circles till dark,' he muttered testily. Using one oar to catch the other he splashed around in the shallows for some minutes before being rewarded with success. He was about to pull it ashore when his attention was drawn to two boats further out in the lake whose male occupants were cheering vociferously. Looking at the cause of their pleasure he discovered it to be the fair Miss Cotterill who, petticoat clad, was hanging her wet dress on a sun-facing bush. 'Queenie!' he squawked. 'What *are* you doing?'

'What does it look like I'm doing? I'm drying my dress, the dress that you drenched, remember?'

'But you've got no clothes on!'

'Sam, I have everything on except my dress. Have you seen the length of this petticoat?'

'It's not the bottom half,' he hissed. 'It's the top! You're nearly . . . well . . . you're nearly popping out and people can see you!'

'Would you be happier if I lay down then? Good God, I'm surely not coming to any harm in the middle of Hyde Park Serpentine at four o'clock on a hot September afternoon!'

'But if you lie down with no dress on, and I'm on the island, what on earth will people think?'

'Sam, I'm not sure how you're going to take this but I think you'd better know now rather than later, I don't *care* what people think. Look, I'll show you.' She seized him around the neck and literally swung on a kiss, much to the whistling delight of an additional two boats now stationary some thirty yards distant. 'The important things to me are my friends and my beliefs.'

'God, but you're like your aunt!' She withdrew her arms from his neck. Legs apart, she put her hands on her hips and stared at him. A vision of naked wet Billie came back to mind. 'And you'll never know how much!'

'I hope you meant that as a compliment, Sam Diamond.'

'You'll do very well if you ever get a better one,' he laughed. 'Now sit down, be quiet, and stop exciting all those toffee-nosed chinless wonders out there in boats.'

She sat down but slipped a strap teasingly from her shoulder, fluttered her eyelashes and pouted provocatively, 'But is it all right if I excite you?'

'I'm not allowed to be excited,' he said with feigned indifference. 'I'm a police officer, and at twenty-six shillings and six a week I can't afford excitement.'

'Ah ha! Then my good name is safe?'

'Your name is safe enough,' he agreed, pushing her gently back on to the grass. 'It's the rest of you that's at risk.' She lay staring up at him, his strong face framed by a cloudless sky. 'It's moments like this that make up for those agonising times when I don't see you for days,' he whispered as he kissed her and lay down beside her. There was a sudden ripple of water as a swan skimmed in to land but other than that, every other sound was so muted. 'I think it's really beautiful here,' she murmured. 'It's so peaceful you'd never believe we were in the middle of London.'

They both closed their eyes and floated rather than slept. To Sam it seemed minutes rather than the hour that it was when Queenie said sleepily, 'Sam, I have to get back soon – and so does that boat unless you want to pay sixpence extra.'

She rose and slipped on her dress as Sam lay back admiring her. 'Queenie Cotterill, you're beautiful.'

'Sam Diamond, you're daft.'

As he rowed the short distance to the boathouse, Queenie asked about Jim and Jane. 'They certainly see each other more than we can,' he replied enviously as he edged the boat to its jetty. 'On the other hand, strolling around scruffy Blackfriars is not quite the same as having your own island in the sun.'

'Cheaper, though, wouldn't you say?' she replied, slipping her arm in his as they walked sedately across the park towards Marble Arch. 'Have you heard about Miss Bardell?' she suddenly asked.

He shook his head. 'The last I heard she was supposed to be in California.'

'She's a very long way from California, Sam, last week she was leading a strike at the East Ham Palace.'

'Strike! East Ham Palace! What on earth was that about?'

'Apparently some of the music hall stars are striking over the low payments made to lesser known acts. It's got quite nasty at times and managers are stocking the shows with amateurs. According to the *Morning Post* she's given up a wonderful contract with Florenz Ziegfeld, the American impresario. He had an American tour planned for her, instead she's leading a strike at East Ham! He's supposed to have said he'll make sure she never plays on any stage in America.'

Sam shook his head in grudging admiration. 'Daft cow! Fancy choosing to be on strike in East Ham rather than singing in California!' After a few moments he raised his hand to his forehead. 'Blimey, East Ham is worse than Stones End!'

'Sam darling, there's my omnibus! I must run, dinner is down to me tonight.' She snatched a quick kiss as, hand on boater, she broke into an unladylike sprint. 'Keep loving me . . . and keep writing!' she called breathlessly over her shoulder.

After seeing Queenie, the walk back to the section house was always an anti-climax, so much so that day that he was tempted to take a tram from Victoria. Yet, for a young man saving pennies for his wedding, a sixpenny fare could be deemed an extravagance. The journey took him longer than he planned as he dawdled over Vauxhall Bridge and wondered what he and Queenie would do on their precious afternoons together in mid-winter. For a while, the thought filled him with despair. A home shared with Queenie seemed nothing more than a dream. As he entered the section house, Jim was about to leave. 'Where've you been?' asked his friend. 'I've been looking for you everywhere.'

'You were hardly likely to find me,' retorted Sam. 'Because I've been with Queenie in a boat on the Serpentine.'

'I know and that's where I looked! I borrowed a cycle from one of the lads and cycled all over bloody Hyde Park. I went twice round the sodding Serpentine but you were nowhere to be seen.'

'Ah!' exclaimed Sam as realisation dawned. 'We were on the island. Queenie got wet and had to hang her dress up to dry and . . .'

'. . . and Billie Bardell crashed ashore in a boat, I suppose?' Jim gave a sigh. 'I dunno, Sam Diamond, it's always the same. I only have to turn my back on you for a few minutes and you get young ladies undressed! How d'you do it, I want to know!'

'Jim!' snapped Sam testily. 'Will you kindly tell me what was so important that you cycled all over Hyde Park this afternoon, please?'

'The chief inspector came into the mess room just after you left. He said he'd been procrastinating – at least that's what I think he said – about Sergeant Dale's report concerning your transfer. He said he didn't want to transfer you but he felt he had no choice. He said if you wanted to put your case, the superintendent would be available at Stones End until five o'clock but after that time, don't bother.'

'It's gone six already,' said Sam worriedly. 'Perhaps he may still—'

'Sam, I hate to tell you this but he's gone. When I couldn't find you in Hyde Park I called into Stones End but he was already leaving and wouldn't speak to me.'

'Whose bike did you use?'

'Jock Russell's. It's the one over there by the shed.'

'D'you think he'd mind if I used it?'

'If he let me ride around Hyde Park all afternoon on it he'd lend it to anyone. But if it's going to make you feel better, why don't you take it now and ask him later . . . by the way, I take it you can ride a bike?'

'Sort of,' called Sam as he raced across the yard. Jumping on the machine, he made progress with a series of alarming squiggles and lurches and was about to ride out of the gate when Jim, with appalling timing, called, 'How's Queenie?'

Turning his head, Sam beamed and yelled: 'Beautiful,' but this response was lost on the inquirer who was more intrigued as to how the cycle could possibly miss the gate post.

Fifteen minutes later Sam wobbled into Stones End station yard and propped his cycle against the wall. He raced upstairs to the chief inspector's office and met Sergeant Hawkins coming down. 'If you've come in for what I think you've come in for, boy, yer too late. You've to report to Tottenham police station nine o'clock Monday next. Sorry, son. Personally I think you'd 'a' been an asset here. For what it's worth, the old man thinks so too and he's not enamoured of a certain station sergeant, I can tell you. But there it is, son . . . sorry.'

Chapter 10

'Okay, Nafan,' said Reg, 'I don't want this meetin' goin' on all bleedin' night 'cos I've got a little party at 'ome fer the old lady. She's eighty years old termorrer, bless 'er cotton socks. Lovely ol' gel, ain't she?' He looked sharply around the meeting for support which flooded back with indecent haste. 'Is there anyfing that's too important to put back ter next time? No? Very well then . . .'

'Perhaps just one thing, Reg?'

He gave an impatient sigh, 'Wot is it now, Sid?'

'It's Max. I think we should decide to make our final decision.'

'Max?' echoed Reg. 'Wot decision is there ter be made?'

Sid shuffled uncomfortably. 'He's now been down in that hole for two days. I should think he's learnt his lesson. So do we let him out this evening?'

'Two days?' Reg chuckled. 'Didn't realise it was so long. I bet 'e bleedin' stinks! Nothin' like sinkin' a few bevvies an' not bein' able ter go ter the carsey fer two days.' The thought obviously appealed to him, as his genuine laughter rang out long after the forced hilarity of his companions. Or rather it *did* ring out until he cut it instantly short with a fist crashing on the table and, a loud: 'NO!' Reg glowered around the room. 'He stays,' he hissed.

'But, Reg . . .' began Buster Slingsby. 'We thought we were only putting the scares into him. If we're not careful, we're going to have a dead 'un on our hands.'

'No, we ain't,' replied Reg confidently. 'You only 'ave a

dead 'un when you *find* a dead 'un. No one's goin' ter find that thievin' git until they knock all those old warehouses down an' that's donkey's years away yet.' He eyeballed everyone in the room for seconds at a time. 'Max was playin' a dangerous little game an' I 'ad to award a foul.' He shook his head with great deliberation. 'If yer don't play ter the rules yer can't complain when yer gits yer come-uppance. Oh, an' by the way,' he added, 'I don't expect anyone ter be payin' 'im no little friendly visits neither. That's where 'e is an' that's where 'e stays. I'm takin' me old mum away to Scotland fer a couple weeks and I'm leavin' Nafan in charge so, providin' nuffin' dramatic arises, I'll see yer all back 'ere . . .' he studied the wall-calendar '. . . Friday 27th, three weeks to the night. Meetin' adjourned.'

Sam arrived back at the section house without recollecting a second of the journey. During his ride his mind had raced through almost every minute of his brief spell at Stones End. Tottenham! He was not even sure where the place was. Other than the football team, he knew nothing else about the area. He would certainly miss working with Jim, they had worked together since they left school, but more importantly, what about Queenie? How far was Tottenham from St John's Wood or, for that matter, Hyde Park? In the ten minutes it had taken him to cycle he had mentally resigned from the force; reinstated himself; demanded to see the commissioner and thumped Station Sergeant Dale particularly hard – he had enjoyed that bit. To his surprise, the first person he met in the yard was Jim Forsythe.

'I thought you were off to see Jane?' asked Sam, leaping off the cycle with newfound expertise.

'I was but she'd never forgive me if I left without hearing your latest news.'

Sam recounted the tale and was pleased at his friend's genuine disappointment. Together they pored over a map to calculate distances but their conclusions were not promising. 'I'm going to ask for permission to marry,' said Sam suddenly.

'But you have to have two years service,' pointed out Jim.

'What's that's got to do with it?' argued Sam. 'Life's not like that, at least it shouldn't be. Queenie and I wish to marry, I wish to stay in the force. If I'm doing a satisfactory job and we are both happy, does it matter a toss whether I have two years or two days service? The whole thing's too ridiculous for words!'

'Don't shoot me, I'm just the messenger,' said Jim defensively. 'But nevertheless, that's what they are going to tell you, mate, so be prepared.'

'I'd better write to Queenie straight away.'

The Tuesday early turn parade lined up a little sleepily at 5.45 a.m. next morning. As the duty officer entered the parade room, Sergeant Binns called: 'Appointments!' Each man dutifully held up his whistle, truncheon and pocket book for view. Inspector Alfie Taylor glanced briefly along the row of a dozen men.

'Are we all present, Sergeant Binns?' The sergeant assured him they were indeed all present. 'Probably too much to hope that we're also all correct. Still, never mind, we're at least halfway to being efficient. Any local dramas we should be knowing about, sergeant?'

'No, sir, there were a couple of robberies last night but two locals have been nicked for them. Oh, yes, a Suffolk Punch has gone missing from the coal wharf stables.'

'What's a Suffolk Punch, sergeant?' asked the puzzled inspector.

'A big ginger horse, sir.'

'Well, there you are, lads, see anyone riding a big ginger horse covered in coal dust, you'll know what to do. Okay then, out you go. Except for you, PC Diamond. I want a quick word with you in the inspector's room directly after this parade. Right – parade, 'shun! Left turn, quick march.'

As the men trooped out into the overcast Borough High Street, Sam followed the duty officer into the bowels of the building. Alfred Jeremiah Taylor was one of the most popular inspectors in the whole division. A burly figure with a large moustache, he always inspired confidence and never appeared ruffled and, whilst being more than able to impose discipline, never appeared to find the necessity to do so. 'Sit down, son, make yourself comfortable.' The inspector came quickly to the point. 'I did hope, indeed I was sure, that you and your mate Forsythe would make good members of this shift. I'm not best pleased at the way things have turned out and if I had a slightly greater say in the matter, it would have been someone else who was packing his bags and not you. However . . .' there was a pause as he rolled a cigarette. 'Where was I? Oh, yes, however that's not to be. It's a discipline service and I wouldn't want it any other way. You're a young man but I'm sure you'll recover because you've got the right approach.' He put a match to the end of the cigarette-paper and the flame singed his moustache before he was satisfied and gave his first deep draw. 'You'll find Tottenham a wee bit rural after this place but don't turn anything down, boy. Get your experience and show those who need to be showed exactly what it is you're made of. I think that's all I've got to say, except that you can have Sunday morning off to make your move to Tottenham section house.'

'Can I ask you something, sir?'

'Fire away.'

Sam then recounted his problems concerning his engagement to Queenie and his aversion to waiting two years in order to marry.

'No one should be in a hurry to marry, boy. If you only knew the number of men who have blessed the job for giving them two years to change their minds you'd be amazed. Yet I can see you're probably not one of those.' He sat thoughtfully for a moment until his cigarette went out. Undaunted, he put it to his lips again as if he hadn't noticed. 'I'm a great believer in if-you-don't-ask-you-don't-get, so why don't you put in for permission anyway? After all, you've got nothing to lose. Come and see me half an hour before we finish duty today and, between the pair of us, we'll knock out an application that'll fetch tears to the eyes of the commissioner himself.' Finally realising his cigarette was spent he cast it nonchalantly into a waste-bin. 'Okay, lad, off you go.'

'One last question, sir?'

Taylor nodded and searched for another cigarette paper.

'Everyone knows, no matter what the reason, the mere fact that I've been transferred, so early in service, will cause eyebrows to be raised. Do I have any redress, sir? Can I take this complaint to anyone, or any department? It is just so unfair otherwise.'

'There is no redress at all,' the inspector confirmed as he struggled with his tobacco pouch. 'Basically, within the police discipline code, you have no rights at all. My frank opinion is that the force is storing up a great deal of trouble for itself. We are now eight years into the twentieth century and men will not accept this state of affairs much longer. But at the moment those are the rules and, until they are changed, that is how we will work. Sorry I can't be more help. Anything else?'

'No, sir, thanks for your time.'

Taylor nodded and put a match to his cigarette.

For Sam the week dragged by. Finishing duty at 2 p.m., Jim would make the most of the free evenings to see Jane. Sam on the other hand had never had so many early nights. However, on Friday he had decided to accompany Jim in his trip back to Inkerman Place and hopefully see his mother before his move to the wilds of north London. As it was a pleasant autumn evening, the lads decided on a leisurely walk. They had plenty of time because Jane would be working until six o'clock. As they approached The

Crown in the gathering dusk, the open door of the public bar appeared particularly inviting. 'Quick pint?' suggested Sam. There was no argument from Jim and very soon the pair sat supping ale at the bar.

With no chance to see Queenie before his move to Tottenham, a mood of melancholy had already settled on Sam and he stared silently into his ale. His meditations were eventually interrupted by his friend. 'Don't look up too quick, but isn't that Show-Off Roff over in the saloon bar, just leaving with Buster Slingsby?'

Sam raised his sights from his beer glass. 'Yes – and what a recovery!' he marvelled. 'Look at him, he doesn't even have a limp! How long since we pulled him out of that hole?'

'It was a little over three weeks ago. A bull-shitting show-off he may be but, credit where it's due, he is some tough geezer that one!'

Reg Simmons had enjoyed his two weeks in Scotland, particularly Edinburgh. He felt it had the sort of class that Blackfriars sadly lacked. A great one for class was Reg. Well, it showed in his choice of car, didn't it? He had decided whilst strolling Princes Street that it was time he changed his address. It was all very well having such a car but when Speeches Smith collected him from his front door, such a vehicle looked somehow out of place in Belvedere Buildings. Not that the buildings were bad – they weren't. He'd slice the ears of anyone who said they were. It was the name that was wrong. It seemed to lack that certain ring.

Reg parted the lace curtains of his mother's parlour. Sure enough there was old Speeches. Reliable lad Speeches – more than could be said for some of the others. Funny bloke really, sometimes went days without speaking. Still, that suited well. Nothing worse than some tosser who prattled on all day about sod all. Better say goodbye to the old girl. 'Just orf for a business meetin', Ma. Probably be a bit late. Don't yer wait up, mind. See yer termorrow, sweet'eart.'

Speeches had put the headlights on as he turned into the Buildings. Reg always liked that, gave it a sort of dramatic approach when the full power of the lights swept the pavement and road. The glare temporarily blinded him as the car rolled to a halt but it would have been silly to have nit-picked when the whole effect had been so impressive.

'Evenin', Speeches, I could 'ardly see a bloody fing,' he began. 'Still, it's certainly a wonderful sight.'

Reg slid into the vast back seat and took up his customary position in the centre. In truth, he was not really sure where the owner of such a vehicle *should* sit. If he sat at the side, it was as if someone else was expected to share. Reg was very jealous of his car and sharing with anyone, other than Mum, was not in his agenda. The fact that Speeches' view via the inside mirror was nil never entered his head, and Speeches would not have bothered to mention it anyway.

'Okay, Speeches, to The Crown.'

Reg's lack of knowledge about cars was only matched by his understanding of geography. It was amazing how little he knew of the area in which he was born and raised. He always left the route to the driver and Speeches hardly ever went the same way twice. Reg thought he was probably showing off his knowledge. Well, there was nothing wrong with that. Who knew? There might well come a day when such knowledge could be vital. They had made three fairly sharp turns when Speeches headed into a street where the wheel-base was almost as wide as the road. Two dark figures walking away from them glanced quickly over their shoulder and were obliged to separate to allow the car to pass. Reg thought there was something vaguely familiar in the way that one of them walked but, before he could study him too closely, Speeches thoughtfully turned off his dazzling headlights. The car began to ease past the pair at little more than a walking pace: suddenly they each snatched open a door and leapt into the rear of the vehicle.

'Speeches!' screamed Reg, feeling quickly for his knife. 'Help me!'

But not only did the driver not speak, he seemed not to hear either. Besides, the garrotte that was slipped so expertly around Reg's neck curtailed further conversation. A few minutes later the car rolled to a halt alongside a silent riverside wharf opposite St Paul's. It was by now quite dark and the only audible noise came from the occasional lapping of the tide against the flat bulk of a solitary anchored barge.

'This seems a nice spot for our little chat, wouldn't you say, Reg?' asked the larger of the two men. The rope was so tight around Reg's neck that he could barely breathe, never mind answer. 'Oh, your tie is a little uncomfortable, is it? Oh dear, Mr Slingsby, what *can* we do to assist the poor man? D'you think we might slacken it a mite?' There was a moment's silence before the speaker tut-tutted and continued in a solemn voice, 'Oh dear, what shall we do! Mr Slingsby thinks we can't loosen your tie after all. Bless me,' he sighed. 'It's just one bleedin' thing after another, isn't it, Reg?'

Reg stared in disbelief at his inquisitor. 'I know, Reg, amazin', isn't it? All I can say is, I think our policemen are wonderful. There I was, three weeks ago, all but dead an' buried, yet here I am now, safe and sound and as bright as a button. Restores your faith in humanity, doesn't it?'

Reg turned his head from side to side in desperation but the team had chosen their spot well, there was no one in sight. 'Well, Reg, now you recognise me,' Max continued, 'let me tell you how I have just saved your life. See that barge out there?' He wrenched Reg's head round to face the river. 'Mr Slingsby here wanted to slip you underneath it. Fancy that! And you not a swimmer, either. I can't think what you must have done to upset him so much.' He gave a deep sigh. 'You must'a been a real little tinker. Anyway, Reg, tell you what I've planned for you.'

Max swung Reg around so they were face to face and barely inches apart. 'As you can see, I'm really lookin' quite well, everybody says so, and d'you know why I'm so well? I'll tell you. I'm so well 'cos of the nice rest you gave me. The two days I spent bound and trussed under those floorboards were real relaxing. Gets you away from the cares of the world, you might say. So I thinks to myself, Max boy, I thinks, poor old Reg is lookin' a bit peaky, why don't I give him a rest, just like the one he gave me? And you know what? Everybody I spoke to agreed with me. Nice that they all had your welfare at heart, ain't it? So that's where we're off to.' Max leaned forward confidentially to his captive and whispered, 'Lot safer there than in the river, Reg. You won't bleedin' drown that's for sure.'

He turned to Buster. 'We don't want him gettin' a cold, Buster, so wrap him up nice and firm like, because he could be there for some little time.'

'Like twenty years?' offered Buster.

'Twenty years?' echoed Max. 'Now that really would be a nice long rest, wouldn't it? I reckon you'd enjoy that, Reg. Off we go then, Speeches.'

By the way Reg protested it was obvious he did not believe Maxie's assurances as to his good health. There was nothing that the pair could not handle in the rear of the car but when Speeches reversed into the yard alongside the derelict shop, Reg's protests increased dramatically.

'It's no good appealing to his better nature,' observed Max sadly. 'We're gonna have to duff him.'

Judging by the way Speeches suddenly leaped into life, there was obviously something in the prospect of duffing Reg that struck quite a cord with him. So much so, that Max had finally to drag the chauffeur off the unconscious figure. 'I said *duff* him, Speeches, not *stuff* him!' he admonished.

Within a few minutes Reg lay sleeping peacefully in his bindings. The original floorboards had been torn away by the endeavours of Sam and Jim but there were still ample sections of planking to cover the old mattress that they tucked carefully around the prostrate figure. Several nails were hammered home and the trio departed.

'Speeches,' said a grateful Max, 'your days of sittin' outside in the motor are finished. You'll certainly be driving it, because you are the only bleedin' driver we've got, but from now on, old sunshine, you'll be *inside*. And not only that, you don't have to wear that stupid outfit anymore. Okay, first stop The Crown, and I wouldn't be surprised if we don't meet a few more puzzled people. You know, I think I'm going to quite enjoy this.'

Ten minutes later the car rolled slowly to a halt outside The Crown. The three men alighted and strolled leisurely through the saloon bar to the door of the committee room. Speeches knocked and threw it open in one arrogant move.

'I know,' said the smiling Max to the three occupants, 'I do look like him, don't I?'

'But you're—' began Long Tom.

'Dead? Don't you believe it, Tom. Like an old geezer once said, the reports of me death have been greatly exaggerated. Now, in the absence of Reg, I would like to call the meeting to order. Nathan, what have you got to say?'

'Don't play games with me, Max,' replied the white-faced Nathan. 'Come to the point.'

'The point, Nathan? I'll tell you the point, shall I? The point is that there are going to be some changes around here and bloody big ones at that.'

'Where's Reg?' asked Sid Green. 'We can't make changes without Reg.'

'Well, Reg's gone off to do a little digging. Oh, what's the word I want, Buster?'

'Archaeological, Max?' offered Buster.

'Yeah, that's it, nice word that, he's gone on a little archaeological dig, and he 'specially requested to be left alone with his thoughts. He reckons if he likes it he might not come back, and in my opinion he's going to like it a lot.' He shrugged and turned out his palms. 'So personally, I don't see him comin' back. I've taken the liberty of makin' three little changes right away, if that's all right with you gentlemen? Speeches here is the only one of us who can drive, so, as the car actually belongs to the committee, I've given it to him on the committee's behalf. Old Buster here, well, he has all the flair of a good deputy chairman, so I've appointed him deputy chairman. For the last change, I thought, well, if Reg is going to keep being away like this, we need someone a bit more permanent as chairman, so guess what? I've appointed meself!'

'You said there would be other big changes, Max,' persisted Sid. 'What are they?'

'Well, contrary to me first thoughts, I'm not goin' to razor the bastards who shoved me underground. I'm going to be – what is it, Buster?'

'Magnamanious, Max.'

'Yeah, that's right, magnamanious. You can each come with the new format, or stay out, please yourself. If you come in then all is forgiven. If you stay out . . .' He shrugged again. 'Who knows?'

'Your first problem's going to be with Frank Cootes,' said Nathan. 'He was close to Reg. He's on tour at the moment with Sandow but he's not going to take kindly to this when he returns.'

'I'll deal with Frank when the time comes. P'haps he might like to take up archaeology and go and look for Reg, who knows? Listen, what I'm proposing is we move out'a this tuppenny ha'penny little racket we've got here, into something more rewarding.'

'Such as?' asked Sid.

'Girls for starters. Reg was a weird sod. He was always uncomfortable dealin' with any female except his bleedin' mother. There are also about a score of bookies' pitches around the manor that we could show an interest in. We're fairly close to the docks and we've got thousands of outlets in the slums around here for any gear that may come our way. With luck, and certainly within a year or so, we could be the biggest team in South London.' He looked around the room for signs as to what effect his words may have had. 'Tell you what,' he offered, 'Buster, Speeches and me will go out into the saloon bar for a drink. You three can have a little gathering of your own and then tell us what conclusions you've came to. Can't say fairer, can I?'

The door had no sooner closed on the trio than an icy silence fell on the room.

'Let's not all talk at once,' snapped Nathan acidly. 'Right, Sid, you first.'

'The way I see it,' said Sid, 'is that Reg was getting more and more power mad. As long as I get an assurance that he won't be making an unexpected return, I'm in favour of forming a new team.'

'Tom?'

'Likewise,' agreed Williams. 'My reservations are about Frank Cootes. He's not going to be at all happy about this and he can be a bloody psychopath at times.'

'I agree,' said Nathan. 'Cootes is the worry. On the other hand, what's our alternative? If Max has come back from the grave with Reg's chauffeur *and* Buster Slingsby, you can bet your last quid that wherever Reg is now, we've seen the last of him. If we can be given that assurance, then we're happy to go in with Max. Agreed?' Both nodded in acknowledgement. 'Call them back in, Sid.'

Max listened to their concerns carefully before replying, 'You're right to be concerned. Cootes is a fucking psycho, but he can be a really handy boy to have around, providing he's handled right. His reputation alone can work wonders. I propose to have just one meeting with him. There'll be no debate, I shall give him the one option – he'll be with us or he won't be . . . in any way.' He studied his watch for a moment. 'By this time tomorrow Reg Simmons will probably have decided to remain an archaeologist, so you'll have nothing to worry about.'

'In that case,' said Nathan, 'can we postpone our decision *until* tomorrow? It would certainly ease our minds.'

Max smashed a fist angrily down on the table. 'NO, YOU CANNOT! Just what do you think I intend running here, the Band of Fucking Hope? This is going to be a rough tough big boys' school. There's to be no fart-arsing about. Listen to me, Nathan, when I was under those floorboards the idea of slowly disembowelling you passed away many a long hour. My patience with you has reached the station buffers, it has nowhere else to go! Decide now, all of you!'

'Put like that, I think I get your point,' responded Nathan. He glanced at his two colleagues. 'Agreed, gentlemen?' The gentlemen agreed.

The Stones End duty sergeant always awoke from his bed a happier man on Saturday mornings, for one very important reason – the Borough Fruit and Vegetable Market was closed! In 1276 City elders had claimed it was a traffic nuisance and matters had deteriorated steadily since. In 1671 Charles II was so fed up with it, he designed new boundaries though this availed him little. Stalls were pulled in a little bit here and pushed out a little bit there, yet the traders survived every attempt to close them down. The market was an anachronism in the early twentieth century, situated as it was at the foot of London Bridge. Without the market, traffic was usually only horrendous; with it, it was a nightmare. Every morning, from the early hours onward, hundreds of barrows, carts, wagons, trolleys, horses and lorries, would edge forward, roll back, tip over, refuse to start, run away, leak, pee and collapse. And every morning a sergeant and nine constables had to attempt a feat that had been recognised as impossible for six hundred and fifty years – keep the traffic flowing. It was worse than a haystack search for needles because in this particular haystack there were no needles.

As a result of these two days of tranquillity, the Stones End manor was therefore relatively quiet, with just an occasional murder, odd rape, dozen robberies, score of brawls and the inevitable five hundred wife beatings. Now whether five hundred wives were genuinely beaten up, or whether, as some coppers claimed, it was just ten wives being beaten up fifty times each, no one was sure but for a newcomer to the area, wife beating had all the characteristics of a thriving cottage industry. The rule-of-thumb basically seemed: 'If things go wrong, belt the missus.' The best aspect of the early-turn Saturday shift was, not only was it free from the hassle of the market but, certainly early on, it was also reasonably free from all the other crimes and misdemeanours. Wife beating tended to be a late in the day occupation; the same could be said for murders, rapes and brawls. So, other than an intermittent robbery, Saturday early turn beat duty was the nearest time of the week to tranquillity on the Stones End patch. Indeed, quite a good day for a young recruit to spend his last nostalgic stint on the manor.

Sam and Jim walked at a slow, relaxed regulation pace as they made their way to their distant beats. Skirting the quiet market they found themselves on the corner of Clink Street. 'Remember the last time we walked past here, Jim?'

He smiled. 'Yes, wonder how old Max is feeling now? I'd be surprised if we ever see him again, wouldn't you? I think he's had such a scare put into him that he won't be seen on this manor for many a long day.'

'I know,' reflected Sam bitterly. 'That's what makes it so bloody maddening that I'm being transferred. If you hadn't wanted a smoke . . . oh, well, can't be helped now. Don't want another smoke before people start moving about, do you? Might be the only chance you get.'

Jim was at first indecisive but the proximity of the warehouse entrance proved too strong. 'Just a quick 'un then.' They glanced quickly up and down the road before making their second entrance to the old Victorian warehouse. This time, in the daylight, they could better appreciate the state of the place.

'He was one lucky lad, that Max, y'know,' observed Jim as he drew up two large boxes. 'Not many got out of here alive.'

'What are you talking about, "not many"?'

'This place,' explained Jim. 'It's Clink Street, the site of the old medieval Bishop of Winchester's palace. Five hundred years ago they used to incarcerate religious prisoners here.'

Sam chuckled. 'That's bloody ironic! I doubt they had such an irreligious git in their entire history as Maxie Roff! If truth be known, I bet the old bishop is turning in his grave at the thought of it.'

The friends spread themselves comfortably out on the two boxes for the few minutes it took Jim to finish his cigarette. 'Where did we actually find Max?' he asked. 'Everything looks so different in daylight.'

Sam nodded towards a wall. 'A yard or so in from that window there, where those new planks of wood are lying.'

'Those planks are fresh aren't they? I don't remember them being here before.'

Sam rose to his feet, stretched and yawned. 'The council, I s'pose. The whole bloody building's a danger. Probably to stop kids, vagrants or even dozy coppers falling in. Come on, James, let's go for my last walk round before I get the freedom of Tottenham.'

Ten feet distant and four feet down, Reginald Slicer Simmons had already had his last walk round. The only question remaining – can one really get the freedom of hell?

Chapter 11

Sam's first five months at Tottenham had not actually flown by. True he had spent comparatively little time at Stones End but Inspector Taylor had been right, the new posting was certainly rural in comparison. He had found it strange that one of his first assignments had been to deal with poachers on Tottenham Marshes. Poachers indeed! It was probably more than two centuries since anyone had marched a poacher into Stones End police station. His section house was something of a plus though, placed as it was just above the police station. The noise nuisance was more than offset by those extra minutes that could be spent in bed on early turn duty. He had finally managed to work out a system for seeing Queenie twice each month, even though strolling arm in arm on Hampstead Heath could get very chilly in December. Sadly, efforts to see his mother had proved particularly difficult. Without a day off, there was barely time at the end of a shift to make a journey anywhere other than locally in north London. He had submitted another application for permission to marry, and, not to be outdone, so had Jim Forsythe. Jane had suggested a double wedding but secretly Sam had wondered if the chances of two constables obtaining permission to marry before the completion of their first two years' service were not halved for that very reason.

Although the Tottenham manor may not have pleased him, the company certainly did. He enjoyed his colleagues and, with several old soldiers in their ranks, many a long night duty was passed with tales of derring-do from such faraway places as Mafekin, Burma, Kabul, Egypt, Khartoum and China. If he had any persistent complaint about Tottenham, it was the temperature. He seemed to overlook the fact that his arrival had coincided with an early winter and so had retained a mental image of the Thames as a sort of thermal barrier, with a sub-tropical south and an arctic north. In fact he rarely ceased complaining about it and soon incurred for himself the temporary name of Shivering Sam. On the other hand, his sheer enthusiasm ensured his popularity. He had certainly taken Inspector Taylor's words to heart and had never turned anything down. In consequence he was soon as experienced as most young coppers could ever hope to be.

The 23 January 1909 had dawned for Sam as a typical Tottenham winter's day. There had been yet another complaint about poachers and he had tramped the marsh for hours without seeing so much as a solitary duck, let alone anyone hell-bent on shooting the things. Hunching his shoulders, he huddled even deeper into his dead weight police greatcoat. He had never known it so cold. 'Y'should'a bin in Afghanistan!' his old Devonian colleague Frank Newman, alias Wolf of Kabul, teased as he left the station three hours earlier. 'Cold? Don't be daft, 'e don't know the meanin' o' the word.'

For those three long hours the biting wind that whistled across those barren marshes had stung his face raw and sought every gap and crevice of his uniform. Turning the icy corner of Chestnut Road, he fondly imagined he could smell the thick smoky tea that simmered permanently on the glowing coals in the old station fireplace. Stewed it would almost certainly be, but at least it would be hot. Having forsaken breakfast for those extra precious minutes in bed, it seemed an eternity since anything hot had passed his lips. He sniffed deeply in anticipation before quickly giving way to nose-wrinkling disgust. It wasn't tea, real or imaginary, pervading his nostrils but rubber! God how he hated the smell of rubber. It brought back those childhood memories of the old rubber apron his mother kept around the kitchen for dirty household jobs, like attending to nine vomiting kids. He could still feel her rough hands pressing his head tightly against the dreaded apron as he bucked and retched into the chipped enamelled bucket kept for such occasions.

Schnurman's rubber factory dominated the street and was just yards from the station front steps. Before he made the sanctuary of those steps he would need to pass the warehouse gates. He found it ironic, having spent twenty of his twenty-one years amidst the stench and filth of a Victorian slum, that his second posting in the Metropolitan Police should be to the comparatively airy suburb of Tottenham where, two buildings up from the station, was the smell that sickened him most – bloody rubber! Lost in a hot breakfast fantasy, the unaccustomed sound of a motor-horn caused him to leap in alarm as a limousine rolled slowly into the kerbside. Young as he was, when it came to automobiles, Sam was a horse-loving traditionalist. He glowered first at the peak-capped driver, then secondly and even more ferociously at the fat comfortable occupant of the rear seat.

I bet he's had a hot breakfast, thought Sam enviously, as he circuited the vehicle. He had almost climbed the station steps when the first shots rang out. The three explosions were so loud that at first the noise seemed to be all around him. Sam's initial reaction was that someone was firing inside the station. He leapt the four remaining steps and crashed through the door, promptly colliding with PCs 'Watt' Tyler and Frank Newman who had taken in the whole scene via the front office window and were running in the opposite direction. 'Wrong bloody way, ye shiverin' sod!' yelled Frank.

Pivoting, Sam saw the chauffeur had staggered back to

the open car door. Further down the street, two thickset men were racing away, each clutching an automatic pistol in his right hand. The shorter of the two also held a small gladstone bag firmly to his chest.

'Stop thief! Stop thief!' came the cry from the car.

Even as Sam watched, a young male passer-by attempted to retrieve the bag but the second of the pair shot him quickly through the head. The youth slumped silently to the pavement. As Tyler, Newman and Sam began their pursuit, the taller of the two men stopped running and, as if he had all the time in the world, calmly took aim. The first bullet grazed Tyler's bull-like neck and the second passed through Newman's tunic flap. The three policemen froze in their tracks.

'The car! Quick, the car!' called Sam, gesturing towards the vehicle. Crouching, all three officers scuttled towards the limousine where the white-faced chauffeur was busy inspecting a bullet-hole in his cap. 'The bastards shot at m . . .'

'Get in and after them, quick!' commanded Tyler.

'Don't be stupid, man! They're shooting people!' objected the driver. 'I don't want him shootin' at me again. I'm lucky to be alive as it is!'

'Do as I say,' snapped Tyler as he thrust the luckless chauffeur back behind the wheel. With Tyler sitting alongside the still protesting driver, Sam and Frank piled swiftly if inelegantly into the rear.

With two large coppers almost on his lap, Isaac Schnurman was in a dilemma. The factory payroll of eighty pounds was disappearing fast towards Epping Forest and Isaac wanted it back. On the other hand, the bullets that now seemed to be flying so regularly were a powerful argument for letting it go. Meantime, the distraught driver had still to start the car. 'What should I do, Mr Schnurman, please?' he bleated.

Schnurman quickly calculated that his position in the

rear of the vehicle, three large coppers flanking him, plus an intention not to alight under any circumstances, probably gave him the best chance of all five. He made an instant and fateful decision. 'Chase them, Keyworth! Get that bloody money back!'

The precious seconds it took to crank-start the car enabled the bandits to vanish, though their trail was emblazoned at each street corner by small groups of open-mouthed pedestrians. Horses and carts, ponies and traps, costers and barrows, swerved, reared or leapt aside as the pursuing car broadsided frantically into the first three junctions. The chauffeur's early terror melted away as the thrill of the chase took over.

'There they are!' yelled Tyler as he pointed to a pair of fleeing figures. 'Quick, man, quick! I'll teach the bastards to shoot at me.'

The bandits, visibly tiring, were bumping into indignant shoppers from a nearby market. The proximity of this market, plus the steady increase in pedestrians, caused the chauffeur instinctively to reach for the car horn. Before Tyler could stop him, a quick blast attracted not just the shoppers' attention but also that of the gunmen. Paul Helfeld, small-time Russian anarchist and big-time Stepney gangster, ceased running for the second time that morning. He slowly and deliberately hooked his left forearm across his line of vision. Resting the pistol just above his wrist, he took careful aim and fired three shots. The first bullet buried itself in the radiator, which promptly erupted in a cloud of steam, whilst the remaining two sliced through the windscreen. Miraculously driver George Keyworth escaped yet again with but a graze.

Whilst Helfeld had paused to shoot at his pursuers, Jacob Meyer, fellow anarchist and crook, had concentrated on the gladstone bag. His grip if anything had tightened. As a shower of large vegetables fell harmlessly about him, he wheeled nervously, pistol pointing. Without bothering to take aim, he fired generally in the direction whence they came. His panic shot comfortably missed the lady who had thrown them but buried itself deep in the heart of Ralph Joselyn, an over-curious ten-year-old who should have been at school.

The car slewed and collided with two market stalls before finally coming to rest in a sea of assorted vegetables and early forced rhubarb at the nearside kerb. This was just as well for George Keyworth because he had rapidly come to the conclusion that six bullets in his direction was at least half a dozen too many. Even Tyler, his tormentor, could expect no more. The old copper threw open the front passenger door and, with anger overcoming discretion, roared abuse at the icy cold Helfeld. The rear passenger door also opened and Frank Newman ran once more with foolhardy determination towards the gunmen, this time using the cover of a brewer's dray. It availed him little. The first shot removed part of Newman's jaw, and the second, most of Tyler's brain. In spite of the fatalities, a hue-and-cry had begun and a daring, ever-increasing number of folk jogged at a respectful distance behind. Sam realised that as long as he could stalk the killers, by keeping them in view, time was on his side. Unhappily for him, Helfeld and Meyer arrived at the same conclusion.

The pair released a barrage of disturbingly close shots before a passing tramcar cut off their line of fire. Meyer was the first to realise their good fortune. After a sharp word to Helfeld, the two bandits raced into the road and clambered aboard the tram. The driver, slightly more astute than his conductor, had the good sense to leap from the front of the car as the pair gained access at the rear.

Though Helfeld's instructions to conductor Willie Murfield were in broken English, his gestures were crystal clear – drive the tram or be shot. The little Scot hated arguments at the best of times and this was anything but the best of times. Willie, with great good sense, therefore drove the tram. Meyer meantime had turned his attention to the three passengers, a young woman, a small child and an elderly man. He waved the barrel of his gun towards the upper-deck staircase. The woman needed no further bidding. Picking up the child, she ran screaming to the steep steps. With Meyer's attention momentarily distracted, the old passenger made a brave but unwise move. It was a move that, because of winter clothing and nagging arthritis, was never going to be quick enough. Meyer shot him without hesitation or thought.

Sam was now desperate. Once the tramcar built up speed, he would not possibly be able to keep pace with it. Breaking cover, he raced towards the unguarded boarding platform. When but a few feet away, he stretched out his fingertips for the brass hand-rail but the tram gathered speed and the gap did not close. He gave one final great surge and, as his fingers touched the cold brass, Meyer appeared on the platform. From a distance of eighteen inches, he took easy aim at Sam's helmetless forehead. Sam stared breathlessly up into the gun barrel. 'You never hear the one that kills you, boy,' old Frank had told him. Sam never did hear it. What he heard instead was the metallic click of an empty magazine. As much in exhaustion as terror, the young man lost all coordination and crashed empty and weeping to the cobbled track.

Meyer and Helfeld now had a breathing space. With the latter keeping his pistol to the head of the conductor, the former slowly slid his foot beneath the badly injured passenger and disdainfully rolled him from the speeding tram and into the road. From a flapped inside pocket, he then took a handful of shells and inserted them into his magazine. Exchanging guns with Helfeld he repeated the task.

'Git up, boy, or are you planning on lying there all day?'

Big Jack Eagles, a burly old copper who looked as if he had never hurried in his life, stood over the now sobbing recruit. He held a pistol in one huge meaty fist and with the other pulled Sam effortlessly to his feet.

'Sorry, Jack,' blurted a distraught Sam. 'I've let them get away. They've shot Frank and Watt and . . . and . . .' His voice began to rise on every word: 'I'VE LET THE BASTARDS GET AWAY!'

'No they ain't, boy. No they ain't. Calm down, calm down,' soothed the newcomer. 'They ain't got away, they're just out of sight that's all. They simply *think* they're safe, at least for the moment. But a tram can't fly, boy. It can only run on rails and as long as they are on those rails, they can't hide, can they?'

'I don't understand.'

'Look.' Jack placed a heavy arm around Sam's shoulders and pointed with the other. 'There's a tram a'coming already. We'll swing it around and follow them.'

Sure enough, from the same direction that the renegade tram had disappeared in, came another clanging monster on the parallel track. At the sight of the pistol-brandishing copper the driver stopped immediately. White-faced, he pointed behind him. 'Just back there,' he panted. 'I've just passed one of our trams and . . .'

'Never mind about that,' cut in Jack sharply. 'Is there any way we can turn your tram round?'

'Eh? Well, there's a turning-table a hundred yards or so down the road, we could turn it there, I s'pose – but why? You're surely not thinking of . . .' His voice trailed away, as if he couldn't bring himself even to think about it.

'No time to explain. Sling every bugger off and get this thing turned, double quick, understand?' Jack gave the gun an extra wave for emphasis and a dozen cloth-capped passengers tumbled from the platform. 'Don't sod off yet, I've got a job for you lot,' he called. Moments later, with the help of the same twelve pressed men, the tram was speedily turned. The pursuing group, now fourteen in number, were suddenly joined by two poachers who had been duck shooting on Tottenham Marshes. The pair leapt aboard as the pursuing tram gathered speed. For Sam this was the supreme irony. For a moment he stared at them dumbstruck. He had spent three hours looking for them, then, when he finally gave up, they joined him out of nowhere by jumping on his tram – and each carrying four dead ducks!

'Hey!' he demanded. 'Where'd you get those bloody ducks from?'

'Shot 'em on the marshes,' said the older of the two cheerfully. 'But this is more fun, ain't it?'

'Shot 'em on the—' began the exasperated Sam.

'Leave it, boy, leave it,' cut in Big Jack. 'If they put a capful of bird-shot up yon bandits' arse-holes, then for my money they can have every fucking duck in Essex.'

By now reinforcements were arriving from all quarters. It had been the first occasion the telephone communication system had been so dramatically used by the Metropolitan Police and, by and large, it had worked well. Over the next few minutes Jack Eagles assessed their total armaments. In addition to his own police issue gun, there was another pistol, mysteriously purloined from somewhere along the route, plus the shotguns and catapults of the two poachers.

The tram rocked and swayed as it gathered speed until finally, a hundred yards or so ahead, and with the now familiar figure of Meyer clearly on the rear platform, the bandits' tram came into view. 'Now we'll have the bastards!' exclaimed Eagles, delighted that his idea had worked so well. 'You two with the shotguns, upstairs! I don't want to be shot at from the front *and* rear. But whatever you do, don't shoot the tram driver or the union will complain!'

The stunned Meyer assessed the situation in a flash and ran to the front of his tram to tell Helfeld the chase had resumed. Helfeld's response was to jab his pistol even deeper into the conductor's neck. 'Faster! Faster!' he snarled. 'Or I'll blow your stinking head off.'

Willie Murfield had been a conductor on that route for ten years and a driver for only ten minutes but even he knew the fast-approaching bend could not possibly be taken at their present speed. Decelerating, he opened his mouth to explain. 'You bastard!' hissed Helfeld, his trigger finger tightening.

'No... Please!' begged Willie, instantly deciding to chance the rails rather than the trigger. The wheels screamed in protest as centrifugal force took over the tramcar. The vibration as the vehicle left the rails and bounced over the cobbles jarred the very eyeballs of its occupants. However, though the jumping car leaned at almost sixty degrees, amazingly it did not topple.

'They've the luck of the seven blind bastards,' muttered Eagles who, cupping his hands, yelled up to the crouching poachers: 'When they jump off that tram, give them everything you've got. We may not get a better chance.'

As the bandits leaped clear a volley of bird-shot fell about them. Futile it may have been but it was an ominous reminder that the rules had now changed. Helfeld gestured to where a pony and trap stood outside an ironmonger's. The pair raced towards it and, tugging the reins free, jumped aboard. As Helfeld lashed the creature, Meyer took up his customary sniper's position at the rear of the cart. The terrified animal reared as the lash landed repeatedly across its flanks. The very trap seemed to scream in sympathy before Meyer realised the wheels were still chained. Yet, even with this knowledge, he still continued to lash in the hope the links would part. Though this wish was soon granted, they did not part until the wheel-spokes splintered. With nothing to support the axle, the trap tipped and the poor frothing creature slumped half-dead across the shafts. Though Helfeld bounced clear,

Meyer was caught a ferocious crack across both ankles. Half lifting, half dragging his accomplice, Helfeld staggered to where a narrow path led to a footbridge over a canal. Meyer limped slowly across the bridge whilst Helfeld took up a firing position yet again. As his pursuers came into view, he decided to make a particular target of their leader. Lining up dead centre on Jack Eagles' massive chest, his fingers had almost closed on the trigger when two shots rang out behind him. Spinning around he saw Meyer on the far bank standing in a scattering of half-bricks. His pistol was still raised in his right hand, whilst his left clutched at a profusely bleeding forehead. Meantime, a limp apron-clad figure was ricocheting untidily down through four floors of factory scaffolding.

Helfeld paused long enough to ensure Meyer was once more under way before resuming aim at Jack Eagles' torso. The bullet that cracked against the parapet, inches from his head, told him his interest in the constable's anatomy was now belated. Realising his position was now particularly exposed and noting Meyer's increasing inability to make ground, he fired two defiant rounds at his tormentors and began a twisting, crouching retreat across the bridge. Jumping the flight of steps at the far end, he followed his friend along the narrow road into a left-hand bend. Their luck, which had begun to fade at the bridge, finally vanished at that bend. Not only were the pair exhausted but, in venting his fury on the courageous bricklayer, Meyer had dropped the payroll. Worse, the twelve-feet-high deal fence that ran at right angles to the pavement told them the worst possible news – they were in a cul-de-sac!

Meyer shook his head and, staggering forward the few yards to the foot of the fence, flopped down with his back to the planks. He was obviously going no further. There appeared no need for conversation as both men sensed each other's thoughts. Giving his friend the merest nod, Helfeld stuffed his gun into his own shirt and, backing off as far as he dared, ran determinedly at the centre of the fence. He would not have been within feet of the top except for a young plane tree whose bare winter branches hung down from the opposite side. He had but one jump and he knew it.

He gripped a branch with an ease that surprised him. His difficulty came when he attempted to gain a foothold. In spite of numerous scrambling attempts, his shoes continued to slide infuriatingly over the smooth deal planks. Finally, and in desperation, he swung sideways and managed to hook one foot along the top of the fence. A few seconds of frantic wriggling, plus two handfuls of enormous splinters, enabled him to roll exhaustedly over the top. Crashing to the ground and sick with pain and fatigue, he was at first unable to move. Meyer watched long enough to see his friend gain the relative safety of the opposite side of the fence, then, eyes closed and mouth open, slumped sideways to the ground. The bandits were back to back and inches apart, with a twelve-feet high fence between them.

'The bastard's made the fence!' panted Eagles. 'If we're not careful we'll lose him for sure.'

'If he can do it, so can I,' responded Sam quietly. His earlier terror had vanished and been replaced by a bitter and burning hatred. Though almost as tired as the fugitive, Sam was ten years his junior and naturally fit. In addition he had the advantage of a much longer reach. His forecast proved correct. Without giving the prostrate Meyer a second glance, he too reached the branches, he too slid on the planks, he too gathered splinters, and finally, almost inevitably, he too reached the top. As he paused to look down triumphantly at the now dismayed Helfeld, Meyer slowly opened his eyes. He could see nothing but the silhouette of the jubilant policeman. The scream of warning Jack Eagles gave was about half a second too late. Meyer's first bullet entered his back just above the shoulder blade and the second clipped his skull, neatly removing an inch of ear on its journey. With a great sad groan, Sam crashed to the ground, inches from his quarry.

It must have been a very close decision whether Jack Eagles shot Meyer or simply tore him apart with his bare hands. The fact that the policeman's finger was still wrapped around the trigger probably tilted the balance. The last man Jack had shot had been a blindfolded Boer spy in the Transvaal nine years earlier. It had been a dawn firing squad and a 'lawful' execution. As he pumped two bullets into the twitching Meyer, he considered it merely another execution. He did not much care if it was lawful, just as long as it was permanent.

The distraction of Sam's wounding had been the spur Helfeld needed to send him scuttling across the sparse garden of a small tumble-down cottage. The door stood invitingly open as Eliza Rolstone emerged from behind a line of washing to discover the cause of the mid-morning commotion. It was only when she turned to shepherd her four small children back into the house that she glimpsed the silent figure slipping furtively through her front door. Keeping her head, she talked normally, if somewhat loudly to her brood, as she made her way slowly towards the increasing number of blue uniforms scaling the fence, a fence that had an unlocked gate that neither pursued nor pursuer appeared to have seen. Within ten minutes this thin blue line had all but encircled the cottage, watched through dimming eyes by a blood-soaked and breathless Sam.

After a last check, Jack Eagles strode defiantly to the front of the house. 'You'd better come out here, mate, or we a'coming in an' I'm gonna blast your balls off!' he boomed through cupped hands.

This directive was answered by a smashing of glass and at least three quick shots. 'At least we know where the bugger is,' muttered the old copper, gesturing to a first-floor bedroom window. Several men rushed the now closed front door and forced it open with ease. Moments later, Jack, together with two other constables, stood with gun poised outside the frail door of the bedroom.

'Listen,' whispered one of the pair. 'It sounds just like he's laughing.' Sure enough, from deep inside the room came an eerie cackling. The laughter was interspersed with foreign-sounding oaths and intermittent shots. For some reason the occupant appeared impervious to their presence. All his attention seemed to be fixed on the thin cordon outside.

'Well,' whispered Jack to his companions, 'we won't get a better chance . . . ready?'

They nodded. The old Transvaal Ranger hurled his eighteen-stone body at the door with all the power he could muster. Not just the door but the whole frame and plaster surround caved in as he crashed face down on to the floor of the room. The demented figure at the window pivoted swiftly and uttered his loudest laugh yet. He pointed with glee to Jack's own pistol which had slid partially under the bed and tantalisingly out of reach. Then he slowly raised his own gun as if to inspect it. Apparently satisfied, he began to quake with mirth. Turning the barrel, he fired his last shot – straight into his own head. The awful laughter instantly ceased but was replaced with a terrifying grin that remained fixed for the seconds it took him to die.

Seizing the corpse by the scruff of its bloodied neck, and refusing all aid, Jack bumped it unceremoniously down the tiny uneven staircase, out of the door of the cottage and across the frost-hardened garden to where Eliza Rolstone cradled the now delirious Sam to her frail pinafored bosom. 'Here y'are, boy,' he announced. 'I thought you'd like ter see the wicked devil's body afore you die.'

'Shame on you, you heathen!' snapped Eliza. 'And you a policeman too.' She wiped away the worst of the bloodstains from the young man's face. 'He's goin' to be fine, I tell you. You mark my words, he's goin' to be fine.'

'Tell Queenie I'm going ... to be ... fine ... see,' whispered Sam breathlessly, and closed his eyes. There was a strange silence for a few moments broken only by the creaking of the tree's branches. The young policeman slowly reopened his eyes. For a few seconds he just stared up at the branches with a puzzled expression, then, turning to the tearful Eliza, he whispered, 'It's *our* tree though, Mum, isn't it? We're all allowed to play on it . . . ain't we? Tell the man, Mum . . . tell him it belongs to all the kids . . . won't you? All . . . the . . . kids.'

Chapter 12

The final scene of the carnage was difficult enough to reach on foot but the newfangled motorised ambulance finally gave in some two hundred yards away. They had tried to reach it via the canal but the tow-path had not been wide enough. After talking to Eliza as a child to his mother, Sam had convulsed for a moment or two before rolling over apparently lifeless. If there were any hopes as to his survival, it could confidently be assumed that Jack Eagles did not share them. Jack dealt in certainties not hopes and had been present during the demise of many a man, both friend and foe. Usually, if Jack said someone was dead, then they were dead, or at least that had been the case in the Transvaal. But then in the Transvaal he had not had to deal with any Elizas. For, as she logically pointed out, Tottenham was not the Transvaal and neither was Sam 'one of your pagan fuzzy-wuzzies'. It was doubtless fortunate for the young man that Jack's current calling was constable and not grave-digger, because then Sam would have had more than an even chance of being buried long before life had officially been pronounced extinct.

'He's dead an' that's all there is to it,' Jack announced.

'I tell yer he's not dead!' Liza insisted. 'He's too beautiful to die.'

Jack, whose study of beauty had been confined to odd evenings in a Port Said brothel, was a little thrown by this declaration. He had never thought of any man being 'beautiful'. He began to wonder if Eliza too had been shot in the head. The debate continued for some time before the police handcart arrived to remove either the person or the body, depending on your point of view, to the still marooned ambulance. Jack bent down and picked up Sam as if he had been a small child. 'I still say he's dead, ma'am,' he persisted. 'But he was only a young lad so don't worry, I'll look art'er him well.' He lowered Sam with surprising gentleness on to the cart and trundled it away across the frozen garden.

'He's going to live, I tell you!' she called as Jack pulled shut the ambulance door. 'He's going to live!'

The furore about the shooting gathered momentum daily. Every ingredient was present for a wonderful newsworthy pudding. What made this particular drama stand apart from the one-day wonder of comparable stories was Sam's medical condition. One day he appeared to be mending, the next on the verge of death. And all this time there was the heart-warming story of his love for Queenie. Newspaper columnists and letter writers all attacked the heartless rule that prevented two young people, so much in love, from marrying. The situation was further complicated by the request for a double wedding. The deputy assistant commissioner eventually spent some time with the surgeon attending Sam and came to the conclusion that he would never recover. In his present state, he was told, Sam could not live longer than another two weeks and, even if there was some miraculous recovery, he would never again be able to take up constabulary duties.

This then, explained the deputy commissioner to a policy meeting, was the answer. Let them marry. Either he wouldn't live long enough to make the walk up the aisle, or, if he did, he would be in such a state that he would no longer be a policeman anyway. So how about the double wedding? he was asked. Yes, he could see a problem there, he admitted, but if Sam died it would surely be in bad taste for the friend and the deceased's sister to engage so soon in matrimony, therefore no precedent need be set. All in all, it had been a rather neat episode. The money had been recovered; the assassins had been executed and – other than the loss of a tramcar – without too much public expense; the new telephone communication system had worked well; half-a-dozen street coppers had emerged as heroes and Scotland Yard was about to show it had a human side after all by permitting the wedding. All it now needed to be truly poignant was for Sam to die peacefully in his fiancée's arms a few days before the wedding, preferably in the presence of a reporter and photographer.

Faced with the prospect of Sam's imminent death, Queenie decided to leave her job in order to spend as many of his declining days as possible at his bedside. Whether it was her presence or his own in-built cussedness no one knew but, obstinate as ever, Sam confounded his doctors by not dying within the prescribed period. As if that wasn't enough, within two months he was once more on his feet and the wedding was back on the calendar. By midsummer, not only was the wedding date arranged, but Sam appeared as healthy as ever. The romance had long passed out of the newspapers and therefore the public eye but the deputy commissioner thought that as withdrawing permission to marry could easily rekindle interest again, this time unfavourable, permission was best allowed.

'You understand of course,' Sam was told, 'that this is a concession so, whilst approval is granted, we cannot encourage others along a similar path. I'm afraid we are unable to offer you married quarters.'

Married quarters were in fact the last thing on Sam's mind. The world had thought him dead. Well, he wasn't and now he could at last have his Queenie to himself which was all he sought.

'So can I take it I will be allowed to return to work, sir?'

'No I'm afraid you can't. That's a matter still to be decided,' came the reply.

Jim, whose wedding plans had run in tandem to Sam's, had been more fortunate. He too was refused accommodation but had obtained a two-roomed sixth-floor old tenement flat in Queen's Buildings almost opposite Stones End Station. The Diamonds' accommodation was a problem that still needed to be solved and it was certainly one that bothered Queenie. Swallowing her pride, she went to the rent office in Waterloo Road and, after much grovelling, finally obtained a basement flat in Inkerman Place.

Sam was appalled. 'But I've spent all my life dreaming of leaving that hell hole and now you're asking me to take you, my new bride, back there?' he protested. 'Surely not? Before you know it, you'll be epileptic again.'

'Sam,' she said quietly as she leaned across him and took his hand, 'since I've loved you I haven't had the slightest trace of epilepsy. In any case, where do you think I've been living since I left my job?'

'I don't know,' he answered. 'Stupidly enough, it never occurred to me. So where?'

'I've been sleeping at your mother's place, with your sister Jane.'

'But you're too good for . . .'

'Sam! Don't even *think* that! Oh, I know I'd be lying if I said it didn't come hard at first.' She shrugged. 'But I've got used to it. If you love me and wish to marry me, then at least for the time being, you've no choice. There is nothing else for us. We'll get out one day, Sam, you'll see.' She leaned forward and kissed his creased brow. 'C'mon, let's talk of brighter things. Let's talk about our honeymoon, shall we?'

During Sam's early incarceration in hospital, several kind souls had sent cards and letters and some had donated money. In fact the grand total of thirty-nine pounds, seven shillings and threepence ha'penny proved sufficient money to pay for the wedding and some second-hand furniture without going into debt. In addition, and just days previous, an anonymous benefactor had donated the best and yet most worrying present of all: a three-day honeymoon in a Ramsgate hotel. It was worrying because never in his young life had Sam so much as crossed the threshold of a hotel, least of all stayed in one. He had a nagging idea that pistol-firing anarchists would prove less daunting.

It was a warm still day on 10 July. Family, friends and neighbours had spread evenly around the pews to make up for the lack of family from Queenie's side. As the two grooms walked up the aisle, Sam's attention was caught by a fleeting glimpse of an attractive woman who for the moment he could not place. She was neatly dressed and indications of former beauty were very clear to see. He turned his head for a better view. She also turned and faced him. Good God, it was his mother! Where was the tired look? Where the frayed pinafore? Where was the wispy grey hair that fell permanently over the forehead? Where were the cap, shawl and slippers? This woman was handsome enough for Ascot! His startled look puzzled her at first. She nodded to him with an air of anxiety. 'You all right, Sam?'

He shook his head in mild disbelief. 'Ma!' he exclaimed. 'You're absolutely lovely!'

His opinion was immediately backed up by Jim Forsythe, who, pretending to turn away, whispered, 'When your sister arrives, tell her I've run away with her mum.'

Within a few moments Sam's sister did arrive and any mention of an elopement with Mum ended instantly. 'What is it about my family today?' whispered Sam. 'They're all so bloody beautiful!'

'There's another young lady who's going to take some beating though,' said Jim, nodding to the second bride following instantly behind Jane.

Sam was genuinely amazed. He had seen Queenie in different moods, attires and situations and had thought she could never be lovelier than the time she had lain sleeping in his arms in Billie's house, but he was wrong. As she joined him at the altar, he turned to her and, without any attempt to lower his voice, said, 'You're a real "Diamond Queen" and I think the world should now stop because it can never improve on this.'

She blushed beautifully as a great wave of warmth surged through her. 'I love you, Sam Diamond,' she whispered.

Before he could reply there was a partial echo from his other side: 'And I love you, Jimmy Forsythe.'

Any doubts that Sam had harboured concerning a double wedding vanished as he glanced at the two girls. Reality in the shape of Inkerman Place, Stones End, Tottenham Marshes and Queen's Buildings may lay in wait outside that solid church door but for a few precious hours four young people were free beyond such cares.

All too soon for the brides, the ceremony was finished and the register signed. If the congregation's attention had not been so naturally centred on the brides and grooms, they might just have caught a glimpse of a stunning fair-haired woman who, arriving late and leaving early, flitted ghost-like from the back of the church and into her waiting carriage.

Nell Diamond, meanwhile had a lot on her mind. Her problems arose from the wedding reception. Number 14 Inkerman Place was never going to be big enough to accommodate the guests, though the Flynns at 12 and the Graingers at 16 generously threw open their kitchens and sculleries. In spite of this, it was still going to be a fairly rough and ready 'do' and Nell's twin dreads were Queenie and the weather. Queenie because she was afraid the girl would find the whole thing sordid – the Flynns were not the most hygienic family in Blackfriars – and the weather because running in and out of the three sculleries in pouring rain with pork pies, plates of pickles and pieces of ham was too dreadful to contemplate. Unfortunately Nell had contemplated little else all week.

But her fears proved groundless with Queenie not only

mixing to the manner born but pounding out many a tune on the Graingers' old piano that had been pushed out under the tree for the day. So with the piano, sunshine and three barrels of beer, Inkerman Place thought it the best wedding for years.

It was mid-afternoon when a cabbie strode across the yard and asked for 'Mr Diamond'. Sam greeted him to be told that a cab to London Bridge Station was part of the arrangements for his three-day honeymoon in Ramsgate and, if he wished to catch the 3.55 p.m., he'd better look smart about it. It was generally agreed that, apart from Blanche Slye who was, according to Nell Diamond, 'no better than she ought to be', no one had ever left Inkerman Place in a cab for a hotel honeymoon before, and even the dubious Blanche had only gone bed-and-breakfast in Southend. As cheers rang out for the departing two, Jim and Jane took the opportunity to steal quietly away to their own flat in Queen's Buildings whilst everyone's attention was elsewhere.

On a flick of the whip, the dappled mare whisked the cab swiftly away from the well-wishers. From the cabbie's verbosity, Sam realised that during the short time he and Queenie were packing, that gentleman had wasted no time in topping himself up from the barrel. Perhaps now might be a good time to discover the name of their benefactor? 'Oi doan' know, sur, that wur paid ter my firm, not'a me.'

'Where is your firm?' asked Sam.

'Watta-loo stay-shun, sur.'

'And *when* may it have been paid in?' Sam persisted.

The cabbie removed his high hat and scratched his head. 'Oi wur told about this jar'b couple o'days ago, so I reckon it must'a bin Thursday marnin' sometime.'

'Is it so important, Sam?' asked Queenie. 'Why can't we just accept it for what it is – a lovely gesture?'

'If I'm indebted to any man,' he said with an air of pomposity, 'then I like to know who he is, that's all.'

Whoever he was, he had certainly done a thorough job because not only had the fare been paid but so had the tip. The cabbie also handed Sam an envelope containing two return train tickets to Ramsgate.

The Cliff View Hotel, Ramsgate had a plush Victorian splendour and staff in abundance. Sam's eyes barely left Queenie as he looked for signs, nods and indications as to the right move to make or the right word to say. His biggest difficulty was when an ancient old porter painfully picked up their luggage and made towards the staircase. 'Just a minute, sir!' Sam found himself saying. 'Let me do that for you.'

'Nay, sir,' panted the old fellow. 'It's me job, sir. I'm paid to be a'doin' this for you.'

'He's right,' whispered Queenie. 'It *is* his job and you won't be doing him any favours by not letting him do it either.'

'But—' Further protests were cut short as she placed her fingers firmly to his lips. Methuselah, as Sam later called him, led the way to their second-floor bedroom and, by the time they arrived at the door, Sam firmly believed they would have to lay the old chap down to recover his strength. 'Here y'are, sir,' he panted as he dropped the cases to open the door. 'The bridal suite.' He obviously took greater delight in conducting the guests around the room than he did in carrying up their cases. His pride as he listed the various amenities was very apparent.

'An' this, sir, is the bathroom. It's the only suite in the hotel with its *own* bathroom. All the others are at the end of the corridor. And then there's the view, sir. The view is one of the very best in . . .'

'Yes, thank you very much indeed,' said Queenie, cutting him short. 'I think we'll find out the rest as we go along, don't you?'

'As you wish, madam,' he answered politely. 'Mealtimes

and everything else you'll want to know are on the notice on the back of the bathroom door. Any problems, or anything you can't manage, just call down to reception.'

The door clicked and he was finally gone. Queenie hugged herself and spun round on tip-toe. 'Oh Sam, Sam, it's just so beautiful! And he was right, just look at that view!' She moved to the window. In the distance, the sunshine shimmered on the distant Goodwin Sands.

Sam slipped his arms around her waist. 'I can't believe this is really us, you know.' He gestured about him. 'This room, this view, this bed.'

'What time's dinner?' she asked suddenly.

'Dinner?' he echoed. 'You're not hungry surely?'

'Not at all,' she agreed. 'I just thought that if it was . . . oh . . . say in a couple of hours time, we could have a lovely bath together. We won't have many opportunities after Tuesday, will we?'

'I think that's the most marvellous idea I've ever heard!' he enthused as he began unlacing his shoes.

'Sam!' she laughed. 'You'll need hot water first, darling.'

He had both taps running almost before she had finished speaking and soon the mirror was heavily steamed. 'Oh, that's annoying,' he complained as he sat on the stool and completed the task of removing his shoes.

'Why is it?' she said, stepping out of her dress.

'Because I'd love to see you naked in the mirror. It would be just . . . well, it would just be nice, that's all.'

'Sam! I'm sure that's a very naughty thing to say.' She picked up a small face towel and quickly wiped off the worst of the vapour. 'You'd better remove the rest of my clothes before it steams up again. I would hate you to miss anything.'

Sam had rarely moved quicker in his life and within moments she stood leaning back against him, naked in front of the large gilt-edged mirror. She reached her arms back over her head and pulled his face down to hers. When the subsequent kiss was to her satisfaction, she lifted his hands and placed them over her breasts.

'What do I do first?' he asked. 'Love you in there, or bath you in here?'

'Bath me first, Sam, then love me to pieces, darling.'

He reluctantly released her whilst he tested the water, then, satisfied as to the temperature, sat in the bath. She lowered herself between his legs and once more leaned back against him. He scooped up the water in his hands and trickled it down over her perfect shoulders and breasts and soon began to massage her with the fattest bar of soap he had ever seen. His hands skimmed and slipped across her smooth body and, after some fifteen minutes of this, with her nipples rock hard, she slowly but firmly eased his hands away from her breasts and said, 'Sam darling, I now have the cleanest tits in Kent. Would you care to try somewhere else?'

'You know,' he said thoughtfully, moving his hands lower down her body, 'I've just realised the advantage of bathing a girl. Not only can I soap you everywhere but I can dry you everywhere too. Two bites of the cherry, as you might say.'

In spite of these observations, it is doubtful if Sam spent too much time on the second 'bite of the cherry' because when he carried Queenie into the bedroom she was still quite wet. 'Let me get this right,' he queried as he laid her out naked beneath him. 'I've never been in a posh hotel before. Is this what's called the love-you-to-pieces stage?'

'Oh, yes,' she agreed. 'At least, I understand that's what it says on the notice behind the bathroom door. But if you do find anything you can't manage, you just call down to reception.'

'So what do I do about my dinner?'

Reaching up, she gripped him tight and twisted over and within a second or so had reversed their positions. 'I'm sorry, my love,' she said as she began to kiss his mouth, 'but there's no dinner for you.' Slowly her mouth inched downward as his moans of pleasure escalated. 'Or supper . . . or breakfast . . . or lunch . . . or tea.'

'Then hand me that bloody notice,' he whispered. 'I've got to call reception.'

Pounding his chest, she fell off into an uncontrollable giggle.

By chance, seventy-five miles away, Jim and Jane Forsythe were also in bed, without the luxury of a bath needless to say but equally happy and without the slightest desire to eat. They had loved each other into a warm afterglow and were half dozing. 'Did everything go as you wished today?' he asked her sleepily.

'It was wonderful, Jim, bless you,' she murmured. 'The only thing that bothered me was Sam.'

'Sam, why?'

'What's going to happen to him, Jim, after today I mean? He certainly seems to have recovered but what is he going to do for a job?'

Jim suddenly sat bolt upright. 'My God!' he exclaimed. 'It was such a marvellous day, I completely forgot.'

'Forgot what?'

'I've got a message for Sam. He's to report back Monday week at 9 a.m. and, because of the difficulty in getting to Tottenham from Inkerman Place, he's to transfer to Tower Bridge . . . and I forgot to tell him!'

'Well, I wouldn't worry too much at the moment,' she said reassuringly. 'Right now he's probably so busy with Queenie you'd have to unravel them to speak to him.'

Jane was almost right. The beautiful Queenie was at that very moment sitting naked across Sam's heaving chest, stuffing a torn-up notice into his mouth between his stifled laughs.

'After the Lord Mayor's Show' had been a favourite expression of old John Diamond's and Sam remembered it for the first time since the old man's demise as, with his new wife, he turned the corner of Inkerman Place. Any greater contrast than that between the Cliff View Hotel and Inkerman Place it would be difficult to imagine. It was back to earth with a vengeance. One blessing was that 11a's former tenant was the recently deceased Flo Reddington, a single lady who had spent most of her life in domestic service and, in her ten years in Inkerman, had made the flat sparkle. Nevertheless, Inkerman Place was still Inkerman Place. A verminous hovel is still a verminous hovel, clean or otherwise.

As the couple approached the door Sam could not resist a wry smile. Apparently, the tenant before old Flo had lost his wife and three children in a typhoid epidemic and, though boiling his drinking water had never entered his head, changing his door number from 13 to 11a had. Who knows? Perhaps there was something in the theory. After all, he'd managed to avoid typhoid. It was such a shame he went insane.

The steps to the basement were steep, twisting and without a guard-rail, far too chancy to carry a bride down. 'Never mind, Sam,' said Queenie. 'I've already been carried and I'm sure it was a lot more fun.'

Hands clasped, they opened the door for the first time to be greeted by stark reality. A damp sweet musty smell pervaded the small flat. Queenie screamed and reeled back in horror as next-door's cat watched with mild curiosity. 'Oh my God, Sam! What's that on the door-mat?'

Chapter 13

The curiosity of the cat was suddenly explained as her four dead rats were seen proudly laid out for inspection. Unfortunately at least two of them had been displayed a couple of days too long for the July temperatures, though not for July flies. 'Ugh!' shuddered Queenie.

'Sorry about that, luv,' came a call from on high. They looked up to the first-floor window to see a fat-faced woman with just one visible tooth. She was known in the Place as Fat Lil. 'It's Sarah, our cat, luv,' she explained. 'Ever since she was a kitten she's done that. We don't like ter discourage 'er because she don't 'alf catch some bleedin' rats. But on the ovver hand, as you can see, she will fetch the buggers back 'ere and it's nearly always down in your flat.'

'But how did she get in?' asked the stunned Sam.

'I'm afraid it was yer brother-in-law, Jim. He let himself in the day arter the weddin'. He said he had a message for you and was leavin' a winder wide open to let in some fresh air. You can't do that, Sam, 'cos if you do, Sarah will dump her bleedin' rats on you. What you have to do is only open the windows a tiny bit.'

'So you're saying it's a choice between damp smells and dead rats, are you?'

'Something like that, luv.' She sniffed. 'Tell you what, though, we didn't half enjoy your wedding. We thought it was really smashin'.'

With several old newspapers provided by Fat Lil, Sam

wrapped up rats and maggots and burnt them as far away from the houses as possible. 'I'll be back in a minute,' he said to Queenie. 'I'll get some carbolic from my mother.'

'I'm sorry, Sam, but I can't stop here on my own, not at the moment anyway,' she said tearfully. 'I promise you I will get used to it but give me time, Sam, please. Give me time.'

'Of course,' he whispered as he put a comforting arm about her and led her away. 'It won't always be like this, girl, y'know. You'll see. Once we're settled in we'll have it like a little palace, I know we will.'

'Will we, Sam?' she asked sadly. 'What will you do, drown the cat?'

Queenie lay in bed that night enveloped in the smell of carbolic. As crisp and clean as the sheets were, she still felt reluctant to touch them. In fact she was now reluctant to touch anything in this place, yet it was her home, hers and Sam's.

What had happened to her life? Within a few short months she had slipped from luxury into a stinking rat-infested basement slum. All her brave words seemed empty now. Sam moved his arm across her body and began to caress her breasts.

'No, Sam, please. Not tonight, darling. Give me time to adjust, eh?'

'Of course,' he murmured and held her tight. 'It will get better . . . I promise.'

She was just about losing herself in sleep when she was aware of Sam's arm slipping away and felt him easing slowly out of bed. 'What is it, Sam?' she asked anxiously as he fumbled for matches. A candle suddenly flickered into life.

'Fat Lil said Jim called with a message. He knew we weren't here so he must have left it somewhere. I was just falling asleep when I thought of it.'

'Sam, it'll keep surely? Can't it wait till morning?'

'*It* might, *I* can't,' he replied simply as he fumbled in the shadows. 'Here it is, under the armchair. It must have fallen down . . . 'Queenie! I'm back! I'm to report at Tower Bridge at nine o'clock next Monday! Things will definitely get better now, you'll see.'

A few minutes later, as she lay in his arms, a tiny chink of light could just about be distinguished at the end of a particularly dark tunnel. 'I'm good at my job, Sam, and I know I could get work again.'

'But your work is all of the live-in type,' he protested. 'I'd never see you.'

'I know, Sam, I know,' she soothed. 'But it won't be forever will it? After all, wherever I work in London, I can get back here easily enough. True, not every night. Perhaps only once a week? But it would be worth it, Sam. We could find a better place and start a family, and life would be so very different for us . . . and our children.'

Her enthusiasm settled some if not all of his doubts and it was with a good heart that he reported for duty the following Monday. Except for the docks, which ran the entire length of the Thames along its north side, the Tower Bridge manor was not so very different from Stones End. With many large factories and rows of tiny two-up and two-down houses, the poverty level was about equal.

By Monday, 11a Inkerman Place was certainly smelling sweeter although the predominant aroma was still one of carbolic and lysol, but the curtains were fresh, the furniture shone, the linoleum gleamed, and for the first time since their return from honeymoon, Queenie had felt relaxed enough to make love. Shortly after 8 a.m. they left the flat together, Sam to go east on his walk to Tower Bridge, Queenie west on her search for employment.

In the days of large policemen, Chief Inspector Tucker was the exception that proved the rule. He was red, round, short and bald with large square teeth, a crimson nose, and a compulsion to call everybody of lower rank 'mister'. This greeting had nothing to do with respect; quite the reverse. Tucker could make 'mister' sound like an insult with no effort at all. He sat studying Sam's record for some minutes whilst the young constable stood to attention in front of him.

'Looks to me, mister, as if yer could be a whole lot of trouble. Y'ain't bin in the job five minutes and there's just one bloody report after another on yer file. Bit of an hero, are yer?' He scowled without looking up. 'Well, in my book, mister, heroes are always bloody dangerous, not so much to themselves but to every other bugger.' He pushed back his chair and for the first time looked up at Sam.'Hmm, well, if it was down to me, mister, I wouldn't have yer. But it's not and I've got yer. But watch yer step. I don't stand on ceremony. If yer fucks me about, then I fucks you about. Do yer job properly and yer'll get by. Any questions?'

'What relief am I on, sir?'

Tucker reached for a clipboard and studied it for some time. 'Night duty relief, mister, they seem to be a couple short. Anything else?'

'Is that tomorrow, sir?'

'No, it's bloody not tomorrow, mister! It's tonight!'

'But I've not had time to make any arrangements.'

'Arrangements? Arrangements? What are you then, some sort of bloody undertaker? I'll tell you your arrangements, mister. Your arrangements are to leave this place now and return for night duty at 9.45 p.m. There, that's a nice simple arrangement I've made for yer, wouldn't yer say?'

'Sir,' Sam acknowledged through clenched teeth.

'Off yer go then, mister, an' don't be late.'

Realising Queenie would not yet have returned, Sam remembered that Jim was also due to start night duty at

Stones End and would hopefully be home now. He made his way up ninety-six stairs to be greeted by his old friend as if they had not met for months.

'Did you enjoy your honeymoon, you lucky sod?' Jim asked.

'Honeymoon?' replied Sam ruefully 'What was that? I think I've almost forgotten it by now.' With that he recounted the events of the past few days.

'You've got to do something, Sam, and quick. She's a great girl that Queenie but she's never cut out for Inkerman Place and you know it. Tell you what, the old fellow opposite is trying to get a ground-floor flat because of his arthritis. If he goes, who knows? I'll ask about it next time I pay my rent if you like?'

'That would be great, Jim, but don't say anything in front of Queenie in case nothing comes of it. The disappointment would only make matters ten times worse, okay?'

Jim agreed and wished him luck and Sam dawdled his way home. As he negotiated the steps of 11a he could hear Queenie singing to herself through the partially open door.

'Sam!' she greeted him. 'I wasn't expecting you home so soon. Now you've spoilt everything. I was going to be the dutiful little wife and have your meal almost ready when you came home this evening. Oh, Sam, I have this wonderful job and I can start whenever . . .' She stopped short and stared at him for a moment. 'Sam, why *are* you so early?'

'I've been posted on the night duty relief, luv. I don't start work until ten o'clock tonight.'

'Tonight?' she blurted. 'But, Sam . . . I can't . . . can't . . .' Shaking her head, she suddenly burst into tears.

'What is it, Queenie, what is it?' he demanded, seizing her in his arms.

Composing herself, she said calmly, 'Sam, I cannot sleep

in this place on my own. I've thought about it a great deal and I just know I can't do it. Every rustle, every creak, every puff of wind will be a rat. I'd imagine them on the floor, on the table, in my bed . . .' She trembled uncontrollably. 'I'd go out of my mind, I know it.'

He released her instantly and shook his head in bewilderment. 'But you're my wife, Queenie! This is your home, this is where you belong! A third of my police service will be night duty. Are you going to disappear every time I work nights? Our marriage is not part-time, it's for keeps. Least, that's what we promised, didn't we?'

'Sam!' she cried. 'I love you and I'll do anything for you, but please don't ask me to do this – do not ask me to sleep alone in this flat at night!'

'So what are you asking of me?'

'Sam, darling, I can sleep in at this new job. It's only at Westminster. I can walk home in thirty minutes!'

'But this flat was entirely your idea! I told you I never wanted to return to Inkerman Place, I only came back because of you, and now you're telling me that it's okay for me to sleep here – but not you!' His tone changed from one of protest to spitefulness. 'Oh, no, certainly not you. It's nowhere near good enough for Lady Muck. The first problem she encounters, she's buggering off to Westminster!' He glared at her for a moment then added angrily, 'Well, I tell you this, woman, it's not on. Here *we* are, here *you* stay.'

She reached forward and took his hands. 'Sam, listen to me, darling, please. I know, oh, *how* I know, that it was my idea. I meant well, I really did, but you must get it into your head that I simply cannot *take* it.' In desperation she searched his face for a glimmer of understanding but there was none. A knot suddenly tied itself in the pit of her stomach. As much as she loved him and as much as he undoubtedly loved her, they were up against an enormous fundamental difference in both background and outlook.

He simply could not understand that she, as a married woman, was still an individual. He would love and protect her to his last breath, of that she had no doubt, but from the moment she had said 'I will' in that church, he'd seen himself as the final arbiter of her life.

'Sam,' she said quietly as she stared him straight in the eyes, 'this is not even a discussion. I . . . me . . . Queenie Diamond – yes, that's right, your wife – am telling you one simple fact. I am not sleeping in this house on my own. Not tonight, not tomorrow, not ever. I love you, Sam, but you must accept it.'

'In that case there *is* a problem, because I *don't* accept it . . . so where does that leave us now?'

She dropped her gaze in tearful sadness. 'It leaves us lost, Sam. It leaves us lost.' Without further ado she went to the cupboard and began to collect a few clothes whilst he picked up a newspaper and pretended to read. A few minutes later her footsteps made for the door. He waited for a slam but there was only the faintest of clicks and she was gone. Dropping the unread paper, he turned and stared with streaming eyes round the empty room.

The postings were being called out on the first night of the night duty parade.

'599 Diamond.'

'Sergeant,' acknowledged Sam.

'By rights you should be learning the beats,' said Sergeant Bevington, 'but I understand you know the area very well. Are you happy to start out on your own?'

There was nothing Sam wanted more that night than to be on his own. He needed those quiet and still early hours when it was possible to sort out his thoughts. 'I certainly am, sergeant.'

'Good. You've got eight beat, by the riverside running along Bermondsey Wall. Two main things to remember: don't get lost and don't fall in. By the way, there's a complaint here as well. Folks at number 13 Malacca House are complaining about the Swains at number 15. Apparently he comes home from the pub every night and knocks his missus about. I think her screams spoil their cocoa, so wander down there and have a look at it, will yer?'

'Sergeant!' he acknowledged.

It was a little after eleven o'clock before Sam found Malacca House. As a riverside property, it had probably been quite desirable when it was planned some fifty years earlier but something had gone terribly awry between the cup and the lip because the finished article was hateful. It was three storeys of superbly situated, appallingly designed squalor. Number 15 was a two-roomed flat at the top and in the corner. There were certainly no screams and Sam was undecided as to whether to leave well alone or knock to let them know he was about. Seeing a glimmering light decided him on the latter. His knock was eventually answered by a frail, ill-looking wisp of a young woman with sunken eyes and a thick, freshly cut lower lip. In fact her thick lip was about the only part of her that appeared to contain body-fat of any description. The rest was five foot nothing and stick-like. With her haunted look and tattered nightdress, she was the epitome of poverty. 'Yeah?' she croaked hoarsely.

'I've come to see if you're all right, luv,' he greeted her. 'But I can see now you're not.'

'Oh I'm all right, mate,' she whispered as she began to push the door to.

'Hang on a minute,' urged Sam placing his foot on the step. 'Who did this to you? Your husband?'

'No, no. Me 'usband had a little fall and his 'ead caught me lip. There's nothin' else to it. I'll be all right in the mornin'.'

'I'm sorry,' said Sam. 'But I can't leave you like this because—'

'Will yer please mind yer own business!' she snapped.

'I'm all right, I tell yer. In any case,' she added, 'he's gorn out so p'haps me an' the kids can get some sleep now.'

'Let me see the children before I go then?' bargained Sam.

She shrugged and led the way across bare wooden floorboards into the back room where, with the aid of a flickering night-light, he could see one rumpled dirty double bed with a sleeping baby, and two single beds each with children top and bottom. The smell was nauseating.

'You sure I can't do anything?' he asked.

'No,' she insisted. 'Nothin' at all. Fanks fer lookin' in but just leave us in peace, will yer, please?'

Sam took one last despairing look around the room and walked out into the night air, gulping gratefully at the foul aroma wafting in from the Thamesside mud. It was a few minutes later, as he stood staring pensively at the inky black river, that a voice cut into his thoughts.

'Ain't lost yourself yet then, Sam?'

He turned to see the wide smiling face of Sergeant Claude Bevington. In fact, everything about Sergeant Bevington appeared wide. His face, his shoulders, his hips, even his silver grey head seemed wider than it ought to. Sam thought he was a man it would always be a pleasure to see. 'All correct, sarge,' he greeted him.

'Bin to that complaint yet?' asked the sergeant.

Sam recounted the tale and the sergeant shrugged helplessly. 'Absolutely nothing you can do, boy,' he said sadly. 'These women'll never agree to go to court, or if they do, they'll change their minds in the morning. They're terrified out of their minds, most of 'em.' He gave a great wide sigh. 'Some coppers get used to it but I never can. I know him at number 15. He's a stinking fat docker six times her size. He'll kill her one day and then perhaps we might be able to do something. She won't be able to refuse to charge him then, will she?'

They exchanged a few pleasantries about the river before

the sergeant bade Sam goodbye and continued his rounds. Sam was just deciding which route to take when he was aware of running footsteps. He turned to see a pretty young girl obviously heading towards him. 'Are . . . you . . .' she panted. 'Are you . . . policeman . . . called . . . number 15 Malacca . . . House?'

'Yes, luv, why?'

'He's back . . . must be . . . killing . . . poor cow . . . screams . . . terrible!'

'You take your time, love,' he said. 'And if you think you're all right to make your own way back, I'll go on ahead, okay?' She nodded furiously and he ran.

Though the block was silent on his arrival Sam took most of the steps three at a time. The door to number 15 was ajar and he walked straight in and directly to the bedroom. The woman sat sobbing on the bed with her nightdress torn and her tiny left breast bleeding.

'Where is he?' demanded Sam.

'No, don't, please. Please, I beg yer, don't. 'E'll be all right when 'e's sobered up, 'onest 'e will.'

Seeing the perpetrator was obviously not in the flat, Sam spun round to leave the premises. The woman then leapt from the bed and seized his legs. 'No, please, no. Don't nick 'im!' she begged. 'You'll make everythin' worse. I'll sort it out wiv' 'im termorrer, you'll see, mate, you'll see.' Gently but firmly Sam removed her grip from his ankles and strode out of the door. Reaching the bottom of the stairs, he realised that because of the river wall, if he had not met the culprit on the way in, then there was only one other route for him to have taken. Sure enough, a short distance ahead and only just visible in the flickering street lamp was a large fat man urinating heavily against that very lamp. He was fumbling with his buttons when he suddenly heard Sam behind him.

''S'all right, mate,' he assured the young constable. 'Got taken a bit short that's all.'

'Are you Mr Swain from 15 Malacca House?' asked Sam.

'Er – yeah, as a matter'a fact I am. What can I do for yer?'

'Well, you can do your buttons up for a start.' Sam waited for a moment or so until his request was carried out. 'Feel better now?' he asked.

'Yer, fanks very much.' The man laughed nervously. 'I feel a 'ole lot better now.'

'Good!' said Sam, removing his helmet. 'Because I'm just about to put that right.'

Seizing the man by his lapels, he lifted him on tip-toe. 'Listen, you stinking fat bastard! I've just been to your flat and seen the most pathetic, terrified creature I've ever seen in my life. She's been slapped, punched and head-butted. She's like a starved dog but she begged me not to nick you . . . well, if it's any consolation to you, I'm *not* going to nick you, but what I am going to do is to give you a little of what you managed to give her. Cop this for starters!'

He drove the man backwards across the cobbled lane in a series of ferocious body punches until he slumped, tearful and quivering, into the far gutter. Then Sam pulled him into a sitting position and dumped him on the kerbside. 'I've been told it's no good taking you to court, so you've had a hiding instead. But if you lay just one more hand on that girl, then the next time I call you'll be in the river. Don't forget, just one more hand. D'you understand?'

The man nodded and leaned forward until his head was on his knees. Retrieving his helmet, Sam resumed his beat.

For the rest of that night Sam was haunted by a mental image of the woman from number 15. Could that have happened to him and Queenie? Did the place that you live finally make you as evil as itself? Maybe the Swains were in love once, maybe she did not want to live there, maybe he insisted she did. Then he dismissed the idea by telling himself he could never act like Swain.

Sergeant Bevington ticked the weary night duty constables off his list at 6 a.m. next morning. 'Hang about till I've accounted for everyone, Sam,' he called, 'I'd like a word afore y'go.'

Once all his men had crawled away to their beds, Claude Bevington closed the door. 'I was patrolling down by the river again a couple of hours ago, Sam.' He paused and studied the young man's face. 'Found a bloke sitting there, just as it was getting daylight t'was. Looked like he'd been hit by an 'orse and dray. I quizzed him for some time but he reckons he'd had a drop too much and had fallen down some stairs. Funny that.' He shook his head in mock wonder. 'I don't remember him from early on. And guess what? He happened to be the bloke from number 15. You know, Sam, the one that knocks his old woman about. Retribution, as you might say, I suppose. He was adamant that he fell down the steps, which is just as well. I mean, I wouldn't like to think that someone, y'know, perhaps a neighbour or someone like that, took matters into their own hands and gave him a pasting. After all, a black eye is one thing. Knocking seven bells of shit out of someone is a totally different matter. Wouldn't you say, Sam?'

'Yes, sarge,' he agreed quietly.

'So if on your wanders, Sam, you happen to bump into someone . . . you know, someone who thought he might like to even the score a bit, you will point out that he's been bloody lucky this time and not to push his luck again, won't you, Sam?'

'Sarn't.'

'Good lad. Sleep well and don't be late tonight.'

It could have been that Sam's little chat with Fatty Swain had worked because for the next few weeks there were no more calls to Malacca House. Sam was certainly pleased by that. With his personal life in such disarray he had immersed himself in his police duties. He'd confided in Jim Forsythe soon after Queenie left but it had taken almost a week for Nell Diamond to discover she was minus a daughter-in-law. Each day he entered his flat Sam looked for the letter from Queenie that would announce her return. Each day there was none.

On Sunday 21 November, he had hastened home after an early turn to join the rest of the family in celebrating Nell Diamond's birthday. Jim and Queenie were due to call soon after three o'clock and the trio were to join the rest of the family at number 14. On the stroke of three Sam had just changed into his best suit when the knocker crashed on the door.

'You're a bloody nuisance, you're early! Go away and come back tomorrow?' he called jokingly. Again the knocker crashed but this time with a feeling of urgency. Sam opened the door to see a uniformed police inspector and sergeant standing before him.

'Diamond?' the inspector asked.

'Yessir,' Sam acknowledged.

'Are you a police officer, Diamond?'

'Yessir.'

'Are you by chance married to one Queenie Maria Diamond?'

'Well,' Sam faltered, 'yes . . . s'pose I am.'

'Then I'm sorry to tell you Mrs Diamond has been arrested and is in custody in Bow Street police station. You realise that, as a serving officer, this is a very serious matter for you?'

'Yes, sir, but—' For a moment Sam was at a loss for words. 'But *why* has she been arrested? And when and where?'

'She was arrested along with several other suffragettes when they ambushed Lloyd George, the Chancellor of the Exchequer, with an armful of fruit in the Strand earlier today. I suggest you attend Bow Street as soon as possible and we'll inform your chief inspector by telegraph.'

The pair had barely left when Jim and Jane arrived. 'We'll come with you. Mum'll understand,' said Jane, and thirty minutes later all three of them were on the well-trodden granite steps of Bow Street police station.

'Mr Diamond? This way, please,' said a young-looking police sergeant. 'I think our chief inspector would like a word with you.' All three of them were ushered into a small room at the rear of the front office where a fierce, military-looking type sat upright at a scrupulously tidy desk with hands clasped in front of him. Chief Inspector Stanley Pomeroy stared in silence as they settled. 'You are PC 599M Samuel Obadiah Diamond of Tower Bridge Police Station, I assume? Who are these others?'

Sam made the introductions and inquired immediately as to the welfare of Queenie.

'Mrs Queenie Diamond has been arrested for a relatively minor offence,' said the chief inspector. 'The one person who *is* in serious trouble is you, young man.'

'Me?' Sam asked incredulously. 'But I've been early turn at Tower Bridge all morning! I've been nowhere else!'

'Your duties this morning are immaterial. You'd better listen carefully to what I have to say. When Mrs Diamond was first arrested she refused to give any particulars. However, on being searched, the name of her employer was discovered. I take it you do know the name of your wife's employer, Diamond?'

'It's written down somewhere at home, yes,' he agreed.

'You see nothing wrong in that?'

'No, sir, why should I?'

'For the simple reason, Diamond, that the young lady is the wife of a serving police officer and as such, under police discipline code, she is not allowed employment.'

'I'm afraid I don't understand, sir,' answered the bewildered Sam.

'It's simple,' came the reply. 'If they're married to a policeman then they don't work. Got it?'

Jim realised instantly what Jane was about to say but she was sadly just out of kicking distance. 'Well, *I'm* married to a police officer and *I* work!' she announced proudly.

Both Sam and Jim closed their eyes in unison and groaned inwardly.

'Well, Diamond, I'm pleased to say this isn't my responsibility but I've been in touch with your chief inspector and he'll doubtless want to see the pair of you at 9 a.m. tomorrow. I can't understand for the life of me how you've both slipped through the net, but there you are.' He shook his head in disbelief. 'It's happened. Now, as to your wife. She refused to walk of her own accord and was therefore carried into the charge room here. A few minutes later, she suddenly fell to the floor in some kind of fit.'

'Where is she now?' cried Sam rising to his feet.

The chief inspector raised his hand. 'She could not be revived and a doctor was called who in turn called an ambulance in which she was conveyed to St Thomas's hospital. I spoke to him a few moments ago on the telephone and he states she is still in a coma and appears to be seriously ill. All I can do for you is to say that, as up to that moment, she had not been charged with any offence, nor is she now likely to be. That may be of some comfort to you. I would suggest you catch a 35 tramcar and make haste to St Thomas's whilst there is still time. I'll therefore detain you no longer.'

Jim was first to his feet as Sam still sat stunned. 'Have we got enough money between us for a cab?' asked Jane worriedly.

'I doubt if we've enough for a tram,' replied Jim ironically. 'But it'll not take long. Come on, Sam, snap out of it.'

Sure enough, within twenty-five minutes they were sprinting up the steps of St Thomas's where a pleasant nursing sister showed them into a waiting room. For the best part of an hour a large old wall-clock ticked the slow minutes loudly away. Eventually a curtain was thrown back and a surprisingly young white-coated doctor appeared before them.

'Mr Diamond?' Both Jim and Jane pointed quickly at Sam. 'Mr Diamond, your wife has had a serious fit but she has now come out of it. I understand from her she has had many of these fits in the past, is that correct?'

'Yes, doctor, but not for some little while,' he said. 'Why do you think it has returned?'

'That's the easy part,' said the doctor. 'Her type of fits are always likely to recur at moments of great stress. Being arrested, for example, is bad enough, certainly for an apparently respectable young lady like your wife, but with her other complication, it is doubly dangerous. You should never allow her to get into these situations, Mr Diamond, because, sooner or later, she is going to go into a coma from which she will not emerge.'

'I don't understand, sir,' began the perplexed Sam. 'What complications? You mean about her leaving home and such?'

'Leaving home, man? Good God, no! I had no idea she'd left home.' He shrugged 'Well, I don't suppose that helped matters. No, I'm talking about her pregnancy, she's expecting a baby and she's not having a good time of it either.'

'A baby!' exclaimed Sam. 'But . . . but . . .' he dropped back on to a chair and shook his head.

'One way and another,' murmured Jim, almost to himself, 'it's been an interesting time. Your wife's left home, been nicked, is epileptic and pregnant. We've missed your old mum's birthday party and both look like getting the sack. Anything else to say, doctor?'

'Well, she's sleeping and it would not be advisable to wake her. So we'll keep her here for a couple of days and you can collect her, say . . . Wednesday morning. We'll let you know.'

Jim stood up and put his arms around the shoulders of Jane and her brother. 'Come on, gang, let's go celebrate before we really get some bad news.'

Chapter 14

Nell Diamond drew the curtains against the afternoon sun, tucked her daughter-in-law comfortably up in bed and quietly closed the door. Tip-toeing downstairs into her kitchen she faced the solemn trio. 'She's certainly in no fit state to return home just yet, Sam. I'll look after her, don't worry.'

'That's all very well, Mum,' protested her son. 'But she's my wife and therefore my responsibility.'

'Oh, Sam, shut up and don't be so bloody pompous!' interrupted Jane angrily. 'If Mum say's she can look after her, then for God's sake LET HER! We've so many problems between us you can do with all the help you can get right now!'

'She's right, Sam,' added Jim quietly. 'If your mum can have Queenie for even a week or so, it'll give us a chance to tackle all the other aggravation.'

'The first thing you boys have to settle,' said a worried Nell, 'is your work. Before Jane gives up her job, you'll need to know whether you two lads still have a job.'

'We should hopefully know within five days, Ma,' said Sam. 'We're suspended on half-pay until the hearing on Monday afternoon, but I'm not hopeful.'

'What on earth will you do?' inquired Nell.

Jim shrugged. 'We can always try paving again I s'pose. Anyway, it's not all gloom, Ma. The old boy opposite our place has moved out and the rent-office say Sam and Queenie can have the flat.'

'What's it like, Jim?'

The young man laughed. 'It's a sixth-floor slum, Ma, but it's Blenheim Palace set against Inkerman Place – and they can move in on Sunday.'

'Does it have rats, Jim?' asked a weak little voice.

All looked up to see a sunken-eyed, white-faced Queenie leaning on the door.

'Queenie!' exclaimed Sam as he leapt to his feet and dashed towards her. 'What on earth are you doing out of bed?'

'I'm listening to just about the only bit of good news since I got off the train from my honeymoon,' she replied ruefully as she returned her husband's embrace. 'Well, does it, Jim?'

'Rats? No. It has the occasional mouse, too many bed-bugs, a dingy stone staircase with ninety-six steps. But on the other hand, on a sunny day, if you go up to the flat roof and ignore the smell from the rubbish chutes, the view is so great you'd think you were on a magic carpet . . . wouldn't she, Jane?'

'A slight exaggeration, James,' smiled Jane. 'But I'm sure she gets your point.'

'I'd like to say something to you all,' whispered Queenie. 'No please.' She raised her hand against both Sam's and Jim's interruptions. 'I've given you all quite a bit of trouble and worry and I'm sorry for that. I'm not sorry for leaving 11a though, Sam. I would have gone insane if I'd had to sleep there on my own. But now I'm going to be a mum *and* we look like moving house, my priorities have changed. I simply want to thank you all for your kindness and . . . and . . . d'you mind if I go back to bed now . . . because I'm shattered.' Falling into Sam's arms she allowed herself to be carried up the tiny staircase and to bed.

As the next few days passed, Queenie's health improved greatly and, by Sunday, Sam had the greatest difficulty in preventing her from assisting the entire Diamond tribe on the house-move from Inkerman Place to Queen's Buildings. Two wheel-barrows had been hired at a cost of two shillings and sixpence and, with chairs and bedstead precariously balanced, the contents were trundled the three-quarters of a mile to the new abode. As each child struggled up the stairs with a piece of furniture, the alarm of the couple on the fifth floor, who had visions of a family of nine moving in immediately above them, amused Sam greatly. Finally, by early evening, the lino was laid, the curtains hung, and with the furniture and the Welcome-To-Your-New-Home ribbon in place, the stage set for the grand arrival of the mistress of the house.

Queenie found the ninety-six stairs more exhausting than she anticipated but at least the nausea she experienced each time she turned the corner of Inkerman Place was absent. Later that night, as she lay entwined in Sam's powerful arms, he whispered apprehensively, 'I have a gut feeling both Jim and I are going to need a lot of reassurance tomorrow night, girl. Perhaps you should have a word with the woman next-door?'

'The police force wouldn't *dare* get rid of their two best men, now would they?'

'Wouldn't they?' he asked bitterly 'You just watch 'em.'

In spite of Sam and Jim's protests, both girls insisted on accompanying their menfolk to the inquiry at Stones End police station the next afternoon. The only reservation was Jane's nagging worry about her job. If Jim was sacked she would certainly need it; on the other hand, if she could show she had already resigned, the inquiry may accept it as a token of good faith. Both girls were invited to a waiting room as the men were ordered to stand in the corridor outside the district superintendent's office. As they were about to part, a vaguely familiar figure appeared. At first neither of them could place him. Jane finally realised his identity. 'It's the chief inspector we saw at Bow Street,' she whispered.

'Oh that's bloody marvellous,' muttered Sam acidly. 'As if the case is not strong enough, they're stitching us up with foreigners from north of the Thames.'

The chief inspector suddenly saw them and called the girls back with some urgency in his tone. 'Ah, young ladies! What a stroke of luck. Would you please bear with me for a moment?' He then turned to the two defaulters. 'I've been thinking a great deal about your cases and, with your permission, I would like to advise you and speak for you at the inquiry.' He shook his head. 'Of course I've had very little time to prepare but I know Superintendent Sorrell who is chairing it and I've always found him to be fair. The fact that your wives are actually here is too good an opportunity to miss. I never knew a defence case that could not be strengthened by the presence of two attractive young female witnesses.'

'And one of them . . .' said Jane, more alert than the rest and pointing directly at Queenie '. . . is pregnant.'

'Wonderful!' exclaimed Stanley Pomeroy. 'How extremely clever of you, young lady . . . and such good timing!'

'Sir,' said Jim. 'we'd be very obliged and grateful if you would act for us.'

'Good. I've already taken the liberty of arranging for two other discipline cases to go ahead of us, just to gain a little extra time, so let's not waste a second of it.' He led the foursome into the waiting room and closed the door. 'The first thing I have to say is that you are going to have to admit everything. The only thing I am going to dispute is intent. That, basically, is why I wanted to be here today. I had no doubt in my conversation with you in Bow Street police station that you had absolutely no idea you had contravened regulations. Now ordinarily that is still no defence but in your case the police force was at least equally at fault and, in view of your physical and even mental state at the time of the offence, I think we have a chance. D'you understand what that means?'

'Not fully, sir,' responded Jim.

'It means you will be punished, there is nothing I can do about that and I doubt if it'll be a transfer. You, Diamond, are already on your third station. If we get any result at all, it could be a fine.'

'How much, sir?' asked Sam anxiously. 'Because if it's much more than ten bob they may as well transport me to Australia now.'

'That I can't say, but a recruit's wages being so miserably low, it can't be much.'

'How about me, sir?' asked Jim. 'You can obviously put Sam's illness forward as his defence but it won't excuse me.'

'I agree, and you're going to be the most vunerable of the two, but by bracketing you both together, as the force itself did when it gave you permission to marry, I'm hoping it will also deal with you together. It's our only chance. D'you wish to take the risk? But I must warn you there is no redress at all. Whatever happens in there today is final.'

The young men looked quickly at each other and nodded.

'PC 599M Diamond, PC 613M Forsythe, Chief Inspector Pomeroy and any other witnesses, please report,' boomed a voice from down the corridor.

'That's us. Good luck,' said the chief inspector.

The two young constables were ushered into a wide room where three senior officers sat at a large desk. There was a sergeant already scribbling and the proceedings were brisk and to the point from the moment they entered. The charges were read out and Stanley Pomeroy was immediately on his feet and saying neither officer desired to take up the inquiry members' valuable time. Both officers pleaded guilty and were only there through their own ignorance and the inefficiency of others. 'Others', it must be said, who should have known better. There were two attractive young witnesses who would be more than pleased to clear up any matter that might be bothering the inquiry.

At least two of the inquiry panel perked up at this and the same pair of heads nodded sympathetically as the girls related their story. At the words: 'And that, sir, is the case for our defence,' all three inquiry members looked up at a clock that showed a time forty-five minutes earlier than they could have anticipated. It took three minutes' discussion to reach the verdict: a fine of one week's pay and both wives to give up their employment.

'Neither of the two constables can afford this amount in one payment, sir, particularly as the wives will not now be working,' explained the chief inspector. 'Can they have time to pay?'

'Very well,' agreed the superintendent gruffly. 'Two months to pay, commencing from next week.'

As the quartet and their defender reassembled in the waiting room, Jane was the first to speak. 'I don't know how we are going to manage this, sir,' she said to Pomeroy, 'but I would like to thank you on behalf of the others because without you I'm sure they would have been dismissed.'

'Thank you, young lady,' he acknowledged graciously. 'I'm afraid you're quite right. The discipline laws are archaic and sadly there is no appeal. It's long been a particular bee in my bonnet and I pray I am no longer in the force when it all blows up.' He then turned his attention to the two men. 'So what will you two do? Will you accept this punishment or will you resign? You will need to bear in mind that if you resign, you are required to give notice so they will be able to seize the week's fine anyway.'

The young men radiated indecision.

'May I point a few things out to you that may help you make up your minds?'

'Yes, please do,' begged Jim.

'Firstly, I would suggest you accept this punishment and put it quickly behind you. Secondly I would suggest that you both aim for promotion as soon as possible. For constables and their families, this job is a poverty-wracked killer. It is essential for your own health that you escape from the lower rung as soon as possible. The higher you go the easier it becomes. Sadly, many senior officers who could help change it, have no wish to do so. They believe because they went through biting poverty, everybody else should share the experience.'

'If you were us, would you stay?' asked Sam brusquely.

'It's certainly right in PC Forsythe's case,' agreed the chief inspector.

'But not in my Sam's case?' cut in Queenie sharply.

Pomeroy made no reply at first but for some moments sat staring thoughtfully out of the window. 'Mrs Diamond,' he began, but though his remarks appeared to be directed at Queenie, none of the four had the slightest doubt at whom they were really aimed, 'your husband is a born thief-taker. He should be an asset to any station at which he serves.'

'*Should*?' she cut in. '*Should*? What does *should* mean?'

'Should means that the police force – every police force – is always going to have trouble with its thief-takers. They will always be in the thick of things and usually up to their necks in trouble.' He raised a hand to forestall her protests. 'I don't blame *him*. Quite frankly, I wish he was at my station. Unfortunately for us both, he's not. It is quite possible that if he stays in the force he will become a great thief-taker.' He gave a little laugh. 'One consistent thing about great thief-takers is that they are never easy to handle. They make so many waves that the average superintendent's desk is awash with complaints. As a general rule, superintendents do not care for this, but the fact is that the rest of us ride on the back of these men and, with just a handful at each station, the streets would be safe for everyone except villains and scum.'

'But my Sam isn't like that,' Queenie protested.

'Your Sam, as you call him, is *exactly* like that, Mrs Diamond! He's been in the force just a few months and already he's been courageous enough to deserve a VC, daft enough to deserve the sack, committed at least three discipline offences that merit dismissal, is outspoken when he shouldn't be, obstinate, insubordinate, cussed, acts from the heart and not from the head – and by the way he's headstrong too.' He paused as he searched for other adjectives.

'Is that all?' she inquired sarcastically.

'No, not quite,' he resumed. 'He's straight, industrious and honest, and that, Mrs Diamond, is why I came here today.'

'You'd better add to that list that I'm also quite dim,' murmured Sam, 'because I'm not sure what you're trying to say.'

'I'm trying to tell you, young man, that in future you must, for your own benefit, *think* before you act! You cannot afford another error. You are on a tight-rope and the net's been taken away. So for God's sake, be CAREFUL!' Further discussion was cut short by the arrival of Sergeant Hawkins, the administration clerk at Stones End, who carried a clipboard. His conversation with the chief inspector was kept inaudible from the four friends. As he finished, Pomeroy clasped his hand to his forehead with a groan of disbelief. 'Diamond!' he snapped. 'What's your current *permanent* address?'

'25 Queen's Buildings, sir.'

'So what's happened to 11a Inkerman Place?'

'We moved yesterday,' explained the puzzled Sam.

'Did you tell anyone? Did you ask for permission? Did

you submit a report to ascertain if it was a fit place for a serving police officer to reside?'

'Well . . . no, sir, I s'pose I didn't, but Jim Forsythe here lives next-door at 26 and his flat was passed okay. I suppose I thought if 11a Inkerman Place was considered suitable, anything was!'

'D'you see now what I mean, Diamond? You're not a bloody gypsy! You can't go roaming all over the place, staying wherever your caravan rests or whenever the mood happens to take you! You're in a discipline force, for God's sake and we are supposed to know where you live. What do you think they pay you a shilling a week rent allowance for?'

Sam shook his head and sighed deeply. 'I take it this means more trouble, sir?'

'Diamond, you can't *afford* more trouble,' explained Pomeroy. 'As a matter of fact, you owe Sergeant Hawkins here a great debt. He's been delegated the task of getting your personal records straight and, as far as your file is now concerned, you have lived at 25 Queen's Buildings ever since your marriage. Got that?'

'Yessir!' snapped Sam.

'Good!' He turned to the sergeant. 'Thank you, it was thoughtful of you, and now I'd better return to Bow Street before I'm accused of fomenting sedition.'

'Excuse me, sir,' said Queenie, stepping forward and quickly kissing the chief inspector's left cheek. 'Thank you on behalf of us both.'

'And us too,' cut in Jane, planting a kiss on his right side.

He bowed with just the hint of a twinkle in his eye. 'A man can seek no greater reward than the gratitude of a beautiful woman . . .' he sighed and turned the palms of his hands to heaven '. . . what price two!'

The two young men certainly took the chief inspector's advice to heart, though each found the financial punishment gruellingly hard. The winter was slow to fade and, as her girth increased, Queenie found the ninety-six stairs to her flat more difficult to negotiate as each day passed. Though at different stations, both Sam and Jim were on similar shifts, so at least they could socialise and share hardship tales.

It was soon after 3 a.m. on a Saturday in early April that Sam had cause to shelter in a dockside doorway from a piercing wind cutting straight up the estuary. He gradually became aware of a cyclist wobbling precariously over the granite cobbles. The rider appeared either drunk or totally incapable of riding the machine. As he neared, Sam decided to stop him. Biding his time, he waited until he heard the creaking of the rusty chain before leaping out in front of the crouching, muttering figure.

Claude Bevington lifted his head from its position an inch or so above the handlebars to see the very person for whom he had been searching for an hour, dancing like a dervish in front of him. Never a good cyclist at the best of times, a borrowed bike, dubious brakes and a wonky wheel all proved all too much for the nervous rider. In a desperate attempt to avoid the idiot copper, he crashed painfully into a long abandoned anchor chain.

'Diamond! You bloody lunatic! What d'you think you're doing? You scared the bloody life out'a me.'

'I'm sorry, sarge, but I thought you looked suspicious.'

'O' course I look soddin' suspicious! Anyone riding that bike over these cobbles is bound to look suspicious. Every bump you hit rams that saddle up your arse like a pike-staff.' He stopped complaining long enough to rub his rectum briskly. 'Sod me but that hurts. Anyway, I've been looking for you for ages. Where've you been?'

'Keeping out of the wind mainly, sarge, it's coming off that river like a razor.'

'Okay, boy, now listen. Though on second thoughts, cancel the *boy* bit. I have to tell you you are a boy no longer, because by now you're probably a dad. A Mrs Forsythe came into the station two hours ago to say she'd had to rush your wife to hospital because she was imminent.'

'What-hospital-sarge-because-it's-not-due-till—' began Sam at a gabble.

'Will you bloody *listen* before you go rambling on! Right, now take this bike and go straight to Guy's hospital. Mrs Forsythe said she'll meet you there. You'll need to come back before 6 a.m. so we'll know you're all right and can be booked off. Oh, yeah, one last thing,' he added as he picked up the bicycle and began trying to straighten the wheels. 'Look after the bike. It belongs to the chief inspector and he's off for a couple of days and doesn't know I've borrowed it. Right, off you go and good luck to the new mum and little one. By the way, it's not compulsory to name it after your sergeant, you know. But on the other hand . . .'

Leaping on to the machine, Sam pedalled away for all he was worth. A flood of thoughts began to race through his mind. Was Queenie all right and why was she so early? She should have at least another month to go yet. Would it be a boy or girl? He had no wish to appear ungrateful to Sergeant Bevington but Claude didn't seem much of a name. If it was a girl then he didn't mind Claudia but Claude was definitely out, it sounded like a gormless fishmonger. As he left the docks behind him, the cobbles gave way to a better road surface and within minutes he raced into the quadrangle at Guy's. Wedging the cycle into the railings, he sprinted into reception where the first person he saw was his sister.

'How is she?' he blurted breathlessly.

'There are problems, Sam, I'm afraid.'

He felt his stomach turn. 'Come on, what are they?' he demanded.

'Firstly, you are a father of twins! Secondly, after

delivering the first – a boy – Queenie went into a fit and no one is yet sure if the second, a girl, is damaged in any way. Both babies are very tiny and the doctor wants to see you as soon as you arrive and . . . oh, look, there he is now. Quick, catch him!'

After the dash from the dockside, catching portly doctor Henry McPherson was no problem and soon the fat old Scot was sitting in a cubicle and explaining to Sam the problems with the twins' delivery. 'Other than being underweight, the first wee bairn is fine. As fer the second . . .' He shook his head. 'I dinna know and won't do either, not for some time. That's the first of the difficulties. The second is with yon lassie herself. She's had a severe fit and in my opinion she should nae go through a childbirth again.'

'Can I see her?' asked Sam.

'Weel, nae for an hour or so, laddie, but as soon as she's well enough, ye'll be the fust ter know. Now I must attend to your little girl. She's as bonny as a rose and nae much bigger. Oh, and by the way, ye'd better get used ter this place because they're goin' ter be here for at least a week or two.'

It was a very worried young man who walked slowly into the waiting room and held his sister's hand in anguish. 'Lately I seem to be spending half my life just waiting,' he muttered.

In fact it was just under an hour before a tired-looking nursing sister entered to tell them the new mum could be seen for a few minutes. Leading the way along a corridor, she ushered them into a white-curtained cubicle to where an exhausted Queenie lay on a blanketed bed. She gave them the weariest of smiles before asking, 'How are the babies, Sam?'

He bent over and kissed her before replying, 'They're well, love. Tiny but well.'

She gripped his hand with surprising strength. 'You have

seen them though, Sam, haven't you?' she asked in a voice full of anxiety.

'Of course we have,' he lied, 'and they're both sleeping like tops. You're a very clever girl indeed.'

She closed her eyes wearily. 'Am I? I can't remember anything about it, isn't that sad?'

'I think we must let her sleep now,' interrupted the nurse, already drawing the curtains. 'Come back and see her later.'

For Sam, the next three weeks were a never ending round of work, hospital and sleep, roughly in that order. The close proximity of his sister and Jim caused him to bless the day he had moved next-door. On the other hand, as each day passed he could also see the problems that were bound to arise with two young children, ninety-six steps and two rooms. The twins, David and Emma, began to gain weight and the scare concerning Emma faded. On being given their final discharge date, Sam felt his fortunes had finally changed for the better.

He was convinced of this when he heard that after eighty-one years a rather boyish Home Secretary named Winston Churchill had decreed the police force was at last to be allowed a weekly leave day. To his great delight, his first free day coincided with his family's release from hospital. It was probably the proudest day of his life when he walked through the streets on the way to collect them. His colleagues had held a collection and given him enough money for a suitably large second-hand perambulator and, though he felt a little self-conscious pushing the empty carriage to the hospital, he was more than compensated by the pride of the journey back. He thought Queenie looked beautiful if tired and the twins like two freshly boiled sausages. As they arrived at the entrance to the staircase he paused. Leaning back, he stared up at the high grey walls. 'Do you think you can manage it, Queenie?'

She gave a wry smile. 'I'll have to, Sam dear,' she murmured. 'I'm now a mum and mums have to do these things.'

Late that evening, whilst Sam was experiencing life as a family man, Jim, together with a small contingent from Stones End under Station Sergeant Dale, was holding back the crowds at an artistes' protest demonstration at The Central, a Blackfriars Road music hall. In an effort to break the strike, many London managements had reduced prices drastically and filled the bill with amateur acts. As a short-term novelty, the public quite enjoyed it. Some of the acts were so appalling they were quite entertaining and many of the worst had already built up a cult following. As the protestors were held back at one side of the theatre, a carriage drew up at the front. The manager was the first to see the occupant. 'Sergeant!' he called to Dale. 'That woman is not allowed in my theatre. She's here solely to create trouble. I want her removed.'

Billie Bardell alighted from the carriage with her customary hauteur and made her way to the foyer. 'I told you, I want her out!' persisted the manager.

'Then it's down to you to tell her,' pointed out the station sergeant. 'Only you can do that.'

'Very well, that's easy.' The manager turned to Billie a trifle pompously and raising an arm, rather unwisely pointed at her from a very close vicinity. 'You are not allowed in this theatre, madam, will you please leave immediately?' He emphasised each word by jabbing the finger backward and forward.

By way of reply, Billie placed her hand on the man's chest and dumped him swiftly on his backside. Then, smiling sweetly at the sergeant, she walked serenely past as if nothing had happened. An eruption of cheering broke out both from partisan pickets and neutral spectators. 'You saw it! You saw it!' clamoured the manager. 'She assaulted me. I want her arrested.'

'Just a minute, madam,' said the sergeant in his severest tones. 'You cannot go around pushing people over, that's tantamount to an assault. Furthermore, he doesn't want you in the theatre. You must leave.'

'Assault, sergeant?' she exclaimed in mock horror. 'But I thought the man was going to attack me! He kept pointing at my . . . well, you know, sergeant, you're a man of the world.' She leaned forward and, cupping her mouth to the sergeant's ear, whispered confidentially: 'My breasts. I should think he's probably a seducer of women and a violator of young girls, wouldn't you?'

The manager scrambled furiously to his feet. 'What's she whispering about? I want that woman out, d'you understand? OUT!'

'I'm sorry, madam,' said Dale. 'But any idea of assault by that man is but a figment of your imagination. If you do not leave this foyer I will have my men remove you.' He then raised a finger to curtail any protest and continued, 'Should you then persist, I will have you arrested for causing a breach of the peace.'

Billie's brief flirtation with gentility faded instantly. 'Don't you point that finger at me, old son, or I'll dump *you* on your arse as well!' She turned her venom back to the manager. 'That randy old git is only employing these amateur acts so he can touch up the girl dancers. That's always been his game, that has – dirty old sod.'

'Sergeant, I want this woman arrested for assault!' persisted the manager.

'And I want this man arrested for touching me tits!' insisted Billie.

The sergeant was slowly shepherding her out of the foyer when her gaze suddenly fell upon Jim Forsythe who had been doing his best to avoid recognition.

'James!' she exclaimed, neatly forgetting the trauma of their last meeting as she rushed to wind her arms tightly around his neck. 'James, can you do something about these potty old farts? You're an intelligent lad, order them to let me in.'

She emphasised the embrace with the most passionate of kisses which did more for Jim's standing amongst his colleagues than a dozen good arrests.

'613 Forsythe!' snapped Station Sergeant Dale. 'D'you know this woman?'

Considering her arms were still around his neck, Jim thought a denial would be unconvincing. 'Er – yes, sergeant. Er . . . Miss Bardell is . . . an old friend of the family . . . as you might say.'

'Not so old though, luvvy, eh?' murmured Billie as, with arms still around his neck, she provocatively embraced him.

'631!' roared Dale who was now approaching apoplexy. 'If you haven't got rid of that woman in one minute, I'm nicking her for indecency and disciplining you for idling and gossiping.'

'Billie, please leave go!' whispered the young constable as he tried to wriggle free. 'You'll get me the bloody sack.'

She threw back her head and roared with laughter, 'Okay, you win.' She turned and faced both Dale and the manager. 'This young man has cleverly talked me out of pursuing charges against you two silly bastards. It's against my better judgement, mind. I just hope I'm doing the right thing, that's all. Now if you let him see me to my carriage, you have the word of a lady that I'll take no action.'

The carriage had been moved on by a constable shortly after Billie alighted and the driver and horse were some sixty yards up the road enjoying a pipe and nose-bag respectively.

'Forsythe!' boomed Dale. 'If you wish to stay in this job, you'll stop this woman talking and get her out of my sight – NOW!' Jim had already decided the incident had gone far enough and knew that just one more word from Billie could tip the scales towards disaster. Placing one arm around her waist and the other hand lightly over her mouth, he led her gently but firmly to her carriage. When a few yards distant, she moved her mouth slightly and, contrary to his expectation, did not try to speak at all but suddenly nibbled and sucked two of his fingers.

A tremor went down his body like chain lightning. 'Will you stop doing that?' he implored. 'It tingles me loins and plays havoc with me duties!'

The cabbie hastily docked his pipe and jumped to open the door whilst Jim assisted her to climb the footplate. Once out of sight of the crowd, her mood changed dramatically. Seizing Jim's arm, she pleaded, 'Tell me about my Queenie and Sam? Where are they living? What are they doing? Are they well?' She shook her head in despair. 'Oh, Jim, Jim, I beg you! Just tell me anything you can about them, please.'

Jim glanced back to where his station sergeant was showing signs of increasing irritation. 'I have very little time so I'll be as quick as possible.' For the next few minutes he gave her a sketchy resumé of the previous eighteen months.

'My God!' she murmured almost to herself. 'Twins, you say? She could have died and I wouldn't have known. Jim,' she clutched desperately at his arm, 'you must do something for me.'

'I think I know what you're about to ask and I must refuse.'

'No, Jim, you mustn't refuse me. Listen. All I want you to do is to keep me informed about everything. I went to the church for your weddings without anyone seeing me, but apart from that I know nothing and it's tearing me apart. Write to me and tell me. I shall want to know about Queenie, the babies, even about Sam. They must never find themselves in that state again without me knowing. Promise me, Jim, promise?'

'Billie, I can't possibly promise you that! Sam would kill

me if he found out, you know he would. Anyway, my loyalty must be to him.'

'But you must, you must!' She looked frantically around as if seeking inspiration. 'Listen to me, Jim, in exchange for this information . . . I'll do anything you ask, *anything* at all, you understand me?'

Jim sadly closed his eyes for a moment. 'You're too proud a woman to beg, Miss Bardell, and it doesn't suit you anyway.' He bent forward into the carriage and kissed her hand. 'You don't have to offer me anything. If it's that important to you, I'll do it for nothing. Goodnight.'

'613 Forsythe,' yelled Station Sergeant Dale. 'We haven't got all day! Get back here this instant, d'you hear me?'

'Sergeant!' acknowledged the young constable. 'On my way.'

Chapter 15

Maxie Roff stared thoughtfully out of his second-floor window straight down the Walworth Road and assessed his situation. He knew the next few months would be a watershed in his life and wanted to make sure he knew exactly what he was doing. It had to be a time of meticulous planning and today was the first stage.

He glanced around the spotless room, searching for his cigar. Cigars were an innovation for him. If he was honest, he was not even sure he actually liked them but they seemed a suitable prop for a budding big-time gangster. Soon the first of his scheduled callers would arrive and Mrs Murgatroyd would show them up.

Max had been born in the little flat two floors above Rosebery's the saddlemakers. When the shop went bust two or three years before, Mr Murgatroyd, who lived on the first floor, had been laid off. He had taken it so badly he gassed himself. Unfortunately he had been a bit reckless in his use of the gas and much of it had seeped through to the bedroom immediately above where Max's mother had lain in the depths of bronchitis. It appeared that coal gas was not the recommended treatment for bronchitis and the coroner guessed that Mrs Roff met her maker a full two minutes before her downstairs neighbour managed it.

Newly orphaned at eighteen, Max had then found the forty-year-old, widowed Minnie Murgatroyd an enormous asset, primarily because she was stricken with guilt, feeling in some way responsible that it was her husband who really killed Max's mother. As a result she took on the responsibility of cleaning the flat and looking after the youngster like a penance. In fact Max could not remember a moment in his entire life when he had liked his mother. If he had thought he could have got away with it, he would have gassed her himself years before. She was a toothless hag, an incessant moaner, and never ceased preaching at him. Whereas Mrs Murgatroyd was still very pretty, never complained, kept the place immaculate and never asked for anything in return. There had been a time when he thought he was in love with Mrs Murgatroyd, he still occasionally woke in the night thinking about her, but to be fair she had never given him the slightest encouragement and he had decided not to risk losing one so valuable by a wandering hand or the mistaking of a bedroom door.

Mrs Murgatroyd had been briefed exactly as to her duties. As each caller knocked she was to show them up politely but not to mention any of the other visitors. Max glanced at the clock then lay back and blew out a long cloud of smoke. All in all, it had been quite a satisfactory day. To be able to sell three horses, four carts and six rolls of cloth that didn't even belong to you was sound economics by anyone's book. Max had started the steal-to-order business almost as soon as he took over from Reg but, profitable though it was, there was still a risk. After all, someone had to steal the goods, or rather commodities, as Max preferred them to be called.

Anyway, this had been a short-term venture. He had intended to remain in the business just long enough to raise the capital for a deposit on the vacant warehouse in Red Cross Street and now he had taken the plunge. He had carefully assessed its potential and it was enormous. Firstly it was in a notorious and densely populated area with exits on four sides. It was the joint highest building in the street so, apart from its north side where Messrs Redmayne & Baxter shared a mutual dead-end narrow alley, it could not be overlooked and all doors and windows were as solid as rocks. The reason for the inbuilt security was the location. Ever since a local doctor had been strangled there for a fiver and dumped on a costermonger's barrow, Red Cross Street had earned the reputation of being second only to the Algiers Casbah. A person, or company, would need to be very sure of themselves before setting up in such a location. Micheldever Brothers had been wildly optimistic when they had opened their furniture warehouse in such a spot, mainly because half the population of Red Cross Street also opened it, usually an hour after it was closed for the night. It was like setting up a whelk stall in a crocodile pool. On the other hand, Messrs Redmayne & Baxter's main product was fairly safe from local marauders, soap being pretty low on Red Cross Street's list of desirable acquisitions. Yet, as Max would frequently say, the smell did add a touch of class to the area.

His thoughts were interrupted by a loud knocking at the downstairs front door. It had to be Frank Cootes who always liked folk to know he was about. He heard the soft muted tone of Mrs Murgatroyd, followed by two sets of footsteps up the four flights of stairs. There was the most delicate of knocks and, in answer to his 'Come in', Mrs Murgatroyd showed the glowering Frank Cootes into the room and closed the door behind him. 'I understand yer want ter see me?' he grunted.

'Frank!' greeted Max. 'How've you been? We've not seen you for months! Sit yourself down and have a drink.' He strolled over to the stone larder. 'Scotch do yer?'

Frank graciously acknowledged that scotch would suffice and sat himself down in one fireside chair whilst Max returned to the other. Then, without the slightest encourage ment, Frank proceeded to swing into greatly embellished tales of his sexual adventures on his recent beer-hall tour of Germany with Eugene Sandow. After listening to a ten-minute recitation of fanciful conquests of fraus and frauleins,

Max decided it was time to cut him short. 'Tell me, Frank,' he began very quietly as he ran a finger thoughtfully around the rim of his glass, 'all these women you talk about, what's the attraction? I mean, nearly all blokes fancy girls but that's not what I'm talking about. I'm talking about something that's an obsession with you. I get the impression from listening to you that you never mention a girl more than once, is that right?'

'O' course,' answered Frank.

'Then why is that?'

Frank shrugged. 'There are so many women out there I need to try them all, I suppose.'

'Nah, Frank, that's bollocks and you know it.'

'I don't understand, what are you sayin' ter me?'

'What I am saying to you, Frank, *is*, that the reason that you never mention a girl twice, is because no woman would ever have a second helping of you. You're an animal and you terrify them. I've seen a couple after you've done with them, Frank, and they've not been pretty. When it comes to women, you're not only an absolute pig but, before we go any further, you'll need to admit it.'

Frank leapt to his feet with his glass still in one hand and rushed forward to seize the sitting Max with the other. Max had sat calmly in his chair whilst he was delivering his verbal tirade against Frank and did not move until his own throat was gripped vice-tight. Suddenly, with all the strength it was possible to muster from a sitting position, he shot a heavy kick upward into Frank's crotch. The strong man instantly jack-knifed and, as he fell to the floor, Max swung the other foot powerfully to the side of his head. With two sources of excruciating pain, Frank opened his mouth in a long silent scream. For some moments Max made no move other than to resume running his finger around the rim of his glass. 'I thought one of the best ways to get you to listen, Frank, would be something like a temporary castration.' He nodded his head almost to himself. 'You've got to admit it was effective?'

Frank made no reply.

'Well, I'm pleased you're paying attention, Frank, because I have something important to say to you.' He paused long enough to drain his glass before continuing. 'When I took over this mob, the first thing I had to decide was: should Frank join dear old Reg? After all, you two were good mates and I thought you might like to be friends for eternity, if you get my meaning. But on reflection, as I've already mentioned to you, you do have some good points. About the best one being your stupid moronic violence. In fact, with the right guidance, you could be quite an asset to someone in my position.'

Frank had begun slowly to straighten his legs which had been screwed up tightly since the first kick. 'Comfortable, Frank? Good, I'll continue then. Old Reg had an inefficient silly little bunch here who thought they were big-time villains, right, Frank?' He again made no reply. 'I'm pleased you concur. You see, it wasn't what I would call economically sound, that was the big problem. So what I propose to do is diversify. D'you know what *diversify* means, Frank?' Yet again there was silence. 'Oh dear, what a shame. Never mind, I'll tell you.

'Diversify means we are going to spread our wings a little. We are going to have a little club with plenty of little creature comforts. Who knows, perhaps a little band, a little gambling, a little drinking, a little wheeling and dealing, and finally some little – no, Frank, make that some BIG girls. Ah ha, Frank! I thought I'd get your interest sooner or later. Tut tut, what a randy sod you are! Now listen particularly carefully here, Frank, because this is where you come in. I am going to put you in charge of the girls. I appreciate it's a bit like putting a drunk in a brewery or a maggot in an apple but I think it might work. Would you like to sit up and I'll explain the job requirements?'

Frank groaned as he attempted to move his jaw from side to side. 'Oh, that's much better, Frank,' continued Max. 'I can hear you now. So, if I put you in charge of the girls, I want no rough stuff with them. I certainly want them to fear you but your reputation will go ahead of you anyway. But get this straight – I am not employing expensive tarts to pander to your perverted pleasures. Once I choose a girl and she is on my payroll, she is not to be marked, you understand? If they look like getting out of order you can give them the odd slap but anything else is to be referred to me. Oh, yes, one other thing. I don't want you shafting them either, that's not what I shall be paying you for. If I see you around any of them with your dick in your hand, then I'll razor it off and shove it in your ear.

'And one final thing. If any of the customers get out of hand, I shall expect politeness at first but then controlled – controlled, mind you – violence. I don't want you doing your nut and half killing them. It's to be arms up their backs and slung out into the alley – and I don't want their pockets picked on the way, understand me?'

The pain at either end of Frank's torso had eased sufficiently for him finally to speak. 'What did you have to do that for?' he complained, rubbing his jaw with one hand and his genitalia with the other.

'Perhaps you forget, Frank,' pointed out Max, 'but *you* had *me* around the throat. In any case, you must be aware right from the start that I'm the foreman of this group so what I say goes. I'm well aware you are not, what might be called, a forgiving man, Frank, but remember any ideas as to paying me back could be fatal for you. I'm not one of your fairies that you usually pick on so let's get our understanding clear right from the start.'

'I wasn't ready for you, that's all,' mumbled Frank.

'My God!' exclaimed Max. 'You of all people aren't going to accuse me of not fighting fair, I hope?'

Frank shook his head ruefully.

'Fine! Now let's decide to work together for the good of humanity – or at least this little section of it. Are you in?'

'Yeah,' grunted Frank. 'What's the set up with the girls? Are they going to be Toms?'

'Yeah, we'll have a few rooms set aside for them to do their tomming, but while I was thinking about it I thought we might be able to fix a couple of observation spots. This would have a double advantage. We could use it for an extra source of revenue and we could make sure exactly *what* was going on behind closed doors.'

'These girls,' said Frank, 'where you getting them from?'

Max shook his head almost sadly. 'It'll be no problem. They'll earn more in a week on their backs here than they will in a year on their feet in any factory between London Bridge and Brighton. In addition the hours are better. To start with I shall want half a dozen young girls, with perhaps a couple of older birds to teach them the tricks of the trade. *But*, and this is important, Frank, I want no kids.'

'Whad'ya mean, kids?'

'I'll know what I mean when I see them. If I see any bewildered-looking tearful kid wandering half naked around the corridor, it'll be your balls on a plate, Frank. That's the responsibility that goes with the job. D'you still want it?'

'How about when I go out of town with the stage act?'

'Yes, I've thought about that and I'm afraid I can't allow it. If you want the job here for twelve quid a week it's yours. But this is my last offer. I think you should remember that you ain't getting any younger and you're hardly an international star coming on during intervals to sell appalling bottles of horse piss to skinny-gutted cretins. Of course, if you want to do the odd job around local music halls and it fits in with my timetable, fine. Other than that, forget it.'

'Okay,' agreed Frank, offering his hand. 'It's a deal. When do I start?'

'I've already got builders working. We'll be opening a month to the day,' replied Max, pointedly ignoring the extended hand. 'So you've got just that amount of time to make your farewells to the halls and give a shafting to all those little "Bolivian Bull" worshippers who might do a turn for you.'

'Just a minute,' protested Frank. 'You don't expect me to be celibate when I'm doing this job surely?'

'I most certainly expect you to be celibate on my time and with my girls. What you do on your own time at your own expense is your business.'

Max accompanied Frank to the door and, as he was about to depart, said, 'I'll be in touch in a few days with the final moving-in date. Stay out of trouble till then, eh? Otherwise the deal's off.'

'Don't worry,' laughed Frank, 'I'll be there.'

As Max closed the door Frank's smile vanished to be replaced by a long low muttering and a look of raw hatred as he rubbed his aching groin with the palm of his hand.

'This way down, sir,' announced the aloof Mrs Murgatroyd, showing no more than a cursory interest in a pervert who talked to himself whilst rubbing his groin.

Rediscovering his cigar, which had been neglected from the moment that Frank had tried to strangle him, Max resumed his pondering. He was already sure of the loyalties of Speeches Smith and Buster Slingsby. After all, they had assisted him in incarcerating Reg. Sid and Nathan Green were still unknown quantities. They were shrewd but they may just feel that it was okay being behind a small-time thug like Reg Simmons but any move higher may make them question the risk. He felt he would not miss Sid in the slightest but Nathan could be a handy lad when it came to organisation, and he was particularly perceptive with a definite flair for diplomacy. Max thought this could be an asset when he moved on to the next stage of his plans which could involve the manors of neighbouring villains. If anyone was going to backtrack, he saw it as Long Tom Williams.

If there had been a knock at the front door then Max certainly had not heard it but there was the definite sound of feet on the staircase. 'Mr Williams and both Mr Greens to see you,' murmured Mrs Murgatroyd as she collected their coats.

'I'm much obliged to you, Mrs Murgatroyd. Come in, lads, and take the weight off yer feet. Scotch, everyone?' There was a mumble of general agreement.

'We thought we saw Frank Cootes from our tram,' said Sid. 'Is he coming to this meeting?'

'No,' answered Max. 'He's already been and we've had our little chat.'

'He didn't look very 'appy,' said Long Tom. 'Though thinkin' about it, I s'pose he seldom does.'

'Oh, yes!' responded Max as if the thought had just come to him. 'He – he had a little fall going down my stairs. Probably upset him. Dangerous on the turn those stairs, y'know. You must remember to be careful when you leave.'

'Okay,' said Nathan, quietly but pointedly. 'We've had our little discussion about the dangers of the staircase. Can we now get down to the main business of the day, please?'

Max spent the next ten to fifteen minutes outlining his plans and when he finished there was total silence for almost a full minute.

'Ambitious,' said Nathan. 'Very ambitious. Did you say toms?' Max nodded. 'Who's working these toms? Are you fetching in a madam?'

'If you see Frank Cootes as a madam, then yes I am.'

'Frank Cootes as a madam? Good God, no!' cut in Long

Tom anxiously. 'But I do see Frank Cootes as a *madman*! You can't leave him in charge of girls, he's an apprentice Jack the Ripper.'

'Don't worry about Frank, I've got him under control.'

'Don't *worry about* 'im?' echoed Long Tom incredulously. 'I wouldn't be able to sleep at night!' He bent closer to Max. 'Listen, you can be as clever as you like but all your plans go straight in the shit-'ouse the minute that nutter gets the sniff of a tart when 'e's randy. You could run your mob like Solomon and he'd ruin it the first moment he fancied a bunk-up.'

'So what are you saying to me?' snapped Max.

'I'm sayin' ter you, count me out. It was risky enough working with him when he was just Slicer Simmons' heavy, but at least he was dealing with blokes then. All yer need is one disembowelled tom and we'd all be in it!'

'Look,' said Max calmly, 'I'm going to need girls. I need them for hostesses at the club and I need them for tomming. Now I can handle blokes when they step out of line but girls are different. I like them but I'm not very good with them.'

'So you think putting Frank in charge is the answer?' asked the bewildered Sid.

'Yes, I do, because Frank is answerable to me. As long as he does his job right and does nothing to interest the local law, then great. But the minute he's out of order . . .' Max drew a finger across his own throat.

'I think you're asking too much of him,' said Nathan thoughtfully. 'Put him in charge of the toms or the hostesses if you must, but not *both*. He's not mentally equipped for the responsibility. You'll need somebody else, preferably a woman.'

'You're telling me nothing I don't already know,' agreed Max. But I don't know a woman I could trust enough to fit the bill.'

'Don't you?' asked Nathan quietly. '1 think you do. Not

only do you know her but from what little I've seen of her I'm sure she would be ideal. If you won't have her in complete charge, then why don't you have her as Frank's deputy? She'll report everything to you and you'll not do better.'

'Who then?' asked the puzzled Max, but as he followed Nathan's eyes he realised the identity of the woman. 'Nathan!' he exclaimed. 'That suggestion's inspired! I'm only angry I didn't think of it first!'

'I hate to ruin your party,' said Long Tom, 'but I don't think this set-up is for me. If you don't mind I'll retire gracefully?'

'Anyone else feel that way?' asked Max with a slight chill in his voice.

Sid Green shuffled his feet uncomfortably. 'Yes, Sid? D'you want to say something?'

'Don't get me wrong Max,' said Sid, 'but I'm inclined to go along with Long Tom. I didn't mind running with Reg Simmons but this is a whole different set-up. It's too risky for me.'

'Bigger risks, bigger rewards,' replied Max as he placed his fingertips together, bent his head forward and appeared to go into deep thought for some moments. He suddenly snapped back to life. 'Okay! I'll count you both out but listen to me first. When I was under that floor, the pair of you were on my hate list. But once Reg was out of the way, I suppose I felt slightly more forgiving. Nevertheless you've been two very lucky little boys. Now you can both leave here without – I almost hesitate to use the term – a stain on your character. BUT . . .' he began to emphasise each word by a thrust of his finger '. . . I do not want to see either of you around my manor again! Not no time! Not nowhere! Now get your coats from Mrs Murgatroyd and get your arses out of here. Mrs Murgatroyd!' he yelled and she arrived within seconds. 'Get these gentlemen's coats and show 'em out, please.'

'This way, gentlemen.' She smiled and ushered them smoothly out of the room.

'. . . And mind those stairs!' called Max. 'I'd hate for you to wind up like Frank!'

Once the door was closed, he was prepared for at least a short embarrassed silence from Nathan but it was quite the reverse. 'Right,' he said enthusiastically. 'What's next?'

'You're next, Nathan,' murmured Max. 'Tell me exactly how you stand in this venture?'

'I stand exactly alongside you,' he replied. 'I think it's a great idea. It's something I always thought could be done but really I despaired because I knew Reg Simmons could never run such a show. You're giving me the opportunity I knew I could handle but never saw myself using. Have you got a name?'

'Name?'

'Name for the club,' he explained. 'As soon as you have a name you're halfway there to having it open. You have something to aim at, it gives you a spur. Come on, Max, you must have a name surely?'

'D'you know, Nathan, that's never even crossed my mind. But you're right, I'll certainly have to give it some serious thought.'

'It's easy, just call it Maxie's.'

Max shook his head in disapproval. 'Nah! That's so predictable it's boring. It's got to be a bit different. Give me a day or two and I'll come up with something. Anyway, in the meantime, let's talk about you. The fact that Sid's gone doesn't influence you at all?'

'Sid's my brother but that doesn't mean we're Siamese twins,' Nathan shrugged. 'As it happens I think he's made a wise decision, it was the best course for him but he can go his way and I can go mine without animosity. We're grown-up, sensible Jewish lads, and now our mother – God bless her – has passed away, we don't have to live in each other's pockets any more. So how much?'

Max laughed. 'I was waiting for that. Well now, that depends. You see, I was hoping you'd stay because you could be an important part of this set-up. Buster Slingsby, Speeches, and to a lesser extent Frank are great for what they are but I do need a bit of academic support now and again, to go with my animal cunning, you understand.'

'So how much?' repeated Nathan.

'A score a week. *Or* . . .' smiled Max.

'Phew!' nodded Nathan. 'That's good! But what's with the "*or*"?'

'The "or" is really an incentive. I'll pay you twenty pounds a week cash in your hand, *or* ten per cent of the profits. There's no rush until we open, take your time.'

'I've taken my time,' said Nathan instantly. 'Ten per cent it is.'

Max offered his hand which Nathan readily took. 'I think you're going to prove a sound acquisition, Nathan, I really do.'

'I take it you're using today to inspect your troops?' guessed Nathan. 'You don't think with just Buster, Speeches and Frank you're a little short of front line soldiery?'

'Possibly, but it's something I can assemble later if I find the need arises. There's no shortage in this area of loyal dedicated blokes who would cut their dad's throat if the money was right. If they can earn two quid a week in a factory, for six pounds a week they'd kill nuns . . . Mrs Murgatroyd!' he yelled. 'Mr Green's coat please!' Max walked to the door of the room with Nathan. 'Take good care of Mr Green going down the stairs, will you, Mrs Murgatroyd? At the moment he's the last person I'd like to see fall.'

Max waited by the open door until he heard the street door close behind Nathan. 'Mrs Murgatroyd!' he called again. 'Would you come up here for a moment? I'd like to speak with you.' He returned to the room and, having once more found his dead cigar, awaited her arrival.

'Ah, Mrs Murgatroyd. Sit yourself down, will you? Scotch?'

'Very kind of you. Just a little water please.'

'Mrs Murgatroyd, I have something on my mind but I will need to ask you a few questions first. D'you mind?'

'No, fire away.'

'Mrs Murgatroyd, what are your long-term plans? For example, how do you see your future, say, five to ten years hence?'

'I daren't think about ten *months* hence, so it's easier not to think about ten years hence at all.'

'Mrs Murgatroyd, if I found myself in a position to buy this property, would you care to work for me and live here rent-free?'

'Of course! But what would I have to do?'

Max spent some considerable time thinking how best to talk around the fact that he wanted Mrs Murgatroyd to be second in command of a brothel. After an intensive mental search of his vocabulary, he realised there was none. 'Mrs Murgatroyd, I am opening a club very soon, I will be catering for many tastes. I need someone to assist me to look after – no, perhaps keep in order may be a better phrase – about half a dozen whores and the same number of hostesses. I can gild the lily a bit and give you a posh name if you wish but the job would still be the same – a madam in a knocking-shop.'

'Could I dress like a tart?'

'Could you . . .' Max shook his head. 'I don't understand, Mrs Murgatroyd.'

She gave a protracted sigh then said, 'I've been a quiet little housewife then a widow for all my adult life. I've always been short of money and lived from one day to the next. I never had children. I'm now forty-three years of age and, as far as I can see, all those boring, poverty-stricken years will one day be considered my best and most exciting times. In reality, other than a honeymoon in a bed and breakfast near Hampstead Heath, I have been dead since I was sixteen. If I could live outrageously, if only for a year, I'd die happy.'

'So what's all this about dressing like a tart?'

She blushed slightly. 'Well, I don't think I have a bad figure and . . .'

'Mrs Murgatroyd!' Max laughed. 'You have a knockout figure! If you do a good job for me you can dress like Lady Godiva for all I care. Now listen carefully. I intend to buy these premises and remain at this address. I shall have a flat in the club but this is where I shall get away from it all, so if you wish to stay downstairs that's fine by me. Your clothing will be free, whatever it is that you finally decide to wear, and so will your rent. In addition I will pay you four pounds a week. Suit you?'

'Oh, Mr Roff!' She rushed forward and kissed him full on the lips. 'You'll not regret this, I assure you!'

'No, Mrs Murgatroyd,' he said confidently, 'I don't think I will. Is there anything else you want to know? If so, now's the time.'

'There are two things really. Firstly, will I be expected to have sex with the customers, and if so do I get extra pay? Secondly, why do you call me Mrs Murgatroyd so many times?'

Max roared at this. 'You're a good-looking woman, Mrs Murgatroyd, but I've not employed you to be fucked by the customers. You're there to see that six other people are! As to your name, quite frankly I'm trying it out. I'm thinking of borrowing it.'

'You mean, you're thinking of changing your name?'

'No, but the club needs a name that sticks in people's mem ory. I thought I might call it "Mrs Minnie Murgatroyd's", how does that grab you?'

'Well, it'll be remembered . . . if only by me! Here, would I get paid extra?' she asked hopefully.

Sam shook his head in disbelief. 'Mrs Murgatroyd ! You

may be a late starter but I see you're catching up bloody quick!' He sniffed suddenly and scrabbled madly down the side of his chair. 'Here, have you seen my cigar? It's alight somewhere!'

Chapter 16

For Queenie, the first four years of the twins' life were little more than a blurred eternity. She had no clear recollection of dates or milestones in either hers or the children's life during that period. All she could remember was the incessant weariness. Living from day to day meant nothing could be planned and every single item could be purchased only when there was sufficient cash in her purse. This in turn meant taking the twins up and down those ninety-six steps three, four, sometimes six times each day. Sam had certainly been a good father but the hated split shifts of four hours on, four hours off, four hours on again, were the bane of every police officer's family, particularly as each constable was forbidden to wear civilian clothes during his four hours off. In effect, with the compulsory wearing of uniform during travelling time, this was a daily fourteen-hour duty. One great blessing was the twins' ability to sleep – which was just as well seeing as they slept together in the corner of the living room with just a curtain to cut them off from a room that served as kitchen, lounge, laundry, bathroom and dining-room.

In conversation with other mothers, Queenie found that the Buildings kids fell into two categories: those who, because of the many noises and distractions, rarely slept at all, and those like David and Emma who slept through just about everything, mice and bed-bugs included. Without this benefit Queenie felt she would be suicidal. She had only three fits during those four years and on each occasion was at home. Her sister-in-law Jane had been a Godsend. In fact, Jane had been wonderful with the children. Not yet having any of her own she practically shared their upbringing. Just a few hearty knocks on the wall was enough to bring her running. Queenie's one great dread was that her neighbours would move house. Jim had recently been promoted and was now a sergeant at Brixton and, in order to remain near his friends, had already turned down one move into police quarters. However, if Jane became pregnant, they would be insane not to move.

As time passed, the two women had become very close, which was just as well seeing as their menfolk were absent for such long hours. For policemen the period was particularly turbulent, with social unrest, Fenian bombs, violent strikes and riots. A persistent source of irritation though was the Suffragette movement. After one particularly violent day of attacks on both police and property, Sam returned home furious and was unable to show his customary restraint whilst discussing the subject with Queenie. What angered him most was the contrast in behaviour with their generally respectable, middle-class background. He had always felt an affinity with workers striking for a reduction from a seventy-two-hour working week but what he could not understand was: 'A load of parasitical toffee-nosed middle-class bitches who have sod all better to do than run around deliberately trying to get nicked. I tell you,' he said, waving a furious finger at his wife, 'they are worse to reason with than six drunken matelots and the next Suffragette who grabs my balls gets my truncheon down her throat!'

Although abhorring Suffragettes as a group, he saved his real vitriol for the Pankhurst family. When Queenie tried to explain that many of these people he scorned so readily performed excellent voluntary work amongst London's poor, he exploded: 'But they're only sodding part-time!

They're playing a game! They do it because it placates their conscience. As soon as things get sticky they piss off to Paris!'

Sensing the rise in temperature, Queenie rose from the table and placed her arms around her husband's neck, whispering, 'It just shows how much I love you that I listen to you talk like that and don't push you off the roof. Kiss me, you prejudiced pig.' For Sam, though the embrace was pleasurable, the gesture of affection was a façade and Queenie well knew it. There was no doubt whatever of their love for each other but the seemingly neverending poverty and the dread of fits and pregnancy caused Queenie to freeze when it came to anything more than a cuddle.

'It's terror, nothing but damned terror,' she confided tearfully to Jane next morning. 'You're either born to it or you're not. I want him to love me, I really do. I want to feel him inside me, I want more of his children, but then I see what's going on around me and I know I could never be as brave as women like your mother.' She gave a forced little laugh. 'It's so ironic that occasionally at night, when I'm weeping with frustration, I can hear you and Jim trying so hard to achieve the one thing I'm terrified of having.'

'Queenie!' exclaimed the red-faced Jane. 'You can't hear us making love, surely?'

'Only if it's particularly quiet,' she assured her. 'Though what old Mother Butler underneath thinks when her gas-lamp keeps jumping around, heaven only knows.'

'Speaking of family additions, you've reminded me,' said Jane, trying hastily to change the subject. 'How do you feel about sharing a cat? It'll keep the mice down.'

'How on earth d'you share a cat?' asked Queenie. 'D'you stuff it and cut it in half?'

'Jim suggested running a wooden shelf between our two balconies at the rear. It's too far for the cat to jump but she could walk across it easily enough, they're very sure-footed creatures. I've noticed several flats have something similar.'

'I can't see much wrong with the idea,' mused Queenie. 'The twins would love it, I'm sure.'

'D'you want to check with Sam?'

'Good God, no! I'm an independent Suffragette woman, I know if I want a cat or not! In fact, that's decided me, I'll definitely have it now. What's its name?'

'Hasn't got one yet, it's only a kitten, but if we want it to catch mice it's got to be fearless. How about "Boadicea"?'

'Boadicea it is then,' agreed Queenie. 'Just a minute though, what's its surname – Diamond or Forsythe?'

'Good point,' said Jane. 'What say we call it Boadicea Diamond-Forsythe?'

'By George! It's never one of the Cheltenham Diamond-Forsythes, is it?'

'*Are* there any others?' asked Jane in a haughty tone as both girls collapsed laughingly into each other's arms.

'A cat?' asked Sam late that evening. 'What on earth do we want a cat for?'

'Mice, of course,' replied Queenie.

'I can catch mice in traps, I'd be more impressed if it could catch bed-bugs, they're as elusive as ghosts. Anyway, how do the twins feel about it?'

'They're so excited I wish I hadn't told them. I should have let it come as a surprise when it arrives tomorrow.'

'Daddy,' came a sleepy voice from behind the curtain. 'Has Bow-ded-derra come yet?'

Sam shot a quick glance at Queenie before turning his attention to the curtained bed. 'Has *who* come yet, sweetie?'

'Bow-ded-derra, our new pussy,' explained the child.

'Queenie,' he whispered, 'what's this Bow-ded-derra she's on about?'

'It's the new cat's name,' hissed Queenie. 'It's actually Boadicea.'

He gave a forced groan. 'Boadicea indeed! There's your bloody middle-class background for you! Why can't you call it "Puss" like everyone else? I can see now why you were a Suffragette.' He went over and parted the bed curtains. David was sound asleep on the far side of the bed wedged firmly against the heavily embossed wallpaper. Four small bed-bugs were making tenuous trails through the regency pattern steadily towards his right ear. Emma was kneeling upright with a pudding round face and wide wondering eyes. 'Can Bow-ded-derra come to bed with me, Daddy?'

Sam leaned across and flicked the bugs into the palm of his hand. 'She's not coming till tomorrow, darling,' he whispered. 'But she won't be able to sleep in your bed with you. Tell you what. How about on my next day off we make her a little basket that she can sleep in, would you like that?'

Emma nodded vigorously.

'Okay, must be quiet now or you'll wake David. G'night, darling.' He gave her one big kiss and gently drew the curtain before stepping out on to the stone balcony floor and squashing flat the quartet of blood-sucking bugs.

A few minutes later, as Queenie poured tea, Sam settled into his old armchair. 'I went to Flat Iron Square today, Sam, and guess who I saw?'

'Give in.'

'Remember that horrible man you fought at the music hall?'

Sam looked up instantly. 'Frank Cootes . . . The Bolivian Bull or some such toffee.'

'That's him! Anyway, he offered me a job. A club opened there a year or two ago and he said they were still looking for staff, young ladies mainly.'

'Which way d'you go to Flat Iron Square? Not by Red Cross Street by any chance?'

'Well . . .' she faltered. 'Yes, I s'pose it was really. It's the only direct way.'

'It's the direct way to getting yourself robbed – or worse! I've told you enough times about that street haven't I? Did you have the twins with you?'

'Well, of course I did! No one's going to rob me, I don't have anything!'

'Don't you?' he asked pointedly. 'What do you think Frank Cootes wanted then?'

'He wanted me to go for an interview, that's all. He gave me a date and a time.'

'You must have had some conversation. Did he tell you what sort of a job it was?'

'No, but I thought if it was a bit, well, you know, out of the way like, perhaps I could do it without the police finding out. If they paid you more than starvation wages we wouldn't need this subterfuge. We badly need the money, Sam, and he said he might be able to fix me up part-time.'

'Oh, he'd fix you up part-time right enough but you don't know how funny that is.'

'So what's so funny about someone offering me a part-time job that I desperately need?'

'The club to which he referred belongs to Maxie Roff. Remember him? My old school mate? Well, it's proving a right pain in the arris for Stones End nick, mainly because whenever they manage to get in, all the evidence has long gone.'

'Oh, I see!' laughed Queenie. 'And you think it's funny that because the local police can't get in to raid it, they should offer me a job without realising I'm a policeman's wife!'

'No, Queenie, strange as it may seem, it's not *that* I find hysterical. What *I* find hysterical is the fact that as soon as I make any move towards your body, you seize up like a petrified clam. But Frank Cootes offers you a job as a part-time whore and you're thinking of going for an interview! Don't *you* think it's funny?'

The horror on her face told Sam his arrow had struck home with an impact he had never imagined. She rose quickly from the chair and ran into their bedroom-cum-parlour, closing the door sharply behind her. Sam was about to follow but paused to check the children. They were sleeping peacefully without a bed-bug in sight. When he entered the darkened room Queenie was standing by the open window, silhouetted clearly against the August night sky. Her perfect figure reminded him exactly why Frank Cootes had sounded her out. He thought had he been a ponce himself he would probably have done the same thing.

She made no move or protest as he eased behind her and slid his arms around her waist, although an occasional tear did drop on to his hands. 'The last time you did this, Sam, I was looking out across the Goodwin Sands and hadn't a care in the world.' She gave a short ironic laugh. 'The joke was certainly on me tonight though, wasn't it? I lay for you in that room in Ramsgate . . . for you to do anything you wished with me.' She turned slowly and faced him, 'I loved you so much I would certainly have been your *whore* if you'd asked me. For the first time in my life I felt totally free and unshackled. I would have done with you, and for you, Sam, anything that two people in love would ever – could ever – do. So what's become of me? Why am I like this now? You were right, you know. What was it you called me . . . a "petrified clam"? Not a bad description, I'd say. Perhaps I needed to be reminded that, after all, you are my husband and you do have rights.'

She ripped so hard at her blouse that the buttons flew off into the dark, striking odd pieces of furniture. He looked on stunned as, crying and sobbing, she tugged and tore until everything she wore was either ripped or ragged. She then threw herself back on the bed and spread her legs as wide as she could. 'What d'you reckon I'm worth, Sam? Thirty bob? A pound? Oh, not that good, eh? Okay, I had two shillings in my purse today. Top it and I'm yours – let's say three shillings, how's that suit you? You're married to a three-bob whore!'

Without a word Sam rose and walked slowly into the living room and closed the door silently behind him. Between her sobs Queenie could hear faint muted sounds of two people next-door doing their very best to swing Mrs Butler's gas-lamp again.

Sam parted the children's bed-curtain and gently lifted Emma across towards her brother. He slipped in alongside her and replaced the curtain. The mere act of closing it caused him to feel removed from the rest of the world. He was a child again, sharing a bed with two other children, just like his childhood had always been. A child ran errands and played in the street, a child didn't consort with bandits, thieves, Suffragettes, wife-beaters and whores. That's it, he would stay a child. He cuddled up to Emma and fell swiftly asleep.

'Is Bow-ded-derra here yet, Daddy?' came the whisper in Sam's ear. He blinked and stared around him. What the hell was the curtain doing? Oh my God! What on earth was the time? He was on duty at 5.45 a.m. and already daylight filled the room.

'Daddy, is Bow-ded-derra—'

'No, love, no, not yet she's not. It's still very early and mummy isn't very well. Turn over and go to sleep again, eh? Auntie Jane will fetch Bow-ded-derra in later. There's a good girl.' Again he searched for the time. He turned over his old turnip-watch that lay on the chair by the bed. Phew! Five o'clock. Could have been worse. He braved a cold-water wash at the sink, followed by an even braver cold-water shave. If he was to arrive at Tower Bridge for a 5.45 a.m. parade, then there was no time for breakfast. In fact there was not a second to spare. Yet he knew he could not leave without first seeing Queenie. The door to the staircase adjoined the still-closed door of the bedroom and he paused. He suddenly felt the same hint of nausea he always experienced whenever he needed to open an unknown door. Gripping the handle firmly he eased open the door. He reeled back in horror and heard a voice he hardly recognised as his own. 'My God, she's dead!'

The window was still open and Queenie lay naked on the bed in the identical wide-legged pose that had not left his mind from those earlier hours. He rushed to her side and was appalled how cold she was. True, the night had not been cold but she had lain unmoving and naked beneath an open window for hours. He closed her thighs, threw the blankets around her and began to rub vigorously.

'Come on, darling, come on,' he kept muttering. As a thought struck him he ran to the wall and pounded it with his fists. He resumed the massage until he heard a nearby window open and Jim Forsythe's sleepily inquiring tone: 'Sam?'

'Quick, Jim – Queenie!' Though the words were brief they conveyed all that needed to be said and within minutes he could hear the hurried footsteps of both his neighbours.

'Sam,' exclaimed Jane as she quickly took in the scene. 'What on earth . . . she's all but naked . . . and half dead. WHAT HAVE YOU DONE TO HER, SAM?

'We had a row but that'll keep. Look, let's get her warm again, for heaven's sake.'

'She must go to hospital,' pointed out Jim.

'But don't you see?' blurted Jane. 'She'll be dead before we get her there! Rub . . . Rub . . . RUB!'

'Listen, Jane,' said Jim urgently. 'We'll keep massaging her here and you run across to Stones End station and get them to telephone for an ambulance. Tell them not to come up the stairs when they arrive but just give a yell. We'll carry her down, it'll be quicker that way. Then get them to telephone Tower Bridge to say that Sam's going to be late, if he arrives at all.'

'But how about the children?' she asked.

'Take a quick look before you go,' snapped Jim with increasing irritation, 'but do get moving! We must get her to hospital!'

'Then either take those rags off her, or put something on her a bit more substantial. They'll think Jack the Ripper's been at her,' she replied with equal irritation. 'And if she's got to go to hospital, take her clothes and a top coat or she'll have to come home nude.'

Before Jane could reach the curtain, a sleepy little voice inquired as to the reasons for the persistent delay of the arrival of one 'Bow-ded-derra'.

Within a few minutes Sam and Jim had bundled Queenie into every blanket available and carried her down ninety-six stairs like a roll of lino. The ambulance threaded its way through the maze of early market traffic and soon entered Guy's hospital. Queenie lay cocooned in blankets from head to foot with her husband holding one hand and her brother-in-law the other. 'How much more of your life are you going to spend taking me to hospitals, Sam?'

'Dunno,' he said with a false air of indifference. 'But if you were a football match, I'd give serious thought to a season ticket.'

'How are the twins?'

'They seemed okay, Jane's looking after them, but it's going to be a long time before she forgives you for telling Emma about that bloody cat.'

'And David?'

'David doesn't give a damn. I think half the bugs in Queen's Buildings were after his ear last night but he just sleeps through it. Queenie, what happened last night? I don't mean our fight. I mean what happened after I slept with the twins? Why did you not go to bed, or at the very least dress?'

'Er – I'm afraid I can't leave whilst we're still moving,' interrupted Jim. 'But if you two would like to be on your own, I'll leap out at the hospital gates.'

'No, stay where you are, Jim, please,' requested Sam. 'There can't be much you haven't guessed anyway.'

Queenie propped herself up and stared at her husband in apparent puzzlement. 'But I thought I did go to bed! Anyway, what are you talking about? Why did you sleep with the twins? What fight? And why am I so damn' cold?'

'You mean you have no recollection of last night at all?' he asked incredulously. 'You remember no conversation, no tearing of clothes?'

'Get me out of here, Sam, I've simply had a fit. I'm over it now and we both know there's nothing more that hospitals can do. Just take me home and get me warm. I want you to tell me exactly what happened last night.'

In truth, the Guy's staff were more than pleased with Queenie's request for an immediate discharge. They made a token protest but once she had received a statutory roasting from matron, no obstacles were placed in her way. By the time the trio left the hospital arm-in-arm, the sun was already promising a bright warm day. Queenie's body temperature, though by no means normal, climbed rapidly. Jim chatted freely on the slow walk home but Sam remained deep in thought as, over and over, he ran though his mind the obscenity of the previous night.

The threesome were greeted at the flat by a very impatient four-year-old who announced that, together with her aunt, her brother and a large cardboard box, she was off to purchase a Bow-ded-derra. 'I'll keep them for a couple of hours or so,' whispered Jane. 'Give you a chance to settle.' Jim too made his farewell and joined his wife and the children descending the stairs.

As the footsteps faded, Queenie made to slip off her coat but when she was halfway through the move Sam pinned her arms to her sides. 'You swear you have no recollection of anything you said here last night?' he demanded.

'Do I have to swear to you now, Sam?' she asked quietly. 'Once you would have taken my word for anything.'

He released her immediately and raised both hands in apology. 'You're right, I'm sorry.'

'So what *did* take place last night?' she asked.

He sighed deeply. 'A lot of things were said that would have been best left unsaid. If you have no recollection of them then I'd say you're fortunate. I suggest you take the opportunity for a little nap before the children return. I'll need to go to work soon so the place will be quiet.'

'Sam, you're telling me a conversation took place here last night between us that seems to have upset you more than anything I can remember. Are you also saying I am now not to know it? Which of us said these terrible things, you or me?'

He shook his head. 'Dunno, perhaps we both did. Look, it's forgotten now except that the distress of it caused you to have another fit. D'you realise how lucky we've been? If it was any time other than August you would have been dead by now.'

'Why did you not sleep with me, Sam?' she asked. 'Why did you sleep with the children?'

He seized her roughly. 'It was all part of it, don't you see?' he demanded. 'The fact that you can't remember means we're halfway to a cure. All it needs now is for me to forget . . . and I'm working on that. But I'll not bloody manage it if you keep trying to prise it out of me every few minutes. Now go to bed and let me go to work.' He gave her the lightest of kisses and was gone.

It seemed she had not been asleep for more than minutes when the distant sounds of children's chatter reached her. 'Eighty-nine . . . ninety . . . ninety-one . . .' Emma had yet to count the entire ninety-six steps correctly.

'Fifty-four . . . fifty-five . . .'

'Auntie Jane, he's made me lose count! He's always doing that. Mummy said he's very naughty.'

'Hush! Mummy may still be asleep. We'll tip-toe in and see, shall we?'

'And can we show her Bow-ded-derra?'

'Oh, I should think so, dear.'

As the key turned in the door Queenie saw at least three hours had elapsed since they had left. She slipped quickly out of bed and ran to her sister-in-law.

'Oh, bless you, Jane,' she cried, throwing her arms around her. 'I don't know what I'd have done without you these last twenty-four hours. You've saved my sanity.'

The children were full of excitement about the new kitten, though whether the animal shared this excitement was questionable. Both women sat on the edge of the bed drinking tea. In answer to Jane's inquiry as to her health, Queenie faltered badly.

Jane suddenly turned to her friend and said sharply, 'Queenie, look me straight in the eye and tell me you are fine.' She made no reply but turned her head and gazed over the rooftops. 'Do you want to talk about it? You don't *have* to, y'know, but they say it helps.' Jane shrugged. 'Not sure I agree with that. Sometimes it makes matters ten times worse but at the moment I think you'd chance anything.'

As Queenie began to recount the events of the previous evening, her friend listened in ever increasing horror. 'So did you faint, have a fit, or what? You're never normally comatose for that length of time, are you?'

In spite of the heat of that August afternoon, Queenie shuddered. 'Yes,' she agreed, 'I did have a fit. I must have been unconscious for an hour or so, I suppose. But then I slowly came around and . . .' Her voice trailed away.

'And?' prodded Jane.

'I lay there and began to think about my own inadequacies, about Sam, about the children, about the future

. . . and, although I was so cold, I wasn't uncomfortable. I somehow felt detached. I hadn't moved from the time I threw myself on to that bed and I suddenly thought perhaps this could be the best answer. The only thing that bothered me was dying with my legs open! It seemed so undignified. I was in no pain, in fact I was almost comfortable, I just felt a little numb, that's all. I remember reading somewhere about Scott in the Antarctic. It said if you are trapped in the cold you must never fall asleep or you won't wake up.' She gave a hard little laugh. 'Never waking up suddenly seemed very attractive.'

'And that's why you pretended to Sam you had no recollection of last night?'

'Yes.'

'But how about the children?' persisted the bewildered Jane.

'I just thought they could have a better life with you.' Queenie shook her head in frustration. 'I can guess what you think of me, Jane, but I can't begin to tell you how desperate I felt. It just eats away at me all the time.'

'But why didn't you tell Sam, or even me, how badly you felt?'

'Your brother's a lovely man, Jane, he'd walk through fire, fight lions and doubtless even die for me. But what he's totally incapable of doing is making any move at all to *understand* me. I don't blame him for that because it's just not in him. Did your father ever attempt to understand anything at all about your mother?'

Jane sighed. 'No,' she agreed reluctantly. 'I must grant you that. But how about me? D'you think it's not in me either?'

'Dear Jane, of course it's in you. That's why you're sitting here now listening to me and that's why I'm telling you.'

'And Sam . . .' asked Jane. 'Will you tell him?'

'No, but don't worry, it'll never happen again.'

'How can you be so sure?'

'Because of Emma and a kitten in a box. As soon as I saw her I knew how weak I'd been. From now on I've stopped lying down and I'm a fighter. If it's me and my kids against the rest of the world, then so be it. I tell you this, Jane – and you're the only one I would tell – if I knew a way where I would not conceive again, I'd be round to Frank Cootes' club in an instant. I'm poor and I hate it.'

Jane stared at her sister-in-law as if she was seeing her for the first time. 'Yes, I think you're quite right, I think you have stopped lying down and you and your kids may well take on the world. I just hope my brother sees it your way, but I doubt it.'

'And you, Jane, how do you see it?'

She smiled and, leaning forward, kissed her sister-in-law on the cheek. Her answer was interrupted by hastening footsteps on the staircase outside. 'That's Sam,' exclaimed Queenie, shooting a quick glance at the clock. 'He was so late for work that I never expected him home for hours yet. Hope he's all right.'

David, who could now just reach the latch, also recognised the footsteps and ran to open the door. Sam ruffled the child's hair but his face betrayed concern in a way his vocabulary could never match.

'Sam! Whatever's the matter?' asked Queenie, rising from the bed.

'All our little troubles have been placed into perspective now, gel,' he said wearily. 'They've sent many of us home for a few hours because our free time in future may well be limited.'

'But why?' insisted Jane.

'As from today, 4 August, we're at war with Germany. They're saying it'll all be over by Christmas but I'm not so sure. I just hope all those buggers in government know what they're doing . . . but I doubt it.'

Chapter 17

Most of the day clients had left and the early evening ones had only just begun to sidle into the club as Max made his way around the card tables and into his compact and secure top-floor office. Since he had opened two similar clubs in Fulham and Battersea, he had been spending less time in Minnie Murgatroyd's and had decided to make up for this neglect.

It had been a hot and sticky summer and Max was not sorry to see it drawing to its close. The one big mistake made in the extensive renovations had been in the ventilation, or rather lack of it. Though tolerable in winter, with a crowded attendance and a hot evening it could be stifling in summer. This was not helped by the fact that, amongst his particular clientele, those who gambled most, washed least. A huge brass-bladed fan hung from the ceiling and swished slow lethargic circuits but it did little else to disturb the heavy air.

He unlocked the solid office door and was once more grateful for the huge chimney-stack that shaded his window from the full glare of the sun. Having taken off his jacket, he had begun to unclasp his case when he noticed a scattered pile of post lying on his desk. One problem with dividing his time between three locations, four if he counted his flat, was this problem of post. Sometimes urgent matters could easily be overlooked. He had begun to thumb through the envelopes when he was interrupted by the collective entry of Buster Slingsby, Frank Cootes,

Speeches Smith and Minnie. 'Nathan's on his way up,' informed Buster. 'He's on the staircase at the moment chatting to Glasgow Gert.'

'After a staff discount, y'reckon?' suggested Speeches in thoughtful observation.

'More like a scab on 'is dick,' muttered Frank in a rare attempt at humour.

'Yeah? Well, don't even joke about it, Frank,' snapped Max. 'Because any girl who puts as much as an *itch* around this place is out in the street in a flash, which is exactly one split second after you.'

Before they had a chance to discuss the respective merits of Nathan, Glasgow Gert and the pox, the door swung open yet again to reveal the smiling and splendidly suited Nathan Green. 'Nice you've decided to join us,' said Max, without looking up.

'That's some suit!' marvelled the impressed Buster. 'You look like a pox doctor's clerk. What d'you wear for encores?'

'I think higher management should always look the part,' replied Nathan haughtily.

'Nathan, Nathan,' said Max. 'Let's keep our feet on the floor, eh? You're not "higher management", you're a ponce, Nathan. A ponce, geddit?' He shook his head in mock reproach. 'Nothing to distress yourself about, being a ponce, Nathan. It's an ancient and honourable occupation. Ask Frank. As long as there are toms and clients there'll be ponces, and never more so than in wartime. You are doing your bit for your country just as much as those poor buggers on the Somme. By the way, if you've a scab on your dick, you're sacked.'

Having suitably deflated Nathan, Max addressed himself to the main business of the day. 'Okay, lads and Minnie, pay attention, I've been doing a bit of research. How long has this war been going on for?' He looked expectantly around his audience.

'Two years?' offered Frank.

'V-e-r-y good, Frank,' encouraged Max. 'Two years it is, and do you know where most of our money comes from now?'

'Toms?' said Nathan.

'Dead right,' said Max, warming to his subject. 'With all the brave soldiers in town you couldn't really odds it. However, if you cast your mind back a couple of years, they were telling us that the war would be over within four months. Well we're into our third year and we're deeper in the shit than ever. Now if there's one thing that's really got worse, it's the food shortage. There's a lot of people ready to pay a lot of money for the right gear and I think it's time we did something about it.'

'There's one obvious big difficulty with that,' commented Nathan quietly. 'It's space. Where are you going to store it?'

'We're not going to,' replied Max. 'Apart from lack of space, it's too risky. What we are going to do is go into the wholesale business. We'll find out what's wanted in bulk – in bulk, mind – and we'll collect it from source then deliver it to whatever outlets require it. That way we'll have no property other than the vehicles. Our risk will be cut by two-thirds, I reckon.'

'So who's delivering?' asked Speeches suspiciously. 'Seeing as I'm the only one who can drive.'

'Don't worry, Speeches, old son, you'll be fire-proof.' Max rose and walked over to the window. 'Out there, in South London alone, are scores of well-trained drivers who are just itching for a chance to drive again *and* we'd be doing our bit for our country in the bargain.'

'So who are all these "well-trained-drivers", and how d'you know they'll want to work for us?' asked Buster.

'They are drivers who've been invalided out of the army. There were two hundred of them in London alone after the first four months of the war. Okay, so many of them are too disabled to drive again but likewise many of them are not. What could be better? An ex-hero driving our lorries. Not only are we helping them find their feet again but what hard-hearted copper would question a hero? Good God, they'd string him up to a lamp-post round here.'

'So how about my toms?' scowled Frank. 'What's happening to them ?'

'Frank,' said Max wearily, 'for the umpteenth time, they are not *your* toms and I should think most of them would be appalled if told they were. You're just their minder. Anyway, it's nothing for you to concern yourself with. Black marketeering is not your currency. In that game you have to bargain and to bargain with someone you need to be polite. That rules you out straight away, Frank. While you're here though, tell me, are we getting many Empire troops in the place?'

Still smarting from Max's tongue, Frank was at first slow to reply but eventually conceded, 'We get 'em in bursts. I fink they're a bit suspicious about crossin' the river on their own. They fink they might get their froat cut or somethin'. Trouble is, they come mob-handed and, if they're a bit pissy, they're a real pain in the arse.'

Max grunted an acknowledgement before addressing the others. 'Seeing as we're a bit away from Piccadilly and such like and particularly seeing as we can't very well advertise, this place has got to be sold to customers on word of mouth. This is especially so with Empire troops. So make a fuss of them.' He turned to Minnie. 'Get the girls to keep the odd bottle of scotch in their rooms. You know, hospitality and all that. I don't want it full, mark you, just a few inches at the bottom. It could be a good investment.'

'Who'll be paying for it?' asked Minnie.

'Paying for it?' echoed Max. 'Just get it from the bar, it's easy.'

'No,' argued Minnie. 'It's *not* easy. If I order five-bobs

worth of scotch from the bar, he'll expect me to pay five bob. Then if I do that, there are at least three girls here who'll sell half of it and water down the rest.'

'All except Glasgow Gert,' muttered Speeches mournfully. 'She'd piss in the bottle and sell the lot.'

Max gave a long sigh and raised his eyes to the ceiling. 'What the fuck am I running here?' he exploded. 'This is not a cheap knocking shop, this is a high-class *expensive* knocking shop and I expect high-class behaviour, not scruffy Scots whores pissing in bottles!' He shook his head in disappointment. 'Okay, scrub the free booze idea but it certainly looks like I need to spend a bit more time here in future.' He glanced down at his watch. 'Anyone got anything else they'd like to fetch up while the opportunity's here?'

'Turbans,' said Frank. 'I'm 'avin' problems wiv' geezers in turbans. I'm never sure wot ter do wiv 'em. Should I sling 'em out?'

'What's the matter with turbans?' asked the puzzled Max.

'Well, very few of 'em drink for starters and they don't want girls, they want boys. I don't really know what ter do. Should I try an' get 'em some young nancy boys from somewhere?'

'No!' Max thundered. 'I want no boys or kids, understand? We're not in the market for that sort of thing. So in future, the house rule is *no turbans*! Is there anything else?'

'Max,' said Nathan, 'if we are going to maintain any sort of standard here, we definitely need more staff.'

'What sort of staff, I thought we had enough girls?'

'Oh, girls are no problem, they're ten a penny. Two months here and they think they're millionairesses. No, it's cleaners, bar-staff and errand-runners we want. We've deliberately avoided employing too many local people for security reasons but we're getting desperate.'

'Wait a minute, what's an errand-runner?'

'Well, sometimes a client might want cigarettes, newspapers, a stamp or even a letter posted. If they're a good customer and spending well, it's more economical to send someone out to a local shop for them.'

'Letters posted!' exclaimed Max 'How many of them come here to write letters, for heaven's sake?'

'*They* don't write them. Many of our clients are illiterate and not all our girls are stupid, y'know. At least four are very well educated.'

'Surely they don't pay a tom good money for her to write letters!' persisted Max.

'You'd be amazed,' corrected Minnie. 'Big Rita has a regular Queenslander who has yet to lay a hand on her. He just stands and watches while she sits in the nude writing letters for him – sometimes even *to* him – though for that she usually charges extra.' She shook her head sadly. 'And as if that's not bad enough, the poor sod can't read.'

'This . . . er . . . Queenslander, how often does he come here?'

'Certainly every week. Actually we do quite well out of him because we put him in a room with an observation panel and rent out a couple of viewing slots for five shillings each.'

'Let me get this straight,' said the confused Max. 'You're telling me we have people who pay, to watch people who pay, to watch people write letters to the people who pay?'

'That's about the strength of it,' agreed Minnie 'Then they pay an errand-runner to post them.'

'And just think,' said Max philosophically, 'my mum wanted me to be a postman!'

'This is not helping me in my quest for new staff,' said Nathan irritably. 'Can I enrol local folk or can't I?'

Max sucked on his teeth for a moment. 'I think I'll give

you a reluctant yes on that one, Nathan. If you say we need them, then we need them. But let's see if we can be a bit selective though. We'll try to use dependants of blokes who are away at the war. They'll be grateful for the extra money and less likely to blow the whistle on us.'

'I'm pretty well known locally, I'll interview a few if yer like,' offered Frank.

'Good God, man, no!' responded Max. 'They'll take one look at you and they'll think you're recruiting for the Kaiser. Thanks, Frank, but no, this is the perfect job for Minnie. So go to it, girl, and remember, no errand-runners under ten years of age and only those whose dads are soldiers or sailors. Got it?' Without waiting for a reply, Max rose to his feet and placed his papers in his attaché case. 'I'm off to Fulham but I'm back here tomorrow.'

The rest also began to rise and Max was halfway to the door when Minnie reminded him that his letters remained unopened. 'Been there for several days some of them have,' she admonished. Max returned to his chair and, placing his feet on the desk, methodically sliced through each envelope. His face remained impassive until he reached one sporting an official-looking stamp. His expression changed first into a frown then into one of horror as he slowly absorbed the full significance of the contents.

'MINNIE!' he yelled at the open door. 'MINNIE! Come quickly!'

The quick patter of feet told him urgency had been conveyed as the breathless woman soon stood, bosom heaving, before him. 'Whatever is it?'she asked anxiously.

He slid the letter across the desk towards her and her eyes quickly scanned the short formal paragraphs. 'It's wicked!' she announced 'They can't make you. Request to see your MP.'

'It's my bloody MP who's partly responsible,' complained Max. 'As I have no interest in this sodding war, other than keeping the troops happy, I can't see why I should be expected to fight in it. Let those who want it have it, I say, but keep the rest of us out of it.'

'Still, you never know,' she said hopefully. 'You may fail the medical, then they won't need you.'

Max obviously saw no hope of salvation in that. 'Look at me, do I look like I'd fail a medical?'

'No,' she wavered. 'But you never know with medicals.' She waved generally at his torso. 'All sorts of things could be wrong in there without a soul knowing it.' She studied a small diary she kept in her pocket. 'What's that date of that medical again?'

'Monday week,' he said in a tone that showed it was already engraved on his mind.

At first she searched for something sympathetic to say. Failing that she suddenly asked, 'What would happen if you didn't attend?'

'That wouldn't work,' he said. 'It tells you on the back that failure to report means you'll be in the nick within the hour.'

'But how about if you were so very ill that you'd be wasting everyone's time if you appeared, what then?'

'You couldn't just *say* that,' he pointed out with increasing irritation, 'because if you could, everyone would be doing it. You'd need something like a doctor's certificate.'

'So what's the problem?' she asked.

'What's the—' he fumed. 'What doctor would give me a certificate for God's sake? I'm twenty-eight years of age, six foot two, thirteen stone and tough as old boots. I'm doomed, I tell you, bloody doomed.' To emphasise the exact degree of impending doom, he buried his head dramatically in his hands.

She leaned over the desk and kissed him lightly on the crown of his head. 'On the contrary, don't give up hope yet, I have an idea.'

He raised his head instantly. 'Minnie Murgatroyd, if you can get me off the hook on this one, I'll—'

'You'll what?'

'Never mind that now, just tell me what you have in mind.'

'I won't *tell* you but if you are here in, say,' she glanced at the clock, 'an hour and fifty minutes' time, you may understand a whole lot better. Okay?'

He nodded in mute obedience.

'Don't worry,' she said, turning at the door. 'It's going to be all right, trust me.'

As he sat alone in the small room, he suddenly realised the war might yet turn out to be a personal experience. Previously it had been something for others to concern themselves with. Little over a hundred miles distant, over a million had already died, yet he had felt so far removed he wasn't even an interested bystander. He was like a soup seller outside a stadium whose only interest in the game was to sell his produce to those flocking in. The bigger the game, the more he sold. Well, this war was a big game right enough and so far millions had flocked in. The way it was going, millions more could well follow them. There was a fortune to be made on the outside, nothing on the inside. In any case, he knew he would never make a good soldier. Taking orders was not his forte. In a face-to-face combat with some fat Jerry he would be fine but buried deep in mud whilst a distant kraut did his best to hit him with a ton of high explosives never appealed.

He went through the motions of reading the dozen or so letters that littered the desk and even produced a pen at one stage with the intention of replying to some but he never went beyond 'Dear Sir' and the date.

It seemed an eternity before Minnie returned to lead him mysteriously downstairs into a dingy and none too clean first-floor store-room. 'Remember now, you must not speak.' A remark she emphasised by placing her left forefinger upon his lips.

He followed her around numerous tea-chests and boxes until they arrived at a wooden partition that ran from floor to ceiling. Halfway up the wall in large painted letters read the word 'SILENCE'. Twin black velvet curtains hung down from the partition, each partially covering a high wooden stool. She ushered him on to the left stool and tucked the curtain completely around him whilst he gathered from her movements that she had joined him on the right.

A thin slot was cut into the partition and, whilst narrow, was some nine inches in length and gave a surprisingly clear panoramic view into the next room. He heard a well-spoken male voice giving directions, though the sound was not sufficiently clear for the orders to be decipherable. In the centre of his field of vision was a large double bed and laying face down and naked upon its covers was the buxom Glasgow Gert. For a second or two, Max was puzzled as to her actions. She appeared to be simulating intercourse, but why? Then he suddenly realised that directly beneath her was a new young Cornish girl, who, being somewhat slimmer, had not been immediately noticeable. Even at the distance he was from the frolicking pair, their spectacularly artificial moans of pleasure caused him to squirm with embarrassment. Great whore she may be, he thought, actress she's not. Again there was an indecipherable command and, in response, Glasgow Gert began to move her mouth slowly down and around the young girl's body. Max had the feeling that this action should have been at least slightly erotic but although he could not see either girl's face, he had the feeling there was a grave danger of both bursting into giggles. As the Scots whore's mouth reached the thighs of the young girl, a third party appeared. It was the owner of the well-spoken voice. He was a round-faced man of about fifty, quite portly and of average height with thick centre-parted silvery hair. He was a gentle, kindly-looking soul who looked about as at home naked in a brothel as a hedgehog in a nudist colony. As the kindly-looking soul knelt behind the bent posterior of Glasgow Gert, his serene appearance was to bely his libido. Seizing her more than ample hips, he raised them from the bed and began to thrust himself forward in a series of rapid small jerks. The Cornish girl, her task now complete, slid from beneath the pair and left them the full comfort of the bed. 'Comfort', however, was something that Gert seemed to be singularly lacking in, especially considering her years as a trollop. She slowly eased herself forward until she was lying face down and flat on the bed whilst her partner continued to ride her. Max felt a light touch on his shoulder as Minnie gestured to him to leave the cubicle. They did not speak until they were once more outside on the staircase. 'Well?' she asked eagerly. 'What d'you think?'

Max looked puzzled. 'I'm running a brothel! What am I supposed to think?'

'But he was buggering her!' persisted Minnie. 'That must make the difference surely?'

'Look, that particular activity is not obligatory in this establishment, it's not even recommended, but if the girls agree to do it for a few bob extra, that's their choice. I don't see what it's got to do with us.'

'Good heavens!' she exclaimed, holding her hand to her forehead. 'You haven't got this at all, have you? You don't know who he is, do you?'

'Should I?'

'If you read the papers you would! He's Doctor Arnold Vincent Shipwright. He was in the Duchess of Whichester's divorce case recently. They reckoned up till that moment he had a good chance of becoming the royal physician. The divorce ruled that out but he's one of the most respected doctors in the country.'

'Not here he's not,' said Max. 'Especially if he goes around buggering . . . MINNIE!' He seized her tightly and rained kisses down on her face. 'Oh, what a darling you are!

I see it now! He's my medical discharge from the army, isn't he? I mean, if you're moving around on the fringes of royalty, it's not done to toddle down to Murgatroyd's to bugger old Gert. I don't think his society chums would rate that very highly, do you?'

'Shall I tell him you want to see him before he leaves?'

'You bet!'

'You must be prepared to lose a bit of custom though. He obviously won't be coming here again and neither will his friends.'

'Yes, I'm sorry about that, it's a blow to my professional pride as you might say. I mean, if you can't have discretion in a knocking shop, where can you have it?' Max gave a sorrowful sigh. 'But, as the old saying goes, "When needs must, the devil drives", and I'm afraid the poor old devil was certainly driving hard today.

'Tell you what, Minnie, fetch up a bottle of scotch. I have a feeling Doctor Arnold Vincent Shipwright is going to need a drink.'

Max's prophecy was certainly correct about the doctor's desire for a beverage. After opening with a display of righteous indignation, he slumped into total submission. Three days later, by personal messenger, Max received two letters, the first confirming he had half the diseases known to medical science and a few that were just being noticed whilst the second notified him of the cancellation of his call-up medical. 'Apparently they think just climbing the stairs will kill me and they don't want the responsibility. God, I'm glad I didn't become a postman!'

For Max it was indeed a day of celebration. Whether it was his announcement that he intended to spend more time at Murgatroyd's or just coincidence was unknown but both attendances and profits rose sharply. The new little errand-runners were doing particularly well. There are few more over-generous people than soldiers who are away from home and confronted by young children. Like all good things, though, it slowly became out of hand and soon small gangs of youngsters began assembling at the club doors as soon as they were released from school for the day. Though surprisingly few complaints were received by Stones End station, the afternoon congregation had obviously not been unnoticed and soon some of the newly formed women's police section were instructed to take an interest. Though the club was not on Sam's manor, his daily journey to and from Tower Bridge took him close to the premises and his reservations about the ability of women police officers often caused him to detour past the club out of nothing more than sheer curiosity.

'I can't see how they expect women to do a job that they're so obviously unsuited for,' he complained as he climbed into bed with Queenie one evening.

'Sam,' she sighed. 'Two years ago, before they disbanded to support the war effort, you would moan regularly about the Suffragettes, about how negative and destructive they were. Now many of those Suffragette types are wearing *your* uniform and doing *your* work. You can't have it both ways. Do you want them on your side or don't you?'

'You could have a point, I suppose,' he agreed grudgingly. 'But they make me feel inadequate. I just wish they were doing something else, like driving a bus or planting spuds.'

'Inadequate? Why should you feel inadequate? You've been working twelve hours a day non-stop for two years for two pounds eight shillings a week! If you feel anything at all you should be feeling positively saintly!'

'Yes, but I still come home every day and, except for the Zeppelins, no one is trying to gas me or blow me to bits. Also, those poor sods in France are getting even lower wages than I am.'

'Speaking of Zeppelins, Sam,' said Queenie, pummelling her pillow into shape, 'as their raids are becoming more frequent, I think we should be giving some thought to letting the twins sleep in the air raid shelter. We are six floors up and if bombs fall we've a long way to the ground.'

'Air raid shelter?' he queried. 'Where's that?'

'It's downstairs in the basement. They've reinforced the ceiling and everyone can crowd in there during a raid.'

'The basement! You'd be in more danger from the plague down there than ever you were from the Jerries up here. No, if they're sleeping let them sleep. David would sleep through an artillery barrage and I'm sure one bloody bomb's not going to wake him. We'll all stay upstairs . . . hand me that alarm clock, please.'

'That's exactly my point, Sam,' she said quietly. 'After just one bomb he might never wake again and just because you want to assuage your conscience by being in the firing line, you shouldn't expect the same from our children. No, Sam, I'm sorry but we are *not* staying upstairs. If you insist on staying, you do so on your own. As soon as those Zeppelins arrive, me and my kids are heading for the basement. You can either join us down there or go up on the roof and chuck bricks at the Germans. The choice is yours. I choose the best for me and my children.'

As they said their good nights, it was obvious to them both that the little day to day differences between them were multiplying rapidly. The strain and frustrations of war, long hours and little pay, did not help but overriding everything else was their increasing inability to relax in each other's company. During the depths of her depression, Queenie had repelled all of Sam's advances, now he no longer made them. As a couple, they simply lived together. Their sleeping was just that, sleeping. It wasn't actually back to back but there was never a touch between them. Sam did not want to lose her but had no idea how to tell her. She wanted love but could not tell him. All either had was emptiness.

* * *

As Sam alighted from the tram early next morning, he turned a corner to stumble over a soldier lying partially in a shop doorway. It was obvious by his location, barely a hundred yards from the police station, that he had not been there all night. Sam toyed with the idea of pushing him further into the doorway in the hope he might sleep it off before the premises opened. The problem with that was that the man might be ill or injured. To hide someone in a doorway at 5.30 a.m. who is found to be dead at 7 a.m. might provoke embarrassing questions. With any luck, once roused, the man might wander off on his merry way or at least on to someone else's manor – though Sam was not hopeful.

Taking everything into consideration, he reluctantly uttered one of the street copper's most often repeated sentences: 'Come on, mate, you can't sleep there!'

Mate obviously thought he could sleep there and in a strong Australian accent said as much, though louder and more forcefully. As a general rule, sleeping drunks don't move, come quietly, or else want to fight everyone. Sam's discovery did not just want to fight everyone, he also wanted to *tell* everyone that he wanted to fight everyone. Trouble was, they were the only two people in the street. The drunk considered this a direct challenge to summon as many others as possible so he could tell them he wanted to fight them. Sadly, his sporting offer to take on the world obviously had to be satisfied with the stupid copper bent over him. Assessing the situation, he promptly threw one great swinging punch. Not only did he miss, he woke up ten minutes later in the charge room at Tower Bridge.

'Hope you're impressed with this, sarge,' Sam told the station officer ruefully. 'I'm not even due at work for another six minutes.'

'Turn his pockets out, Sam,' ordered the station officer. 'He don't look capable of doing it himself.'

Within a few moments the charge desk was littered with an assortment of three nations' currencies, army documentation, one filthy handkerchief, two postcards of sepia-toned, coffee-coloured, shy young female Egyptian nudes, plus an assortment of letters. At the station officer's request for the prisoner's name and unit, Sam browsed swiftly through the contents on the desk. 'What are these for, mate?' he asked the Australian as he slid over the letters.

'They're written to me by me girlfriend, cobber. They're a bit saucy an' I'd thank you not ter be a readin' of 'em . . . so there!'

'They're nursery rhymes, sarge,' whispered Sam.

The old sergeant shook his head and sighed. 'Takes all sorts, I s'pose.' He then turned his attention to the young soldier. 'Right, pay attention and listen to what I'm going to say to you.'

He read out the charge and Sam stood, pen poised, to note the young Queenslander's reply, which was: 'Why ain't you yeller bastards over there fightin' the fuckin' Jerries, instead of 'arassin' those of us who've come over 'ere ter fight 'em for yer?'

'Okay, shove him down the cells, Sam,' ordered the station officer, closing the charge book. As there was no audible reply from Sam, the sergeant looked up for a visual response, again there was none. Instead the policeman stood staring with a distant expression out through the grimy window. 'Sam!' repeated the sergeant. 'D'you hear me?'

'Er – yes, sarge, I'm sorry . . . what d'you say?'

'Wake up, boy! The cells, put the prisoner in the cells.'

'Yes, sure thing, sarge,' responded Sam as he turned to the prisoner. 'Come on, Digger, you can get your head down until the court opens.'

Because of time spent with the drunk, Sam had missed the early turn duty parade and, at ten minutes after six, presented himself to the early turn duty sergeant. 'All right if I walk up to London Bridge as soon as premises open this morning, sarge?' he asked politely.

'Why, lad?' replied Claude Bevington.

'Because I think that Digger was quite right. It's high time I joined the army.'

Chapter 18

'Sam, tell me this isn't true. Please, please! With the hours you work the children barely see you now! Is this your way of removing us from your life forever? If so, at least have the guts to say it!'

'You don't understand me, Queenie, do you?' he asked wearily. 'Right from the start I've felt ill at ease about my part in this war and it took a shitty drunk to set me straight.'

'Your *part*!' she echoed. 'This isn't a play or a game, Sam! It's not your *part* I'm concerned about, it's your *death*!' Her eyes suddenly narrowed in realisation. 'That's it, isn't it?' she demanded. 'You've got a death wish, haven't you? That explains why you chased that tram at Tottenham! It explains your insistence on staying six floors up during air raids! It explains this present insanity of rushing off to France for yet another attempt to get yourself killed. You're right, I'm afraid, I *don't* understand you. I thought I did, I even told myself I did, but it was just self-delusion. No, I don't understand you, Sam Diamond, and I don't suppose I ever will.'

'You not only don't understand me, gel,' he said quietly, 'you don't even give me a chance to talk. If you'd let me finish, you would have learned that I'm not going to France, leastways not as a soldier. Because they don't like this scar on my head, they've put me in the bloody navy.'

'The navy?'she asked in astonishment. 'What on earth do you know about the sea?'

He gave an indifferent shrug. 'Used to hire a row boat in Hyde Park, didn't we?'

Before Queenie could reply there was the sound of running footsteps on the staircase, followed by a quick, familiar knock at the door. 'That's Jane,' said Queenie, glancing up at the clock. 'Wonder why she's running? I hope nothing's wrong.'

As Queenie opened the door, her sister-in-law fell breathlessly into her arms. 'Jane, darling, whatever's the matter?' Queenie asked anxiously.

Jane threw back her head and laughed loudly. 'Matter? Bless you, sweetie, nothing's the matter, other than I'm fit to burst! It's just that I'm so happy and Jim's not home yet and I need to tell someone – I'm going to have a baby at last! Isn't that wonderful news?'

'Yes, of course it is,' said Queenie, giving her a loving hug. 'I'm so happy for you. Jim will be absolutely delighted.'

'So will old Mother Butler,' pointed out Sam, ruffling his sister's hair. 'She might be able to get a bit of sleep now.'

'I do hope that's the last time you run up ninety-six stairs for a little while though,' chided Queenie.

'Yes, I know it wasn't very bright. I promise to be a steady old mum in future. I shall take my time, complain about the stairs and pause for breath on every landing. How's that suit?'

'If I know your Jim, he'll insist on chairs placed on every flight of steps so you can do that very thing,' smiled Queenie. 'When's he due home?'

'Any time now! I can barely wait!' Jane wrapped her arms tightly around her own waist and hugged herself in delight. 'I want to shout out to him the moment he turns the corner of the street. Jim Forsythe, you're going to be a dad!'

'Why don't we do it then?' said Queenie enthusiastically.

'You do it from your window and I'll do it from ours! I bet he'll fly up those steps.'

The maternal instinct already began to manifest itself as Jane crossed the room to peep through the curtains at the sleeping twins. 'You're going to have a new little cousin, you two,' she whispered to the slumbering pair. 'And if he or she's as good as you, I'll be more than delighted.' She leaned over and kissed each child lightly on the forehead. Emma murmured slightly in her dreams and David slept on impervious.

They had but a short time to wait. Fifteen or so minutes later, with head buried deep in a newspaper, the father-to-be strolled leisurely into the street. At first, though he heard the voices, he placed no significance on their message. It was only when the words were taken up by smiling passers-by that he glanced up from his paper. As he looked quickly from one to another, wondering how they knew his name, he followed the direction of the pointing fingers. Seeing the two laughing women at the windows, he broke instantly into a sprint. If there was a world record for skimming ninety-six steps, picking up, swinging around and kissing a slightly pregnant woman, then Jim Forsythe left it in tatters. Their happy laughter echoed down the dungeon-like staircase almost to the street. Soundly though the twins slept, the delighted adults decided to leave open the doors and finish their excited conversations in the Forsythes' flat. It was there, minutes later, that Queenie disclosed the news of Sam's enlistment. 'When d'you leave, Sam, and where have you got to report?' asked Jim, coming slowly back to earth.

'Monday week, Chatham Dockyard. As I finish in the police on Friday, it means I'll have my first time off for over two years! I've promised the kids I'll use it to fix up the plank for the cat's walk between our two balconies and I think Queenie has a couple of other little tasks for me. At this rate, and if I'm not careful, I shall become quite domesticated. Almost worth joining up for, wouldn't you say?'

'It might be if you weren't going to Chatham,' responded Jim. 'I went there once, I thought it the most dreary place I've ever seen.'

'At least it's not far,' said Sam cheerfully. 'It could have been Portsmouth, Plymouth, or even Scapa Flow. I can get to Chatham almost as quick as I could to Hyde Park.'

'True,' acknowledged Jim. 'Except they don't call you back in after an hour and take your boat away.'

Even with the euphoria of Jane's great news, Jim could sense the fraught atmosphere between his two friends. 'Come on, Sam,' he said. 'Let me take you round The Winchester for a celebration pint. After all, we shan't see so much of you from now on.' He gave Jane a quick kiss. 'Won't be long, "Mum". Just two pints and we're home again – honest!'

It was during the short time he spent with Jim in The Winchester that Sam realised how badly he had needed someone to confide in. Since Jim had been promoted, changing both shifts and station, they had seen much less of each other. It may have been that his marriage would not have deteriorated into its current state if his old friend had been accessible to balance Sam's own obstinacy.

'I had no idea you two were in such a mess!' said Jim sadly. 'I know our wives are particularly close so Jane couldn't fail to have heard about it. I just wonder why she hasn't mentioned it to me.' He reached forward and held his friend's forearm, 'I couldn't be more sorry, Sam. Other than my Jane, you're my dearest friends. Looking back, I feel almost mean to have been so happy when I ran up those stairs.'

'The pity is that I joined the navy today,' said Sam regretfully. 'If I had heard Jane's good news first I probably wouldn't have done.'

'Why?'

'Because Queenie is going to be so lonely. What with me away and you both moved on she'll—'

'What d'you mean "moved on". Where are we supposed to be moving on?'

'You're not remaining in Queen's Buildings surely? I understand you're eligible for married quarters now. You'd be barmy to stay here when you can do so much better for yourselves elsewhere, you know you would.'

'I know no such thing,' denied Jim indignantly. 'In any case, if your Queenie can cope with six-year-old twins, my Jane can cope with a new baby. Of course neither of us has to stay there forever. If I know your sister, now she has learnt how it's done, she'll be trying for two or three others. I'm not sure what old Mother Butler will make of it though! What I would suggest is that we suspend any decision until the war is over. You'll be back home again then and we can all talk about it properly. What d'you say?'

'Jim boy,' said Sam philosophically, 'whether or not you know it – although I'm sure you do – you are destined to go far up the promotional ladder in the police force. I on the other hand, am not. I am absolutely delighted for you but I also know that promotion is not for me. We may have been lifelong friends but there comes a time when you must think about yourself. If you don't, it's not fair to you and it's patronising to me. If you're honest, you'll admit as much.'

Jim smiled ruefully. 'I think the girls may have something to say about that but I'd be lying if I pretended I couldn't see your point. Look, how about if we stay at least until Jane has the baby? That way they can look after each other during Jane's pregnancy and your absence.'

'And if the war lasts another ten years, what then?'

'If the war lasts another ten years then none of this'll matter anyway because there'll be no one left to worry about it, so drink up and have another.'

During the next few days, the relationship between Sam and Queenie appeared to stabilise and on his last night before his departure, she awakened around two o'clock to discover his arm around her. This lost something of its significance two hours later when, again awakened, she found him sleeping on the edge of the bed and facing the wall.

Breakfast turned out to be chaotic. Sam's train to Chatham was at 8.10 from London Bridge station. Because of the proximity of the station to Queen's Buildings and the children's school, David asked if they could 'see Daddy off to war'. Sam had a niggling suspicion the boy expected at the very least a pipe band. Queenie thought she could hardly refuse the lad's request but the children's excitement did not make for a peaceful mealtime, especially with the customary arrival of two of their friends. These two youngsters had been orphaned in an earlier Zeppelin raid and were living with their respective grandparents in a neighbouring block. Grace Melia was a pretty little olive-skinned charmer who was already showing signs of inheriting the outstanding beauty of her mother. Jack Kirton too was unusual. He was a quietly spoken nine-year-old with a pretty, almost girlish, face. Yet this was misleading because he was also authoritative with the physique of a child several years his senior and, being three years older, undoubtedly the leader of the quartet. Jane tearfully kissed her brother farewell, and with the best wishes of dozens of neighbours ringing in their ears, all six trooped off determinedly, if not merrily, to London Bridge.

It was debatable whether the children's main interest lay in seeing the hero off to the war or staring open-mouthed at the galaxy of snorting, steaming engines. As with any busy wartime station, the hustle and bustle, whistles and hisses, captivated the children's attention until they had to be reminded to kiss their father goodbye. Soon came a distant whistle, the roar of an engine, a cloud of hissing steam, and for a few seconds the train barely inched forward, as if unsure as to whether it should really leave. However, once having made up its mind, it gave a reverberating roar and, gathering momentum, curved away to disappear down the shining silver lines towards Deptford. For a moment there appeared to be a strange respectful silence but yet another distant whistle blew and the whole cacophony began again.

As they left the station, Queenie was thankful for the children's excitement as they regaled each other with railway tales, real and imaginary. It left her lost in thought as they left the precincts of the station and walked into the early market traffic. She had heard the motor-horn for some seconds before realising its warning was aimed at her. If the vehicle was impressive, so were its occupants. The driver was stern of face but smart of appearance and the passenger was a powerful young man with a smiling open countenance and an expensive suit. Assuming directions were needed, she began to prepare her apology for her lack of local knowledge. 'I'm sorry,' she began, 'but I only know the names of the main roads round . . .'

'It's Sam Diamond's lovely young wife, isn't it?' asked the passenger.

The children were stunned into a reverential silence. First a railway station and now a big man in a big car actually knowing Mum! 'Er . . .' began Queenie, slightly flustered. 'Do I know you?'

'I certainly know you, my dear,' replied the man. 'My name's Max, Maxie Roff. I never forget a beautiful woman, especially when she's married to a friend of mine. Let me put your mind at ease. We met one Saturday night in The Feathers. I was about to attempt to seduce you with my charm when Sam informed me you were already spoken for.' He put his hand on his heart and gave a long sigh. 'Story of my life, I'm afraid.'

'Oh, yes, I remember you now, you're an old school friend of Sam and Jim's!'

'Quite correct, my dear, but I've met them both since. The second time in, shall we say, their professional capacity? Did Sam not tell you?'

'If by professional capacity you mean work, then no. Sam wasn't a great one for talking about his work.'

'Wasn't?' he queried with a puzzled expression. 'What do you mean wasn't? Is something wrong with him?'

'You could say that,' she said with a hint of bitterness. 'He's just gone off to join the navy.'

'Join the—' He shook his head in bewilderment. 'Look, get in the car all of you. We'll drop the kids off at school then you can tell me all about Sam.'

The words were hardly uttered before all four children were in the car like long dogs. Heaven indeed! David pressed his nose tight against the car window in a desperate search for school friends to impress. Charles Dickens primary school was barely three minutes' drive from London Bridge but the children milked the journey for all it was worth. Royal tours have known less excitement. They may have scuttled into the car like whippets but they emerged like Maharajahs, nodding condescendingly to any school friend rash enough to catch their eyes. As they ran joyously into the school playground, Queenie smiled warmly as she watched them go. 'Thank you, Max. What with the war and the shortages, it's not a good time to be a child. That little group haven't been so happy for a long time. You can drop me here, I can walk home easily enough, thanks again.'

'Just a minute!' he said, putting out a restraining hand. 'You haven't told me why Sam's run away to sea. Look, we're on our way to my club, it's only round the corner. Why don't you come and have a cup of tea and tell me all about it, eh?'

Queenie needed no second bidding, for in truth she was not only flattered but as excited to be in such a car as either of her children. Everything about Max reeked of affluence and, for Queenie, affluence was a long forgotten experience. Minutes later, he led the way through the chair-piled tables up to his office. Once she was seated, he left to order some tea and returned minutes later with a well-laid silver tray.

'Right, young lady, we shouldn't be disturbed for a while, so fire away. I want to hear it all, mind.'

An hour or so later, with Queenie still talking, Minnie Murgatroyd knocked to remove the tray. 'Ah, Minnie!' sang out Max. 'Just the person! Minnie, how many cleaning staff do we have working here?'

'Eight usually but they're not here all the time. Some come in the evening, some in the morning.'

'Who supervises them?'

'I suppose I do from time to time but—' She shrugged. 'In reality no one does. If we have a complaint we just sack one and hire another. I don't really have time to be chasing cleaners,' she protested.

'Of course you don't and that's why, starting tomorrow, I propose to hire Mrs Diamond here in a purely supervisory capacity. She lives close by so she can pop in for an hour or so in the morning and no doubt for the same amount of time in the evening. Will you make sure she has a key before she leaves today?'

Minnie, feeling words were not needed to convey her total lack of enthusiasm for the idea, carried out the tray and settled for the briefest of nods.

'Excuse me, Mr Roff,' said Queenie coolly, 'there are two things here which are worth mentioning. Firstly, that lady is hardly ecstatic about the idea. Secondly, I don't want the job.'

'If you don't want the job then there's no harm done,' said Max soothingly. 'I just thought with you living so close by, Sam away and you having two kids to look after, you could do with three quid a week. You could suit yourself as to hours. After all, you don't need to stand over them, just make sure the cleaning is done satisfactorily before they go home.'

'Three pounds!' exclaimed Queenie suspiciously. 'Look, I'm not stupid. Three pounds a week is more than my Sam was getting for working twelve hours a day, seven days a week. I fully realise some of the things that go on in this place and I'm not whoring for three quid a week, you know!'

'I do hope that's a joke,' said Max tightly. 'Whores are whores and ladies are ladies. I don't get them mixed up and neither should you. I am offering you a proper job for what I consider proper money. Okay, let's put our cards on the table. I happen to know you are just about on the breadline and, with two kids and your complaint, there's little you can do about it. So, if there *was* a job for you anywhere, it would have to be part-time and small change. I'm offering you a job that I think needs doing. Someone has to do it so it might as well be you. Satisfied?'

'But *why* me?'

'If it's your honour that's bothering you, forget it. You're a fine-looking woman, though I would guess you've forgotten that. Ordinarily, I might well have considered trying to bed you. Not *whore* you, you understand, just bed you. Whores come to me, I don't go looking for them. You see, contrary to what some folks think, I do have standards. The reason for my gallantry is that your Sam once saved my life and I owe him. So although I well fancy his missus and I'm offering her a good job, my hand is never going up her skirt. And for that matter, whilst she is in this club, neither is anyone else. [illegible] pounds two shillings a week and that's my final offer, take it or leave it.'

'Could I ask for one condition?'

'You can ask, I'm not sure if you'll get it. What is it?'

'That if my Sam – sorry – *when* my Sam comes home, not

only do I not have to report here but he is to remain ignorant of the fact that I even work for you.'

'Sure,' he replied. 'But how long do you think it'll be before he finds out? The Queen's Buildings Bush Telegraph is better than Reuters. Still, if that's what you want, that's what you can have. Anything else you'd like cleared up?'

She gave just a hint of a smile before replying. 'Just two things more. I sensed an instant atmosphere directly your lady – Minnie I think you called her – saw me. What's the situation there?'

'Minnie?' he laughed. 'Minnie is my self-appointed protector. She fancies me rotten but probably thinks she's too old for me, which is possibly right. Instead she just loves me silently and thinks I don't know it. I've known her for some years now, we actually live in the same house, but not once during that time has she ever called me by any name. Not Max, not mister, not darling . . . nothing. I'll either have too much to drink one night and wake up one morning in her big comfortable bed. Or . . .' He left the sentence unspoken.

'Or?' prodded Queenie.

His smile faded. 'Or she'll stumble on me with some other woman and bury the biggest knife she can find in my back. Anyway, what's the second question?'

'How did Sam and Jim save your life?'

'That's between Sam and Jim. If they tell you, fine. If they don't, forget it.'

'What are my exact hours?'

'You have none. Minnie will introduce you to the staff and I'd like you to come in as irregularly as possible. You can work it around your kids by all means, so I'll leave that to you. Oh, and one more thing. There's an animal called Cootes who works here. I keep him because he can be real handy at times, but watch him. He's dangerous. If you have any problem with him, let me know.'

'As a matter of fact, I know Mr Cootes,' said Queenie.

'My Sam once beat him in a fight on the stage of the South London Palace.'

'One of Sandows' fights?'

'That's correct.'

'Phew! Queenie Diamond, I didn't know that, I'm impressed! Cootes can be a killer! Perhaps I should employ both you *and* your old man.'

'Perhaps you should, Mr Roff. I may remind you of that after the war.'

'I'm sure you will, Mrs Diamond, I'm sure you will. Oh, and by the way, the name is Max, not Mr Roff.'

'I'll think about that.' She glanced up at the clock. 'You see, it's not yet eleven o'clock and I've had quite a day already. I've seen my husband off to war, I've been picked up by a "gentleman", I've had my first ride in a Rolls-Royce, I've got a job in a brothel, and now I'm being invited to call you Max! It's enough to fetch on a young woman's vapours, Mr Roff, and I'm not sure just how much more excitement a girl like me can be expected to take.'

Max gave a throaty chuckle and said almost to himself, 'You'll do, Mrs Diamond, you'll do just fine.'

Within the half-hour, Queenie was recounting the day's events to a dumbstruck Jane. 'What's it like in there?' she asked eagerly. 'I know it sounds terrible but I've always wanted to see inside a brothel. They sound so wicked. Do you think you could show me around sometime?'

'Like a conducted tour, eh?' said Queenie teasingly. 'I bet even Max hasn't thought of that one.' Her smile slowly faded and she looked questioningly at Jane. 'Seriously, though, are you sure you could look after the children on the odd occasion when I'll need to go to work?'

'Of course I can, love, don't worry about it. They're not babies any more and, as you say, most times they'll be in bed anyway.'

'Yes, but how about Grace and Jack? They spend nearly as much time around here as my own two. I can't very well stop them but on the other hand it does seem a liberty to ask you to look after two additional kids as well.'

Jane sighed patiently and, taking her friend's hands, looked her straight in the eyes. 'Queenie darling, we are close enough friends to say "No" if we need to. If I thought I couldn't cope, I'd tell you. As I'm sure you would me. But I'm more than happy to be of assistance. I love your children and the other two are almost as good. So, you hussy, go to your brothel whenever you need!'

Queenie gave her a grateful embrace. 'You're bloody angelic, Janey Forsythe, that you are! If you have another ten kids I shall insist on being aunt, god-mother, and, with my new job, benefactor, to each of 'em!'

It was two weeks before Queenie received the first letter from her husband and its news was better than she had dared hoped. After preliminary interviews, he had been selected for training and posted to the Dover Patrol. This was basically a naval force that was set up to keep the Straits of Dover clear of German ships, submarines, mines, aircraft, and any other item that could be thrown, grown, propelled, expelled, dropped, anchored, floated or sailed to the detriment of the thousands of men who criss-crossed those vulnerable twenty-two miles of water each day.

The great advantage of the Patrol was that it was based in the Channel ports, most of them within a ninety-minute train ride of London Bridge. 'Could have been a thousand times worse,' Queenie confided to Max. 'He could have been on a battleship or submarine and I may not have seen him for years!'

'I hate Dover,' said Max thoughtfully. 'I went camping there once with the Poor Boys' Mission. I'll never forget it –

we had a randy vicar. One night he touched us all up and our tent blew down. I've never been so cold in my life.'

'What has that got to do with my Sam?'

Max blinked several times before replying. 'Nothing really, in fact I'd forgotten it until now. I s'pose it was just you mentioning Dover that did it.'

Queenie stared at him silently for some moments. 'You're a strange boy, you know,' she said shaking her head. 'In some respects you're as cold and calculating a person as anyone is likely to meet. Yet in others you're still a chattering kid. You can be as generous as Carnegie and as mean as a cobra. Why have they not called you up for the services?'

'Ah, well,' he sighed. 'I didn't want to tell you really. I mean, it's not something I like to speak of. It'd hardly be in keeping with my reputation as a tough nut.'

'So what is it?' she asked with increasing curiosity.

He placed his hand on his chest. 'It's the old ticker basically. One false move and, pouff, gone!' He dramatically threw his hands wide. 'No doctor can tell me when or where it'll happen, that's the tragedy of it.'

'Oh, I'm so sorry,' said Queenie sadly. 'Forgive me for being so nosy, I'll not mention it again.'

Max, feeling a reply was not needed, settled for a knowing nod.

There was a strained silence for some minutes as Queenie tried desperately to think of something to lighten the conversation. She was saved by the arrival of Minnie who had entered with the same aloof demeanour she always adopted in Queenie's presence. 'Have you told Mrs Diamond about your tea party next week? If you expect her in early she'll doubtless need to be informed.'

'Oh, yes! Good point, Minnie, I'd totally forgotten.' He turned to Queenie. 'It's my birthday next Wednesday and I'm having a tea party for all the staff. Nothing too boisterous, you know, because we'll all be working in the evening. Just a few cups of tea. But I've sent my scouts out and hopefully we'll have some fresh meat sandwiches, genuine cream cakes, some tropical fruit, and, as an additional attraction, Madam Renato! Kick off about 4 p.m., I'd say.'

Queenie stared open-mouthed at just the thought of such a feast. 'Wherever would you get—' she began. Then, thinking better of it, gave a short grimace. 'The timing could be better, that's usually when I meet my children from school. I'll ask my sister-in-law to help out. Subject to her agreeing, I'd love to come. Here, wait a minute! Who's this Madam Renato? We haven't got to watch one of your old toms doing a speciality act with a cream cake and a banana, have we?'

'Funny you should say that,' answered Max provocatively. 'Because you're right. Well, perhaps not quite right. Madam Renato certainly did work for me in, shall we say, an intimate capacity some two years ago? But then she found out, purely by chance because some client paid her to dress up, that she had a flair for telling fortunes. The girls love to have her back from time to time. Of course, mostly she cheats because she knows so much about them and, more importantly, knows what they want to hear. Although many of the newer girls say she's actually quite good. Apparently, every now and again she's absolutely accurate. Personally I think it's superstitious crap but it should be a bit of fun. By the way, when she worked for me her name was Fifi Le Fanu. Before that she worked for Jenner's the brewery and it was Elsie Bone.'

'Of course!' agreed Jane later, in response to Queenie's request. 'You know I will. You can stay as long as you wish, enjoy yourself and I'll see them to bed. Perhaps while they're here, Grace and Jack would like to have their tea with me. Us five could have a little party of our own. Fresh meat and cream cakes might be a little scarce and we won't have a fortune teller, but who knows? I *might* be able to scrounge an apple or two.'

'I simply can't remember the last time I went out socially,' said the grateful Queenie. 'I'll try to sneak home some little treats in my apron pockets.'

It was difficult to say who was looking forward to party-day most, Queenie or her children. The persistent rain did nothing to dampen anyone's spirits and, as Jane hastened the children home from school, Queenie showed the same enthusiasm for her jaunt to Red Cross Street.

'What's for tea, Aunt Jane?' asked the ever hungry Jack.

'Toast and jam,' proclaimed Jane. Two years of war had made the children appreciative of any sweet morsel and their excited cries made it all worthwhile. It was Grace who suggested playing 'I Spy' on the staircase landings. Though forbidden to climb the final flight of stairs to the roof, they could easily and safely look out from the iron-barred landing window and see clear across to the docks. This made it a favourite spot, with St Paul's, The Monument, and numerous other easily recognised landmarks clearly in view. In addition, David and Emma had requested the key to their own flat to collect a few toys that they were anxious to show their friends. Though the key to number 25 had been returned, the door had not been closed. It was therefore natural for David's desire for a pee to take him into his parents' flat and not that of his aunt. Jane meantime busied herself concocting a little suet pudding for a surprise dessert.

The lavatory was situated at the side of the balcony, and, as the child approached, he noticed Boadicea had become seemingly trapped between a flower-trough and the wall in the centre of Sam's recently built cat-walk. Soon realising his attempts to reach the animal were pointless, he returned indoors to seek a chair. In spite of a valiant struggle, even with the chair there was a shortfall. Deciding on one last extra stretch, he eased himself up on tip-toe and plunged over the railinged balcony on to – only *just* on to – the edge of the quivering cat-walk. Boadicea, not caring for this sudden intrusion, strolled haughtily off on to the opposite balcony.

The cat's sudden appearance at Jane's feet caused her to give an involuntary start, before remembering that since Sam had assembled the walk, the cat seemed content to share her days happily between the two dwellings.

By now, stark terror had gripped the boy and it was Emma who was the first to realise his predicament. Her cries brought Jane running out on to the communal staircase, then into the flat and finally on to the balcony, thus almost completing a circuit from her start at her own kitchen table. The alarming sag in the cat-walk indicated David's safety was seriously threatened. Ashen-faced, she straightened the chair that he had used and, with reassuring words in an unconvincing tone, shakily reached out for him.

The boy, frozen with fright, was incapable of assisting her. She was still several inches short of him. Her eyes searched for something –anything – that might be of use before she realised that if she edged closer to the side of the balcony, she could cling on to the brick corner with her left hand whilst stretching forward with her right. It *could* give her those extra precious inches. It was little more than a chance but it was her only one. Inching forward, she touched the boy's hand. This seemed to give her a new impetus. Gradually curling her fingers, she had to decide on the moment when she would have sufficient purchase to chance a grip. Finally, as her fingers met around David's slender wrist, she began to edge him slowly towards the balcony.

Unfortunately, one of Queen's Buildings many structural deficiencies was its reaction to prolonged rain. This was never more pronounced than on painted brickwork and the interior of many balconies could easily sport six or more coats. To this rule of condensation, number 25 Queen's Buildings was sadly no exception. Though the boy was almost at her feet, he was still the wrong side of the balcony railings. To compound the situation, her fingers were slipping and her balance faltering. Meantime, ninety feet below, the spiked railings around the basement flat reached up in silent anticipation.

'Go on, Queenie,' urged Glasgow Gert. 'Ha' yer palm read. A gel like ye wi' all her future before her should have a smashin' readin'.'

'Yeah, it's only a bit of fun, go on,' urged yet another female voice. Her indecision finally broken, Queenie took her seat opposite Madam Renato, alias Fifi Le Fanu, alias Elsie Bone and offered her hand. The bespectacled, bejewelled palmist took the hand and, turning it gently over, traced the various lines with impressive dexterity. She was halfway through the I-see-a-long-and-happy-life-with-a-man-who-loves-you-very-much speech, when she ceased abruptly. She lifted her gaze from Queenie's palm and studied her face for some moments. Then, with a heavy frown, she resumed her original study of the hand. 'I see . . . I see . . . someone close. It's not your husband though.'

A whoop of delight came from the watchers. 'It's the quiet ones who're the worst!' Yet there was something about the changed demeanour of the palmist that suddenly sobered the most boisterous of the women.

'I see . . . I see . . .' she faltered.

Queenie suddenly snatched her hand away and thrust it quickly behind her back. 'No! No!' she cried. 'I don't believe in this mumbo-jumbo anyway. I'm going home!' The chair tipped over backwards as she rushed from the building without even stopping for her coat.

'What were that aboot?' demanded Gert. 'I thought it were supposed ter be fun?'

Madam Renato stared wide-eyed at the still open door. 'I don't know, I've never known anythin' like it before, but whatever it is, I don't want to know anythin' like it again.'

As Queenie raced breathlessly around the street corner she was just in time to see the ambulance door close and a policeman scrawling in his notebook. 'Oy, just a minute!' called the constable to the departing attendant. 'Where did you say you were going?

'Southwark, mate . . . Southwark Mortuary.'

Chapter 19

The killick strode along the three straight ranks of the recruits. His expert glance could, in two seconds, sweep up and down a sailor from boots to cap and still have time to examine everything in between. Having settled for his customary three defaulters from the morning parade, he quickly completed announcements and daily orders. 'Right now, pay attention! With the exception of Ordinary Seaman Diamond, the rest of you will march to the recreation ground for PT. Wait for it, Diamond! Wait for it!' He glowered at the tottering Sam who was having great difficulty in moving back off his toes. 'Ship's company, ATTENTION!. *Now* you can fall out, Ordinary Seaman Diamond! Get it right, man, get it right! A smart right turn, count to one and leave the parade. Smartly, man, smartly! Right . . . rest of you, by the right. Quick MARCH!'

Sam stood at the side of the parade ground and watched perplexed as his comrades marched away.

'To the admin office. See Chief Petty Officer McCawley. Smartly, man, smartly!'

'Yes, Hookey,' acknowledged Sam as he strode off for the main office.

'At the double, Diamond, at the double! No one *walks* across a parade ground, man! You'd have been bloody hung from the yard-arm in Nelson's time! Quick-march-quick-march-quick-march!'

It is common practice amongst all discipline services, civil or military, pointedly to ignore any bewildered recruit who should find himself, for whatever reason, in an administration block seeking help. Important people continually rush by carrying papers, clipboards and serious expressions, each of them more eminent than his predecessor. Sam felt if he asked just one of them for directions, the war could be lost. Just as he was wondering if he would be spending the entire duration there, the killick entered. 'If you've seen the chief then get back with the company, Diamond, don't fritter away your time here. There's a war on, y'know!'

'But I've not seen him yet,' Sam almost wailed. 'I don't know where he is.'

'Not seen—! Bloody hell, man!' he boomed. 'What've yer been doin' here fer the last half hour? Playin' wi yerself! Right, foller me. Left-right-left-right-left-right!'

By the tortuous route they took, Sam became convinced that, had it not been for the killick's arrival, he *would* have spent the duration in the foyer. 'In here, lad.' His companion opened a frosted glass door to reveal a diminutive bald man, with a heavily lined forehead and a slightly askew eye-patch. 'Left-right-left-right-left-right! Ordinary Seaman Diamond, Chief!'

'Thank you,' murmured the chief petty officer in a surprisingly soft voice. He picked up a piece of paper and studied its contents for a moment or two. 'I'm sorry to tell you, Diamond, that I have some bad news. The problem is, its arrival coincided with a great deal of activity over the naval telegraph system. As you may know, the Hun have just bombarded Margate and one or two other Channel ports and, because of the confusion, we cannot work out exactly what your bad news is, except to say it's a bereavement but who-what-when-or-how-many, I'm afraid I'm unable to say.' He raised his eyes from the paper. 'Are you expecting a bereavement, Diamond?'

'Expecting a—' began Sam. 'No, of course not.' Then, as a long afterthought, added, 'Chief.'

The chief gave a long weary sigh. 'Very well, but it is annoying and it's something we could well do without at this time. You'd better go outside to my clerk and he'll give you a rail warrant. In the absence of anything more definite, I shall grant you seventy-two hours' compassionate leave. You'll need to return here no later than three days from midnight tonight. No later, d'you understand, otherwise you could be arrested.'

'You have no idea at all, Chief . . . about the bereavement, I mean?' asked Sam anxiously.

'No, it has come from the police at . . . let me see . . . Stones End Police station. Hmm, is that your local station, Diamond?'

'Yessir, just a hundred yards or so from my home.'

'Sounds very rural,' he murmured idyllicly. 'You're very lucky to be living in a country area, Diamond, very lucky indeed, but don't let it detain you when it's time to return. After all, lad, that's why we're fighting the Hun, isn't it, to keep him from raping our fair land? Dismiss then.'

The dismissal was the sign for the killick to leap into life with a rapid 'left-right-left-right-left-right' away from one office and into another.

For Sam, the two-hour train ride from Dover Marine station to London seemed an eternity. He had deliberately sat facing the engine as if it would speed his arrival. Not once during the journey had he removed his gaze from the window and it was always to the front, as if the merest hint of a side glance would cause him delay. As the cathedral at Canterbury loomed slowly into view, he was convinced the train had taken the wrong route. Surely it should have been at Bromley by now? But no, Sittingbourne, Rainham and Swanley dragged by and eventually the countryside gave way to scattered towns, which in turn gave way to urban sprawl, then cluttered streets, dockside cranes, traffic jams and smoke, and at last – at very long last – the train rolled reluctantly into London Bridge station. Opening the door, yards before the train stopped, he leaped wide and sprinted towards the platform gate.

Easily the first passenger from the train, he arrived before the obese and breathless ticket collector had positioned himself on his stool. ''Ang on a minute, sailor, fer Gawd's! She'll still luv yer, yer know. Two minutes ain't gonna make any difference one way or the ovver!'

Ignoring the fat philosopher, he thrust the ticket towards the man's pudgy fist and raced on. Unfortunately it seems that ticket-collector's fingers can only function when their owners are sitting comfortably upright on their stools. A buttock on and a buttock off is no position for collecting railway tickets from impatient sailors. Long before the ticket fluttered to the floor, Sam was halfway across the concourse and deaf to the collector's: 'OY!' Which was more than could be said for the two military police corporals who were patrolling by the exits. 'Hold it, sailor, hold it!' ordered the harder faced of the two. Unwisely Sam brushed between the pair of them. The next moment he was aware of an enormous thud in his back and the dirty concrete floor jumping to meet his face. This was a split second before every light in the world blew out.

He was aware of muffled voices, a splitting headache and a cold numb feeling to his jaw. As the mists cleared, he realised he was on his back, reeking of strong disinfectant, and someone was dribbling cold water over his face. His gaze instantly recoiled from a bright overhanging light. On a second attempt he realised it was a first aid hut whose customary function was for dealing with severely war injured in transit. The pain spreading rapidly over his face told him he might well qualify for that usage, particularly as a kindly Red Cross nurse was bathing his chin with a blood-soaked swab.

'Oh, yer with us again, are yer?' growled a gruff voice just to his rear. He turned his head quickly – too quickly. A lightning pain flashed across his skull and blurred his vision. Repeating the movement at a more gradual pace, he saw a large military police corporal whom he took to be one of the pair he had seen earlier. But *how much* earlier? How long had he been on that couch, seconds or days? He only had a pass for seventy-two hours and someone close – or some people – God knows who or how many, were dead!

On a table alongside the corporal were laid out all his personal possessions. 'Yer were nearly 'ome, sailor,' said the corporal. 'So what was all the bloody rush about?'

'What happened?' asked Sam.

'We requested yer to stop. Yer refused,' he replied simply.

Sam winced with pain 'So what did you do, shoot me?'

'Yer a lucky little sailor-boy, we could'a done.' The corporal gave an enormous sniff. 'What d'you remember about it?'

'Not a lot,' muttered Sam. 'I remember running, then a sort of push in my back and that's about it really. I suppose I must have landed on my head?'

The corporal shot a quick glance at his colleague. 'That's about the strength of it, son,' he agreed. 'When yer refused to stop fer us, we reached out for yer and that must'a caused yer ter stumble. Anyway, yer've only got a few cuts and bruises and a bit of a shake-up, you'll recover. I've seen yer seventy-two 'our pass and yer compassionate notice. So nah yer conscious, as soon as the nurse 'as cleaned yer up, yer can be on yer way.' He gave another great sniff. 'Perhaps when a military per'liceman asks yer ter stop next time, yer might take a bit o'notice of 'im.' Sam agreed that sounded a pretty sensible idea.

The corporal then pushed the scattered possessions across the table towards him. 'Put 'em in yer pocket, son, an' 'oppit quick before we change our mind and lose our good nature and charge yer.'

'Charge me!' echoed Sam, his temper now rising. 'What

on earth would you charge me *with*? I've got a legitimate pass and I'm lawfully on my way home. I think you're well out of order, corporal, if you don't mind me saying so.'

'Oh, a barrack room lawyer, eh?' He turned to his colleague. 'Oh, we do love them, don't we, Albert?' His tone and mood changed as he turned his attention back to Sam. 'We'd charge yer wiv failin' to stop for our command and we might also sling in a little assault charge on poor old Albert 'ere. Just to spice it up a bit, y'understand?'

'Oh, yeah,' acknowledged Sam, raising his hands. 'I fully understand.'

'I fort you'd see it our way, son,' leered the corporal. 'Most lads usually do.'

Sam looked up at the nurse who had remained impassive throughout the debate. 'Thanks for all you've done, nurse, though I didn't care much for your helpers.'

'You'll need a few stitches in those wounds before you go, young man,' she reproved. 'Or they could turn very nasty.'

'How long will it take?' he asked anxiously. 'I haven't got long.'

'As soon as the doctor returns.' She looked at her watch. 'Say about an hour. Anyway, it wouldn't do you any harm to lay quiet for a while. You've had quite a blow.'

Sam threw off the blanket and swung his feet to the ground. 'Sorry, can't wait. I'll be home in twenty minutes. And, anyway, I'm a quick healer. But thanks all the same, nurse.' He reached for his cap, and as soon as it touched his head, winced.

'Better keep it on, boy,' ordered the corporal. 'Yer improperly dressed wiv' out it an' yer liable ter be stopped by the MPs agin.'

Sam nodded an agreement. 'You're right, corp'. I don't think I could take being stopped twice in a day.' Easing himself out on to the concourse, he resumed his interrupted journey at a fraction of his previous pace. He had almost reached the pavement when a fat female newspaper-seller, squatting perilously on an old orange-box, signalled to him. 'Sorry, gel,' he said, raising the palms of his hand. 'Ain't got time to read today.'

'Don't worry 'bout a paper, sailor,' said the woman. 'I was just wondering how much of that incident you remembered?'

'Not a lot really,' he said, still trying to take his leave of her. 'Why?'

'Well, if yer not interested . . .' She shrugged and turned away.

'Sorry, no offence.' His eyes narrowed. 'Did you see what happened then?'

'There ain't much 'appens on this station that I miss,' she snorted. 'They pushed yer dahn and yer fell on to yer face – yer chin most probably – then the taller of 'em whacked yer twice over the nut with his truncheon. Uncalled fer, I thought it was. Uncalled fer and dahn-right cruel, if yer asks me. But then that's 'is bleedin' game, 'e's always at it.' She nodded as if happy with her conclusions.

Of course! thought Sam. That's why he had injuries to the front and rear of his skull! The wicked bastard! He turned momentarily but, remembering he had already seriously encroached into his precious three days, stored the information in the back of his mind. 'Thanks, gel,' he said gratefully. 'I'm obliged. I'll shove it in my pending file and try to give it some time later.' He broke into a trot and, gathering speed, raced away into the warren of streets leading home.

Minutes later, he turned the last corner and looked up at the tall gaunt grey tenement that was Queen's Buildings. His eyes frantically sought his own window. There was the death sign sure enough, the black drawn curtains. So it was correct! My God, but who? Suddenly he realised the window next-door was also curtained. Perhaps Jim was on night duty and asleep? No, the curtains were the same, thick and black. These were definitely mourning curtains. The idea of a Zeppelin raid entered his head, but where? It couldn't have been the Buildings, there was not so much as a window broken, so where? His injuries caused his skull to pound as he raced, two at a time, up the stone stairs.

Turning the key he opened the door on to a silent flat. Both beds were made and the place was its usual spotless self but except for Boadicea sunning herself on the cat-walk there was no sign of life. He ran next door and pounded on the large iron knocker. There too was silence. Where next? Of course, the police station! They had telegraphed him, they would know.

Slamming the door behind him, he cleared each flight in one jump, and within seconds almost fell out into the street. He was about to cross the road when he heard his name being called. At first he could not trace the voice but its persistence caused him to raise his eyes. There, waving from the window of the fifth floor directly beneath his sister's flat, was old Mother Butler. He acknowledged her and cupped his ear to listen.

'If yer 'adn't bin so bloody quick, yer'd 'ave seen I 'ad the door open fer yer,' she admonished irritably. 'They're at the coroner's court. They said yer'll know where it is.' Her task completed, she withdrew and slammed the window.

The coroner's court was almost as close as the police station and Sam was there in minutes. A portly bewhiskered constable sat in the inquiry window and looked up in recognition as Sam entered the foyer. He nodded in the direction of a large polished wooden door. 'Sorry about the news, Sam,' he whispered. 'The case is on now, started about ten minutes ago.'

Sam eased open the door and his first view was of the witness box where Mr Shinn, the local pathologist, was in the process of giving his evidence. '. . . and therefore, I would say, death was caused by the multiple ruptures of the spleen, heart and lungs, all conducive to impalement from a great height. Death would have been instantaneous. Many of the other injuries to the body were caused by its removal from the railings but, because of the original impact wounds, they have no bearing on the death of the deceased.'

As Sam widened the door he heard a sudden whisper, 'It's my daddy!' He glanced down and saw an eager Emma running towards him arms wide. The coroner, Doctor Montague Neville, raised one eyebrow as Sam smothered Emma's noisy enthusiasm with a fervent kiss and a murmured, 'Thank God!' He searched the rows of benches, saw a white-faced Queenie clutching the hand of Jim Forsythe. So where was David? Suddenly seeing her husband, Queenie turned quickly to her left and instantly the boy's eager face peeked out at him. In fact not only David but those of his friends, Jack and Grace. What on earth were the children doing here? And who was dead – not Jane surely? Though he had yet to ask the question, Queenie's faint nod gave him the answer he did not wish to hear.

For Sam, the next fifteen minutes of the hearing were a blur as his head ached fit to split. He heard voices but they had no meaning. Reality slowly restored itself and he was able to hear the coroner pass the verdict of accidental death on his sister. Then he added how noble it was to sacrifice one's own life to save that of another, particularly a child.

Being nearest the door and still clutching Emma, Sam was quickly into the corridor. He waited for the sad little group to follow. The children emerged first, followed by Jim and Queenie. If it had not been for Queenie's arm, it was doubtful Jim could have made the walk unaided. Sam took his other arm and they made their way to the bench outside in the gardens. It was there that Sam heard the full story. As tragic as it was, it was also apparent that had it not been for the sheer physical presence of young Jack, the inquest would have been delivering two verdicts that day.

'David had made the edge of the balcony but was the wrong side of the bars,' explained Queenie. 'As Jack grabbed him, he slipped. Jack then held him, swinging by his shirt and jersey, with one arm for the time it took four people to run up ninety-six steps to assist him.'

As Jim began to recover, Sam released him. Eyes blinded by tears, he silently hugged the two boys, one in each arm.

'Can we go home now, please?' begged Jim. 'I'd like to be on my own for a while.'

As they left the gardens, there was a whistle and a small police van edged into the kerb. 'Sam!' called the driver. 'Taff Jenkins said you might be able to use a lift.' Not for the first time in his police service Sam found himself blessing the thoughtful Welshman and, within a few minutes, having allowed the children to play in the street, they had climbed to the relative peace of their own homes.

'Sorry to be a drag, Sam,' said Jim, 'but I'm absolutely beat. Since it happened I've hardly slept. If you don't mind I'll try to have a little nap. See you later, eh?'

As anxious as Sam was about his friend's welfare, he was relieved to be alone with Queenie. There were just too many questions needing an answer.

'Sure, Jim,' responded Queenie. 'I'll wake you with some tea about six o'clock.'

The door had barely closed before Sam turned to his wife and hissed, 'So why did *my* sister need to be in *my* flat, saving *my* son from his death? Where was *my* wife and his mother?'

'Where do you think I was, Sam?' she answered quietly. 'Cruising the Mediterranean with my rich lover?'

'Don't you dare be funny with me, woman,' he snapped. 'All I want to know – in fact, have a right to know – is why *my* wife wasn't looking after *my* children?'

'Just listen to yourself, Sam, will you?' she requested. 'It's *my* this, *my* that. Everything about you is *my, me, mine*! Sometimes I think they're the only words you know. Yes, I am *your* wife, same as you are *my* husband, but I don't think your being my husband means I have to possess you mind, body and soul, no more than you should possess me. You're not going to like this, Sam, so get yourself prepared. I was out working when Jane died. I work most evenings and most mornings – not for long, just a couple of hours here and a couple there. Jane knew this and agreed, in fact requested, to have the children. What happened to her could as easily have happened to me.'

'But it didn't happen to you, did it? It didn't happen to their bloody *mother*, it happened to their bloody *aunt*! Even worse, an aunt who was expecting a baby! Your neglect killed two people, you selfish cow!'

Queenie walked slowly over to him. 'Oh, wait a minute now, Sam, don't let me down so lightly. You could do a lot worse than that if only you'd ask me *where* I work.'

Uncertainty clouded his face. 'What do you mean, *where* you work? Where the hell *do* you work?'

She placed her hands on her hips and, thrusting out her breasts, stood facing him, feet astride. 'Queenie Diamond, wife and personal possession of Police Constable Samuel Diamond, London's leading bigot, works in a brothel owned by one of London's most notorious club owners. How's that grab you, Sam, eh?' He stared at her open-mouthed. 'Nothing to say? Then perhaps I'll continue, because it gets even better, or worse, depending on your point of view. She works there to save her kids from starving. After all, why shouldn't she work in a brothel? The hours are short and the money's good.' She turned sideways on to him and ran her hands quickly and smoothly down over her breasts, belly and back on to her hips. 'The clients pay their money and once their time is up, they make no further demands on her, they don't consider she's *their* personal property. Of course they might say something like, "Yer a great fuck, dahlin', see yer next week," but that's about the limit of their demands. They certainly wouldn't say, "But in the meantime, don't leave the house or talk to any strange men." You see, Mr Diamond, your wife gets more consideration from ponces and whore-mongers than ever she does from her own husband.'

Sam took a pace forward and, with one swipe, knocked Queenie staggering across the room into the children's bed-curtain which fell upon her as she lay motionless on the bed. Striding over to her, he pulled her to her feet and shook her violently. 'My sister lies dead in that mortuary and all you can talk is filth! We may have come from the gutter, my sister and me, but we would never show the disrespect that you've just shown. You've spat on her memory and I'll never forgive you for it.'

Through bleeding lips and with dry eyes, she whispered, 'You know *nothing*, Sam Diamond, absolutely nothing! For if you did, you'd know that your sister was the greatest friend I will ever have. I can't remember the number of times I've cried myself to sleep in her arms. She was kind, she was loving and she was gentle. I loved your sister in a way you could never love anyone. I have many regrets in my life, Sam, you've seen to that, but the greatest one is that it was her hooked on those spikes and not me. If it had been me, it wouldn't have mattered. She would have been the only one to have missed me and she would have loved and looked after my children in a way that I will never now be able to love and look after hers. I don't really care what you say or think of me, it's no longer important to me, but don't you *ever* accuse me of disrespect to her memory.'

'How dare you talk of my sister like that!' He nodded to himself rapidly, as if now he understood everything. 'I should have guessed what you Suffragettes were really up to. I always suspected you were all bloody queer. I understand it all now, that's why you wouldn't let me near you! That's why you're going whoring. Just so long as you get paid for it it doesn't matter. Why should it? It doesn't mean anything to you anyway.' He pushed her back on to the bed in disgust and reached for his coat. 'Where is this whore-house?'

She made no reply but suddenly the light of recognition dawned on him. 'It's Red Cross Street, isn't it? Of course it is! It's bloody Murgatroyd's!'

'No, Sam, no!' she implored 'Don't go there, please!' But he thrust her aside and walked straight out without bothering to close the door.

A feeling of total despair swept over her. Because an emotional dam had been breached she had decided many things needed to be said but the vitriol and spite in Sam's tone, indicated the whole thing had got out of hand. Feeling a faint sensation on her wrist, she glanced down to see a trickle of blood meandering its way across the back of her hand. As she looked in the mirror to examine her cut lip, she was aware of movement behind her. She swung round with alarm and was relieved to see Jim standing there. He might not have slept long but he had certainly slept heavily.

'I'm sorry but the door was open,' he said blearily. 'I was asleep but I thought I could hear a commotion. Is everything . . .' he suddenly stared and changed his tone. 'What have you done to your mouth? That's quite a gash, you should clean it.' He came over and lifted her chin. 'Keep still a moment.' He gently eased her bottom lip away from her teeth. 'That's a nasty gash you have there, young lady.' He looked her straight in the eyes. 'Sam?'

'Who else?' she responded. 'Look, Jim, Sam's gone to Murgatroyd's and I'm frightened. The mood he's in, he's liable to do anything.'

'Whyever has he gone there?'

'Because I told him I worked there and . . .' she faltered for a moment '. . . he thinks I work there as a tom.'

'*WHAT!*' exploded Jim incredulously. 'Wherever did he get that impression from?'

'Me, I'm afraid. I've bottled up things for so long and today he pulled the cork. But he's not in their league, Jim. They'll kill him.'

'I'll get my coat. You stay here and clean up that cut. But don't worry, Sam can take care of himself.'

'Wait!' she implored. 'You'll never get in the place without me, I have a key. I'll ask Grace's grandparents to keep an eye on the children till we return.'

As Sam stormed down Red Cross Street, he saw the Jenner's brewery cart with its two great nose-bagged shire horses standing patiently outside the club. Two sturdy, leather-aproned men were heavily engaged in the process of rolling a forty-gallon barrel of bitter down from the cart on to the pavement. A delicate task at the best of times, it had taken a wobble and it was now taking all their strength and attention to set the barrel back on its tracks. Picking up two of the beer crates that littered the pavement, Sam carried them through the door and up the staircase. Each door he passed had been propped open for the draymen and he did not meet a soul until the third floor where a pinafored girl with a mop and bucket almost collided with him. 'Yer a bit early, sailor, we ain't open yet. Come back in an hour or so.'

'Oh, er – I've come to see Mr Roff about some business.'

''E's in a meetin' at the moment in 'is orfice.'

'Yes, I know,' said Sam. 'I'm late, I'm afraid, can you direct me? He is expecting me.'

'You takin' them crates to 'im then?' she asked.

'Oh no,' laughed Sam. 'I was just helping the draymen, they've got a bit of a problem with a barrel . . . in his office, you say?'

She sighed. 'As if I don't 'ave enough ter do, I'm a bleedin' guide nah! All right then, this way.'

They made their way up several stairways before the girl stopped at a final flight. 'It's at the top o'them stairs, yer can't miss it. Take the big door in front 'cos the little 'un at the side is a lavatory.'

She was already on her way down before he had a chance to thank her. As he climbed the last few steps he could hear muffled voices through the door. He paused and, slowly turning the handle, edged open the door in an attempt to decipher either words or number of people present. Before he could do either, he heard the click of the lavatory door and his arms were suddenly pinioned in a vice-like grip. Someone with exceptional strength then propelled him on tip-toes into the room.

'Yer never know whatcha gonna find when yer go fer a piss, do yer?' asked Frank Cootes. 'I found meself a little sailor boy. Ain't that nice?' Giving an extra wrench to Sam's arms, he snarled, 'Say 'ullo to all me friends, sailor boy, but make it quick 'cos you've got an appointment wiv' another little pal o' mine.'

So saying, he swiftly transferred his grip by pulling back Sam's chin with one hand and placing a knife against his throat with the other. 'You've fucked me abhart once too often, me old fruit, and no one – not no one – is allowed to do that ter The Bolivian Bull!'

Chapter 20

Sam cursed himself for his stupidity and instinctively began searching for an escape. He surveyed the room to find he had entered by the only door and the solitary window was small, specially reinforced and high. If he was going anywhere, it had to be the way he had entered. Maxie Roff appeared to be holding court with three other men and a reasonably attractive middle-aged woman, none of whom Sam knew. Max peered at him for a second or two before recognition dawned.

'Well, I'm—' he began. 'It's Sam Diamond! What're you doing here, Sam?'

''E's listening at fings that 'e didn't orta be a listenin' at. Ain'tcha, me little sailor boy?' asked Frank with yet another agonising wrench.

'Okay, Frank, let go of him,' ordered Max. 'We'll see what it is he wants. Apart from anything else, I'd like to know how he got in here.'

'Oh, no, Max!' snapped Frank. 'Not this time.' He pushed the tip of the blade against Sam's throat just firmly enough to make a small incision. 'I owe this bastard one and now he's going to get it.'

'FRANK!' thundered Max. 'Let him be! If you kill a copper the local law would put us out of business in days. Let him go and we'll sort it out.'

'No, Max! Sortin' out time's long gorn. Don't worry, when they find 'im they won't know if 'e's a copper, sailor, or a tub of jellied-eels.'

Sam knew if there was to be any salvation, it could only come from his own efforts. Even if Max wanted to help, he was too far away and Frank Cootes was in no mood for compromise. On the other hand, by the very position of the knife, there was no way that Sam could make the slightest of moves without getting hurt. The trick was to hurt himself as little as possible. That meant he would only have one chance because Frank was behind him and Sam could only feel his whereabouts. Clenching his fists as tightly as he could, Sam raised them to the side and brought the knuckles down as hard as possible against Frank's lower ribs, at the same time wrenching his own head away to the right. He was momentarily aware of a sharp burning sensation to his throat but at least he was free. The knife had clattered to the floor and Frank, clutching ribs too painful to breathe, was open-mouthed and defenceless. Jane's death; Queenie's confession; the military police and the knife at his throat – all went into the two almighty blows Sam delivered to the gangster, the first to his jaw and the second to his solar plexus. Frank tumbled like a pole-axed bullock. Whatever else Sam had in mind was shelved as the earlier beating, plus the combat with Frank, suddenly took their toll. A wave of nausea suddenly flooded over him and he felt as weak as a kitten. Staggering forward, he clung to the edge of the table whilst the blood flowed freely from the wound to his throat. He was sure he was about to faint but also knew he was incapable of fighting it.

He glared around the table where everyone sat calmly staring back. He turned to Max and knew he wanted to ask him something very important but for the life of him he could not remember what it was. His hands slipped slowly from the polished surface and he crashed to the floor alongside the unconscious Frank.

Max rose from the table, nodding approvingly. 'That,

gentlemen, was very impressive. I wonder if he'd like Frank's job when he comes to? Though perhaps I should find out what he was doing here first.'

'He's a copper, ain't he?' said Buster. 'He was obviously spying on us for a raid.

'He's not that sort of copper,' explained Max. 'Anyway, he's a sailor now and his missus works here so he don't need to spy.'

'So what did he want?' asked Nathan.

'Buggered if I know,' replied Max, scratching his chin. 'But I tell you something, he don't like Frank, does he?'

'No,' agreed Nathan. 'And when Frank comes to, Frank ain't going to like him much neither.'

There were hurried footsteps on the stairs and the door was thrown open to reveal a breathless Jim and Queenie. Seeing the two figures slumped on the floor, Queenie raced to Sam's side and discovered the blood. 'What have you done to him, Max?'

'What have I done?' asked the incredulous Max. '*I've* done sod all! He bursts in my place uninvited, gives my minder a right spanking, falls arse over head, and you're blaming me! I don't even know what he's doing in here anyway.' He leaned forward and peered into Queenie's face. 'And what's the matter with you? Everyone seems to be going around spanking everyone else today. Is there something going on that I don't know about?' He turned irritably to Minnie. 'I thought this place was impregnable but it's getting more like Hampstead Heath. Do something about it, will you? Oh, while you're at it, get that doctor of ours. Tell him we've had a shin-kicking competition or something and we've got a few abrasions that could do with his expertise.'

'Supposing he doesn't want to come?' she asked.

'He'll come all right, don't worry about that. But *if* you get any problem, tell him we'll pay well then casually mention Glasgow Gert. He'll come for sure then.'

As Minnie made her exit Max appeared to notice Jim Forsythe for the first time.

'James!' he cried. 'I was so sorry to hear about Jane. She was such a lovely girl.'

'Thanks,' said Jim curtly. 'But the first thing we have to do is stem Sam's bleeding. Have you got anything to plug that hole in his neck? At a pinch, a clean handkerchief will do.'

'Clean handkerchiefs might be a bit rare amongst my mob but I'll give it a try,' responded Max doubtfully.

Jim pointed at Frank who had not moved since he hit the floor. 'What's up with this git?'

Max shook his head thoughtfully. 'I'm not really sure. I think it's getting to the stage when I've got to make a decision about him, though I could give you a valuable piece of advice.'

'That is?'

'When he revives, he is going to be narked with Sam – and I really mean *narked*. So as long as this bloke's around, Sam and his family will need to watch their backs. Cootes isn't going to let this go in a hurry, I tell you!'

'Then I'll nick him and charge him.'

'Jim, Jim,' soothed Max. 'Evidence, son, evidence. There are no witnesses, none of us saw a thing. As for Sam, well, I ask you, y'know what he's like. He's a stubborn obstinate git, always has been. Do you seriously think he'll charge Cootes?'

'Then I'll take a chance and nick him anyway,' snapped Jim. 'Because that animal's got to be seriously put away.'

'Okay, for old times' sake I'll make you a promise and it's this – Frank won't be any trouble for a year or two, how about that? It's time he had a lay down anyway. Now I can't say fairer than that, can I?'

In the absence of a first aid kit, and much to Nathan's displeasure, Max considered that his own immaculately white pocket handkerchief was the cleanest item of linen on the premises. It was therefore plugged into Sam's wound to await the arrival of the gang's 'appointed' physician.

Doctor Arnold Vincent Shipwright seemed to have dismissed from his mind the exact circumstances of his retainer and threw himself into the treatment with the enthusiasm of a first-year locum. He stitched Queenie's mouth, Sam's neck and skull, and for Frank suggested 'some opening-medicine and a tonic' which seemed to be his stock in trade for most ailments.

'He revels in this,' whispered Nathan. 'He thinks he's a bloody frontier doctor, silly old sod.'

Speeches and Buster escorted home the tottering Frank, together with his jug of quinine and a week's supply of laxative. Meanwhile Max insisted on discovering the real reason behind Sam's invasion. When he heard it he was grim-faced. 'I don't know what went wrong with you four,' he said to Jim sadly. 'Your double wedding was great! It fetched out a real romantic streak in me. Now you're a widower and this idiot thinks his missus is on the game!' He rose to his feet and took out a notebook. 'Listen, Sam, although you and I are at opposite ends of the scale, we trust each other, am I right?' Sam gave a guarded nod. 'Well, I'm going to write down here exactly what your wife does in this establishment and roughly her hours. I'm going to show it to you and you can wander wherever you like around this building and confirm it with any employee, starting with Nathan and Minnie.' Queenie began to protest but Max would have none of it. 'No, I insist. Go on, ask anyone you wish.'

Queenie watched and listened, devouring every word. She was willing her husband to refuse Max's offer but in her heart knew he would accept. As he bent to listen to Nathan's whispered reply she felt Jim's hand upon her forearm. 'He's just dead beat, that's all. It's been a bad time for everyone. It'll be all right soon, you'll see, just trust him.'

'You think so, Jim?' she asked with a weak smile. 'Take me home then, please. I've got to collect the children and I've had all the trust I can take for one day.'

'But how about Sam?'

'Sam has a mission,' she said. 'And when Sam has a mission, he needs no one else.'

The children were in bed when Sam finally returned home. Queenie stood wearily at the sink trying vainly to remove a blood-stain from her blouse collar. Though hearing his key in the door, she deliberately failed to acknowledge his presence.

'Now I've discovered exactly what you did at that club,' he announced triumphantly, 'I've told Maxie Roff you're never setting foot there again. What I can't understand is why you would want to make up such a dreadful lie.'

She turned slowly with hands still holding the soapy garment. 'Can't you, Sam?' she said quietly. 'No, now I come to think of it, I don't suppose you ever could. But you needn't have bothered, I've returned his key.'

'That's fine!' he replied. 'And I refused to accept the three quid he offered for your wages for this week. Now we're not beholden to him in any way whatever.'

She stared at him for a moment before shaking her head in disbelief, 'Sam, d'you remember a thousand years ago when we had a honeymoon and you actually loved me?'

Suspecting a trap he made no reply. 'Well, who paid for it?' she persisted.

'I never did find out,' he answered doubtfully. 'I suspected it was Billie.'

'Just another little matter you were wrong about. Max paid.'

Sam's first reaction was to respond angrily but feeling there could be more revelations he did not wish to hear, he kept his silence. 'I called into Stones End Station on the way back,' he said, desperately seeking a change of subject. 'And they contacted my unit. I can't get an extension for the funeral. I've got to return in two days' time. Would you like us to go out somewhere, the zoo perhaps?'

'The zoo is closed for the war,' she said wearily. 'But if you have any time at all, I suggest you spend it with your children and your brother-in-law because all of them, your son in particular, have just lived through a nightmare.'

The last thing any warring couple requires is to share a bed whilst their anger rages. Yet exhaustion dictated otherwise. At nine o'clock, with Sam aching for his leave to pass quickly, they fell into bed. Queenie lay awake until the stroke of ten, when she fell asleep wondering why both God and Jane had forsaken her.

Queenie was right, the zoo had closed. In fact children's entertainment was non-existent, which probably wasn't surprising in a nation which had so many other concerns after more than two years of war. Sam had taken the four children, together with a bag of rock-hard mildewed crusts, to St James's Park lake to feed the permanently hungry ducks. But even ducks have standards. The crusts hit the water like slivers of shrapnel and were, as far as the ducks were concerned, about as interesting. Still, at least the pigeons were inquisitive. Though nothing is guaranteed to amuse children quite so much as pigeons: 'Doing a pooh on Daddy's hand.' Ironically, when Sam swished his soiled fingers in the lake, the ducks showed more interest in that particular flotsam than ever they did in the crusts.

In spite of these light-hearted moments, the last two days had been agonising for Sam. As each day passed he felt he was moving further away from Queenie yet could not understand why. It wasn't as if he wanted to. All he knew was that he was continually on edge in her presence. He even began to feel ill at ease with Jim. It seemed unfair that a couple as devoted as Jim and Jane should have been torn apart by helping two people incapable of helping themselves.

'He won't bend, Jim,' confided Queenie. 'He won't bloody bend and I don't know what to do. I really do love him but he acts like he's God. He continually makes rulings for me and cannot even begin to understand why I get so angry. I swear, one day I'm going to wake up and find he's sold me – and not even to the highest bidder – probably to someone who meets his own high moral standard.' She sighed wearily. 'He's only home for three days and we are both looking forward to his departure.'

'Are you going to see him off at the station?' asked Jim.

'No, it'll be late in the evening and I'm reluctant to leave the children now. Could you do it for me?'

'Of course,' he assured her. 'I have compassionate leave until after the burial.'

'What will you do then, Jim?' she asked.

'I honestly don't know. The bottom has fallen out of my life. Being in the force, there were obviously times when I wondered how Jane would cope without me but it simply never crossed my mind that one day I might have to cope without her.'

'Will you stay next-door?'

'Certainly for the moment. Although I've decided to try for as high a rank as my education will allow. At least being a station sergeant has one great blessing. I shan't have to return to the single men's quarters. I don't think I could face that again.' He looked at her a little awkwardly. 'Look, Queenie, can I ask you a personal question?'

'You can ask me anything you like.'

'It's a bit embarrassing but, now Jane has gone and I have to work such long hours, it occurred to me, since you've now lost your income from Max, perhaps you'd care to keep my place a bit tidy? After all, you already have our – I mean my – key. I'm afraid I won't be able to match Max's three quid a week, but then for a lot of the time I shan't be here and . . .'

'Jim!' she interrupted. 'I was going to do that anyway. It's the very least I could do. I don't want your money. It's just your presence we want. Me and the twins, that is. They'll miss Jane terribly and what with Sam away in the navy, the last thing I want is for them to lose you, too!'

'Good, except for your payment, that's settled. I feel a lot happier in my mind now. What time are you expecting Sam and the children home?'

She glanced at the clock. 'Any time now but word's gone round the grapevine that Hicks the greengrocer's are expecting some potatoes about this time so I'm off to get a place in the queue. That'll take a good hour and a half. If Sam takes the children out tomorrow, would you like me to accompany you to the undertaker's?'

'No, Jane's mum has asked to do that but thanks for the offer, it was thoughtful of you.' He gently touched her hand in gratitude as she departed.

As Jim moved the old iron kettle across to the centre of the flames, his attention was drawn by the chatter of the children climbing the stairs. He was already at his door as the group reached the final flight. 'Hullo, gang,' he greeted them. 'I'm about to make tea if anyone's interested.'

The children flopped gratefully down on his settee and began to chatter loudly amongst themselves. Sam moved over to join Jim on the fireside chairs as they waited for the kettle to come to the boil. 'I used to think when you and I were slinging those paving stones around that it was bloody hard work. Then there was those long walks along the river when I was coppering at Tower Bridge. But I tell you this,' he gave a weary sigh, 'there's nothing more shattering than looking after four kids. God knows what possessed my mother to have nine! I think she should have stopped after having me and never had another.' It was out before he realised and he screwed up his eyes tight in instant regret. 'Oh God, I'm sorry, Jim! I didn't mean to . . . well, you know what I mean. I wouldn't have missed having Jane for a sister for the world.' He shrugged and fell into silent despair.

Jim smiled and lifted the boiling kettle from the stove. 'Don't let it worry you, Sam, of course I know what you mean. In fact I'm quite pleased you made such a gaff. You see, it gives me the opening I've been looking for.'

'I don't understand?'

'Oh, I wouldn't dispute that for a second, Sam. If there's one thing I'm absolutely sure of, it's that you "don't understand". I'm referring to you and Queenie. You were – I should say are – my greatest friends but I'm sad at what I'm seeing.' He stirred the old brown pot with a large spoon and eased it carefully away from the dancing flames. 'Maxie Roff was right, you know. I thought between the two of us we had scored the greatest win-double two fellows could ever make in the marriage stakes. Now my Jane's gone forever and you seem to be doing your very best to lose your Queenie.'

'You'd better not let her hear you saying that,' said Sam bitterly. 'If there's one thing she can't stand being called, it's *my* Queenie.'

'Yes, but there are ways of saying it, Sam. I'm going to take a chance and speak frankly. You are at a crossroads and don't seem prepared to do anything about it.'

'Wait a minute! Wait a minute! It wasn't until yesterday that I found out how much she confided in Jane. So what's she going to do now Jane's dead – confide in you? Don't forget she's my wife and if there's one person she should be confiding in, it's me! That is, unless she's actually talking *about* me!'

'There you go again, you see! Anyway, how is she supposed to confide in you when you're not here?'

'Yes,' Sam cut in. 'But *you* will be here, won't you, Jim? That'll be very convenient, won't it?'

Jim stared at his friend in total dismay. 'I'm sorry, it was a mistake to discuss this matter. It was neither the time nor the place. Accept my apologies, Sam, I'll not mention it again.'

The cold silence between the friends was masked by the giggling of the children. Jim blew on his hot tea and decided to chance a change of subject. 'What time are you leaving tomorrow?'

'I'll leave as soon as the children are in bed, there's no point in stopping after that. It seems if Queenie and I are alone for any length of time we only argue. It may be better not to draw out a farewell, wouldn't you agree?'

Jim refused to comment, replying simply, 'I shall be around and I'd like to see you off if that's all right with you?'

Sam nodded and called to the children to say goodnight. In spite of himself he felt a deep pang of jealousy at their obvious affection for Jim.

It was a little after midnight when the distant sound of gunfire disturbed Sam's sleep. He turned to the window to see Queenie, already standing there in her nightgown, gazing away across the rooftops where the occasional flash lit the far night sky.

'Zeppelins?' he asked sleepily. 'How close?'

'I don't think they're going to trouble us tonight,' she replied. 'It's been like it for some time now and they haven't come any nearer. If anything, they're going further away.'

'Why didn't you wake me?' he asked.

'I would have if they had come closer but I think the worst is over. It's nowhere near so noisy as a few minutes ago.' He joined her at the window where, on a fine day, they could see clear to the docks. 'It's eerie standing here feeling relatively safe, yet knowing a few miles away some poor souls are actually dying,' she added.

The intervals between flashes gradually lengthened until it was obvious the raid had finished. He turned to say as much, when he saw her face still staring out into the distance. For the first time he realised how much the passing years had changed her. When they had first met, she had been a truly lovely young girl but now that youth had faded. Yet, in its place, was a real beauty of a woman. A sad delicate beauty for sure but nevertheless a beauty that, in the shadowy moonshine, could still take his breath away. His instincts told him to reach out, hold her and soothe away all her fears and doubts. Several times he almost did just that, yet in spite of these instincts he remained incapable of movement. The moment of closeness soon passed and he knew then it would never return. It was as if fate, tired of his obstinate stupidity, had woken him in the night to award him one last chance. If that was so he had failed miserably. 'G'night,' he mumbled as he crawled back into bed.

The twins, using the dry crusts kept specially for such purpose, scraped the last remnants of porridge from their bowls as their two friends called before school. 'Daddy is taking you to school seeing as it's his last leave day, so behave yourselves and no fighting,' said Queenie. Giving each child a quick check, a lightning brush and a big kiss, she released them on the world.

The twins were excited to be able to show off sailor dad to their admiring classmates whilst many of the young mums, delivering their offspring at the schoolgates, were equally appreciative. The hubbub of the playground had finally faded as Sam turned for home.

'I thought I might find you here,' said a familiar voice. 'It's made me glad I don't have kids. I hate it when people always know where to find me.'

Maxie Roff was sitting nonchalantly on the bonnet of

his limousine. The sheer casualness of the pose, for pose it was, radiated assurance and wealth. 'I'd like to have a little word with you, Sam. What say we pop along to the Borough Market? The pubs will be open there. I think propositions always sound better over a pint, don't you?'

'I'm not sure if anyone's given me a proposition before,' replied Sam matter-of-factly. 'But I've got a spare hour and if the treat's on you . . .'

Five minutes later the car rolled to a halt at the kerbside opposite the Southwark Tavern public house. 'I think it's very civilised to be able to get a drink before ten in the morning,' pronounced Max as they entered the saloon bar.

Sam nodded an agreement, then added, 'But it's even more civilised if you turn up in a Rolls-Royce – and seeing as you're about to ask me, I'll have a pint of best.'

Two minutes later, having settled into their chairs and taken their first swig, Max spoke. 'My proposition has nothing to do with our old friendship, or what happened one night in a certain derelict building, it's entirely business. Not charity, you understand, but definitely business. Last night I got thinking about Frank Cootes.'

Sam snorted. 'With the whole world to think about, why pick on that arsehole?'

'Frank Cootes, or someone like him, is handy to me in my line of work. To be honest, I hate him and this time he is well out of order. What I really need is someone who could do Frank's job but in a slightly more civilised way. That's the proposition. I'll pay you four times your copper's wages and there'll be plenty of other perks.' He gave an expansive gesture. 'Groceries, coal, soap, women. What say you?'

'I've just joined the bloody navy!'

'Then desert! The war'll be over one day and no one'll be looking for you then.'

'You just don't understand, do you, Max?' Sam shook

his head in frustration. 'I'm in the navy because I volunteered. I volunteered because I thought it was something I ought to do.' He gave a deep sigh. 'I'm tempted – very tempted. At the moment I haven't a spare farthing but I know I could never live with myself if I deserted. I like you, Max, but really you're everything I'm against. You and I could not be more different. I'm all bloody principles and you . . . well, you're . . .' he searched frantically for words.

'The most totally unprincipled bastard you know! Isn't that what you were trying to avoid saying?' Max raised a finger and pointed directly at Sam. 'You and I come from almost identical backgrounds. Same age, same school, played in the same street, same build, same intelligence, at times we almost look similar. Yet you are a fifty-bob a week copper, living in a slum with two kids and a wife, and I am a £5,000 a year, Rolls-Royce-owning employer of some thirty odd people – and do you know *why* that gap between us is so wide? It's because you have principles and I have none. So you tell me what your bloody principles have done for you?'

'Well, they've caused me to lose this argument for a start!' replied Sam with a rare wry smile. 'But let me ask you this. You say you are totally unprincipled – yes?' Max nodded. 'Cootes has caused you bother and you will have no compunction about trampling all over him?' Again Max nodded. 'Then if you are so totally unprincipled, how come you have put yourself out so many times for me – by the way, thanks for the honeymoon. I know me and Jim saved your life but according to your philosophy that should mean nothing to you at all, yet it obviously does.'

'Sam, I agree I owe my life to you two and, if it was within me to have close friends, it could easily be either of you. But it's not. If I thought you deliberately got in my way I would smack you down without a moment's hesitation.' He paused as if he wished the words to sink in before adding, 'If you came to work for me you would need to be very aware of that fact.'

Sam drained the last half of his glass in one long gulp. 'Max, I've learnt more about you over this one pint of bitter than I have in our previous twenty odd years. I'll not work for you till this war's over but if you have a vacancy then I might well be obliged. Does that rule out a second pint?'

'Bloody well ought,' Max muttered ruefully, collecting the tankard. 'But deep down I suppose I'm a softie. Can I give you a lift anywhere after?'

'No, I'm having a quiet day before I win the war for king, country, and all you parasites who stay behind and ponce.'

'So whose just ordered the second beer that he's not paid for?'

'If ever I'm sensible enough to work for you, you can stop it from my first week's wages.'

They drank the second pint and then Sam rose to his feet and said farewell. Deep in thought, he strolled slowly back to Queen's Buildings. He was dreading the afternoon because, try as he might, he could think of no words to say to Queenie. His fears were groundless as, on his return, she pointed out the very least he could do on his last afternoon was accompany his mother and brother-in-law to the undertaker's. He took the chance almost gratefully until the mortician casually asked if he would, 'Care to see the deceased, sir?'

Sensing his apprehension, Jim whispered, 'It's okay, her face is unmarked. I know how you must feel but your mother would be upset if you didn't go in to pay your respects.'

Knowing the truth of that observation, Sam accompanied Clem Botwright into the inner chapel. His sister lay with her head and neck exposed, and the fearful wounds that had deprived her of her young life were blessedly not visible. Old Botwright had done a fair job and, impassive though it was, the face remained beautiful. For some minutes Sam stared down with tear-filled eyes before Clem, by virtue of a tactful cough and a shuffle towards the door, made it clear that time was up.

It was a silent trio who returned to Inkerman Place from where, after a cup of tea, the two friends made their way home. They were about to pass Stones End station when a ground-floor window was thrown up and they were hailed by the melodic voice of Taff Jenkins. 'Sam lad! Heard you were home, how are you?'

Sam liked Taff a great deal but at that moment had no inclination for cheery conversation, so with a polite acknowledgement he kept walking. 'Hey, Sam,' persisted Taff. 'You know Frank Cootes, don't you?' The friends froze in their tracks. 'He's a guest of this establishment and not too happy about it either by all accounts.'

'What's he in for, Taff?' said the pair in almost perfect unison.

'Anonymous call said he had a load of black market gear at his home address.'

'And did he?'

'Oh, yeah, he had it right enough, mon. But you know Cootes, can't leave it at that, can he? He has to have a go and he's taken off half of the good Sergeant Dale's ear! It was his clean one too!' chuckled the old Welshman. 'Thought that might cheer you up. Look after yourself, boyo!'

'Sometimes I think there *might* just be a God after all,' whispered a grateful Sam.

'But how can God find time to make anonymous telephone calls when there's a war on?' asked Jim.

'Y'know,' said Sam thoughtfully, 'I think he may have done it just after he bought me a couple of pints in the Southwark Tavern.'

The news of Frank's arrest and Sergeant Dale's torn ear

certainly put renewed enthusiasm in their stride, though Sam's faded noticeably as his own front door came into sight. As he entered he glanced at the old mantelpiece clock. A whole two hours to go! Whatever was he going to talk about with Queenie for two long hours? The twins were deep into some serious eating as they scraped and dug hungrily into their basins. 'Smells good!' exclaimed Sam enthusiastically. 'What is it?'

'Oh, it's a real cordon bleu job, this one,' said Queenie as she busied herself at the stove. 'It's posh title is "bone-and-broth-mash". Actually it's spuds, a few bones and half a kettle of hot water, but if you don't care for it, there's always a salt and pepper sandwich.'

'No, no,' Sam quickly insisted. 'The cordon bleu'll do just fine.'

Contrary to his initial dread, the time passed quickly as Queenie postponed the twins' bedtime until his departure. The children were further delighted when he also discovered he was able competently to recite two of only four fairy stories he had ever known in his life. Suddenly it was 7 p.m. and Jim was knocking at the door. Sam hugged the children for some seconds before kissing Queenie lightly upon the cheek. He took one last look around the room, swung his kit-bag over his shoulder and was gone.

The pair covered the short distance to London Bridge in a few minutes and, after stopping at the George Tavern for a pint, were still ten minutes early. No matter what the hour, terminal stations in wartime always seem to be seething with people. Sam wondered where they were all going and what they did when they reached there. Suddenly his eye was caught by two smart military uniforms. The smaller of the two appeared to be chatting up a plain-looking female porter who seemed flattered by the unaccustomed attention. The familiar taller figure stood apart from his colleague and gave an impression of bored embarrassment. 'What's your platform?' asked Jim, cutting into Sam's concentration.

'Eh? Oh, number seven, just there, where those two military coppers are.'

As he spoke, the taller of the two soldiers whispered in his colleague's ear and strode off towards the small urinal situated between six and seven platform.

A half-plan began to formulate in Sam's head. 'Look, Jim,' he said quickly. 'It's nearly time and I could do with a quick piss before I leave, so I'll say my goodbyes now. Thanks for everything, old mate.' He swiftly gripped his friend's hand in brief but genuine warmth. Even so, Jim was slightly taken aback by his abruptness.

A mutual 'Look after yourself' and the friends parted, Jim to the exit and Sam, kit-bag on shoulder, to the urinal.

The whistle blew and doors slammed as the 20.10 to Dover Marine groaned, creaked and inched its way down the platform. The compartment's sole occupant, a delicately scented, exquisitely millinered old lady sadly decided there was to be no one to share her journey and searched for her book. As the train gathered momentum, to both her surprise and delight the door flew open and a breathless young sailor first hurled in his kit-bag, then followed it with himself and fell panting and smiling in the opposite corner. 'Sorry, madam, cut it a bit fine, I'm afraid. Didn't upset you, did I?'

'No, young man, not in the least. I would have been quite disappointed to have travelled alone. I take it by your time-keeping you've been on leave?'

'I have indeed, ma'am, and it certainly looks like you know sailors.'

'I have three grandsons in the navy so I ought,' she replied proudly, offering him some dark chocolate. 'And did you have a nice leave?'

Did I have a nice leave? thought Sam. Well, I got beaten up, my throat was cut, I slapped my wife, my sister is dead, I rowed with my best friend, and my marriage is in tatters. But, on the other hand, I got offered a job and I have just left the second greatest bastard I have met in my life lying head down in a railway urinal, so in conclusion I would say: 'Yes, thank you, madam. All things considered, not bad at all.'

Chapter 21

Sam stood rigidly to attention as the killick finished his tirade. 'The fact that some supercilious shit from the army gets stuffed upside down in a piss-hole and probably got everything he deserved, is of no interest to me at all, Diamond. What I'm concerned about is the amount of good navy time wasted in the search for the offender. D'you know how long it's taken the admin staff to work out who was responsible for that little trick? No? Well, I'll tell yer – six weeks. SIX BLOODY WEEKS! The proper sailors among us could have sunk half the Kaiser's fleet in that time. Instead they've all been poncing around trying to trace you! Are you still disputing it?'

'I am, Killick. Very much so!'

'If you come clean and admit it, it'd be so much better for you, yer know?'

'Oh, I'm sure it would, Killick, but unfortunately I know nothing of the poor soldier. That's to say, nothing other than he knocked me over, smashed me twice over the head with a truncheon, split my chin, lied to me, and still failed to find the faintest evidence to arrest me.'

'So you deny attacking him in revenge?'

Sam put on his most hurt expression. 'But he was an *army* corporal, Killick! I wouldn't dream of attacking an *army* corporal – even if he did beat me to the ground. I should think that would almost be treasonable.'

'Right, you remain there at attention and think about how long you're going to spend in Portsmouth's Naval

Detention Centre, while I go in and have a word with the chief.'

It was difficult to know exactly what Chief Petty Officer McCawley would consider a legitimate interruption to his day. Whenever the killick had reason to call on him, he always felt it was like asking Nelson to look at his watch two minutes after he had lost an arm.

'Yes?' the chief answered irritably as he looked up with his one good eye. 'What now?'

'It's this case of young Diamond, Chief. I thought I'd have a chat with him, to prepare the ground as you might say, before the navy began anything official. But he's denying everything.'

'That's preposterous! We all know he did it. He was on the railway station at that period and had already fallen foul of the patrol. It was obviously nothing but a callous revenge attack. Disgraceful carry on for a young seaman, absolutely damn' disgraceful.'

The killick gave a deep sigh. 'That's as may be, Chief, but the fact is the two military police should have been patrolling together and they weren't. The injured corporal caught a vague glimpse of naval bell-bottoms but nothing else. There were between fifty and sixty naval personnel on the train that night. In theory it could have been any one of them.'

'But in practice?' urged the chief.

'In practice it was undoubtedly him but unless we can bluff him into admitting it, we're never going to prove it.'

'So what are you trying to say?'

'Well, Chief, after all, it was only the *army*. I mean, it wasn't as if it was the naval provost or anyone important like that. Also, they had taken a right liberty with him three days previous. If you ask me, I'd say it's ended all square.'

'That's all very well, man, but I can't just let him think he's got away with it!'

'I agree, Chief. So why don't you tell him you're taking

into account his obvious distress at his bereavement and therefore not going to charge him. But, as a token of your displeasure, when he leaves here in a couple of weeks, he's getting a lousy posting. After all, that's not difficult, we've got no shortage of them.'

The chief looked thoughtful for a moment. 'Hmmm, that's not a bad idea in the circumstances. You're right, we can't prove it, and by a stroke of luck I've got just the posting for a clever dick like him. Came in yesterday. It's here somewhere.' He rummaged through a high-piled tray of correspondence. 'Ah ha! Success!'

He offered the sheet of paper to the killick who scanned it quickly and gave a low whistle of sympathy. 'Poor sod!' he murmured. 'And just look who's skipper! Personally I'd sooner spend the rest of the war rowing in a minefield!'

In the absence of witnesses, Sam had known from the start there was never going to be sufficient evidence against him. However, he had not deluded himself into thinking that would be the end of the matter. When the list of the new postings was eventually pinned to the ship's company notice board, it meant little to either him or his fellow recruits. Running his finger down the list he saw he had been drafted to mine-sweeping duties on board the *Bristol Princess* operating out of Ramsgate under Captain Galileo Falkener-Jones.

With the course ending on a Friday, it was customary for recruits to have weekend leave before reporting for ship's duty on Monday morning. Sam was not too upset when this privilege was denied him. To ease his conscience, he wrote a long rambling letter to Queenie and the twins, deliberately allowing it to take up most of his Saturday evening. He was told there was a steam pinnace leaving the training school at midnight and, war duties permitting, he could obtain a lift because it was due in at Ramsgate harbour 2000 hours Sunday. These launches were wooden-hulled antiquities of some eighty feet in length, staffed by two volunteer reserve officers, a couple of engineers and four or five deck hands. Most of the officers came from overseas and were used on such boats when it was suspected their talents could be deficient if applied to anything larger.

They had not been at sea for more than thirty minutes when Sam noticed the whole eastern sky lighting intermittently in horizontal flashes. He turned to a squat pipe-smoking engineer who had just emerged from the tiny claustrophobic engine-room and was leaning on a rail.

'Whatever's that?' marvelled Sam. 'Aurora borealis?'

'Not unless the North Pole's moved, it ain't,' answered his greasy companion, biting firmly on his pipe. 'As it's in the east, it's probably a gun barrage on the Somme.'

'British or German?' asked Sam, before realising the stupidity of the question.

'If you were in the bloody trenches you'd be so deep in the mud you probably wouldn't know yourself,' replied the engineer. 'Never mind being eighty miles away in this old tub.'

'What does the navy use this old tub, as you call her, for?' asked Sam.

'The navy uses this heap when it don't want to risk losing anythin' worth more than five quid. In other words, we're totally expendable. If anyone's broken down in a minefield, they send for us; stuck on a mudbank fifty yards in front of a Jerry coastal battery, us again; decoys, that's us too. I hear that next week they want someone to paddle up the Rhine and shout "Bollocks to the Kaiser" – guess who's favourite for the job?'

Sam laughed and asked, 'Are there many boats like this in the Dover Patrol?'

'The Dover Patrol, lad, is full of bleedin' boats like this. It's boats like this that keep it going. Battleships'd be more hindrance than help. In fact, it shouldn't be called "The Dover Patrol" at all, it should be called "The Dover Expendable Scuttle" 'cos that's what we do – we scuttle.

We scuttle here, we scuttle there, we scuttle all over the soddin' place. Battleships don't scuttle, see, they take about two miles to turn round. That's no use if you're scuttlin', son, is it?'

Sam was beginning to sense a little mist on his rose-coloured spectacles. He had long guessed that the *Bristol Princess* was not going to be the admiral's flagship but he was getting slightly apprehensive about exactly what sort of craft it might be. It took a while before he could pluck up sufficient courage to ask the question he suspected he did not want to hear answered. 'Er – I'm joining the *Bristol Princess* at Ramsgate. You don't happen to know what sort of craft she is, by any chance?'

The old engineer sniffed and tapped out his pipe on the rail. 'Well,' he began thoughtfully, 'if they gave it a lick of paint, new engines, new superstructure and a new skipper, I'd say it might be improved to the standard of a decent shithouse. But as it stands at the moment . . .' He gave another sniff. 'Well, personally, if I was joinin' her, I'd tie meself to two sacks of coal and jump in the sea.' He blew the dead ash from his pipe and lowered himself backward into the engine room.

It had been an unusually quiet night though at dawnbreak they did see a Zeppelin feeling its way, cloud to cloud, back home across the Channel. A few optimistic bursts of machine-gun fire were tried but most of the time they couldn't even see the thing. It was extremely doubtful if the airship had even been aware of their presence. Sam suddenly heard the now familiar voice of the old engineer rising from the bowels of the boat and presumably complaining to his colleague. 'Oh, yeah, bleedin' wonderful, ain't it? Now we're bleedin' Zeppelin fighters! Give the admiralty a few minutes to put their brain in gear an' when they find out we ain't shot it down, they'll probably send us up to look for it.'

It was dark when they tied up on the quayside. One of the

hands gave Sam some fairly clear directions and within ten minutes he experienced his first glimpse of his drafting. If anything, he thought, the engineer had underestimated the craft. Certainly the one thing he had *not* expected the *Bristol Princess* to be was a paddle-steamer – and a rusty one at that!

As far as Sam could see at first glance, the rest of the crew appeared to be only marginally more experienced than himself. One young matelot, who looked like he should only be here with his mum's permission, led him to his hammock-space. He was a thin, tall, intense-looking boy, with a permanently open mouth. 'Hello, my name's Walter,' said the youth. 'Or Walter the Defaulter as most people call me.

'Normally the skipper would see you but I don't think that's advisable right now. He's – er, he's a bit tired tonight and he'll probably see you in the morning. But on the other hand . . .' he threw up his hands '. . . he might not.'

'What do we do?' whispered Sam, trying hard not to let his feeling of anti-climax show. 'You know, when we're out at sea. After all, we can hardly fight battleships can we?'

'Mainly we mine-sweep and I'm sea-sick,' said the lad solemnly. 'In fact, in any sea other than dead calm, I'm sick most of the time.'

Sam studied him suspiciously. Was this the customary 'new recruit wind-up'? On the other hand the boats he and Queenie used to hire in Hyde Park looked far more formidable than this steamer. 'You a defaulter?' asked the lad suddenly.

'Well, that's a matter of some debate,' replied Sam. '*I* don't think I am but I have a feeling the navy could see it a mite different. Why'd you ask?'

'Well, this seems to be a defaulter's boat. It's a fifty-year-old paddle-steamer that was sent for scrap in 1909 but they dug it out of the breaker's yard to use it for mine-sweeping. There are only nine of us on board and most of us have had a bit of trouble at one time or another.'

'What's your trouble?' asked Sam.

'Well, at first they said they were going to charge me with desertion and shoot me. But they didn't.'

'They didn't shoot you?' responded Sam, still not sure if he was being taken for a ride.

'No, of course they didn't!' exclaimed the lad with the first hint of irritation. 'Thinking about it, they decided not to charge me with desertion. They simply charged me with going absent without leave. They can't shoot you for that, you see,' he explained.

God, I hope there aren't many on board like you, thought Sam. 'So what did you do to merit this threat?' he asked.

'I didn't feel well and I went to the doctor's.'

'And they claimed that was desertion?'

'Well, I popped home to my local doctor because he's quite used to me. I get these bilious attacks, you see, and I didn't think the navy doctor would be any good for them. As I only live in Canterbury, I thought no one would mind. Unfortunately they did.'

'So *you* thought they wouldn't mind – and *they* thought they'd shoot you? Got that a bit wrong, didn't you?'

'Yes,' agreed the lad sadly. 'But I thought they were very good at my court martial. That's when they decided not to shoot me but send me here instead.'

'I can well understand you being very pleased with that verdict,' nodded Sam. 'I think most people would be. But tell me about the captain?' he said, desperately seeking to change the subject. 'Is he a defaulter and how does he treat the rest of the crew?'

'I don't think he's a defaulter,' said the lad. 'But he's ever so old and a bit barmy. He swears and hollers at people a lot, but he's not bad really. He spent most of his early years catching pirates in the South China Sea and there are times when he still thinks he's doing it. He retired from the navy about 1901 so they re-commissioned him.'

'They didn't dig him out of the breaker's yard too, did they?'

'Oh no!' replied the lad seriously. 'They found him in Berrynarbor in north Devon. Is there anything else you'd like to know?'

'No, I don't think so,' said Sam. 'I think that's quite enough to be going on with. I doubt if I could absorb much more. But are you sure I shouldn't report to the captain until tomorrow morning?'

The lad glanced quickly about him before leaning forward and whispering confidentially, 'He's a bit worse for wear tonight. He'll be a whole lot better in the morning.'

'But . . .' began Sam. 'Supposing we have to put to sea in an emergency, what then?'

'We never have emergencies on this boat,' explained the youth. 'It takes too long to get going. It's quite all right though, the admiralty knew all about it. That's why we mine-sweep. Y'see, if we get blown up it's not very important.'

His easy matter-of-fact tone suddenly caused a chill to run down Sam's back. What had almost seemed like a music hall comedy was actually a matter of life and death. He suddenly felt very tired. He had missed an entire night's sleep on the patrol from Dover and it had suddenly caught up with him. Perhaps if he crept into his hammock he would wake in the morning and find it had all been a dream and he was back meandering round the Tower Bridge manor. But if it *was* a dream, that cockroach, currently feeling its way down his hammock netting, looked surprisingly real.

Whether it was the stuffy air or genuine exhaustion, Sam had no means of knowing but he slept solidly for the entire night, though unsure whether he felt better for it. After ablutions and breakfast, he was just putting the final touches to his appearance before seeking the captain when a booming voice announced the captain was seeking him. 'Ordinary Seaman DIAMOND! Where are yer, yer lazy cur? My cabin at once! AT ONCE, D'YER HEAR?'

Sam had heard right enough but because the sound had reverberated around the boat, he had little idea of its point of origin. The ship, though not large, was certainly confusing with twists, turns and gangways leading in all directions. The old *Princess* had spent the majority of its early years shunting day trippers from Bristol to Weston-Super-Mare and it showed. 'DIAMOND! ARE YOU BLOODY DEAF?'

Sam knew by the last outburst that he was close. Two twists, a five-foot ladder, a short gangway and he was there. Captain Galileo Falkener-Jones sat at his desk in his tiny cabin facing the open door. 'At bloody last, man!' he yelled. 'Right, I like to know everything there is to know about my men, so tell me about yourself. What are you doing in the navy and how come you're on my boat?'

Sam mentioned as much about himself as he thought fit, carefully omitting all mention of London Bridge station.

'That's pretty impressive, Diamond!' acknowledged the skipper. 'In fact, it's so damned impressive I wonder what you're doing on this ship. Could it be there's a little something that may have escaped your mind?'

Sam was quick to realise the old man must be aware of the reason for his posting and decided to take a calculated risk and mention it. 'Well, there was a little difference of opinion between myself and a military policeman on London Bridge Station, sir. But I think he made a meal of it.'

The captain looked thoughtful for a moment and tapped his forefinger on his front dentures. 'Hmm, I'm not sure what the best phrase for being upside down in a gents' urinal is, Diamond, but whatever it is, "Making a meal of it" doesn't spring readily to mind. However . . .' he dropped his hand from his mouth and leaned back in his chair, '. . . the whole thing smacks of initiative and that's what this damned war needs – initiative! Well done, lad, well done!'

His enthusiastic tone dropped as he suddenly changed subject. 'Now, to other things. Firstly, dress. If there's one thing the navy likes it's a bit of gold braid and shiny peaks. Probably taught you that in Chatham and Dover, I daresay.' Sam nodded a polite agreement. 'Well, forget it, because if there's one thing us minnows of the Dover Patrol dispense with, it's gold braid and shiny peaks. Dress is totally informal, it has to be. There will also be times when you'll need to sleep on deck. Therefore, your first requirement is security. Always make sure you have enough rope to secure yourself to the ship. The second is warmth. As long as you can do the job asked of you, I don't give a damn what you look like but I will not tolerate any complaints about being cold or wet. As long as we can clear mines, you can wear a rubber eiderdown if you wish. Mines, you see, are a coward's weapon. They can't even be there and face you whilst they are trying to blow you to Kingdom Come. Typical of the damned Krauts. By the way, have you any idea how we sweep their mines?'

'No, sir, none at all.'

'We usually link a cable to another craft astern of us and, between us, we drag it through the minefield in a long loop. This hopefully cuts the cables and the mines pop up to the surface. So what's the obvious next problem, Diamond?'

'I assume we have to be careful in case they explode, sir?'

'Good God, man, that's what we're here for, to explode the buggers! We get our rifles and fire at them! You'd better get used to rather large bangs because on a good day we get a lot of them. Finally, as you may already have become aware, we are expendable. We are a slow easy target and any Kraut fishing off the end of a pier could sink us with half a brick and a beer bottle. But don't even begin to think about whether it's fair or not, just accept it for what it is. After all, if you were an admiral, what would you rather lose, a battle-cruiser with hundreds of men or us? However, I have no great desire to die yet and it's my task to ensure we live. But, I *am* seventy-two years old and I *do* have my off days. Any questions?'

'When do we start, sir?'

'We leave in a couple of hours. As the newest member of the ship's company, it's your job to go quickly around town and buy anything we may be able to cook while we're at sea. The cook keeps a kitty for that purpose. Anything else?'

'No, sir.'

'Well, I've got a question. Why are you the only man I've ever interviewed on this boat who has not asked me about leave? You're a husband and a father, I understand?'

'At the moment things aren't too great between me and the missus. I'd like to postpone it for a while if it's all the same to you, sir.'

'Matters not the slightest to me, lad. But don't you think about your children?'

'I've thought a great deal about them, sir, but we only have two rooms and if me and the missus keep rowing, well . . .' Sam gave a deep sigh. 'The kids are better off without me.'

'Very well, lad, dismissed.'

Sam had never been the best shopper in the world and the navy had not improved his talents. But it was generally considered that his purchase of four swedes, a dozen turnips and six sheep's heads had provided a reasonable culinary test for the cook. It was also agreed the cook failed miserably.

Three miles out of Ramsgate, the *Bristol Princess* rendezvoused with a fellow paddle-steamer, *Duchess of Lithgow*. They made their way due east to mid-Channel where it was believed several German U-boats had laid a small minefield. The reason for this guesswork was that the

Germans had recently perfected a new system of laying mines that the royal navy considered unsporting if not unethical. Previously, for a submarine to lay mines in a busy shipping lane close to shore was considered risky. After all, submarines are not at their best on the surface. But a recent development allowed them to lay mines whilst submerged. This meant that any water deep enough for a U-boat, no matter how close to shore, was extremely vulnerable. The sweep had only been under way for thirty minutes when the first mine broke surface. To the disgust of the *Bristol's* captain, it was exploded by a rifleman from the *Duchess*.

'Hooligans!' ranted Falkener-Jones, firmly believing his crew should have the first shot.

Soon several more mines emerged and eventually a dozen or so were bobbing ominously about in the choppy waters. Several shots rang out from the *Duchess* before another explosion took place. Suddenly, Falkener-Jones left the bridge and strode determinedly to the bow of his boat where, bellowing directions to his bridge, he removed a large pistol from a holster and began to take aim. 'In closer, you damned fool!' he yelled over his shoulder. The steamer changed course and headed straight toward the bouncing mine.

'Surely he's not trying to explode it at this range?' asked the incredulous Sam. 'He'll blow us all up!'

'He blows 'em up at shorter ranges than this,' complained Walter. 'Sometimes we get bloody drenched. The best place to be at this time is at the stern of the boat. It's less . . .' Sam assumed the lad was about to say 'dangerous' when an enormous explosion took place off the bow of the steamer. The blast rocked the vessel and, before Sam could regain his balance, he felt a sizable chunk of the Channel cascade down.

'Bloody idiot! I'm soaked through!' he moaned, as the icy water inevitably found the gap between neck and collar.

'Whatever you do,' warned Walter, 'don't let the old man hear you complain when he's minesweeping. If you do, he'll keep you on deck for hours to teach you to be wrapped up and watertight.'

Before Sam could reply, a second deluge found the one dry spot missed by the first. Within moments he had gone from feeling snug and warm, to soaked and wretched. For the first time, he began to seriously wonder if tipping a corporal upside down in a urinal may not have been a trifle indulgent. After the fourth mine had exploded and Sam was beyond salvation, he watched the old man shoot the mines with increasing admiration. He would pause only to cuff his nose, take a swig from a hip flask and reload his gun. Then, pouring a torrent of abuse on everything German, would resume his one-man war.

'Does he ever let anyone else have a shot?' asked Sam.

'When he's finished his flask he may do,' said the second engineer. 'By that time his aim's going anyway and he'll start telling everyone that he's been firing at Sumatran pirates. Though just why he thinks Sumatran pirates explode when you shoot them, God only knows.'

Sam knew that he should have been appalled at the behaviour of a man who was responsible for the lives of nine people, to say nothing of the steamer. Yet he knew that Captain Galileo Falkener-Jones was just what the old boat needed and the engineer on the steam launch was wrong. The worst possible man for the job would have been a young flyer, or perhaps a bitter captain, fallen from grace through behaviour or injury. To be skipper of the *Bristol Princess* may have carried less status than the captain of the Woolwich Ferry, yet the captain was perfect for the role and, in spite of their words, the crew knew this too.

As days turned into weeks, Sam realised the old man's speciality act of blasting away at mines allowed the crew to share a bravado that could not normally be experienced on such a boat. This, in turn, gave them a team spirit that many larger and more sophisticated crafts could only envy. Sam's only complaint was that, personally, he still felt removed from the war. He had joined the service through anger when his pride had been stung. His aggressive strength was at its best in tight face-to-face situations, not blowing up inanimate mines, laudable though it was. He was an attacker not a defender and he needed to be at the sharp end of the action. What he wanted – in fact, needed – was to *hurt* the enemy but he failed to see the opportunity to do that whilst sweeping mines on a paddle-steamer.

It was a mid-April morning and, as they tied up at the Dover quayside, Sam sensed something in the offing. There was a huge flotilla of small boats in the harbour and all the captains had gone swiftly ashore after giving rigorous instructions for checks of their craft. Before Falkener-Jones left the boat he had told them, once their inspection was complete, that they were to get as much sleep as possible. Sam had never found it easy to 'store' sleep, he was either tired or he was not. He found the idea that one could sleep for two days, then remain awake for three, ridiculous. With this in mind, he decided to make the rounds of the local shops to see what could be scavenged.

'Where you off to, lad?' came the captain's booming voice, as Sam was about to leave the gangplank. 'And why aren't you resting?'

Sam explained his inability to indulge in prolonged sleep and was apprehensive when the captain ordered him to his cabin. 'I've been meaning to speak to you for some weeks now, lad, sit down.' The captain poured himself a particularly generous rum, though making no offer to Sam. 'You are the only member of my crew that has not taken leave and I'm concerned about it.'

Sam sensed there was little point in arguing and kept his silence to hear the remainder of the address. 'You're a good crewman, Diamond, apart from a stubborn streak that can be maddening at times, but I've noticed a change in you recently. I usually have no time for chats but d'you want to tell me about it now, whilst I have a minute?'

After a moment's thought, Sam confessed to his feeling of frustrated inactivity which pushed a fleeting smile across the old man's features. 'When you have experienced the establishment's attitude to the fighting man, son, you will learn one very important thing. As soon as they start to take an interest in your welfare, *watch out*! Now, a few hours ago you had orders to rest. Since you have been in this navy, has anyone ever told you to rest?' Sam shook his head.

'And they're not damned likely to!' pointed out the captain. '*Unless* they know something about the immediate future that you can't possibly know. Are you following my drift, lad?'

'Yes, sir!' responded Sam, with the first tremble of excitement.

'Good! But to take this further, not only are they concerned about your physical well-being, they are also applying themselves to your cultural needs – how about that? This afternoon, in the temporary theatre, they have laid on a two-hour concert. So, what with a concert AND a directive to rest –' the old man shrugged his shoulders '– need I say more?'

'No, sir, no, indeed! I'll get my head down straight away.'

Five minutes later, with turbulent mind and tightly closed eyes, Sam lay as far from sleep as a birthday child. In spite of his doubts, he must have dozed because when the call came to parade on the harbour, he awoke bewildered. As the ship's company formed a single line, Sam glanced along the quayside to see similar scenes enacted from scores of other boats. There was a great deal of speculation as to the purpose of the intended assembly and Sam, not wishing to betray a trust, said nothing. Wild rumours ranged from an issue of suicide pills to a lecture on venereal disease. 'How can I git the pox in the middle of the Channel?' complained one hairy stoker, 'I couldn't even git it in Port Said!'

It was not until every seat in the theatre was taken that a lieutenant commander walked on to the stage and raised his hands. 'Gentlemen, we are extremely lucky today to have a group of artistes from London's variety theatres who have travelled down at great expense and personal inconvenience to entertain you. When they finish here, they have to dash back to London's theatreland to appear at their respective evening performances. So can we give a great naval welcome for these wonderful people who will be accompanied at the piano by Lancelot Merrill.'

The curtain parted to reveal a squat, bearded man at a large grand piano who rattled out a medley of popular tunes of the day, beginning with 'Pack Up Your Troubles' and finishing with 'Anyone here seen Kelly?'. This was a less than subtle introduction to the Irish comedian Kaidon O'Kelly who, on completion of his stint, acted as M.C. for the rest of the show. There were eight acts in all and when the penultimate act had disappeared into the wings, the all too familiar bars of 'The Boy I Love' began. There were few in the audience who did not know the identity of the singer associated with *that* particular song and, before she could be introduced, an explosion of cheers and whistles erupted. Kelly's witty words were completely drowned as Billie Bardell swept majestically on to the stage.

Sam could not believe his eyes. It had been years since he had last seen her and, if it were possible, she looked even better than when he had first lifted her from the sand pile on Brixton Hill. The sound almost lifted the temporary roof as she led a thousand voices in 'Whose Your Lady Friend?' and then sang a moving version of 'Poor Butterfly', so poignantly softly that most were frightened to breathe. As the storm of appreciation faded, Kaidon O'Kelly could be seen gesturing from the wings that it was time for a finale. Never an act to leave early, Billie decided to give her last song 'You Made Me Love You' from amongst the audience.

It was the one thing Sam had been dreading. A thousand people there may well have been, but he knew for certain she would find him. What amazed him was just how quickly she did it! She had reached '. . . I guess you always knew it—' when the faintest lilt in her voice betrayed her. The pianist gave an instinctive glance but she recovered her composure instantly. Leaning her low neckline over two open-mouthed worshipping matelots, she plucked Sam from his seat to roars of enthusiasm. Tugged by his collar, he followed her trance-like to the stage where she commandeered a chair left by a juggler and sat the young sailor upon it. She turned to the audience with the coyest of looks, 'I've been looking for this lad fer ages y'know,' she said, with finger in mouth. ''E's bin ever so naughty. Me dad said, after what he's done ter me, I need a weddin' ring.' She then sat on his lap, placed her arms around his neck and reprised the song. When she reached 'Give-me-give-me-give-me-give-me, what I asked for . . .' the response from the audience was so great that, for the first time to Sam's knowledge, it was impossible to hear her voice. As the last note ended, she turned slowly towards him and kissed him fully and passionately on the mouth. O'Kelly had been waiting desperately for such an opportunity and rang down the curtain. 'Billie, c'mon!' he demanded. 'Our train leaves in twenty-five minutes and we've all got our shows to do!'

She finally slipped her arms from Sam's neck. 'Quick, come to my cubicle while I change. I want you to update me because I've lost all contact.' The 'cubicle' was little more than a corner and a curtain but for two or three minutes he sat recounting events whilst she calmly undressed then re-dressed in front of him.

'Billie! Billie! Will you please *HURRY*!' came the urgent demand.

'Look, Sam, I must go,' she said softly, as she scrawled out a note. 'But come and see me when you are on leave in London. That's where I'll be appearing for the next couple of months – promise?' She stuffed the note quickly into his pocket.

'I'll do my best but we don't get much leave here.'

'Then write to me, but we mustn't lose touch again, d'you understand?'

'Billie! If you don't come we'll have to leave you!'

She kissed him again and was gone. As he walked back to his stunned ship-mates he took out her note. It contained two fivers, the name 'Palace Theatre' and a big kiss. 'I hope the entertainment's not left you too dreamy, Diamond,' said the voice of the captain, 'because in three hours exactly, your war starts good and proper.'

Chapter 22

The first thing the *Bristol*'s crew noticed as they returned to their ship was a huge open box with a tall metal-framework attachment. As they scanned the harbour, they could see most other boats were similarly equipped.

'Right, lads, pay attention,' boomed the captain. 'I hope you all enjoy a good firework display because that's what we're going to give tonight. We're gonna entertain Jerry with coloured starlighters, pretty Roman Candles and the odd whizz-bang.' The crew began to wonder if the old man had really crossed the line this time but he continued, 'Mr Brock, he of firework factory fame, has got all his little chaps to fix us all up with an assortment of pyrotechnics. So tonight, Diamond, even you should not be bored. Anyone want to place a little bet as to what we're up to? I warn you, it's ingenious . . . I just hope it bloody well works!'

He glanced around for takers. 'No? Pity, I was hoping to make a guinea or two. Right, then listen carefully. We have intelligence reports that Jerry is planning a night raid on Folkestone and Dover. As you know, there is no moon tonight and, out there in mid-Channel, it's like looking for a dead fly in a dark coal-mine. So all he has to do is stop a mile or so offshore, let rip, then scuttle for home when he's finished bombarding. Unless we can catch him at daybreak or he gets lost, he's reasonably safe.

'Well, tonight he's not going to be safe. Is everyone with me so far?' There appeared to be universal comprehension so he continued, 'At a given signal, every boat in our group will ignite their box and five Royal Navy destroyers and two monitors, who will be at our stern, will get stuck into Jerry – who by then *should* be clearly illuminated. Any questions?'

'What's a "monitor", sir?' asked a puzzled, rosy-cheeked lad. 'At my school it was someone who filled inkwells and collected the milk money.'

'Well, our monitors are a bit more potent than that, Richardson,' explained the captain. 'Monitors are one of the strangest craft you'll ever see. They're a bit freakish-looking and rather waddle along. They move sluggishly, steer awkwardly, they're full of noise, and the recoil from their guns can knock over the crew and break crockery. But they are so low slung they are difficult to see and they are like an armoured citadel with guns bulging out of her side like blisters. They are of a shape so difficult to hit that they are one of the safest ships you could wish to sail in, but they fight like bulldogs. If I was a Jerry captain, I would definitely not be happy about the presence of a couple of monitors. Incidentally, if they are firing from behind us and the noise doesn't scare the shits out of you, have a word with the MO because you're in need of treatment.' He looked around. 'Anything else?'

'Sir,' began an engineer, 'other than lighting the sky, what else do we do?'

'Unfortunately the wise Admirals never actually worked that one out. I would say our first action will be to get out of the bloody way of the destroyers and their torpedoes. Our second will be to convince Fritz that he should be trying to sink some other bugger than us. Because when he gets walloped he's going to be really annoyed and, if you're annoyed, a nice slow-moving obsolete paddle-steamer is a gift from the Gods. Hit it and you can claim you have sunk an enemy ship. You don't let on it was only a hundred-and-fifty-ton, fifty-year-old paddle-steamer with a septuagenarian captain and a crew of nine defaulters. As far as any German captain is concerned, we will be the battleship

Nelson with a crew of two thousand and a dozen assorted admirals. So as far as I am concerned, once our last little sparkler fades, we fade too – and fast! There will only be one crew out there concerned with our welfare and that will be *us*. Remember, when those fireworks first light up the Channel, not only will we be able to see Fritz but Fritz will be able to see us. I'm hoping when he sees the destroyers racing in, he'll lose interest in the *Bristol Princess* but you never know with these Germans, they are so bloody untrustworthy. Yes, Diamond?'

'S'posing, when we're busy lighting up the sky, the only Germans about are those in submarines. What then?'

'Then, Diamond, we're in big trouble and I sincerely hope the navy shoots whoever dreamed up this idea so he can accompany us to our after-life and carefully explain his theory.'

'How long will this firework display last, sir?'

'Difficult to say, larger boats have larger displays, but it'll probably last long enough for our destroyer force to obtain the enemy's position.'

The skipper was certainly right about the darkness. It was so thick it seemed chunks could be hewn out of it. After some fifty minutes' steaming, the skipper announced they were in position and it was twenty minutes to zero. The signal was to be three maroons fired in quick succession. The *Bristol*'s only armament was a Boer war machine-gun that was reasonably accurate for fifty yards but after that lost interest. However, as the captain pointed out, the Germans wouldn't know that and it certainly sounded ferocious.

The minutes dragged until the final ten seconds were reached. Someone's time-piece was a little out because, with six seconds still remaining, three powerful maroons tore up into the dense blackness. Within a further few seconds night changed to day and, sure enough, less than a mile north-east, a German force of six destroyers and several torpedo craft could clearly be seen. Sam spun to face the opposite direction and was more than relieved to see a similar number of British destroyers together with a slightly lower number of escorting boats.

With the British gunners having the advantage of surprise, a great salvo of shells could already be heard whistling overhead. The first salvo fell slightly short but the second neatly straddled at least two of the enemy ships. By now the German gunners were in place and, as expected, an ancient churning paddle-steamer presented an irresistible target.

'Shove that damn' firework display over the side, Diamond!' called Falkener-Jones. 'We've done all we can do here, we'll achieve nothing by sinking.'

As Sam ran to the stern of the boat he stopped open-mouthed as two torpedo tracks raced straight towards their rear from the direction of the British destroyers *Swift* and *Broke*. His first reaction was to leap over the guard-rail before he realised the torpedoes were passing either side of the boat with barely three yards to spare. He watched in fascination as the starboard torpedo struck the nearest German destroyer. The first explosion was severe enough but the torpedo must also have struck the magazine because a secondary blast hurled the entire mid-ships up into the display of star-shells that still abounded a hundred feet above the sea. 'WILL YOU DUMP THAT BLOODY DISPLAY, DIAMOND!' yelled Falkener-Jones. 'OR YOU'LL BE UP THERE WITH THAT LOT!'

It took all Sam's strength to manoeuvre the framework to the edge of the stern and finally, with a great hiss, most of the apparatus fell into the foaming paddle-wash. Though the sky remained bright, the fact they no longer carried their own illumination made everyone on board feel slightly safer. The German destroyer hit by the second salvo obviously had its main armaments put out of action but a heavy machine-gun from somewhere aft had no such hindrance and was making its presence felt amongst the smaller British boats of the flotilla. Suddenly it also ceased firing and its two gunners could clearly be seen running for the side of the ship. Before they reached it, a roaring searing flame engulfed the entire deck and the ship rolled swiftly over, submerging dozens of scorched men beneath its capsized hull. Though they were the enemy, Sam froze in horror.

He was aware the *Bristol* was turning sharply as the captain tried to move from the brightest part of the sea. Now there was nothing they could do except make for the dark edges, still some three miles distant. The noise was deafening, as missiles fell around them like rain and not all of them German-made.

Within ten minutes they were away from the thickest part of the battle and into the relative darkness. The confusion was immense with ships sinking, firing, and exploding. To Sam's inexpert eye, it did not appear that any boat would escape unscathed except perhaps the larger of the German destroyers which seemed to have held a charmed life. As the enemy turned for home, guns still blazing, the *Bristol*'s crew looked in fascination as the *Broke* closed in on it at high speed. At first Sam could not understand why the Royal Navy ship would need to be so near but the angle of the boats soon made it clear. The *Broke*'s guns were out of action and it was attempting to ram its opponent! There was a terrible tearing sound as the bow of the *Broke* buried itself just to the rear of the German destroyer's funnels and both ships became locked. Immediately small arms crossfire began from both German and British boats.

'Blast!' yelled Falkener-Jones as he changed course back to the fray. 'Bloody idiot! What's he think he's playing at. I'd kill him if it was my ship!' It was full steam ahead for the old paddler as she made straight for the collision. 'There're going to be a lot of people in the water, lads,' said the captain. 'We'll need to pick 'em up quick. That sea's still perishing.'

'What do we do about Germans, sir?' asked Walter.

'If any look like the Kaiser, throw them back! As for the rest, take them as they come, you'll probably not know the difference anyway.' There was suddenly a huge grating sound as the *Broke* slid back from the side of the German ship. The hole it left was enormous and the sea poured into the destroyer causing a rapid list to port. As the *Broke* eased away, the small arms fire continued until the Germans began to abandon ship. The fate of the earlier crew was fresh in everyone's mind as boats were lowered, rafts thrown and men jumped by the dozen into the cold sea. The *Broke*, though relatively successful, obviously had problems of its own. It signalled it was breaking off its action and leaving survivors to be picked up by the *Bristol* and other small craft.

'No one comes on board this boat without my approval!' yelled Falkener-Jones to his crew. 'Don't forget, *no one*!' He ran to his cabin and unlocked four rifles and passed them out amongst the crew. 'There are only nine of us and scores of them buggers, so be very choosy!'

There were two paddle-steamers, two steam launches and a monitor threading their way through the men in the water, each boat reluctant to stop whilst the battle still raged. Nets were tried but eventually the small craft stopped and the grateful survivors scrambled aboard. With a total of some sixty prisoners, Falkener-Jones ordered the uninjured German prisoners below into the various cabins where they could be better guarded. Meanwhile the injured were made as comfortable as possible on deck. Whilst a good idea in theory it was more difficult in practice because of the inability of anyone in the *Bristol*'s crew to speak German. It took some time to find an English-speaking prisoner and, by then, all prisoners had long guessed what was required of them.

In the main, the prisoners followed the captain's instructions but there were at least a dozen who, feigning injury, remained on deck. The starlight and fires had now lost their brightness and the search was becoming more fruitless by the minute. As the third consecutive man hauled aboard turned out to be dead, the tiny flotilla turned for home. Because of their injuries, only one guard was placed on the deck prisoners. If there was to be any threat at all, it could be expected from those below where two guards were placed on the companionway and one in the engine room.

The uninjured prisoners remaining on deck knew every minute was precious. The longer they left it, the closer they came to an English port and prolonged captivity. If they were to take any action at all, it had to be done whilst as near to the coast as possible and in the confusion of battle. Sam was still tinkering with the remnants of the firework apparatus when a dozen Germans swarmed all over Walter, who was busy being sea-sick on the steps to the bridge.

All things considered, the young defaulter put up a reasonable struggle and managed to shoot one attacker and vomit on another before he was overpowered. With the element of surprise lost, the prisoners were unable to take over the engine room and became indecisive as to their best course of action. Sam suddenly found this whole operation unforgivable and was blindingly incensed by the sheer ingratitude of it. He thought it typical of the Germans, without realising it was exactly the ploy he would have attempted himself should the situation have been reversed.

In ferocious anger, he seized a loose pole from the remnants of the firework-platform and raced to the German with the rifle, battering him ferociously to the deck. Too blind with temper to pick up the gun, he turned on the remainder of the prisoners and, wielding the pole like a claymore, herded them towards the bow of the boat. His towering temper was more frightening than any weapon and it was this that led to his downfall.

One of the gravely injured prisoners had sat groaning since he was rescued wedged upright against the side of the companionway. Feeling Sam had gone out of his mind and would kill them all, he stretched to his limit and finally reached the rifle. Firing the bullet into Sam was the last thing he did before slumping to the deck dead.

Before the prisoners could regroup, a machine-gun from a monitor was trained on them and they were ordered to surrender. To a man they obeyed.

Captain Galileo Falkener-Jones was not best pleased. Walter the Defaulter had been sea-sick at his post; no one had checked the prisoners for injuries; one of his crew had been shot if not killed; and he had almost lost his ship to the confounded Germans! For a moment he had had visions of having to sail the *Bristol Princess* into some terrible German anchorage to be exhibited as a trophy of war.

With the assistance of four heavily armed seamen from the monitor, he tore into the 'injured' prisoners and, none too gently, ripped open their clothes to examine every wound. Having found at least six who were unmarked, he ordered them to collect the dead body of their comrade plus the unconscious body of their enemy and carry them both to his cabin.

Sam's wound was quite messy and, without expert medical help, impossible to diagnose. The bullet seemed lodged in the rear of the shoulder and it was just a question of whether or not it had penetrated a lung. One thing was sure, the bunk was in a mess. Shame really, he had quite liked the young man. His aggressive instincts would have been useful for combating Sumatran pirates.

The naval hospital in Ramsgate was at the south end of

town and, if anyone was well enough to enjoy it, had excellent views across the shallow flats of Pegwell Bay. The view was wasted though because if anyone had reached a stage where they could actually enjoy the scenery they were returned to combat next morning.

The bullet that had buried itself deep in Sam's shoulder had not been his main problem. If it had, he would have been back in service within weeks. His problem had been that the impact of the shot had thrown him forward on to his head, reactivating his old injury. This was to cause him several months of amnesia plus blinding headaches. His days were a bewildering mixture of good and bad. On a good day, he would look out of the window and stare nostalgically across the Goodwin Sands. He would remember those few golden hours when he was happier than ever before in his life. Why did everything seem so easy then and so difficult now?

On bad days, blankets of dark depression smothered his every thought and neither threats, promises nor cajoling would move him from his room. Sadly the one visit made by his family coincided with such a day and his refusal to see Queenie or the twins angered her and distressed the children, particularly as she had called with the news of his mother's death. Nell had not been in good health since her husband had died and had gone downhill steadily since that date. It seemed her distress at hearing of Sam's injuries finally tipped the balance.

Queenie's excuses to the children on the journey home barely masked her fury. When Jim called on her later to inquire after his friend's progress, she took the opportunity to unburden her frustrations upon him. 'His mother had died and I wanted to talk to him about it. Instead of which it's flung straight back at me. I just don't care any more, Jim!' she cried. 'I spent every penny I had to take my children to see him today and he wouldn't even leave his room! How much longer can I keep throwing myself at someone who treats me like dirt? Even if he hates me, why does he take his spite out on the children? They've talked of nothing else but seeing him for days. Look at them – they're crushed. Well, he won't crush me!'

'But, Queenie, the man is ill,' protested Jim. 'He's been badly injured and he's obviously going to need time to recover.'

'I don't have that sort of time, there isn't that sort of time in the world. This injury has nothing to do with whatever ails Sam, it's just brought it to the boil, that's all. I have tried so hard but now I'm at the end of the line. Sam needs someone he can walk over and inflict his moods upon. Someone who will be happy when he's happy and sad when he's sad. Someone who will like the people he likes and hate the people he hates. He doesn't want a wife, he wants a mirror image of himself, just like his father wanted – and sadly got – from his mother.'

She stopped her tirade and, falling back on to a chair, said softly, 'Poor Jim. I'm sorry that I had to burden you with all this but since Jane's death I haven't been able to talk to anyone.' She suddenly shook her head and buried her face deep in her hands. Her hair fell forward, muffling her quiet sobs.

Jim stood undecided for a moment then knelt down beside her and slowly lifted her chin.

'Queenie . . . please . . .' In truth he did not even know what he intended to say. All he knew was that their faces were inches apart and, at that precise moment, they needed each other desperately. He brushed back her hair and saw she was holding her bottom lip firmly between her teeth. He reached forward and gently eased it away, where it remained slightly parted and full. She closed her eyes and leaned forward.

The kiss they shared was at first so gentle it was nothing more than a touch. Then, as he slid his hands around her waist, it slowly increased in intensity until every part of him responded. He had no idea how long they kissed but when they finally eased away, he began to stammer an apology. She quickly put a finger to his mouth and urgently whispered, 'No, don't speak yet! Whatever you do, don't speak yet.' Closing her eyes, she fell wearily against his pounding chest.

When the young doctor heard of Sam's refusal to see his family, it prodded him into a course he had been contemplating for some time. 'Sam,' he said, 'I think it's time we changed your treatment. I propose to give you some new surroundings. We are going to send you to London. No!' he added hastily. 'Not to your family but to a convalescent home in Hampstead. We have done all we can do for you here so we are going to pass you on. D'you understand?' Sam nodded. 'And as part of your treatment, I am going to let you make the journey on your own. I'll give you very detailed instructions, d'you think you can make it?'

Until that moment Sam had had no idea *what* he wanted. He just felt he had been buried in a swamp with sloping sides and every time he made to escape he fell back further into the slime. Yet the instant the doctor had started to speak, he knew this was what he wanted. He needed to get to London, he needed to break out. He needed to be free of everything that reminded him of what might have been. Well, he was sick of wondering what *might* have been. This time he wanted to know what was *going* to be. There was only one place to find out and that was London.

Wydmore Clinic in Hampstead had been completed in September 1914 and was intended for the confused and elderly rich. The idea was good but the timing lousy. Any well-furbished clinic completed six weeks into a world war is not in luck. Before a single paying client was admitted it had been requisitioned by the government to house at least some of the wounded from Mons. Its undoubted success, particularly with head wounds, then led to the navy sending their wounded also and after the Battle of Jutland there was always a strong naval presence.

The young doctor's idea proved inspired because, with relatively little hospital care, Sam improved enormously. The only thing that delayed his return to his unit were his occasional lapses, though these were becoming fewer. On the other hand, when Sam did have a lapse it tended to be pretty dramatic. His speciality seemed to be black marketeers.

When he had a mood, he would haunt local markets looking for any character offering rationed merchandise. He would then quietly point out that seamen were dying in their thousands to bring such items to port and it ill became anyone to make a profit from the deaths of such men. As a group, black marketeers were not susceptible to such moralising and frequently said as much. This was *not* advisable. The resulting fracas usually saw most of the goods strewn everywhere and the local police called. Cap-and-shawled women, who would not ordinarily take a crust that did not belong to them, considered these scattered articles fair game and most items usually disappeared up jumpers or petticoats long before they hit the pavement.

Though the local law did not know of Sam's constabulary background, their treatment of him was sympathetic, but after the eighth or ninth disturbance representations were made to the clinic for a curtailment of his vigilante activities.

Apart from these excursions, the biggest worry about Sam was his refusal even to acknowledge the existence of his family, in spite of Queenie's bi-weekly visits. He had gone from being miserly in his mention of them to outright denial they even existed.

'I don't believe it has much to do with his injury,' explained the doctor to Queenie, reinforcing her own suspicions. 'I think it is something that was already there and the injury has simply aggravated it. Whilst you're here I must ask you, how do you feel about having him home?'

'Having him home?' she echoed. 'But how can I? He doesn't even admit to us!' She paused before replying again. 'What would happen to him – if I said no, I mean?'

'That's easy. If you said no we would simply discharge him and he would have to make his own way in the world.'

'What exactly does that mean?'

'You've seen them, haven't you? It's the same after any war. They tramp from place to place, day to day, year after year, searching for God knows what. They have no base, they have no home. In effect they are lost souls. Salvation Army Hostels are full of them.'

'But he can be violent and I have two children! How *can* I have him?'

'Does he have no other family, parents for example?'

'His parents are dead and a young sister is already having difficulty coping with the rest of the family. If he came anywhere it could only be to us.'

'How about giving him a quiet room in a corner of the house, perhaps somewhere he could be on his own for part of the day?'

'There are four of us in two rooms on the sixth floor of a tenement, doctor.'

'I'm very sorry, m'dear. I know I can offer you no comfort but there will inevitably come a time soon when we must discharge him. Probably within a month or two, I'd say, but let's not be too pessimistic. There is the chance he will recover.'

'Be honest with me, what are the real chances of that, doctor?'

'I would have to say remote ... remote but not impossible.'

'Well, he's my husband so of course I'll take him but there is something I must point out to you, doctor.'

'Yes?'

'I know my weaknesses and I know I can be unforgiving,' she said calmly as she rose to her feet. 'Therefore I must tell you this. As I would defend him, so I will defend my children. If he harms them in any way, any way at all, I shall kill him. Good day to you, doctor.'

'I don't think I heard you say that, Mrs Diamond. But good luck to you anyway.'

One perk that the walking wounded enjoyed from the Wydmore Clinic was the complimentary passes that were issued to them. These enabled the holders to see many shows, films and concerts in the cheaper seats of central London without charge. This concession was also helped by the accessibility of Hampstead to London's West End. For Sam, it was only a matter of time before he led his little group of free-wheeling socialites to the matinee at the Palace Theatre. It was possible that he would have left it at that but, during the interval, when a Scots lad drooled over a picture of Billie Bardell in the bar, he could not resist mentioning he knew the lady. Hoots of disbelief met his claim and he immediately realised he had snared himself. If he was to keep face, he needed to be as good as his boast.

'Very well,' he said, scrawling two quick lines on the back of her note to him. 'I bet you she gives me a wave during her act.'

As the final notes of each song faded, so did Sam's confidence. By the fifth she had given no indication of knowing he was there. It wasn't until the spotlight suddenly fell on all six of the sailors and she sang 'The crew I love is up in the gallery . . .' that he breathed properly. As far as his colleagues were concerned, he could not have received more plaudits if he had sunk the Imperial German Navy single handed. To pile treat on treat, Billie invited them to her dressing room for a drink, then arranged for a taxi to return them to the clinic at her expense.

In spite of his protests to the contrary, word rapidly

spread around the clinic that Sam had been a stage-door Johnny prior to the war and he found himself inundated with request for tickets to the most unlikely functions. This soon became a great embarrassment to him and he began to avoid the clinic's social outings. It was during one such afternoon, when he had the recreation room to himself, that an awe-struck young nurse told him a 'posh' lady visitor awaited him in the conservatory. By the girl's demeanour, he knew it could only be Billie and suddenly felt overjoyed to see her. As he walked through the beaded curtain, he saw her sitting, or rather posed, legs crossed and smiling, in a beautiful white silk dress at the end of a red leather settee. Yet, for the first time since he had known her, he felt relaxed. In fact, not only relaxed, he found her stunningly attractive and said as much. Then, pulling her to her feet, he kissed her warmly.

'Sam Diamond!' she exclaimed. 'Tut tut . . . and you a poor wounded sailor too!'

He kissed her once more and said, 'Oh, Billie, you've no idea how wonderful it is to see you again!'

'But you only saw me two weeks ago at the Palace matinee!'

'That didn't count and you couldn't have come at a better time for me. I'm really beginning to think I'm on the mend. I've not lost my temper or sorted out those bastards – sorry, I mean *traders* – for nearly two weeks now. A few more days like this and I'll be back on the Dover Patrol. Hopefully not on that bloody paddler!'

'Sam,' she said, unclipping her handbag, 'I've carried this cutting around for months now and I've been meaning to do something about it. Now I'm finally here, perhaps you should read it.' The headline read MARRIED WOMEN TO VOTE. It went on to say that in a step towards universal suffrage, married women over the age of thirty years would be allowed to vote from Wednesday 6 February 1918. Sam looked puzzled.

'Don't you see, you oaf!' she chided. 'All those years Queenie fought for the vote, and now she's in the first group to get it! She was thirty years old on Monday. I bet she was ecstatic.' She stared at him for a moment. 'Sam, you're not listening to a word I say!'

'On the contrary,' he disputed, 'I'm listening to every syllable.' He looked up at her. 'D'you know, I saw that at the time and it never registered. Yet directly I saw it in your hand, it clicked in my mind instantly.'

'And do you know what I came here to say?' she asked.

'I think so. You came to suggest this could be a good excuse for me to visit and congratulate her. An ice-breaker so to speak.'

'Well, excuse was not the word I was looking for but you're not far wrong.' She gripped his arm. 'Sam, can't you see? It means I could see the children! Sod you two, if you're both daft enough to get yourself into your current mess that's your own bloody fault, but it's not a good enough reason for me to be deprived of the twins.'

He gave a great long sigh. 'But we've changed greatly since you first knew us, Billie,' he said. 'We're not star-crossed lovers any more. I think Queenie could have coped with everything but the poverty. It was that which told in the end.'

'I think you delude yourself, young man,' she said softly. 'I know that girl as well as she knows herself and I would say she could have coped with poverty. Maybe not easily, but still she could have coped. But what she would have needed to have helped her through was love and a bit of thoughtfulness. If I had to guess, I would say those two commodities were a bit rare in her married life.'

Anger appeared on his face but he did not speak. There was silence for some moments, then he said, 'There, you see, I am improving. Two weeks ago I would have knocked you down for that. But now . . .' he shrugged. 'Who knows? Perhaps you're right.'

She looked excited. 'So you'd come with me to see her?'

'Yes. I shall need to do it sooner or later anyway. I'll always regret it if I don't. When do you have in mind?'

'Sunday's the best day for me. Pick you up ten o'clock?'

'I can't see why not. Sunday it is then.'

'But you can't just walk in on the girl, Sam. You'll need to write first.'

'Whatever for? If she's nothing to hide, why would I need to write?'

'Because you deliberately buggered off and left her flat broke in the middle of a war with two young kids, *that's why*! You can't just come wandering back because it suddenly suits you! Good God, Sam, if you can't see that, you can see nothing and this reconciliation is going to be bloody hard work!'

Before he could make a reply they were interrupted by a third voice. 'Sam, could you introduce me to Miss Bardell? I've been a fan for years.' The clinic's doctor strolled slowly towards them.

'Er – oh, yes. Miss Bardell, this is Doctor Devlin. He looks after us here.'

'Miss Bardell, I have applauded you till my hands have ached on many, many occasions and it's a great privilege to meet you. I had no idea Sam moved in such exalted circles.'

'Thank you, doctor,' she replied. 'Sam has surprised very many people, believe me.'

'I shan't interrupt you for long,' he said, 'but I couldn't help but overhear part of your conversation and you, Sam, may be able to cross a little bridge for me. I'll need to give you a thorough examination, of course, but how do you feel about returning home for good? We can do very little else for you here and Sunday may be a great opportunity to test the water. What d'you say?'

'You really *did* overhear, didn't you, doctor?' said Sam with a wry smile. 'I knew I had to face this problem sooner or later. Each day I've been going to ask you and each day

I've funked it. So while we're at it, when would I go back to my unit?'

'You won't, Sam,' said Devlin. 'Your navy days are over. A loud barrage or battle could finish your sanity for good. From the moment you are discharged from here you're a civilian, though I'd give you two or three weeks on your certificate to enable you to settle down again.'

'So where does that leave me and the police force?'

The doctor shrugged. 'If I was the police medical officer, I would have no hesitation in employing you again. After all, even the police force doesn't fight sea battles. By the way, I'm more than happy to put that in writing. Unfortunately I don't work for the police, but I'll certainly do all I can to help you. I suggest you pop in to see me first thing in the morning and I'll give you a final check up. I'm sorry to have intruded, and thank you again, Miss Bardell, it was charming.' He bowed graciously, kissed her hand and left as unobtrusively as he arrived .

'Sam!' exclaimed Billie excitedly. 'You realise what this means? It means you're almost mended!'

'Does it?' he said quietly. 'It also means that if just one little thing goes wrong, I could be single, crackers, jobless and homeless.'

She tip-toed up and gave him an enormous kiss. 'And that, sweetie, is why you're a pessimist and I'm an optimist.'

Chapter 23

In spite of his original agreement, Sam's enthusiasm for his reunion with Queenie waned as each hour passed. Yet the spirit that flourishes in military hospital stood him in good stead as to a man his fellow patients arrived to wish him luck. His send off was almost royal as the blind, limping or limbless collection of humanity cheered Billie's arrival and the pair's departure.

'Wot a lucky bar-stard 'e be,' said a stoker from Norwich shaking his head in disbelief. 'Not only duz 'e's missus looks loike an angel but 'e toddles orf wi' Venus 'erself! If oi could 'ave a whole night wi' that wench, the ole Kaiser could 'ave me other leg.'

Billie heard the remark just as her chauffeur was closing the door. Sliding quickly from the rear seat and, much to his obvious embarrassment, she confronted the man face on. He began to bluster but she would hear none of it.

'Sorry I can't give you a whole night, me old dumpling,' she smiled. 'But would you settle for a big kiss instead? It's quite free!'

The dumpling thought it was the best deal he had had since peacetime and, to the cheers of his colleagues, threw down his crutches and kissed her whilst wobbling defiantly on one leg. Sam was always uncomfortable at such times and turned to stare out of the opposite window. Once more the chauffeur assisted Billie into her seat and, to even greater cheers, the car eased away. She leaned across to

Sam and, laying her head on his chest, pointed a disapproving finger. 'You're an old prude, Sam Diamond, you really are . . . and don't deny it, it's written all over you.'

'I think it cheapens you, that's all.'

'But, Sam, that's my real character!' she protested. 'Those lads weren't cheering me because I'm a *lady*, they were cheering me because I'm *cheap*! Cheap, cheerful and a bit tarty to be exact. In any case,' she teased, 'if I was a lady, I doubt I would have had anything to do with you for starters.' She tugged his arm and wriggled close to him. 'I'm determined you're not going to upset me today, Sam Diamond, I've been looking forward to it for too long for that. C'mon, gimme a little cuddle and tell me you've finished sulking, eh?' She looked at him with such an excited happy smile that he was forced to grin.

'I don't know how you do it, you cow,' he said, shaking his head. 'You have this infuriating knack of turning my emotions upside down. I could have walloped you back there, and now . . .'

'And now?' she echoed provocatively.

He shook her off. 'And now I think you're the most infuriating bitch I've ever met because I find myself wondering–' he glanced quickly out of the car window '–what the penalty would be for having a woman in the back of her car, at ten-thirty on Sunday morning in Regent Street?'

'Well, if you think it's cheaper in Regent's Park we could always turn back,' she replied, staring him straight in the eye and toying with the top two buttons of her dress. 'I'll have a word with the driver, shall I?'

'Sod you!' he muttered. 'One day I'm going to call your bluff over these obscene little remarks you make.'

She threw back her head and gave a great laugh. 'Oh, my poor Sam. I really shouldn't tease you today, should I? It's too big an occasion. Let's just relax and simmer down. I can't believe how excited I am about seeing Queenie again,

I hardly closed my eyes last night and as for the twins – well! C'mon, tell me, what did you say to her in your letter?'

'I didn't say anything.'

She looked puzzled. 'I don't understand. How could you write a letter and not say anything?'

'Simple. I didn't say anything because I didn't write anything. I couldn't see why I should. Look, I'm not here today to make a grovelling apology. I'm here to try to patch things up. The best way for us to do that is for us both to start off on equal footing. She'll see me as I am and I'll see her as she is. Otherwise it's like when they paint railway stations the day before royalty arrives. D'you know, Queen Victoria never saw a rusty nail?'

Total horror showed in Billie's face. 'If I had a rusty nail right now, Sam Diamond,' she screamed, 'I'd poke it up your arse about as far as I could get it!' She pounded his chest. 'Oh, you fool, you bloody pompous bigoted fool! D'you mean to sit there and tell me that girl has no idea that we're coming? Is that it?'

'That's right. As I say, she'll see me as I am and I'll see—'

'If you say that once more, Sam I'll . . . I'll . . .' she clenched her fists and trembled with temper '. . . I'll fucking knife you, I swear I will! Can you not see, you moron, that YOU KNOW YOU ARE GOING THERE!! THAT POOR COW DOESN'T! How can you possibly be on an equal footing? That's about as equal as Mount Everest and your stupid brain!' She clapped both hands to the sides of her head. 'I don't believe I'm hearing this.' She leaned forward and slid back the glass partition.

'George!' she called to the driver. 'Take us to Hyde Park and stop somewhere in Carriage Road, I've got to think.'

'Look, Billie—' Sam began.

'Don't!' she shrieked. 'Don't even begin to speak to me yet. I'm not going to allow you to destroy this day for me,

Sam, but I've got to think first or by God you will, I know it!'

George stopped the car by the Serpentine Bridge and asked if Billie wished to remain in the vehicle. 'No, I'll go and sit by the lake for a while and sort out my thoughts.'

Meanwhile, Queenie Diamond had just taken the twins and their two friends to Sunday school and was hastening back to prepare their dinner. She had almost reached the block entrance as Jim Forsythe turned into the street on his bicycle.

'Jim!' she exclaimed. 'It's amazing. We live four feet apart and I go days without seeing you. How've you been? You look tired.'

'I think the whole country's tired, love,' he said wearily as he followed her up the staircase. 'But for me it's this four hours on and four hours off which is the killer. In effect, it's a seventeen-hour day, seven days a week, year in, year out. I'm sorry I've not called to ask about Sam but I'm no sooner home than I fall into bed. That reminds me, I owe you for two weeks' cleaning.'

'Don't worry about that.' She smiled. 'Cleaning your place is easy. You're either not there or fast asleep. Come on, I'll make you a quick cup of tea before you drop off.'

'Heard from Sam lately?' he asked.

'Certainly not *from* him,' she replied. 'But I've been to the clinic many times and they say he's progressing well, though he'll never go back to sea again.'

'Does he know that?'

'I'm not sure, though the doctor says he hopes he may be able to return to the police force. It will depend a lot on how the next few weeks go.'

They had reached the top landing and Jim slid the old cycle from his shoulders. 'Phew, what a relief. After a full day's work and a cycle ride home, those ninety-six stairs can be the last straw.'

'Go and get yourself ready for bed and by that time the

tea will have drawn. I wouldn't mind a five-minute sit-down myself before the children come home. I'll leave the door, pop in when you're ready.'

Jim busied himself by laying out his clothes and cleaning his boots. This was followed by a wash and a decision to shave. In truth, the shave could have waited until the morning and, if it had not been for Queenie, probably would have. With tunic off and slippers on, he pushed the open door and trundled into number twenty-five. They exchanged small talk for some fifteen minutes before Jim's red-rimmed eyes noticed the mantelpiece clock. 'I'm sorry, Queenie, but if I don't go to bed soon, it won't be worth going at all.'

'Yes, of course, I shouldn't have kept you up, it was selfish of me. The children will be back soon, leave the door as you go.' She collected the tea cups and moved towards the sink. To leave the flat, Jim would have needed to go in the opposite direction, instead he followed her. She was unaware of him until she felt his arms slip around her waist from behind. She made no protest or sound but just closed her eyes and lay back against him. 'Queenie,' he breathed, 'I know after I kissed you last time we decided it wasn't fair on Sam or the kids, but I think circumstances have changed now.'

'Have they, Jim?' she murmured. 'Convince me. I desperately want to be convinced.'

'The children hardly know him,' he began. 'For that matter neither do you. I realise, to a certain extent, you and I have been thrown together by fate but I also realise that you mean more and more to me each day. Life is not only hard for you, apart from the children, it's empty. I could fill that emptiness.'

She turned to him. 'Oh, you could, Jim Forsythe, you most certainly could. But, what you have conveniently forgotten is the discipline regulations of the police force. Anyway, Sam and I can't divorce. First of all we couldn't afford it, and secondly, working-class people don't do it anyway. I knew it was for better or worse and he's my husband so I must stick by him. Besides, you'd be classified as having a relationship with the wife of a junior officer, one who's been wounded in the war as well! Heavens, man, they'd not only sack you, they'd dump you in the Tower for the next fifty years!'

'I'm prepared to take that chance,' he said. 'Are you?'

She shook her head. 'No, I'm not,' she said firmly. 'It would be very romantic but I can't afford romance. In any case, if the worst happened, I'd be trading one misery for an even greater one and you'd never forgive me anyway.'

'But how can you say that?' he demanded. 'You know exactly how I feel.'

'It's because I know exactly how you feel that I do say that,' she explained. 'In spite of everything that has happened, you love the job that you do. I think that's wonderful because few people can say that, so can you imagine how you would feel if you lost it? Every time you saw me you'd think of it. It would poison everything we have. No, Jim, I love you more than you know but I can't go through with this.' She paused to hold back the tears. 'You see, if you love me like I think you do, you won't ask me ever again because I tell you now, I would say yes – and that "yes" would be the greatest diaster to befall either of us.'

There was silence for endless minutes before he spoke. 'That's the first time you've ever admitted you love me,' he said quietly. 'But you're right of course. Not only that but Sam and I grew up together and I'd always feel a thief.' He squeezed her hands. 'Perhaps I'm just tired, I'll be more sensible when I've had a sleep.' He leaned forward, kissed her forehead and turned to the door.

'Jim!' she whispered urgently. 'You will still be my friend, won't you? I'm not brave enough to give up everything.'

'You just try to get rid of me, that's all.'

She ran towards him and threw her arms around his neck. 'Just be there from time to time for me, Jim, don't matter what else happens. Even if you meet another girl – and I'm sure you will – just let me talk to you once in a while, eh? I think I might just survive then.'

He kissed her gently until distant footsteps could be heard on the stairs. 'C'mon, wipe your eyes, you can't let the children see you've been crying, now can you?'

'You don't know them as well as I do, Jim. I bet they won't even notice.'

'You're on,' he said, placing a reassuring arm on her shoulder and turning towards the door. 'Penny bet says they'll spot it straight away!'

As the door swung open, Sam Diamond stared at his red-eyed wife and his jacketless, slipper-clad friend. 'Well, well!' He spun around and faced Billie who was three steps behind him. 'Write to her, you said, give her warning you are coming, you said. Why? So she would have time to get rid of my children's uncle and my former best friend? It looks like the cat's been away and the rat's come out!'

'Sam!' exclaimed Queenie nervously. 'I had no idea you were coming. I—'

'That's *very* obvious,' cut in Sam who then turned to Jim. 'I suppose because you've lost your missus and you thought mine wasn't being used, you could move in and help yourself, did you?'

'SAM!' shrieked Billie. 'Have you gone completely mad? You've barely set foot in the door and you're full of poison!'

'And that surprises you?' he asked. 'How come, if she's the wonder wife that everyone tells me, I find she's got this bastard, as comfortable as you like, settled in my flat? Perhaps you could explain it to me, because if this is how flagrant they are at eleven o'clock on a Sunday morning, what are they like all night? While my kids are sleeping soundly in one room, their uncle is fucking their mother in the other!'

Queenie turned quickly to Jim. 'Leave us please, I'd like to talk to Sam.'

'Not yet, I have something to say first,' he replied, turning to Sam. 'Whatever conclusion you come to in your own warped mind is for you to live with. I feel sorry for you because you never used to be like that, but you cannot condemn everyone else just because you're sick. Your wife happens to be about the most honest person I've ever met and God knows you don't deserve her. However, she'll stay by you right or wrong and, if you had any sense at all, instead of pouring this torrent of sick filth on her, you'd go down on your knees and beg her to stay. Though why she should is beyond me.

'I'm leaving now, Sam, because she asked me and for no other reason.' Turning to Queenie, he added, 'Don't forget, give me a knock if you think you need me. Goodbye to you, Miss Bardell. Sorry our meeting couldn't have been happier.'

'Oh no you don't!' hissed Sam, seizing Jim's shirt-front. 'It's not as easy as that, me old son. You can't just abuse my trust and pretend you're all indignant and hurt when you're found out!'

'Sam, let go my shirt, please,' requested Jim coldly.

'Admit it then,' he snapped. 'Admit what you've been up to with my wife.'

'Sam, for the last time, let me go!'

'Don't be so bloody stupid, Sam,' demanded Billie. 'Let him go, for God's sake.'

By way of a reply Sam threw an almighty punch to Jim's face. When they'd wrestled and scrapped in their younger days, Jim's speed had always been an asset and it stood him in good stead now. However, the room was cluttered with furniture and space was at a premium and soon he was trapped between a cabinet and the open door. Sam's superior strength then told as he crashed two fierce blows to his opponent's ribs. Before he could take further advantage, Queenie's screams suddenly reminded him of his mother's reaction to the beating he had received from his own father. In that second he realised he had become a replica of the hated old man. Fists poised, he checked momentarily, which allowed Jim the split second chance he needed to send Sam crashing unconscious to the floor.

'My God!' screamed Billie. 'Look at his head!' A pool of blood, rapidly increasing in size, spread out beneath the skull of the fallen sailor as his face drained white. Jim's anger instantly evaporated as the blood-stained corner of the cabinet told its own story and he fell sobbing at the side of his former friend.

The screams of the two women attracted several neighbours from the flats below and between them all they carried the comatose Sam down the stairs and into Billie's limousine. Jim and the two women accompanied the car to hospital whilst two of the neighbours volunteered to care for the twins.

'Listen,' said Billie to both Jim and Queenie, 'this is vitally important. Sam only received one blow – okay?'

They both nodded in agreement. 'Very well. Therefore no one knows, or can know, *exactly* what happened. I doubt if Sam would even know himself. So he fell, you understand? He fell! Because, and without being too dramatic, with Sam's recent medical history the chances are he won't recover.' She paused to let her words sink in. 'Nothing, absolutely nothing, would be gained by anyone knowing the truth. All three of us know that this amounted to a self-inflicted wound. As much as I am capable, I love that bigoted fool but this was entirely of his own making and therefore our first allegiance must be to you, Jim. The last thing you two want is for the real reason for the fight to emerge. Can you imagine how it would look? "Police inspector kills alleged lover's war hero husband!" You wouldn't have a snowball in hell's chance. Quick now, what d'you say? We've only got two minutes before we have to tell the doctor's what happened.'

Jim made to speak but was interrupted by Queenie. 'Jim,

she's right, you don't even have a choice. Unless we agree that he fell, tripped, call it what you will, you are done. You must leave it to us. Remember, you weren't even there when it happened. It was our screams that fetched you. Now all we have to agree is what *did* happen.' She looked helplessly at Billie.

'Right,' said Billie, 'listen carefully. Sam arrives home . . . finds kids at Sunday School . . . decides to put up a sign above the door to greet them on their return. Gets a chair but because he's been ill he's still a little weak. He topples from the chair, hits his head . . . yes! Yes that's it! He topples from the chair and hits his head on the base of the cabinet as he falls to the floor. There are even blood stains there to prove it!'

Jim shook his head violently. 'We'll never get away with it, and not only will I go down but you will too. Can you imagine what the newspapers would make of your presence? They'd slaughter you!'

'Rubbish!' she retorted. 'The papers might slaughter me but the public would flock for miles to see the old brass who got caught up in a love triangle. You've lost the vote two-to-one so shut up and hold your tongue. Queenie and I are in charge, ain't we, gel?'

'But what's going to happen to Sam if he recovers?' asked Jim. 'He was hoping the police would accept him back. He'll have no chance of that now, will he?'

'I don't know,' replied Billie. 'It's not that cut and dried. The medical officer at the clinic recommended the police re-employ him and just before we came away Sam was handed a note saying they had agreed to do so from the date of his discharge. If he recovers then he has a job.'

'And if he doesn't recover?' persisted Jim. 'What then?'

'For heaven's sake, Jim!' exploded Billie. 'Why are you bloody coppers always so pessimistic? You're as bad as Sam! Look, on the law of averages something has to go right sooner or later. Fingers crossed, this is it.'

With Sam's medical history he was rushed straight into the operating theatre and it was obviously going to be a long wait. Billie took the hospital vigil on for herself and sent Jim home to get some sleep and Queenie to care for the children.

'It's the only day of the week when I can help,' she pointed out. 'So let me do it, please?'

Jim arranged to call in on his way to work later in the day and Queenie also insisted on returning once the children were abed.

It was early evening before she felt rational enough to explain the day's happenings to the twins. She sat on the side of their bed and stuck with the story that the women had concocted for the doctor. 'So if Daddy had not been putting up a notice for us, he wouldn't have fallen down?' asked Emma.

This was an aspect that Queenie had not considered. The child sounded as if she felt responsible. As she faltered for a reply, footsteps could be heard on the staircase. Grateful for the reprieve she looked anxiously at the door, hoping the knock was going to be for them and not Jim. She was in luck as a short rat-tat diverted the children's attention.

'I'll go, Mum!' yelled David, leaping from the bed. He opened the door to reveal a smiling Billie Bardell.

'Well, aren't you a proper little Diamond, young man!' she exclaimed. 'You're obviously David, so where is Emma?' She glided into the room and joined Queenie at the side of the bed. 'Right, if you two children come and sit next to your – what am I, an aunt?' Queenie nodded. 'Yes,' continued Billie, 'your aunt. So if you come and sit with me . . . and your mum goes and makes some tea . . . I will tell you the good news, see.' The children chuckled and took to her instantly. Within seconds they were sitting either side of her and chatting away as if she was an everyday visitor.

'So what is it?' asked Queenie anxiously. 'Is he going to be all right?'

'With any luck, your daddy's going to be fine. He's going to have some stitches in his head and he's got to be quiet for a while but soon he will be home as right as ninepence. There, isn't that good news?' The children agreed it was indeed good news as Queenie finally caught Billie's eye and received a reassuring nod in response. After Billie taught them a little song that their mother prayed they would forget by morning, the children settled and the bed-curtain was drawn.

As the two women finally sat by the fire, Queenie begged in a whisper, 'Now tell me everything.'

'He certainly has a nasty cut,' said Billie. 'Twenty-five stitches in fact. But they think the impact simply concussed him, as it would have done even without his war injury. In other words, the two injuries are separate. Of course he'll need rest but his recovery should be good.'

Queenie closed her eyes in relief. 'I'd better tell Jim, he'll be off to work soon.'

Billie gave a quick glance to confirm the children couldn't hear. 'Queenie,' she whispered, 'what are you going to do about him? If Sam comes home things will never be the same again, you know that don't you? Sam is a very unforgiving man.'

Queenie gave a bitter little laugh. 'Tell me something I don't know!'

'All right, I will,' said Billie quickly. 'In spite of your delusions, anyone can tell Jim Forsythe loves you and you probably love him. It stands out a mile and you'd have to be blind to miss it. So what're you doing?'

'Nothing!' she replied curtly. 'I'm married to Sam and that's the be all and end all of it. In many respects he's a good man, he certainly means well.' She gave Billie a fleeting glance. '*You* seem to like him well enough. After all, the first time I see either of you for ages is when I see you both together. I'm supposed to accept that without a murmur but Sam can go mad because he suspects, quite wrongly, that Jim and I are in each other's bed all the time.'

'Well, let's talk frankly then,' said Billie. 'I grant you that there is some stupid chemistry that attracts me to your Sam. But if he was the last man in the world I could never marry him. I know I'd kill him before a week was up. But he does attract me. To be honest, I wish he didn't. I'm old enough to be his mother and a relationship like that can be quite pathetic. I grant you I flirted with him a little this time, but I think it was more to keep my hand in than anything else. Perhaps I'm beginning to feel I need reassurance.'

'Why did you seek him out again? You're not suddenly short of admirers surely?'

'Well, Sam isn't an actual admirer – in fact, he's bloody stand-offish at times! No, the real attraction for me this time was you. That is, you and the children. D'you realise until today I'd never seen them?'

'Well, we both know the reason for that, don't we?'

Billie gave a great sigh. 'Listen, this humble pie lark is a whole new experience for me, so don't make it harder than it is. What I'm proposing is a truce. I'm getting older and you and yours are my only family now. Can we start afresh?'

Queenie rose from her chair and knelt by the side of Billie's. 'I'm not in a position to turn down an olive branch from anyone, especially someone who's been as good to me as you. I'm a bit short of friends right now but – and I know this is going to be very difficult for you – if you promise not to strip off *too* many times in front of my husband, you've just acquired a whole new family.'

'Does that mean I can strip off now and again then?' queried Billie, only slightly facetiously. 'After all, a mature wench still likes to think she's capable.'

'You are a rude incorrigible bitch!' responded Queenie. 'But, okay, you can run naked over Tower Bridge if you like. But not in front of the twins, there's a good aunt.'

'Great!' exclaimed Billie. 'Now firstly, let's see what I can do about getting Sam a proper job because—'

'Whoah! Just a minute!' cut in Queenie. 'A quick late condition to our new agreement. Sam would consider that being a copper is a "proper job", and I'm sure, bearing in mind his previous attitude, you'd be juggling with dynamite to suggest otherwise. Why don't we just contact you if we find we desperately need help? That way he won't feel that sense of obligation he's so scared of.'

Further conversation was interrupted by the sound of Jim's door slamming shut, to be followed by a quiet knock at their door. Billie let him in and, after assuring himself the children were fast asleep, inquired as to Sam's condition. 'Have you got a moment, Jim?' asked Queenie. 'It's really very important.'

Within a few minutes he was quickly acquainted with the details. 'But there is one last thing,' continued Queenie. 'Sam will be coming home and I don't think I need tell you what that means?'

'No, that's true, you don't. Anyway, now you're no longer on your own, you won't need me. My promotion has given me an increase in pay so I can afford a flat.' He laughed ruefully. 'Perhaps a ground-floor one this time.'

Billie showed instant interest. 'I'm on my own! I've got an empty ground-floor flat. You could move in with me and . . .' Catching Queenie's disapproving stare, she raised her hands defensively. 'All right, all right. Just keeping in practice. I thought it might save me running naked over Tower Bridge, that's all.'

'Can I ask you a question before I go, Miss Bardell?' said Jim.

'Fire away, sweetie.'

'Has your chauffeur had so much as a cup of tea today?'

'Dunno,' she replied. 'But I would doubt very much if he has. He doesn't usually.'

'But that's cruel!' interrupted Queenie. 'The poor man must be parched and starving.'

'Not a bit of it,' countered Billie. 'He's like a bloody

doormouse, he sleeps all the time. I don't mind really, it means if anyone nicks the car they'd have to nick him too. It really puts them off, y'know.'

Jim finally said his goodbyes before swinging his cycle on to his shoulder and gingerly descending the staircase. Billie peered at the mantelpiece clock. 'I must leave soon too,' she said. 'I've a new song I must try. Look, I have a three-month tour coming up in a few weeks so I won't be seeing you for a little while. You sure there's nothing I can do before I leave, nothing at all?'

'No, you've been more than kind,' said Queenie gratefully. 'Now you've taken the plunge it would be nice if we could see you from time to time. I'm sure the twins would like it. I bet they bore all their school friends tomorrow with stories of their famous aunt.'

'Well, so long as they don't tell the true ones darling, I don't mind.'

'By the way, why did you two come today? Was there a particular reason?'

For a moment Billie looked puzzled until realisation dawned. 'Oh, yes! We came to congratulate you on being able to vote at long last.'

'Vote? I can't vote! I don't know what you're talking about.'

'Of course you can vote!' replied Billie irritably. 'You've been able to vote since February this year, as have all married women over thirty. I kept the cutting. We thought you'd be amongst the first. Don't tell me after all that's happened you knew nothing about it?'

'I haven't been able to afford a newspaper since the children were born,' she said. 'And, quite frankly, voting is not top of my priorities right now.' Her eyes narrowed, 'Wait a minute. Are you saying if you hadn't kept that cutting you wouldn't have come here today?'

'Probably not,' admitted Billie.

'. . . and Sam?'

'Same, I guess, I took it to show him. He'd seen it but because of his injuries it hadn't registered.' She placed a hand on Queenie's arm. 'Sorry, pet, are you annoyed?'

Queenie gave an ironic little laugh. 'Annoyed? No, I'm not annoyed. Weary and battle-worn, yes, but annoyed, no. You meant well, but I do wonder where my Jim would have been right now if you hadn't kept the cutting.'

'You said "my Jim",' pointed out Billie. 'But I take it you meant to say "my Sam".'

There was silence for a minute before Queenie slowly raised her head. 'I said exactly what I meant to say.'

'Oh dear! It looks like Auntie Billie's made two mistakes, doesn't it?'

Chapter 24

'Sam Diamond,' said Billie, 'you are without doubt the most insufferable, obstinate, cantankerous, pig-headed bugger I've ever had the misfortune to meet! My poor bloody chauffeur reckons he's done more running around for you since they wheeled you out of the navy than he's ever done for me.'

'What's your chauffeur to do with me?' growled Sam, looking up from his bed.

'The hospital's discharged you and he's taking you home. Your children are in the car and your wife is sprucing up the flat. King Teddy couldn't have it better, so move your bleedin' self.'

'Don't come in here giving me orders,' protested Sam. 'You're supposed to be considerate to the poor wounded sailor – or whatever it is I am now.'

'Well, there's a surprise!' she chided. 'Fancy the word "considerate" being in *your* vocabulary! I bet I could have got great odds on that. Anyway, cut the rabbit and put on these clothes your wife sent. I've not got all day.'

Sam swung himself down from the bed – provoking gales of merriment when Billie saw his night-shirt – and reached into his locker. 'It's no good you looking in there,' she exclaimed, handing him the bag of civilian clothes. 'You're not a sailor any more. You haven't been for two weeks. You're now that nice Mr Diamond from number twenty-five, so put on your coat, cap and boots and follow me.'

He made a quick farewell to the staff, though it was

obvious he had not been the most popular patient, and trundled dutifully behind his benefactor.

Having been cheated once, the children treated the promised arrival of their father with some suspicion, showing greater enthusiasm for Billie's presence than for his. David did eventually relax but Emma was having none of it. Billie, sensing Sam's increasing frustration, whispered to him not to force the relationship as the girl sat tight-lipped in the corner. The short drive home seemed to take an eternity but eventually the car rolled to a halt at the bottom of the block.

'Right, you lot, out you get,' chirruped Billie. 'You're all big and ugly enough to take yourselves up the stairs. I'm off now on a tour. You two kids take care of your daddy and perhaps I'll see you when I come back. Do I get a big kiss before I go?'

Emma made no secret of her affection for Billie as she launched herself across her father to embrace the woman. Even David, at an age when kissing aunts was considered sissy, allowed himself a little peck.

Billie made no attempt at a grand farewell to Sam beyond a, 'Look after everyone, you miserable sod,' as the car drove away. The children waved until long after the vehicle was out of sight as Sam waited patiently for them to join him at the foot of the endless steps.

Queenie, who had watched the departure anxiously from her upstairs window, had left the door ajar for their arrival but Sam, weaker than imagined, took longer than usual to make the ascent. He soon realised the climb was not without compensations as Emma began to open up to him. By the sixth floor, they were almost old friends again.

Queenie had rehearsed her opening remarks many times and changed them as often, eventually settling for a simple, 'Hullo, Sam. Nice to have you home.' After a token embrace and an attempt at a kiss, the small talk began. 'Do I have a job?' 'Haven't the kids grown?' 'Where's Jim?'

* * *

About the same time, a mile away, another meeting was taking place but this one of national importance. Lloyd George, the prime minister, was engaged in a long conversation with General Sir Cecil Frederick Nevil Macready, GCMG KCB. It was a long conversation because Lloyd George was offering the general a job – and the general did not want it. The position of Commissioner of Metropolitan Police had been held for some years by Sir Edward Henry, a weak indecisive man. Under Henry's leadership, morale in the force was virtually nil, with constables frequently working upwards of a ninety-hour week for pay less than that of the poorest labourer. In addition, there was no machinery for grievances, of which there were many, and with 2,000 policemen having recently demonstrated in Marylebone, the Metropolitan Police was verging on a strike if not mutiny. Macready was a martinet and a classic nineteenth-century imperial trouble-shooter, having fought in Egypt, Sudan, Transvaal, India and Afghanistan, with the occasional jaunt to Ireland and Wales where he had ordered a bayonet charge against miners. Whenever there was trouble in the British Empire and everyone despaired – Macready was sent. Lloyd George was certainly in bad trouble and wanted the old commissioner out but he could not do that until Macready agreed to go in.

It was said Lloyd George could have talked a dozen duchesses into bed quicker than he took to get Macready to accept the post of commissioner. Eventually, after hours of persuasion, the old campaigner finally capitulated and accepted the post. Once successful, Lloyd George did not waste a minute. He immediately sacked Henry and installed Macready as his successor.

If the force was hoping for an improvement under the new commissioner, it was mistaken. One of his first actions was to announce a plan to transfer 1,000 dissatisfied constables to the army in France, where already 360 had been killed in action, and then sack every striking officer, leaving the army to patrol the streets of London. However, with revolution breaking out all over Europe, the cabinet lost their nerve. As a result, Macready was ordered to swallow his pride and give the men the rise they sought with as much grace as he could muster. Defeat was not a word in Macready's vocabulary but, disciplinarian to his fingertips, he did as he was ordered.

Pay rose to three pounds per week plus ten shillings rent allowance. This was only paid providing the officer lived within six miles of Charing Cross. When asked why the ten shillings only applied to officers living within the six-mile radius, Macready explained that outside that area they would undoubtedly have a garden. When pressed further on this point, he irritably stated that any constable lucky enough to have a garden did not need an extra ten bob! Even so, in spite of such odd quirks, the majority of inner-city ranks found themselves a pound a week better off and deluded themselves they had won. They obviously did not know Macready, who had simply bided his time.

Sam's two-week sick leave was almost at an end when he received the awaited envelope telling him to report to Stones End police station for a medical the following Monday. 'I seem to have spent half my life going for bloody medicals,' he complained. 'I no sooner get back on an even keel than I'm off to see yet another doctor.'

'Sam, you can't possibly go for this medical unless you are absolutely sure you wish to rejoin the force and, above all, are fit enough to do the job. Now whatever happens, don't mislead the man. If you aren't fit for the work, for God sake say so!'

'Listen, gel,' he said, 'I'm older and wiser now. I can do the job right enough, in fact I'm quite good at it. Where I've fallen down in the past is impetuosity. I've acted first and thought second. Now, providing I don't get a whack on the nut, I'm fine. Any case, I'm big enough to ensure that doesn't happen again and since the strike and the pay-rise, a copper with my service can get three pounds, ten shillings a week! Bloody hell, within six months we can be out of debt!'

His enthusiasm failed to convince, though she ceased her protestations.

Days later Sam found himself squinting into a lamp while a white-coated physician attempted to peer into his brain. 'Headaches?' asked the physician.

'No,' lied Sam.

'Fatigued or depressed?'

'No,' he lied again.

'Very well, off you go. I'll submit my report and you'll hear in due course.'

'Can you give me any idea if I've passed, doctor?'

'No, except to say that after the discharged soldiers and sailors I've seen, I've come to the conclusion there's hardly a fit person left in the land. You're as good as any and better than most, so you could be optimistic. Though when any young man says he wishes to *re-join* the constabulary, I suspect brain-damage immediately!'

The doctor's prediction proved correct as a few days later a letter arrived telling Sam to report to Leman Street police station the following Monday.

'I hate to re-start a career with a complaint,' he muttered to Queenie after reading the directions, 'but this is my third posting within ten minutes' walk of the Thames. Who's getting all those plum jobs at Richmond, Hampstead and Hyde Park, I want to know? I could walk round Leman Street's manor for thirty years and not see one tree.'

'What's special about trees, Dad?' asked David curiously. 'Should we have some?'

Sam was about to explain the point of his remark when Queenie's grin caused him to think better of it and settle for a groan of acceptance instead.

After four years, a cautious optimism about the war had

manifested itself throughout the nation. The huge German successes of the early summer had faded and, by autumn, the whole course of the conflict had changed. Successes were announced daily and by late October most folk were hoping for the first peaceful Christmas for years. It was in this euphoric atmosphere that Sam reported for his new posting. The superintendent seemed fairly indifferent, as if there were far more important matters to concern himself with than yet another war-wounded copper revisiting old pastures. He quickly perused Sam's service record as it lay in front of him. 'Hmm, not too impressive, is it? Says here you need close supervision.' He glanced up. 'That true?'

'If I knew who made the entry, I'd be better suited to make a reply.'

'Why would that make such a difference?'

'Because I've known a few senior officers from whom I would accept that criticism, and I've known others who were so stup—' Sam paused. 'Sorry, sir, cancel that. I've promised my wife to cut down on my impetuosity. Though I'd still like to know exactly who wrote it.'

'That's confidential information, lad, but on the basis of it I'm going to put you on Inspector Dale's relief. He's my strictest supervisory officer and they are currently on their first four-hour duty of the day. You'll probably find him in the front office. By the way, your new number is PC 145H.'

Sam raised his eyes. 'Inspector Dale, sir?' he queried. 'Not Clarence Dale, formerly a station sergeant at Stones End, by any chance?'

'Yes, d'you know him?' The superintendent glanced back at the record, 'Oh, yes, I see you also served at Stones End. You two should get on then. Much to talk about no doubt.'

'I don't think I'll be doing a lot of talking to Inspector Dale, sir, and I needn't inquire further as to who made that entry.'

'That's pure conjecture, but I'm telling you I do not expect to see further entries on your discipline sheet. You've had your last chance – understand?'

'Perfectly.'

'And while you're at it,' snapped the chief, 'you might do something about your damned insolence!'

'I'll work on 'em both, sir,' replied Sam in a stubborn attempt at the last word.

He made his way into the front office and spotted Dale who was sitting at a desk and pontificating to one of the new women constables recently incorporated into the force. Though Sam could not hear the words, he immediately recognised the overbearing style. He waited until the lecture had finished before he spoke.

'Told to report to you, sir. Re-join from the navy.'

Dale raised his head without at first recognising Sam. 'Not another bloody invalid surely? I'm getting fed up with some of you blokes who are coming back into the force, unable to do the job properly. Throws a tremendous strain on the rest of us.' He gave Sam a quick up and down glance. 'You *look* all right,' he said begrudgingly. 'Pray tell us, what physical allowances do we have to make for you?'

'Physical?' queried Sam. 'None at all, sir! I don't have a *physical* problem, mine's more what you might call mental. Most say I'm barmy.'

'BARM—' Dale's exclamation was cut short as a faint light of recognition began to show in his eyes. 'I know you, don't I? Oh, yes! I should have spotted your insolence right away. Diamond, Samuel Diamond. Very lucky man to be accepted back in the job in my opinion, Diamond. In fact, if the truth be told, you should have been dismissed when you were at Stones End.'

'If the truth be told, sir,' said Sam, 'then there's *two* people in this room who shouldn't be here, wouldn't you agree?'

Dale's eyes narrowed. 'Let's get this straight. I'm in charge of this relief and I believe in discipline. If I have one example of your well-known misdemeanours, just *one*, I shall not hesitate to fall on you like a ton of manure. Get that?'

'Perfectly,' acknowledged Sam.

'Meantime, seeing as every other constable is out on his beat, you can do a short patrol within half a mile of the station. Come back in two hours when I'll fix you up with someone reliable who can teach you the beats.'

Sam again acknowledged the inspector before making his way, with no little gratitude, out into the relatively clean air of the most sordid area of London. Ambling down one alley after another, he eventually wandered into a narrow lane full of tiny shops and immigrants. He knew the instant he set foot in the street it was not the sort of thoroughfare where policemen were greeted with open arms.

There were numerous shabby little cafes with mysterious figures huddled at grimy tables, yet no matter how close he looked, he never once saw anyone actually eating. Heads would turn but no one appeared keen actually to catch his eye. Having entered the street part-way down, he had been unable to see its name. He studied each shop for a clue but, though some numbers were displayed, the street name was absent.

'Lost, darlin?' came a throaty female voice. 'I give good directions, 'speshully fer the boys in blue. Ten bob fer 'alf an 'our or five visits fer two quid.'

Sam peered deep into the doorway that adjoined a Chinese cafe to see a hefty woman clad in a red kimono with a yellow dragon winding itself around the waist. Though 'clad' may not have been the right phrase as most of it was parted to reveal frayed pink underwear that, having seen better days, had certainly not seen a wash since. She was so deep in the doorway, she looked like a mole evading the light.

'What's the name of this place, luv?' he asked.

She gestured around her as if the name was the most obvious thing in the world. 'Moe Ling's. I fort all you coppers knew that? We're all Chinese and yer know what they say abhat Chinese gels, don'cha, luvvie?'

Sam thought the nearest she had been to China was probably Wapping High Street but curiosity got the better of him. 'No, what *do* they say about Chinese girls?'

'They say they go sideways!' she chortled. 'Fer 'alf a quid yer can find out.'

'Thanks, but it's not what I'm looking for right now. All I want to know is the name of this street?'

The woman looked astonished, 'It's Cable Street, me darlin'. I fort everyone knew that! 'Ere,' her eyes narrowed, 'you're a real copper, are yer? I mean, yer not pretendin' y'are so yer can git a bunk up fer ten bob, are yer?'

'Look,' said Sam with a hint of irritation in his tone, 'just tell me the way back to Leman Street and I'll leave you in peace, I promise.'

By now the woman felt out of her depth and was relieved to hear the constable wanted nothing more than to depart. 'First turnin' left, then left agin, keep goin' an' yer carn't miss it.'

'I'm much obliged to you, ma'am,' said Sam giving the woman a polite salute. 'And I shall never lay sideways again without thinking of you.'

Although the episode was mildly amusing, he cursed himself for his stupidity in leaving himself so vulnerable. He had not been at the station for more than an hour and he already had blundered into an obvious vice area and wound up talking to a whore. It wouldn't need a Clarence Dale to make something of that situation.

Zig-zagging through a winding cobbled alley, he was more than relieved to see the tatty front of Leman Street police station. He was eventually introduced to his mentor for the day, one Hughie Delaney, a giant Scot, and, before he'd had time to gather his wits, was once more off towards the river. 'I've done this trail already today,' said Sam, explaining his short adventure to Hughie.

'Sounds like Nanking Nell,' boomed the Scot. 'But the lassie were connin' ye if she ask for ten bawb. She's normally on offer fer seven and six.'

'But – er—' began Sam.

'Ah, dinna worry,' assured Hughie. 'I doubt if even some

o' the lechers we have at this nick have taken her up. They'd be worried their ears'd fall off. I think her usual clients are Lascars.'

'Lascars?' echoed Sam.

'Aye, they're seamen, mainly from the East Indies. If their boat docks anywhere between here and Tilbury, they come ashore in droves. They're okay unless they've had a wee dram, then they can be bloody dangerous because a lot carry knives. If ye look like havin' trouble wi' any, whack 'em quick. If ye let them get the advantage of ye, ye'll have grief.'

Sam then began to ask questions about the station and was not surprised to learn Inspector Dale was despised by everyone. 'We've met before,' Sam told Delaney, recounting his previous experience. 'I realise now I deluded myself. I knew he was transferred but I had no idea it was on promotion!'

'Aye, he's bin here for some teem now, in fact he's the senior inspector. The problem is, wi' a weak superintendent and nae machinery fer complaint, he can do what he likes and frequently does. The man's an unmitigated bastard.'

As Sam stumbled wearily around the beat, he soon realised he was not as fit as he'd thought. To make matters worse, on returning to the station he was greeted by Dale who told him he was to report back four hours later for a split shift. Cycling home across Tower Bridge, he began to wonder if he still had the ability to do the job. The thought of returning so soon for another stint of duty made him feel nauseous.

Queenie was appalled at the sight of him. 'But look at you, Sam!' she said as he fell into a chair. 'You're simply not fit. You can't possibly return today. Didn't you explain to them?'

'Listen, woman,' he said wearily. 'The reason they took me back is because I told them I *was* fit. D'you think they'd keep me for a minute longer if they found I couldn't manage? Especially that bastard Dale. It's exactly what he's been waiting for!'

'Sam,' she began, 'I wasn't going to tell you this but Miss

Bardell said the offer of a job still stands. Why don't you speak to her?'

'Well, firstly, I object to you discussing me with someone else. Secondly, she's away for months. And thirdly, I will not be a kept man! She's not got a *proper* job at all for me. It'll just be something she's contrived. For a few weeks I'll be her toy. Then she'd tire, drop me, and look for someone else to flatter her vanity. I couldn't possibly work for her and she knows it.'

'Let's not argue, Sam,' pleaded Queenie, busying herself at the sink. 'You haven't the time and I haven't the inclination. Why don't you snatch a couple of hours' sleep? I'll have something for you to eat when you wake, what d'you say?'

Receiving no reply she turned for confirmation but Sam was beyond hearing as he lay slumped on the chair in the sleep of the just.

As weeks passed into months and peace finally returned, Sam slowly built up to his former self. He liked Leman Street as a manor. Though only separated from his previous station by the width of the Thames, there was greater variety of work. The only down side was the eternal watchfulness of Dale, coiled like a snake waiting for a false move, plus of course, the hated split-shifts. The children were growing fast and his relationship with Queenie had stabilised. There had been no physical relationship between them for years but for the first time since their early days, they were at least relaxed in each other's company.

Commissioner Macready, believing in carrots as well as sticks, had introduced a half-hour meal break and reinstated weekly leaves. Yet even these concessions did not balance up the rigid discipline and lack of appeal procedures. Discontent was rife and it was widely agreed that the situation could not be improved until the force formed a union. Unofficial – even illegal – meetings were held with ever increasing support but those attending always ran the risk of serious discipline should their attendance be discovered. A common punishment for this offence was the forfeiture of the reinstated weekly leave. These leaves were classified as a privilege and were commonly withdrawn for the most trivial of reasons. It was during one such cancellation that Sam found Dale had posted him to a traffic point at the entrance to the Tower of London. The rain had fallen in torrents and by the following morning every bit of his uniform remained wet. He put on his spare and, on reaching the station, was agreeably surprised to be greeted by an old acquaintance who had been transferred on a discipline transfer.

PC Baden Benjamin Bates, formerly 515L now 101H, proclaimed his presence with a loud announcement: 'Diamond! Yer owe me thirty bob!'

'Well, I'm buggered!' exclaimed Sam. 'If it's not old Baden Benjie! What on earth are you doing here?'

'Apparently I'm posted wi' you, whilst I'm larning the beats. Though why I should be posted wi' such a welshing bar'sted, God only knows.'

'So what evil did you do to merit a transfer to this nick?' persisted Sam.

'A grave misunderstandin', boy, thass all it were. The guv'nor o' the King's Arms done his money at the Derby an' came 'ome early. 'Is wife told 'im she called me 'cos 'er cat were trapped in the attic but 'e didn't believe it. Didn't wanna believe it if yer asks me. Anyway, what about me thirty bob, yer sod?'

One advantage of showing a newcomer around the manor was the freedom to chat. 'Idling and gossiping' can hardly be alleged when the prime function is to impart knowledge. 'Come on then, Benjie,' instructed Sam. 'We'll take a stroll down Cable Street, it's one of our more interesting locations.'

The pair chatted merrily as they swopped recent histories. Nearing the river, a worried elderly woman told them a dog was trapped in the mud left by the receding tide and was in grave danger of drowning. Reaching the scene, their first glimpse confirmed the animal was well and truly marooned. It was two yards from the water's edge and thirty yards from the nearest steps, surrounded by acres of oozing wet mud. The problem was how to get it out.

'As you're the new man, Benjie,' said Sam, 'I think it's a job for you.'

'Nart on yer life!' Benjie protested. 'Nart only am I senior man but you owe me money. Tell yer waart, *you* git that dog out an' I'll cancel the debt. Can't say fairer, eh?' During the two men's entire acquaintance, Baden Benjamin Bates had made just two suggestions. The first resulted in Sam joining the force, the second was to result in his leaving.

'Okay,' groaned Sam. 'Anything to get you off my back. Let's see how many planks and boxes we can find first.'

With a fair bit of ingenuity, Sam made a path of sorts that led from the bottom of the steps to within a yard or two of the dog. He had made fair progress until the dog suddenly became bored and decided to move. When Sam changed direction, the creature moved again. This game went on for some time, much to the delight of a dozen cheering dockers giving unhelpful directions from the sanctuary of a nearby barge. All his 'Here, Boy', 'Good lad' and 'Bugger yer, yer bastard' fell on deaf canine ears as the animal enjoyed the game to the full by skipping even further across the mud-flats. Eventually it reached the entrance to St Katherine's Dock where it simply swam into the dock entrance, strolled up the slipway, shook itself and vanished. With mud splattered up to his chest, Sam not only looked awful but smelt worse. Much to the amusement of Benjie who finally recovered enough to state, 'Wur the best thirty-barb's worth I've ever 'ad!'

'I can't patrol like this,' complained Sam. 'We'll have to go back to the nick.'

In an effort to avoid too much public attention they filtered their way through an assortment of twisting alleys and narrow passages, much to the discomfort of those passing by. The very person Sam did not want to see was standing ominously on the station steps. Inspector Dale screwed up his nose in disapproval.

'You can't enter this building smelling like a sewer, Diamond, go and change at once.'

Sam pointed out that with a uniform still wet from the previous day, that was out of the question. Dale replied that to have one uniform wet and the other in such a state was dereliction of duty, particularly as the evidence, i.e. the dog, had vanished. It may be that even Dale would not have pursued that particular charge but Sam was in no mood to find out. 'If you hadn't cancelled my day off to put me on traffic-point out of nothing but sheer bloody-mindedness,' he snapped, 'I would have had another uniform, you stupid vindictive bastard!'

True to form, it was the verbal offence which sunk him and exactly the opportunity Dale had wanted. Benjie could only listen in disbelief. He could have given crucial evidence about the phantom dog but he could only destroy Sam if he were to give evidence about the conversation. 'I'm sorry, sir, but I 'eard nuthun',' was all he could muster.

It was three weeks before the hearing. Even the discipline board guessed there were strong undercurrents which did not come out in the evidence but with Sam's past misdemeanours, they felt obliged to back the inspector.

'Sam, you've done it again!' exclaimed Queenie. 'Four weekly leaves *and* a week's pay forfeited! We won't have a penny and we're right back where we started! It's so unfair, can't you appeal?'

'No,' he answered glumly. 'There's no appeal. What's done is done. But there's a big protest demonstration in Trafalgar Square on the third of May, they'll have to recognize us after that. The way most men feel now, we'll have an official union by autumn. They can't keep treating us like this, there's unrest everywhere.'

The day could not come quick enough for Sam. Finishing night-duty at 6 a.m., he snatched a quick nap before joining

2,000 colleagues assembling in Kennington Park for the march to Trafalgar Square. They were blessed with beautiful weather and the several accompanying bands, together with the colourful banners and streamers, gave the whole assembly a festive appearance. Shortly after mid-day, and to prolonged cheers from their families, they set off happily on their two-mile march.

Though the government had stated they would never sanction a police union, the marchers considered this stance an irrelevance. If they could not have an approved union, they would have one that was unapproved, and if that was denied them they would strike. After all, they had won their battle over pay so they would win again over despotism. With the amount of civil unrest in the country, no parliament could govern without police on the streets. Well, that was the theory but Macready had had a year to prepare his campaign and Macready never lost twice. He again gave away carrots in the shape of a £1 per week rise and the abolition of the split shift. He then showed his stick by stating any man joining a union, official or otherwise, would be dismissed. But on a sunny day, with bands playing, crowds cheering and friends singing alongside, it was difficult to imagine defeat.

There was euphoria as they left the park and it remained as they marched proudly over Westminster Bridge and past Downing Street. It was the solitary man, standing on the little traffic-island at the entrance to Trafalgar Square, who caused doubt to creep in. General Sir Cecil Frederick Nevil Macready, GCMG KCB, had left Scotland Yard at noon and walked to the Garrick Club where he had lunched well. Enjoying the sunshine, he had strolled casually down St Martins Lane and across Trafalgar Square where he decided he could see every demonstrator individually by taking up position on the traffic-island. It was there, attired in top hat, spats, frock coat, button-hole and gold-knobbed walking stick, that he eye-balled each and every one of his 2,000 men as they entered the square. The band went off-key, singing faded and gazes fell. First round to General Macready.

There was no doubting the anti-climax that was felt. All the brave speeches, all the promises, all the rhetoric was undermined by the image of the lone dandy on a traffic-island brazening out 2,000 men who hated his guts. Martinet he may have been but the bastard had style. Although he would never have admitted it, even to himself, Sam knew from that moment his days with the police were numbered.

It was a very different crowd that left the square. Most put on a brave face but Queenie saw through it the instant Sam walked in the door.

'Sam, please promise me you won't strike! There's no work out there and for sure he'll get rid of you all. The man scares me witless. He's tough, unemotional, and he doesn't bluff.'

'He can't possibly get rid of everyone, gel. He wouldn't dare.'

But when he returned to work that night his conviction received the greatest blow. Fifteen colleagues who had expressed support for a strike had changed their minds. 'But why?' pleaded Sam. 'Why at this stage? Why, when we finally have the chance to beat the bastards?'

'Oh, yeah?' said one, sliding a circular across the table. 'Then read this.'

Not only was dismissal threatened for striking but two years' imprisonment also for 'causing disaffection'. For most it was the final straw.

A few weeks later, on 31 July, Sam joined 1,080 colleagues on a strike for representation. Of his colleagues, 17,923 did not. The next day, 1 August, 1,080 policemen – among them PC 145H Samuel Obadiah Diamond – joined the three million already unemployed. A second-round knockout to General Sir Cecil Frederick Nevil Macready, GCMG KCB.

Chapter 25

'It's no good, Sam, we must talk. The twins are getting bigger and we're getting poorer. You are going to have to swallow your pride and let me return to Murgatroyd's. Max said I can have my old job any time I want it and I've not had a fit now for a couple of years.' Queenie had rehearsed those three sentences for hours and even prepared the sequel for Sam's customary objection. She was non-plussed when, with one condition, he agreed. 'I have one more job interview,' he replied. 'He's specifically requested an ex-copper. If I don't get it, I'll have no choice, you can work for Max.'

'Great,' she enthused. 'So where's the job, bearing in mind you've had twenty-seven refusals to date?'

'The firm is in the Strand. It has lots of very important foreign business associates, politicians and clients and needs an escort. The boss wants someone trustworthy because a lot of valuables and cash are handled, and the pay – wait for it – is six pounds a week! I have an interview Saturday morning at ten o'clock.'

'Sam, that's wonderful! D'you think you'll get it?'

'Can but try. I'm borrowing Benjie Bates' bowler hat and brolly. He was going to charge me two bob for the loan but he's relented and now it's free. Anyway, the bugger owes me that for getting me to chase that stupid dog!'

Saturday morning found Sam preparing for his interview. The final result impressed even the twins and their friends as they prepared for a trip to the park. 'Mr Diamond!' said Grace. 'You do look a toff! Don't he, Jack? Don't he look a toff?'

Jack agreed. 'You look very smart indeed, sir, and I'm sure you'll get the job.'

'Well, thanks, Jack. That's very kind of you. I understand you're working now?'

'Yes, sir, I work in Mr Roff's office but I get every other Saturday off.'

'It seems everyone works for Mr Roff these days,' replied Sam with a tinge of envy. 'Anyway, mind how you go. And enjoy yourselves, all of you.'

To a cheery chorus of 'thank you's' the children clattered down the stairs. Sam watched them go before murmuring to Queenie, 'That Jack's a strange boy, y'know. He's so polite, yet he always makes me feel uncomfortable. He's so ... what can I say ... unemotional? Yes, that it, he's unemotional.'

'He may be unemotional,' agreed Queenie, 'but Grace is absolutely beautiful. She's going to be a right little heartbreaker when she grows up and I think our David may well be the first to suffer. Anyway, enough of them, are you ready?'

'As ready as I'll ever be. Wish me luck, brush me down, and I'll be off.'

As the morning was pleasant, and rather than risk creasing his clothes on a tram, Sam walked the two miles to the Strand. Riddell, Riddell & Percy was situated on the second floor of an office block near the Aldwych. The receptionist was skinny, toffee-nosed and supercilious. She quizzed Sam at such length that he wondered if her interrogation was part of the interview. She finally appeared satisfied and, after ordering him to be seated, disappeared into the interior before returning to announce reverently, 'Mr Percy will see you now.'

Mr Percy, a well-fed bald little gentleman, obviously

looked after himself well. The office was palatial, with oil paintings, oak panelling, leather seats and an ankle-deep carpet. Other than Mr Percy's, no chair was to be seen and Sam had no choice but to stand in front of his desk like a defaulter. Mr Percy appeared particularly intrigued by his naval exploits. 'Do I understand you have left the constabulary because of your wish to better yourself?' he asked.

'I couldn't "better" myself more than the force, sir,' Sam corrected. 'I did not *leave*, I was dismissed because I went on strike. I wouldn't have left otherwise.'

'WHAT!' exclaimed Mr Percy, rising to his little feet. 'You came out on strike and now have the effrontery to apply to this firm – to *this* firm I say – for employment? Get out, man! Get out at once, d'you hear! You'll not get a job here nor anywhere else, I'm glad to say!'

Sam stared at the man for a moment whilst he considered punching his mouth. Instead he tapped Benjie's bowler back on to his head, hooked his brolly on his arm and politely said, 'Sir, you are a know nothing prat and I wouldn't work for you even if you had manners. Good day.'

As he strode proudly through the secretary's office, she looked up questioningly. 'No, I didn't get the job,' he informed her. 'And I pity you and anyone else working for that pompous shit.'

In spite of his defiant outburst, he knew he was now in serious financial trouble. On his journey to the interview, he walked to save creasing his trousers. On his return, he walked to save the fare. He had long suspected employers had placed an embargo on police strikers and Percy had all but confirmed it. Deep in thought he found himself passing the recreation ground where his children and their friends were playing cricket. Strolling towards them, he realised a confrontation appeared imminent between the four of them and a gang of older boys. At first, he was not too perturbed and simply decided to sit and watch in the hope the youngsters would resolve it themselves. Suddenly matters came to a head. The two largest members of the gang rushed forward at Jack whilst the rest swarmed over David and the girls. A piercing scream caused Sam to leap to his feet and run to help.

He was almost there before he realised the scream was nothing to do with the girls but had been emitted by the larger of the boys attacking Jack. The scream had been so penetrating that the attack instantly ceased. Even at that distance, Sam could see that of the two youths who'd attacked Jack one was now on the ground bleeding from the nose whilst the other was nursing what looked suspiciously like a broken arm. With both leaders out of action, the nerve of the gang disintegrated and they broke into a run. Last of all was the big lad, now white-faced and clutching tearfully at his limp hanging arm. On Sam's arrival, David and the girls still appeared shaken but Jack politely greeted him as if nothing had happened. 'Hullo, Mr Diamond, did you get the job?'

'What was that all about?' asked Sam anxiously. 'And how did he hurt his arm?'

'Oh, they wanted Grace's locket and I said they couldn't have it, that's all.'

'So who screamed?'

'I tweaked his arm a bit but I think he was just making a fuss, Mr Diamond. I mean, I did tell him he couldn't have the locket, didn't I, David?'

'Yes, Dad,' agreed David. 'That's quite right, he did. But they took no notice.'

As the gang had disappeared, Sam decided to forget the matter. Glancing at Jack, he sensed the boy had already erased the whole incident from his mind.

'Jack,' he said curiously, 'just what is it you do in Mr Roff's office?'

'I just do filing and things at the moment but Mr Roff said

I can go out with some of the men when I'm a little older. That's good, isn't it, Mr Diamond?'

'Yes, Jack, that's very good,' replied Sam hollowly. 'Very good indeed.'

All five returned home together with Sam walking a little behind. It was probably the first time he'd had occasion to detach himself and actually study his own children and their friends. Queenie was right, Grace was certainly going to be a very beautiful girl. It was sad that her parents had not lived to enjoy her growing up. It did not take much to see that David was already smitten with her.

Emma, on the other hand, was a proper tom-boy and had been from a toddler. Being so tall, she took after Sam rather than her mother and, though not destined to be beautiful, she would certainly be attractive.

David, on the other hand, had many of his mother's features, with her small mouth, high cheek-bones and slim, wiry, build.

There was no doubt that Jack was a total enigma. Ever since a child he'd radiated power though it was puzzling exactly whence the power came. Though larger than average, his strength appeared to come from inbuilt confidence rather than anything else. Even now, in his early teens, he would be more than a handful for most men. Yet it was his ability to remain detached from events happening around him that Sam found so disquieting. He suspected if he quizzed the boy about the recent fight, there would be no recollection of it. In addition to this, he would smile but not laugh, shrug but not cry, and murmur rather than shout. Because of his misgivings Sam had considered barring the twins from Jack's company, yet they both worshipped him and, judging by the most recent event, with every justification.

He left the youngsters playing in the street as he climbed the steps home. Whilst on the last flight, he could clearly make out a man's voice talking to Queenie. Though too indistinct to recognise the tone, Jim Forsythe came instantly to mind and a pang of jealousy knotted his stomach. He eased his key into the door in order to throw it open without warning and was surprised to see his own chair occupied by Maxie Roff.

'Sam!' greeted Max. 'At last! Well, old son, were you lucky? D'you get the job?'

Sam scowled, 'No, and I bet the bastard spent the entire war on his fat arse. He looked the sort. Sorry, Max, no offence.'

'None taken, mate, but I have no time for pleasantries, so how'd you like to work for me? I'll pay you three times your copper's wages, whatever that was?'

Sam did not hesitate. 'Yesterday I would have told you to stuff your job but today's confirmed what I'd long suspected – there's an embargo against police strikers. They're shutting us out.' He shook his head in disbelief. 'I have no choice. If society doesn't want me in then it'll have me out. I have kids to look after and Mr-sodding-Percy was the final straw today. Whatever it is, Max, I'm in.'

'Good lad! I couldn't be more pleased if—'

'Wait a minute!' cut in Queenie. 'It's not as easy as all that! What *is* Sam's job?'

'Queenie!' he snapped. 'I don't give a sod *what* it is! I'm well past that stage. For years I've been on the side of the angels and today a self-appointed angel kicked me in the balls. I have now changed sides. I have no allegiances, I have no loyalties, I'm a mercenary hired to the highest bidder. Max has just bid three times my wages, therefore I'm Max's. It would be nice if my first task was to set fire to Riddell, Riddell & Percy but I don't expect to be lucky all the time. Anyway, Max, what was the real reason you called?'

'I heard you were out of work so I thought I'd offer your delightful wife her old job back but this is a happier arrangement for both of us, agreed?'

'Agreed,' acknowledged Sam.

Queenie stared at them for a brief moment. 'I'm so pleased you're both happy!' she said acidly. 'Would anyone care to ask me if *I'm* happy? No? I thought not. It's bad enough that you should act as if I don't exist but when I'm actually sitting here listening to you say it, it's absolutely bloody maddening!'

'And on that note, I'll leave,' said Max as he hurriedly gathered up his brief-case and his astrakhan coat. 'I do hate domestic disputes. See you Monday about midday, Sam, we'll have a chat then.'

Queenie waited until Max's footsteps had faded down the staircase before turning to her husband. 'Are you sure this is what you want? It's still not too late to turn back, you know. Heaven only knows what you may be letting yourself in for. I shall worry myself sick each time you leave.'

'Did you worry when I walked the docks every night with only an eighteen-inch piece of wood for protection?'

'Of course I did, you know that!' she protested.

'And did you worry when I went off to fight the Kaiser in an obsolete paddler with a seventy-year-old nutter in charge?'

'But, Sam—'

'DID YOU?'

Biting her lip, she made no reply but gave the slightest of nods. 'Then what the hell is the difference? Except that it's less dangerous and for the first time in my life someone is actually paying me a decent wage?'

'Seeing as you don't appear to know,' she murmured, 'I'll tell you the difference. What Maxie Roff is offering you is everything you were opposed to when I first knew you. I've heard about some of the things that go on – they're evil.'

'Oh!' he exclaimed triumphantly. 'So it's all right if you work for him but not if *I* do, that it?'

'I could live with the work I did, I just hope you'll be able to say the same.'

It had been some time since Sam had entered Max's club. He was surprised how it had changed. It was certainly more extravagantly decorated but also like a small fortress. Sam had the feeling this was not just to deter police raids. Max waved Sam to a large armchair and, exactly on cue, Minnie carried in some tea. During the few minutes she was there her eyes barely left Max. As she closed the door, Sam said, 'I wouldn't like to upset that woman. She looks a classic poisoner.'

Max smiled and gave an exaggerated look at his cup. 'Good observation, Sam. She's still a good-looking wench and there've been many times when I've really fancied her. Do you know what's prevented me from trying?'

Sam shook his head.

'Exactly the point you've made.' He smiled. 'It would be great while it lasted but when the game was finally over I'd be in big trouble. She'd either cut my throat while I slept or top my glass with arsenic. Hence, we're just good friends. Right, Sam, to business.'

His smile vanished and he became almost a different person. 'I now have several establishments throughout town and, with the war being over, many people are trying to find a niche for themself. It's inevitable I'm going to make enemies, that's the first thing. The second is the tranquillity of these establishments. Rivals do like to upset anything that's going well. Therefore some people will try to rock my boat. To forestall this, I occasionally nip in first and sink theirs. It's called early retaliation. You'll find we do a fair bit of that. Are you with me so far?'

'Every word.'

'Well, there are policy decisions that won't concern you but – because we are getting bigger by the week- I need to keep an iron hand on my "employees". As you well know, as long as we keep our battles between ourselves, no one minds. Even the police are happy to do a Nelson. But the instant some innocent party gets duffed up, the bloody wheel comes off. Your job will be to see the wheel *doesn't* come off. I've got some rough geezers out there and they occasionally want a bit of handling. Think you can cope?'

'For a tenner a week? I'll cope.'

'Don't forget the nutter's out soon. I stitched him up last time because it suited me but I can't pull that one again and, to be honest, he's a wonderful frightener.'

'You mean Cootes?'

'I most certainly mean Cootes. Perhaps if the three of us have a little meeting we can work something out. Though he definitely don't like you, does he? On the other hand, he don't care for the rest of the world much either, so I suppose you're in good company.'

'Max, I must ask you one hard question about Frank, and I'll need a straight answer.'

'Fire away.'

'You say I'm in charge? Okay, let's say for the sake of argument lovable old Frank comes back into the fold and refuses to accept that fact, do I have last word?'

'Of course!'

'Whatever word I see fit?'

'Absolutely! And if you think he'll do a better job two miles off Southend pier in a weighted sack, then so be it. But speaking of Frank, there is one vitally important thing to consider. I don't want him working for anyone else. He knows too much and in the wrong hands he could be a time bomb. He either works for us or he goes diving in the estuary. Understood?'

'Understood right enough. Just finally, how about me? How expendable am I?'

Max did not speak for a while but sat tapping a rubber-tipped pencil on a blotter. 'I owe you and Jim Forsythe my life, Sam, but I can't be permanently grateful. I've offered you a job because I'm reasonably sure you can do it. But you're not a fool and you know this isn't a charity. If I'm wrong you'd be as expendable as Frank Cootes or anyone else. Sometimes this game's worse than a war. Being a crook – make no mistake, that's what you are – changes the rules. Sentiment and chivalry have no part. It's not romantic, it's a bloody jungle. You've chosen to live in it. If you want to survive in it, then civilised standards no longer apply.'

'Thanks, Max,' said Sam. 'I wish everyone was that frank. Am I now a fully paid up member of your mob?'

'Uh huh, but remember one little piece of advice because it could one day save your life. No one kills crooks but crooks – so watch your back.'

'Thanks, I'll remember that. When do I start?'

'This evening at 8.30. We've got a little outing arranged to a club over at Battersea. But before then I want you to go to Morrie Elkstein's in Tower Bridge Road. Tell him I sent you and get him to fix you up with a suit for tonight. You can't possibly go on an outing in that one. They'd think you was an off-duty copper.'

With a couple of hours to spare before he visited Morrie, Sam bought a newspaper and strolled over to Gaol Park to sit in the sun as he read. It was only as he sat that he realised how appropriate the location was. Gaol Park was a small recreation ground on the site of a former execution yard at the rear of the old Horsemonger Lane Gaol. Many were the villains who had pondered their past whilst swinging on a rope at that location. He wondered how many of them had claimed they were doing it for their children? Well, so what? It was too late now. And how many of those had had a free new suit?

As Sam entered Max's office that evening, he realised by the smoke and the noise that everyone there had been present for some time. If that was the case, it could only be because Max had wished to tell them all of his new appointee. By now, each gang member would be waiting to assess his ability, perhaps even to test him out. It was a situation where first impressions counted most. He was suddenly grateful that Morrie had managed to fix him up with a dark three-piece that had passed the tailor's critical eye with only minor adjustments.

'Ah! There you are!' announced Max, 'How smart you look! The boys have been waiting to meet you.'

He waved a large hand around the room to where seven or eight powerfully built men sprawled in chairs. Of the group, Sam recognised only two. Max had certainly been building himself an empire in the last year or so. 'I shan't bother to mention everyone's name, you'll pick 'em up as you go along. Besides, where we're playing tonight wouldn't be the best place for name tags.'

A few polite chuckles greeted this as Max continued, 'The boys know exactly what's expected of them and I don't expect the Half Moon Club to be shining for some little while after our visit. I suggest you go along as an observer. But if anyone steps out of line, you deal. Remember, we want their customers to lose their dignity, not their health. There'll be two of our taxis picking you up shortly. Meantime, make yourself at home and get to know the boys.'

Sam glanced at the wall clock. 'If you give it an extra thirty minutes, the shifts will be changing and you'll have less chance of blundering into a copper.'

'We ain't afraid of no coppers,' came a gruff voice from somewhere amid the armchairs.

'It's a risk we needn't take,' snapped Sam. 'So we'll leave it thirty minutes.'

'Good thinking, Sam,' cut in Max. 'Another half-hour isn't going to make any difference to us one way or the other. A thirty-minute delay it is then.'

Though it was Sam's first ever supervisory role, his

natural aloofness enabled him to take to it instantly. He had a quick word with each of them and realised that by insisting on changing the time of the raid, he had surmounted the first hurdle. As they packed tightly into the two taxis, Max bade them farewell. 'By the way, Sam,' he added, 'you don't have to tip, they're our cabs.'

Though Sam had no clear idea of the method of the raid, he had certainly expected some subtlety. Instead they leaped from the taxis and barged straight through the front door. By any standard the club was impressive. It was circular and compact but with the space well utilised so it was in no way crowded. There was an attractive bar with attractive barmaids and a quintet playing attractive music.

Some fifty customers of both sexes and various ages sat at tables or embraced on the small dance floor. In the main, the clientele was well dressed and probably in professional occupations which may have accounted for the lack of screams. At first, the wanton destruction offended Sam's tidy mind. To placate this he turned his attention to the few staff who showed resistance. It was all over in a couple of minutes as Max's gang, task accomplished, began to withdraw.

Just as Sam was about to follow, he saw that one gang member, known only as Jinks, had been seized and pinioned from behind by a fat middle-aged customer. To everyone's surprise, the customer, showing surprising strength, loudly proclaimed he was going to: 'Keep this bastard till the police arrive.' To Sam's horror, he saw Jinks wrestle one arm free and, fumbling in his belt, withdraw a knife.

'Dignity, not health' Max had said. Pushing aside two protesting diners, Sam reached the struggling pair just as the knife was poised. With his left hand he chopped hard at the wrist of his bandit and with his right snatched the knife. Wrenching the couple apart, he gave two quick slashes which severed the customer's braces and a third that ripped open the top of his trousers. The man dropped his arms to his sides in instant confusion as his trousers tumbled to his knees.

'Come on!' snarled Sam, dragging Jinks away. 'Get out, quick!'

As he turned, screams gave way to chuckles and his last sight of the room included a yelling fat man standing astride a heap of clothing in a pair of threadbare combinations and a long-tailed shirt.

The cabs were waiting a short distance down the High Street and within twenty minutes they were all safely back in Murgatroyd's, leaving the drivers to refix the correct licence plates. The adrenaline was obviously in full flow as the gang noisily re-lived the raid in the sanctuary of the club bar. Already exaggerations were creeping in. Sam was only mildly interested when he felt someone at his elbow.

'Pint, guv?' asked an obviously respectful Jinks as he slid the large glass mug across the table. 'Sorry about that but I couldn't get away. He was a strong bastard.'

Sam nodded. 'If anything like that ever happens again, you're out, understand? Going as a team means working together, not wandering about like a brain-dead duck. And the next time you pull a knife on a customer, I'll bury it in your throat. If you kill some innocent party on a raid like that, we'd all be in line for the rope. That's not happening while I'm in charge. The same applies to everyone here. If we're going to work together, let's all be sure where we stand.' He looked slowly around the barroom, staring at each in turn. At least that's one trick I learned from Macready, he thought with some satisfaction.

Sam smelt Max's cigar an instant before he heard his voice. 'Things went well, I hear. Come into the office. I'd like to know more about it.' With a glass in one hand and a clipboard in the other, Max ushered Sam into the office and closed the door.

'It seems like the boys were impressed with your action.

Apparently they seemed to like the way you defused the situation,' he said guardedly.

'Do I gather by your tone you're not quite so ecstatic?' queried Sam.

Max smiled, took a long draw on his cigar and slowly let it out. 'Took a long time for me to get used to these things, Sam,' he said, studying the label. 'But well worth it in the end.'

'Unless I'm mistaken, I sense a little homily approaching.'

'You're shrewd, I grant you that. You see when I first smoked these things I felt quite sick. I only did it for effect, bit like your actions today really. I used to create exactly the impression I sought until the last second when I always blew out the smoke too quickly. You know the sort of thing – long draw in but quick puff out. Small matter, you may think, but it's that detail that gives away the whole show.'

'And I gave the show away tonight?'

'You did indeed. You see, you're going to be like most of us, basically a nice bloke acting like what I call an "ice-man". Somewhere along the line we give ourselves away, just like you did tonight. A real ice-man wouldn't do that.'

'So when did I slip up?'

'You did it when you played sensible adviser to Monkey Jinks.'

'I gave him a last chance, that's all.'

'There's no such thing in this game, Sam. Monkey knew the score. He shouldn't have been on his own at that stage and certainly not with his back to anyone he didn't know. You should have had him out on the street instantly. Now I'm in a difficult position. If I take action against Monkey, I undermine you. And I've just appointed you. D'you see how it snowballs?'

'So what are you saying?'

'I'm saying in a game of no last chances, I'm about to give you one – but not out of choice. I'm giving it to you because

I want you in iron control of this mob by Tuesday week at the latest.'

'What's so special about that day?'

'Well, Sam,' said Max slowly, 'Tuesday week is the day our number two ice-man is released from prison. That's right, Cootes comes out. Think you can handle it?'

Sam angrily realised his heart beat a fraction faster at the news. 'Of course I can,' he bluffed. 'No trouble at all. But you said "number two". Who d'you consider your "number one" because I haven't noticed him?'

'Then you haven't been looking, young sir,' said Max. 'Because I tell you with no exaggeration, he scares me shitless. I've only got him working for me because I couldn't stand the thought of him working for anyone else. One day when they hang him he will be so famous you'll bore people with stories of how you used to be his boss and, I believe, his friend! I tell you, young Jack Kirton is going one hell of a way in this game – should he live that long. And as leader of this pack, from tomorrow I want him under your wing.'

Chapter 26

Throughout Sam's service in the constabulary, he had told himself that when the day came for him to leave, whatever the circumstances, the Godsend would be a regular sleep pattern. No more going to bed when everyone else was just waking, or walking windswept streets when the civilised world was snuggling down for the night. Yet that had not happened. He would frequently wake at 3 a.m., dozing only fitfully till daybreak. That warm Tuesday morning was no exception. 'How long have you been awake?' Queenie whispered thickly.

'Oh, not long,' he lied.

'That's untrue. You tossed and turned from the moment you came to bed and mumbled to yourself even when you appeared to be asleep. What's on your mind, Sam?'

He put his hands beneath his head and watched a bed-bug move slowly down the wallpaper. 'It's a big day today,' he admitted. Then, to his surprise, he told Queenie everything of his conversation with Max ten days before.

'But you don't have to put up with this, Sam,' she protested. 'There are plenty of jobs I can do. We've got by in the past, we can again.

'You don't understand, I'm in too deep,' he said. 'Oh, I can cope with Cootes right enough, I've been dealing with scum like him all my life. It's that kid that makes me uneasy. Max was right, he *is* an ice-man. It's in his eyes. The funny thing is though, I trust him completely. He has an aura about him. He's supposed to be "out with" me but I usually feel I'm "Out with" him. I've never known anyone so calm. I've never seen him ruffled. He's going to join me in my meeting with Max and Frank today and I feel a lot happier knowing he's on my side.'

Queenie squeezed his hand reassuringly. 'Look, Sam, we're obviously not sleeping any more this morning. I'll make some tea.' She tip-toed into the other room and eased her way around the twins' beds. If space in their two rooms had been a problem before, since the twins had been in separate beds it had multiplied.

It was a little after 6 a.m. when she heard the postman's footsteps. With just two flats on the top floor there was always the expectation of a letter when he was so close. Today was no exception.

'Sam!' she stage-whispered in uncontrolled excitement. 'You'll never guess, we've a wedding invitation! Guess who it's from? Go on, guess!'

'How do I know?' he moaned. 'Anyway, I don't like weddings, tell 'em I'm working.'

'Bet you'll like this one, Sam, it's ever so posh! It's at The Grosvenor!'

'That settles it! It sounds expensive, I'm definitely working. Anyway, who is it?'

'Would you believe Billie? She's marrying – let me see.' She scanned the invitation for a moment. 'She's marrying Sir Cedric Hathaway at Caxton Hall on Saturday! Good heavens, that's quick! Hope she's not going to be a menopausal mum. There's an additional note – no presents by request!'

Sam was alert in an instant. 'Hathaway? The clever old cow! He's worth millions! He owned half the music halls in London, recently sold most of them to a cinema chain. You're right, we'll have to go to that one. I take it the twins are invited?'

'Of course!' Queenie laughed. 'Emma would never let us out the door otherwise.'

'Who's talking about me?' came a sleepy voice from behind the curtain. Within seconds all four were wide awake and wondering just who was this superman and had he any idea of the task he had taken on. 'You're not pulling our legs, are you, Mum?' queried Emma. 'It's not a plot to get us all up early, is it?'

'But why marry now?' asked a puzzled Queenie. 'She's a bit past child-bearing age.'

'Perhaps that's why,' said Sam. 'If she hadn't been on the halls she'd probably have had a dozen kids by now and taken motherhood completely in her stride.'

Queenie was still excited as, hours later, Sam collected Jack and they made their way to their assignation with Max and Frank Cootes.

After so long, Sam was not sure what he'd expected from Frank but if he was hoping for a softening he was disappointed. He was the same leering, granite-faced thug who'd departed years earlier, neither diminished nor mellowed. He sat glowering as Sam and Jack entered the room. 'Understand yer nah the foreman?'

Sam nodded an agreement.

'I take it this is yer lad I've 'eard so much abhat?'

'He may *look* a lad,' said Sam, without once removing his gaze from Cootes, 'but if that's what you think, you think wrong.'

'I'll make me own mind up abhat that. Max sez if I wanna come back, I've gotta bury the 'atchet. That's providin' yer don't turn out ter be the barsted who set me up. Then o'course I'd kill yer. Were yer the barsted who set me up?'

'I was not.'

'Very well, shake on it.' He reached out his hand and Sam noticed Jack instantly stiffen. Guessing Cootes would try a vice grip, he tightened his muscles in preparation. It was as well. His grip neutralised the other and with a leer Cootes finally relinquished his hand.

'Okay, you two,' said Max. 'Now we have that settled, I've a business to run. Firstly, Sam, you've an appointment at The Tsar's Restaurant in Mile End Road. You'll need to see a geezer called . . . let me see.' He glanced at a paper in front of him. 'Oh, sod. Stanis-something-or-other. Anyway, he's a White Russian immigrant in a green-painted restaurant. See him because we've had no revenue from there for a month now and he owes us forty quid. Take the lad with you and if the Russkie don't pay, tell him we'll parcel him up in bits and return him to Lenin. Leave the cab here and go by underground. Tower Bridge is a bloody menace to traffic lately. Meantime I've got a special job for you, Frank.'

Unemotional he may have been but Jack Kirton's eyes always lit up at the thought of a trip on the underground. He could go from chilling mobster to child in seconds. It was the moment the train emerged monster-like from the tunnel and approached the platform that thrilled him most. He would always jump back with excitement before stepping forward again with a sheepish half-smile.

'They never come *on* the platform,' laughed Sam. 'They run on rails, y'know.'

The Tsar's Restaurant was almost adjacent to the underground station and sheepish smiles had long faded by the time the pair entered by the green-painted door. The professional smile of the host likewise vanished the moment he realised the identity of his latest customers. He led them to a far corner table away from the afternoon loungers sitting near the entrance.

'I've been expecting you,' said the Russian, 'and I know what you are going to say.' He shrugged, turned out his palms and nodded towards a table containing four loud young men. 'These gentlemen tell me they now run the protection business. So do I listen to you, or do I listen to them? I cannot listen to you both.' He gave another helpless shrug.

Sam pointed precisely to confirm he had the right group. 'Those four?'

The restaurateur nodded.

Sam studied all the clientele for some moments. Then, seemingly satisfied with his conclusions, he whispered to his young companion, rose from his table and strolled the short distance to the rather scruffy quartet. He nodded a greeting as he sat uninvited at the only empty chair. 'Seems t'be a misunderstanding,' he said quietly as he placed two large clenched fists, knuckles down, on the centre of the table. 'Our little friend here,' he nodded at the ashen-faced owner, 'has been misinformed that you are looking after the security of this place. Silly, isn't it? We all know that Mr Roff looks after it don't we? I daresay you've got the wrong premises. Easy mistake to make though, eh?'

His quiet confidential manner obviously confused them at first but, as the quickest of them made to slide back his chair, Sam quickly open his fists and tossed a shower of fine pepper into each of their faces. Within seconds the blows that rained down on their unprotected heads caused each to crash to the floor in a fit of sneezing groans. Sam and Jack then gently eased them back on to their seats.

'Dear, dear. Little hay fever, is it?' Sam asked. 'How unpleasant for you. Perhaps you're allergic to the food here. Does happen, I hear. Never mind, I 'spect if you stay away it'll clear up by itself. Usually does, I find.'

As Sam spoke, Jack had quickly run through the gang's pockets and removed three cut-throat razors, a sharpened chain and a weighted rubber tube which he handed to Sam. 'Tut tut,' said Sam. 'I *am* disappointed! This sort of thing reduces the whole tone of the place. I shall have to ask this gentleman to see you off the premises.' He glanced up at Jack. 'Show them the door, will, you Cyril? I don't think we want their sort here again, do you?'

Whether he disliked being called 'Cyril' or whether he was purely acting, Sam never discovered but Jack seized each with a ferocious intensity and hurled them out of the door and halfway across the Mile End Road. Other than two toppled chairs, a ruffled table-cloth and a scattering of ground pepper, the whole exodus had been completed with the minimum of fuss. 'Now, sir,' said Sam, addressing the proprietor, 'here is Mr Roff's card. Should you ever have a problem again, don't hesitate to contact him. After all, that's why you pay insurance, isn't it?'

Mr Stanis-something-or-other took the card without a word and beckoned Sam to the kitchen where he handed over an envelope containing exactly forty pounds.

Sam and Jack were almost back at Murgatroyd's before Sam spoke again. Even Jack's customary platform leap had failed to amuse him. 'Y'know,' he sighed to the young man, 'as much as I enjoyed sorting out those four thick-heads, I hated taking that fellow's cash. It's going to be hard for me getting used to this job, Jack, that's for sure.'

Max greeted them both as warmly as if they had been absent for months and insisted on taking them to his office and hearing every detail, particularly the role played by Jack. Sam handed the envelope to Max as Minnie deposited a tray of tea. It was the confusion of arms across the table that probably caused the accident. The small pot toppled and in a split-second the desk was awash with scalding liquid. Quick as Max was, he still sustained a steaming streak across his shirtfront. Amidst frantic apologies from Minnie, he ripped his clinging shirt away from his chest.

'It's okay, it's okay,' he insisted. 'I've a spare shirt, no harm done. Just mop this desk while I change.' Minnie tearfully snatched a handful of paper from the waste-bin and began to soak up the spreading pool whilst Sam did likewise with a large blotter pad. As he pressed down, he saw the name Frank Cootes doodled in pencil in the corner of the pad together with an arrow that led to the name

Nathan Green which had been all but erased. He quickly removed the sheet and swapped it with the one beneath. Eventually the desk dried and Max returned, buttoning up a fresh shirt.

By now, Minnie's fawning manner was irritating them both. 'I tell you, don't worry about it,' snapped Max finally. 'It's just a shirt, forget it.' He pointed to the chair where Jack Kirton had sat totally indifferent throughout. 'He has.'

'I'm so sorry, dear,' began Minnie. 'I'll fetch you in another tray and . . .'

'NO!' yelled Max. 'Look, I didn't *ask* for tea! I didn't *want* tea! Now I've got a desk full of the bloody stuff! Will you just piss off and LEAVE US ALONE, WOMAN!'

Having finally understood the message, she gathered up the last of the crockery and scuttled from the room. Max shook his head despairingly as she left.

'Well, it's a blessing in one way. At least I don't fancy the silly cow any more. Anyway, to business.' He looked up at Sam. 'You want Saturday off for a wedding, that right? Anyone I know?'

Sam explained briefly and Max was as surprised as everyone else had been. 'By heaven, he's a lucky old bugger! He's got a million quid and her! She'll kill him within a month! You should have kept in with her, Sam. The only thing better than an over-sexed widow, is a *rich* over-sexed widow! Yes, take the day off by all means. She always did fancy you. And you never know your luck, d'you?'

Sam was finding his new image difficult to maintain yet managed to force a weak smile. 'And how about Jack? He's been invited along with the twins.'

'No, sorry, Sam, I need him. I've got a job for him and Frank that day, but don't let that stop you from enjoying yourself.' He turned to Jack. 'Don't mind, lad, do you?' The lad's smile indicated he didn't mind in the least.

* * *

Queenie always claimed Billie was eternally lucky and Saturday's weather bore that out. It was with no little pride that Sam paid their fares on the 35 tram. Even David looked smart, whilst the three females each personified a different type of beauty. The narrow winner was the lithe and aptly named Grace, who was clad in be-ribboned hat and flowing white dress. But Emma, identically attired and forsaking her tom-boy guise, showed every indication of running her close. As for Queenie, her maturing beauty in a neat two-piece classically off-set the delicate charms of the two younger women.

As the five crossed the road to join the assembling guests, Sam gave them some quick encouragement. 'Heads up, girls, you're the best-looking lasses here today.'

'Oh, yeah?' groaned Queenie under her breath. 'Well, how about that?' She nodded to where a stunning figure in a low-necked, classically cut light blue crêpe-de-chine suit was about to step from a wedding limousine. 'Couldn't you just kill her, the bitch!'

'Bloody hell, Dad!' exclaimed David. 'I don't half fancy my aunt!'

Sam's pride in his family was forgotten as he clapped eyes on the bride to be. He could think of nothing other than he had actually made love to this woman. He had excited her, explored her, played with her, tasted her and had her. It was a chapter in his life he had almost forgotten yet he knew then it was one he would never forget again.

'SAM!' she greeted him, blatantly ignoring the remainder of the congregation. 'Queenie! Emma! David! Grace! How wonderful you all look! You are coming to the eats afterwards, aren't you? Good, I'll speak to you there.'

Queenie had once known most of Billie's friends and guessed that the majority of those present were associates of the noble Sir Cedric Hathaway. So where was the man himself? Undaunted, Emma asked an attendant. When he was finally pointed out to the group, forecasts about the groom's early demise flooded back to Sam. Even Queenie's eyes narrowed.

'Personally,' she whispered, 'I'd be surprised if he lasts the reception, never mind the honeymoon. I'm not being catty but I don't see this as a love match, do you?'

As a group, they could only agree. Because of the crowd, Sam and David stayed outside during the ceremony, though the girls later claimed it was beautiful. It was the reception that interested Sam anyway. A fleet of taxis ferried the guests to The Grosvenor and eventually everyone was seated. The family may have felt slightly overlooked in the seating at the ceremony, but there was no such negligence at the reception. Billie had ensured their position was adjoining the top table and never lost an opportunity for a quick wink at each. A small orchestra had played throughout the meal and was augmented by five more musicians for the dancing. Much to his annoyance, Queenie dragged Sam up for the first dance of the evening, then compounded it by asking him how many present might live in a two-roomed tenement.

'Probably just the groom,' he growled sarcastically.

'Do you mind if I cut in on the smartest man in the room?' asked Billie.

'I would have been surprised if you hadn't,' said Queenie, graciously waving a hand towards her partner. 'But remember, I shall want to hear all the news after.'

As Sam reached for his new partner's hand, he was taken aback when she slipped her arms around his neck and pushed herself in tight to him. 'Now you know you're a lousy dancer, Sam, so why don't you just push into me and sway a little? We'll both enjoy it more. By the way, how'd you get so smart? I still have nightmares about your dad's old trousers. But this –' she tugged the seat of his suit '– this is really the business. It'd be a pleasure to pull them off you.'

'Have you been drinking?'

'Of course I've been bloody drinking! You don't think I'd marry if I was sober, do you? Especially old Cedric. He's eighty if he's a day!

He relinquished his hold and stood back from her. 'Then why on earth are you marrying him?'

'Voice down!' she hissed. 'Because I'm bloody skint! I don't have a brass farthing!' She pulled Sam back tight against her. 'It's a business arrangement. I won't inherit the estate when he goes – his kids have seen to that – but I *will* have an annuity settled on me. Which, for me, is an ideal arrangement.'

'How about your house in Brixton?'

'Gone! I took some expert investment advice, you see.' She gave a hollow little laugh. 'Stay away from "experts", Sam, they'll skin, bone and bury you!'

'But how about your theatre money?'

'The music hall's all but dead and I'm not getting any younger. How much longer will people pay to see a big wench belting out loud songs in a tight frock? Once I could expect a gallery full of blokes praying me tits were going to pop out. Soon they'll be terrified in case they do!'

'Billie,' he said softly, 'you are still an exciting woman.'

'Exciting?' She shrugged. 'Maybe, but so are road accidents and who wants to be one of them? That's why I've decided to be a kept woman instead.'

'How does Sir-whatever-his-name-is feel about it?'

'It was his idea! I think he just wanted a woman he could show off to his friends and, as long as he doesn't expect the dutiful wife, I'm happy to oblige. It's not a bad life, y'know. Of course I've earned the old darling a few bob in the past, perhaps his conscience pricked him. Anyway, tell me all about your lot.'

Though the music had stopped she held on to Sam's arm and walked him back to his table. On reaching it she clapped her hand quickly to her mouth. 'Sam Diamond! I'll lick off Lloyd George if these aren't the loveliest three lasses in London. They're beautiful! Come on, girls,' she ordered. 'You're going to meet everyone. You're much better than those toffee-nosed cows out there.' With that, she tugged the two laughing girls to their feet and whirled them to the top table.

'She doesn't change a bit,' marvelled the watching Queenie. 'So tell me about it, Sam.'

As he recounted the tale, she shook her head in sorrow. 'She was always useless with money,' she said sadly. 'She could earn it easy enough, drive the hardest of bargains, but she just couldn't keep it.'

The evening was everything they had hoped for, the girls in particular felt like royalty but soon it was time to leave. As they were about to say their farewells Billie took Sam and Queenie aside. 'I've a big favour to ask of you two.'

'Go ahead,' said Queenie suspiciously.

'Can I have your Emma to work for me? I'll promise her a good life. I never did get a satisfactory replacement for you, Queenie, though heaven knows I tried hard enough. Your Emma could well be it. Think about it and let me know, please?'

The pair of them looked at each other in surprise and Queenie was the first to recover by putting her fingers to her husband's lips. 'We'll say nothing now, will we, Sam?' she asked pointedly. 'But we'll discuss it with Emma and let you know.'

'I can't ask more,' replied Billie with unaccustomed humility as she gave them all a warm farewell. For the youngsters in particular, the first taxi rides of their lives were icing on the cake. As the cab stopped outside Queen's Buildings, they desperately made a great noise but to no avail. To their disgust, not a curtain moved as they alighted from the cab and entered the block.

Queenie knew she must wait for the youngsters to sleep before she and Sam could discuss Billie's request but with the twins in their beds and Grace sleeping under the table, it took ages for the giggling trio finally to settle.

'I've spoken to Emma and she wants to go,' Queenie whispered eventually. 'I think she's right. She'll have far more opportunities there than we can ever give her. If she remains here she'll stay in that factory for the rest of her life – and for what? Somewhere to go between child-births? Is that what you want for your daughter?'

'No, it's *not* what I want for my daughter but being someone else's skivvy is also *not* what I want for my daughter! Still, I'll not fight you over this one. If she wants to go, let her. Write to Billie to that effect in the morning. G'night.'

Sam certainly fell asleep rapidly but he also woke soon after dawn. He lay for some time thinking over his daughter's opportunity and the more he thought of it the better it seemed. It was a pity that Emma was the one who had had the offer when it was David who was the problem. The boy was already making noises about joining Max's organisation and Sam was unhappy with the thought.

It was a little after seven o'clock when the muted giggling from the other room finally reached its peak. 'Right, you three!' called Queenie. 'As you've woken us, you can feed us. Breakfast is down to you lot. Your father and I expect a good old fry up in fifteen minutes from now. Right, go!' She smiled at the pandemonium that seemed to cause as she lay beside her husband for the next quarter of an hour.

All-in-all, breakfast was a success. Though how much of it had been David trying to impress Grace, was difficult to judge. Emma, ecstatic at her parents' approval, was also on her best behaviour.

'I'm not used to this goodwill,' said Sam finally. 'I'm going for my Sunday paper. Coming, David?'

To his surprise the lad declined.

'Oh, come on, Sam,' whispered Queenie. 'If you were

his age, what would you do? Go with your dad for a newspaper or flirt with young Grace in her skimpy nightie? And if you even have to think about that one, Sam Diamond, then you *really* are getting old!'

Having bought the paper, Sam decided on a quiet read in Gaol Park before returning to the temporary bedlam of home. He was barely past the sports page before a familiar tone bade him, 'Good morning, Mr Diamond.'

'Jack! You're out early this morning, where're you off to?'

'Nowhere, I'm on my way home. I've been working all night with Mr Cootes.'

'Working?' he echoed. 'Working where? Doing what?'

'Working down at Brighton on Mr Nathan Green's boat. It was a bit sad really.'

'Sad? Why's that?'

'Well, I got sent downstairs for something from the galley and Mr Cootes told me Mr Nathan must have fallen in the water. Mr Cootes dived in but couldn't save him. There was a swill bucket there and he couldn't swim. Mr Cootes reckoned he must have tried to throw something over the side and fell in. Was sad, wasn't it?'

'And this was last night, you say?'

'Yes, 'cos we had to call the police, that's why we were back late, but the police agreed he must have fell in 'cos he'd had a lot to drink.'

'Where's Cootes now?'

'He's gone to the club 'cos Mr Roff said he'd be waiting for him.'

'Did he now?' said Sam thoughtfully. 'Do me a favour, Jack. Drop this newspaper off at my flat and tell Queenie I won't be back for a couple of hours, okay?'

'Certainly, Mr Diamond, see you later. 'Bye.'

''Bye, Jack.' Sam rubbed his chin thoughtfully. So Nathan Green was dead. Besides Max, no one else knew anything about the club's finances. How convenient.

The quiet Sunday streets were just beginning to show signs of life as Sam let himself in by the side door of Murgatroyd's. A team of morning cleaners had long tidied the Saturday night litter and the smell of disinfectant permeated every corner. Making no secret of his arrival, Sam whistled as he climbed the stairs. The eternally watchful Minnie had just left Max's office with the equally eternal tea tray. 'Mr Cootes is in with him at the moment,' she said. 'But if you care to wait I'll tell him in a few minutes.'

'Thanks, Minnie,' said Sam. Then politely ignoring her he walked straight into the office. 'Morning, Max,' he greeted. 'Up a little early this morning, aren't we?'

'I'm sorry, Mr Roff—' began Minnie from the corridor.

''S'alright!' cut in Max. 'Don't worry. Just see we're not disturbed again though, eh?' He turned his attention to Sam. 'To what do we owe the honour, seeing as you had the weekend off? If I'd known you were going to waste it by coming in here, perhaps Frank may have been able to put it to better use.'

'I thought Frank *had* put it to better use. I hear Nathan had a good drink and went swimming in the dark. Careless combination, I'd say.'

'They do say accidents happen,' said Max icily. 'Does it cause you some distress?'

'It certainly distresses me when a lad as young as Jack Kirton is involved in a premeditated plot to do someone in. Yes, that distresses me very much.'

'What did I tell yer abhat this creep?' cut in Frank. 'Didn't I say he'd be a waste of space, didn't I? Yer should'a let me finish the git years ago. He's gonna be trouble to yer ovverwise, I'll tell yer.' He turned to Sam. 'You've 'ad one near miss. Yer won't be so lucky next time, sunshine, believe me.'

'Button your lip, Frank,' ordered Max. 'As for you Sam, don't you ever come in here again and take that attitude with me. I knew nothing about any accident to Nathan until a few minutes ago, understand?'

'That's a lie, Max, and you know it. I came to work for you with my eyes open but involving a kid like Jack in murder is not on in my book. I'm resigning, Max. Here's your key. You have my word I'll never shop you, though I'm not stupid enough to think that promise will satisfy. But I tell you this. If you send that turd,' he pointed straight at Frank, 'after me, I'll send you back his black heart wrapped in his white liver.'

'Sam,' replied Max quietly, 'Jack Kirton's no longer a kid. If you think that you're deluding yourself. He's totally ruthless. But as you're his self-appointed protector, that's not my problem, it's yours. What *I'm* concerned about is your accusation of murder. I tell you, I had nothing to do with Nathan's death.'

'No?' said Sam, leaning across the desk and picking up Max's customary pencil. He moved it to the corner of the blotter pad and squiggled a quick circle around the doodle. 'Pencil it in again, Max. You never know, Nathan might get lucky and have a resurrection. If he does, what's the betting his first job will be to shoot Frank Cootes?'

Max glanced quickly at the doodle then shifted his eyes to Cootes who was already rising to his feet. 'No, Frank! Let him go. I'm sure he'll keep his word. After all, with such a lovely wife and daughter, why shouldn't he?'

Sam sighed and turned to the door. 'You're so bloody predictable, Max, but *should* anything remotely like that happen, guess who wouldn't see the day out?' Reaching the door he added, 'And as for you, Frank, I wouldn't dream of telling you who stitched you up for years – would I, Max? No, I wouldn't bloody dream of it.'

On Sam's return home, the hubbub was even greater than when he'd left. In addition to the three youngsters, Jack Kirton was busy tucking into a huge fried breakfast.

'Did you know this boy has been out working all night?' reprimanded Queenie. 'Poor lad was absolutely starving. I thought you'd take better care of your apprentice.'

'Not my apprentice any more,' said Sam. 'Max and I have just parted company.'

Queenie closed her eyes thankfully. 'I can't tell you how pleased I am, Sam. I've always had a bad feeling about that job. What happened?'

As Jack was present, Sam had initial reservations about telling the whole story but changed his mind and finally disclosed every detail.

'Well, I don't know what Mr Cootes done up on that deck, Mr Diamond,' said Jack, ''cos I was downstairs, but I do think you should be very careful now. He really hates you and he always says if he gets half a chance, he'll take it.'

'Oh, Jack,' pleaded Queenie, placing her arm around the young man's shoulder. 'Leave those people, please. I'm sure your mum and dad wouldn't have liked to know you were working at such a place.'

'I'm all right, Mrs Diamond, thank you. I'm old enough to take care of myself. I am a grown lad, you know. But I'll promise you one thing. I'll keep an eye on Mr Diamond for you because you've both been very good to me since my parents were killed.'

Queenie kissed his forehead lightly. 'Thanks, Jack, that's very thoughtful of you.'

'That's okay.' He smiled. 'Thanks for the breakfast, I'd better be off or my gran will be selling my bed. 'Bye, everyone!'

A chorus of farewells followed him as he pulled the door to behind him.

'Sam, I feel uneasy,' began Queenie. 'I think Emma should go and stay with Billie as soon as possible. Even that lad sensed the evil.'

'I think you worry too much,' said Sam. 'But it wouldn't do any harm to speed up Emma's move, I suppose.' He turned to the girl. 'How'd you feel about going as soon as Miss Bardell returns from her honeymoon, sweetie?'

'Anything to avoid that factory, Dad, you know that.'

And so it was. The letters were exchanged and three weeks to the day Emma was packing excitedly for her move to Billie's new home in Hendon. It was halfway through this packing that Grace and David arrived to say they had twice seen Frank Cootes in the locality.

'Oh, that's no big surprise,' assured Sam. 'The club's barely half a dozen streets away. We're bound to lay eyes on him from time to time, especially on a Sunday with fewer folk about.'

'But I've seen him too, Sam,' said Queenie quietly. 'And I had never seen him on the street before this week. Now I've seen him three times in as many days.'

Sam was about to reply when a knock at the door caused them to look anxiously at each other. 'It's okay, Mr Diamond, it's me, Jack,' came the reassuring voice.

Sam inched open the door until he was satisfied and soon Jack was amongst his old friends again. 'Mr Diamond, can I go with Emma today because something strange is going on in the club and I can't get to the bottom of it. I'd just like to make sure she gets to Miss Bardell's in one piece.'

'She'll be okay,' said Sam 'I'm taking her on the underground, though you're welcome to come along for the ride.' He laughed. 'We know how you like trains.'

'Thanks, Mr Diamond. I appreciate that. When are we leavin'?'

'As soon as she's finished packing. Actually you've done David a favour, he was coming with us but now he can take Grace to the pictures instead.'

Goodbyes were said and Queenie watched from the window until the waving threesome had turned out of sight before nervously scanning every doorway.

Intermittent Sunday service had caused a crowd on the Borough Station platform and, as the train neared, Sam couldn't resist watching Jack from the corner of his eye. Neither could Frank Cootes. The instant the train entered the station, the lad gave his customary jump as Sam closed his eyes in silent amusement.

It made little difference that his eyes were shut. It was a ferocious shove that caused him to open them again but by that time it was much too late. He was falling like a stone on to a live line where a monster-like train was to dismember his body.

Chapter 27

'The family swear it was Frank Cootes but he was not identified in an ID parade by witnesses on the platform and he has an unshakeable alibi with at least four people vouching for him,' said Detective Inspector Wilf Bromley.

'So what do you think?' asked Jim Forsythe.

'Well, he certainly had the motive and had been heard to threaten Diamond on many occasions. He's animal enough to do it and this sort of thing would be right up his street. He also makes no attempt to hide his delight at Diamond's death.'

'You say "Diamond's death" as opposed to "Diamond's murder". Why's that? Any doubt?'

'Personally, none, but it was a crowded platform; no one saw him pushed; no one was seen running either to or from that part of the platform; the driver saw a figure stagger a few feet in front of him but nothing else.'

'How about the two people with him, what did they see?'

'The daughter's in a hell of a state, poor kid. All she saw was the gory mess. As for Kirton, he's calm enough but beneath it all appears to be quietly boiling. I know you're a friend of the family but d'you know *him* at all?'

'Oh yes,' said Jim. 'I know young Jack right enough. His parents were killed in the war and he lives with his old gran. He's always been a friend of the twins', even though he's two or three years older. Sam and Queenie were marvellous to him. If they'd had enough space they would have adopted him. He seems totally unemotional but I'd be surprised if his mind's not in complete turmoil right now, even though it probably wouldn't show. Does he have any form?'

'None, he's as clean as a whistle. Though he's been working for Roff for some time and had been working with Diamond 'till three weeks ago. However . . .' His voice faded.

'That's a pretty ominous "however",' said Jim. 'What's on your mind?'

Bromley shook his head thoughtfully. 'I've never met anyone quite like that lad. It's like questioning a statue except that he speaks. Heaven only knows how Sam Diamond worked with him, I find him quite frightening.'

'Okay. Thanks, Wilf,' said Jim. 'If you could keep me posted on developments I'd be obliged. I have no official interest in this case but I was a life-long friend of Sam's and I'm still close to the family. I'm off to see them now.'

'You will point out to Queenie the difficulty we have with the lack of witnesses, won't you?' pleaded the detective. 'She's not taken it too badly but that boy David is becoming obsessed with Frank Cootes. He's just young and daft enough to do something really silly and they are *not* a team to mess around with, as poor Sam found to his cost.'

'Okay. Oh, by the way, do you know when they'll be able to have the funeral?'

'Well, the body's in so many bits and pieces that I shouldn't think there's any point in keeping it much longer. As soon as the inquest is out of the way, they'll probably get the nod.'

As Jim climbed the stone steps he felt he had been away a century or more. Each door he passed seemed to be a memory from his childhood rather than a year or so ago. His knock was answered by Grace Melia and, though the time since he had last seen her had been so short, he could not believe how she had blossomed. The two other occupants of the room looked up at his entrance. Poor Oueenie looked so weary he guessed she had hardly slept since Sam's death.

'Jim!' she exclaimed. 'How wonderful to see you!'

David, who was feeding the cat, also looked up in delight. 'Uncle Jim! Perhaps now they'll arrest Frank Cootes! He did do it! Everyone knows he did!'

'They're doing their best, Dave,' he replied soothingly. 'Where's Emma?'

'Emma's staying with Miss Bardell,' replied Oueenie. 'We thought it best, there's nothing for her here now anyway.'

He bent and kissed her forehead. She seized his hands gratefully. 'How are things for you?' he asked.

'We're picking up, I suppose,' she replied. 'But it would help if we knew that someone had been arrested. Though being an old copper's wife, I realise it's not easy without witnesses.'

'I don't see why it's so important,' snapped David. 'Everyone knows who did it.'

'Oh that it was that simple, David,' she sighed. 'Though the fact that Cootes has disappeared certainly help points the way.'

'Disappeared?' Jim echoed 'Since when? I've just left DI Bromley at Stones End and he knows nothing about it.'

'Maxie Roff told us about an hour ago. He came round to offer his condolences and see if there was anything he could do for us. He reckons Frank hasn't been seen since yesterday. He says he's got people out looking for him though.'

'He's going to get away, Mum, I know he is,' said David. 'And that just shows how interested the police are. They didn't even know he'd gone! It's because Dad was a police striker, that's why. They weren't interested in him getting a job and now they're not interested in his murder. Well, *I'm* bloody interested and when I kill Frank Cootes, perhaps they might wake up!'

'Don't talk like that, Dave,' said Jim firmly. 'It's stupid and you know it. Everyone is saying Cootes killed your dad because he was always threatening to do it. If you keep talking like that, and anything happens to Cootes, they'll be saying the same about you.'

'I'd be proud for 'em to say it.' He picked up his coat and made for the door. 'At least I wouldn't be like some of his so-called friends who are so worried what Cootes might say that they're too terrified to nick him.' He crashed the door behind him.

'Jim, can't you fetch him back?' pleaded Queenie. 'I'm worried what he might do. He's been like that ever since Sam died. He was supposed to accompany Sam that afternoon but he went to the pictures with Grace. I think he blames himself.'

'We needn't worry about him finding Cootes just yet,' said Jim. 'If he's done a runner and gone to ground somewhere, Dave's hardly likely to find him around here. Frank Cootes is a widely travelled man, don't forget. No, the person I'm interested in at the moment is Maxie Roff. What did he want to know?'

Queenie shrugged. 'Well, you know what Max is like. He can be a charmer when he wants. He said he just came to make sure that we didn't associate him with Sam's death. He reckons he was as devastated as we were.'

'Did you believe him?'

'More or less. He said he was indebted to both Sam and you for saving his life and he wanted to nail whoever it was who killed him.' She nodded towards Grace. 'He said when, or should I say if, we ever get back to normal, then there was a job for both of us at his new place at the Elephant and Castle.'

'Did he say what sort of job?'

'Yes, it would be my old job back again. Beggars can't be

choosers, Jim, and really I quite enjoyed it. I know I have to get on with the rest of my life but that's going to be difficult until they find the person who killed my husband.'

'How about you, Grace, what job did he offer you?'

Grace looked sheepishly across at Queenie without saying a word. 'D'you want to tell him, Grace, or shall I?' said the woman.

'Perhaps you ought to tell him, Auntie. It'll sound better from you.'

'Very well,' said Queenie. 'Well, he wants her to be – what is it, Grace? A hostess? Yes, that's right, a hostess. We haven't discovered what exactly "a hostess" does yet, though, and certainly we daren't tell David. On the other hand, you can see she's a real beauty. It's her decision. Real beauty doesn't last forever, especially in Queen's Buildings. As you well know, Jim, these old flats take a rapid toll on beauty.'

'Queenie, are you really sure you want to work for Max again? People may well think it a little odd.'

'Then perhaps I *am* a little odd but after all the mourning and weeping is done, there's still rent to pay and mouths to feed. All the condolences in the world aren't going to alter that. Most widows say you lack for nothing for a month after your husband dies but after that you're on your own. Wives see you as a threat and husbands as a challenge. If that's really the case, then sod them all because I am going to be independent as soon as ever I can. And if that means working for Maxie Roff, so be it.'

'That may explain your reasons but how do you excuse this young lady? She has all her life before her. Is she to spend her best years working as a "hostess" for that shark?'

'If she had any other choice, perhaps not. But she doesn't have that choice. Oh, come on, Jim, it's all right for you to pontificate, you're a man. You may not have had a privileged background but you were able to make the most of what talents you had. You've worked hard and you've done well for yourself. For a woman it's different. But this young lady has a golden chance to escape. Knowing what I do now, I have no doubt at all what I would do in her situation.'

'And when the bloom fades, what then? Haunting dark railway arches because she's afraid to be seen in the light, at seven and six a time?'

'I'd say that's down to her, wouldn't you? If she had a good start and still ended up under Waterloo station, it'd be entirely through her own stupidity. But if she has to raise half a dozen kids in two rooms in Queen's Buildings, stupidity doesn't even enter into it. She'd be in penury even if she was a bloody genius!'

Jim raised his arms in surrender. 'Whoah! I'm sorry I started. Look, I'm back at Stones End on a transfer in a couple of weeks. I don't want to encroach on you, particularly at a time like this, but if you think I can help in any way at all, don't hesitate to come over and ask for me.'

Queenie looked puzzled. 'Why are you transferring back, Jim, that's unusual surely?'

'It's a promotional transfer. From that date I'll be a chief inspector and Stones End is my first posting.'

'Jim, congratulations! It really is local boy makes good, isn't it? I'm so proud of you, and in spite of everything, I know Sam would have been too. He wasn't at all well when you two fell out and . . .'

'I know, I know.' He took her hands. 'Sam was always my greatest friend and I owed him so much. I would never have joined the police if it hadn't been for him, neither would I have married Jane and . . . oh, so many other things besides. Anyway, don't hesitate if you think I can help. I'll be in touch. 'Bye.' He pressed her hand, nodded to Grace and was gone.

Before leaving for home, Jim decided to call in to Stones End to speak to Wilf Bromley. He wondered if the detective would have heard of Cootes' disappearance.

'No, I hadn't,' said Wilf. 'But I'm pleased you called in, for another reason.' He led Jim down the corridor and pointed to the observation window of the detention room. 'Don't let him see you but take a peek at who's sitting in there.'

Jim placed one eye to the small wire-glassed aperture. 'Bloody hell! What's the young fool been up to?'

Wilf shook his head. 'Well he's a lot luckier than he deserves to be. You know how impregnable that bloody club is? Well, he tried to scale the drain pipe. Not only did he break the pipe and get stuck, but a woman in the club saw him. Apparently he wanted to search the place to find Frank Cootes. He's convinced he's still in there. Anyway, Maxie Roff isn't interested in charging him so after he's cooled down we'll send him home. I just wonder if you'd like to have a word with him before you go?'

'Yes, but before I do that, I'll have a word with Max. Can I use your telephone?'

'Certainly, but be particularly careful what you say. I don't *think* Max is in the frame for Sam's death but I obviously can't rule anything out at this stage so I don't want to jeopardise any subsequent inquiries. Do you think you could restrict your conversation solely to the lad?'

Jim nodded a reply as he searched the directory. Two minutes later Minnie's voice answered and three minutes later Jim was running down the station steps.

'Jim Forsythe!' exclaimed Max. 'I can't tell you how delighted I am to see you again.' He turned to three bored-looking blank-faced men lounging in chairs. 'This is the copper I told you about, remember? The one who once saved my life.'

Their singular lack of interest indicated they remembered the story only too well.

'Okay, lads, leave us for a few minutes. Mister – er, what is it? Sergeant? Inspector?'

'Inspector'll do.'

'Inspector Forsythe's an old friend, we have a bit to talk about. I'll see you fellows later. Take a seat, Jim. You're looking well. What can I do for you?'

'It's about Sam's lad, they've got him in the cells. I take it you know he thinks Frank Cootes killed his father and is hiding here?'

'I'm ahead of you, Jim boy,' said Max rising to his feet. 'Come on, follow me. You can search the place from top to bottom if you wish. It's in a bit of a state though. We're moving to our new place near the Elephant and Castle very soon and I'm afraid we've let things run down a little.'

'I'm honoured,' replied Jim. 'I understand few police officers have set foot in this place.'

'Too well run, that's why,' answered Max proudly. 'If it had been anything else they would have haunted the place but with it being so efficient and no complaints made, it speaks for itself, I'd say.'

'So why're you closing?'

'Sodding London County Council! They reckon we've been breaching fire regulations since we opened. Personally I think it's a right liberty. Other than the odd rocket on the roof during Guy Fawkes Night, there ain't been a sign of a fire. They've got more bloody power than you have, you know!'

Jim smiled. 'They do have a bit, I'll grant you that.'

'Anyway, I shouldn't be moaning about such trivia when our old school mate's still unburied. What do you make of it, Jim? D'you reckon it was an accident?'

Jim rubbed his chin thoughtfully. 'Well, it's true, people *do* fall under trains, fairly regularly in fact. When you think of the innocuous places that are heavily railed, then think that hundreds of people stand unprotected only inches away from a speeding train, it's a miracle there aren't more killed. On the other hand, Sam Diamond was not the sort of man to fall under a train. If you are asking "Did he fall or was he pushed?" I'd say he was pushed. Though whether it will ever be proved, I'm not so sure.'

Jim's observations seemed to silence Max for some time and they had descended to the first floor in relative silence before Jim was aware of a movement behind some boxes. He stopped and turned in that direction.

'Hullo, Mr Forsythe, sir,' came a faintly recognisable voice. 'How are you?'

'Why, Jack Kirton! Hullo, Jack, haven't seen you for ages. What're you doing here?'

'I work for Mr Roff now, sir. And, as we're moving, I'm seeing if there's anything worth taking with us to the new place. Terrible about Mr Diamond, wasn't it?'

'Was indeed, Jack. I understand you were with him when it happened. Must have been very distressing for you?'

'Not as much as for poor Emma. She didn't stop crying for days. Davy's taken it bad as well.'

'So I understand.'

'Do you think I could have a word with him, sir? Me and Gracie were his best friends and I've hardly seen him since the accident. He's taken it so bad he seems to have run wild. I thought it might help him if the two of us could just have a chat, like.'

'I think that's an excellent idea. I'll ask Inspector Bromley as soon as I leave. Even better, why don't you leave with me and we can go straight there when I finish with Mr Roff?' He turned to Max. 'Okay with you, Max?'

'Sure! Anything that gets that David off my back's fine by me. Off you go, Jack, see you tomorrow.'

Jim left the young man in the police station foyer whilst he first spoke to Wilf Bromley. 'The search proved nothing. I certainly went in every room but a dozen or more people could have been circling around behind me and I still wouldn't have seen them. It's like a maze in there and there's so much junk in the disused rooms. No wonder the LCC are closing it down.'

'Now you've spoken to Roff, how'd you feel about his potential involvement?'

'I certainly can't believe he knows nothing. He always had the knack of appearing open and friendly, that accounts for his charm and success. The point is, if he knew *anything* then he would have to have known *everything* because the murder – for that's what it was – would have been entirely because Sam wanted out from Roff. Max wouldn't have liked that at all. Sam would have known enough to put most of them away for life. If I had to guess, I would say that Cootes did it with Max's encouragement. Which makes it vital we find Cootes because without him there's no case against Max.'

'Why have you got young Kirton sitting outside?'

'He asked me if he could speak to Davy Diamond. He thinks he may be able to calm him a bit. They've been friends for years and it certainly could be worth a try.'

Bromley nodded an agreement. 'You may as well take them both with you. We've finished with him here. But unless Kirton can work miracles, I'm fairly sure we'll have Davy back here again. Hang on, I'll get him up for you.'

Moments later the detective led a sulking white-faced youth into the CID office. 'Here he is,' said Bromley. 'Perhaps you can get it into his thick head that we have no desire to keep nicking him, because I don't seem to be able. The more time spent on him, the less time spent trying to catch whoever killed his father, but he doesn't seem to want to hear that. Anyway, he's all yours for now.'

'Come on, David,' said Jim, placing an arm around the lad's shoulders. 'I've got someone outside to see you.' He said his farewells to Bromley and led the youth down the stairs and into the foyer.

'Listen to me, Davy,' said Jim, as the station door swung closed behind them. 'I've got a couple of other appointments and I'm well late. Can I trust you to go home to your mother – who's worried sick about you – and not let me down? Jack will look after you but please, whatever you do, stay away from Murgatroyd's. Agreed?'

David gave a sullen nod and walked off towards home with his friend. Once Jim was out of sight his sullenness vanished and he became sparkingly angry as he wheeled on his companion.

'You're as much to blame as any of them!' he hissed. 'How can you possibly continue to work there after what they did to my dad? I thought you were almost part of our family. Instead you're as bad as any of them bastards!'

'I know how you must feel,' soothed Jack, placing an arm around his friend's shoulders. 'I'd feel the same but you must understand. Yes, I worked there, so did your dad. I was on your dad's side not theirs because we trusted each other. It ain't just one happy little team in there, you know, there are all sorts of little wars going on. Frank Cootes probably drowned Nathan Green. Max doesn't really trust Cootes. That woman Minnie is jealous of half of the women who work there. And I wouldn't trust one of the buggers!'

'Is this supposed to make me feel better?' David replied, shrugging off the arm.

'No, I'm explaining the set-up to you, that's all. But I do have something to say that might make you feel better. Want to hear it or are you still mad with me?'

'Go ahead.'

'If I had to guess, I would say Frank Cootes killed your dad. But, as we now know, Frank has done a runner, though I'd guess Max knows where he is. He'll come back, he always does when he needs money. If I know him, he'll come back before they move to the new club at the Elephant and Castle because he'll be a bit out of touch and won't know exactly who's likely to be where and what the full set-up is.'

'Jack!' exploded David. 'You didn't have to be a fucking genius to know that Cootes done it, and if Cootes done it then Max *had* to know about it, so what're you telling me that's new?'

'Just this. I've never studied anything like I've studied the set-up at that club. For months I had complete access to everything. There's nothing I don't know about it. At first Max thought I was too young to worry about, but when your dad arrived he thought it wiser to move me out with him. By that time I'd discovered Nathan Green was robbing him blind. That was why Max sent Frank Cootes to drown him. Now I can carry on working there and get my wages, they do pay well, you know, and when I find out when Frank is returning, I'll tell you and you can tell Mr Forsythe. With any luck they'll catch them both together. Max won't be able to deny it's anything to do with him then, will he?'

The whole thing was starting to sound a little out of David's depth. He didn't mind suddenly jumping Frank Cootes and taking revenge for his father, but making deep laid plans were not part of his make-up. 'Why can't we just bash him?' he asked.

'Two reasons,' said Jack. 'The first is we can get rid of Cootes *and* Max, with no danger to ourselves. And the second is–' he gave a leer that sent an instant chill down David's back. It was a look he had never seen on anyone before, least of all his best friend. '–*I* can run the place.'

'YOU!' exclaimed David. 'But what do you know about it? You're just a lad—'

'WRONG!' cut in Jack angrily. 'That's what they all thought at first but now they know different. The two geezers in my way were Max and Cootes but with the plan I've just told you I can get rid of them both, Cootes forever and Max for a bloody long time. I can run a club better than all of them put together.'

'But I still don't see how you can run a place like that?'

The leer had gone and was replaced by his customary contrived, slightly lost look. 'I can run it because I know absolutely everything there is to know about everyone there, customers *and* staff. You see, I once found an interesting note-book that Max keeps in his safe. But, most important of all, I know exactly what I want and where I'm going. In addition' . . . he gave a long pause '. . . I'm really quite ruthless,' he added calmly.

Chapter 28

'You're quiet this evening, David,' said Queenie. 'Aren't you going out with Grace?'

'Perhaps you haven't noticed, Mum, but I see less and less of Grace nowadays. I think she's looking for bigger fish.'

Queenie smiled at her son before replying. 'Grace probably thinks she has a lot of catching up to do. She didn't have the happiest of childhoods so I suppose it's inevitable that she'll want to look at what's on offer first.'

'Meaning I'm not much of a catch, I suppose?'

'That's not true, son and you know it. But if Grace is ever going to get out of Queen's Buildings, this is the age she must do it. If she doesn't do it now she never will.'

'So where does that leave me?'

'Just don't force her. It's wonderful to know there's always someone dependable you can lean on. I doubt she'll meet many of those. That will probably be a bigger asset for you than you realise.'

'Oh, so it's good old reliable Dave, is it? Well if that's what she thinks, she's got another think due. Sod her, I'll look elsewhere.'

'David, you are still young and—'

'Mum, I'm nineteen!'

'But you have plenty of time! Fellows *have* time, girls don't. Anyway, let's not argue. Tell me, have you seen Jack lately?'

David thought carefully for a moment. He wanted to mention Jack's plan. Without question Mum deserved to know but then she would almost certainly spoil it by claiming it was too dangerous. He finally disclosed part of it. 'He's keeping a look out for Cootes. Soon as he sees him, he's going to let me know.'

She lowered her knife and fork to the table. 'Okay, so he tells you – what then?'

'I contact Uncle Jim, that's all.'

'David, listen to me, this is very important. A few weeks ago there were four of us here in a close knit family. Your dad is now dead, your sister no longer lives here and I'm terrified something will happen to you. I know it's difficult but until the whole case is solved, I implore you stay away from Jack and anything to do with that place. I'm asking this as a favour to me, d'you understand?'

'One minute ago you told me not to "force Grace", now you're asking me to stay away from Jack?' he protested. 'Do I have the pox or something? In any case, Jack's almost one of the family.'

'*Almost* but not quite. I'm beginning to think there's something strange about him. I honestly can't put my finger on it but just lately I've realised that boy has depths I can't understand.'

David thought they had discussed Jack long enough, anything more and he was liable to divulge too much. It was therefore with no little relief that he heard muffled conversation and footsteps on the staircase. He looked up expectantly and was not disappointed when the knocker thudded and Billie Bardell's voice was heard. Queenie was first to the door. She was quite shocked, never having seen Billie so subdued. There was almost a lost look about her and she appeared to have aged several years. She did not even speak as she entered the flat but simply put her arms around Queenie and buried her face deep against the younger woman's neck.

'I'm sorry I didn't come earlier,' she said apologetically, 'but I just couldn't bring myself to it. Emma has been a Godsend to me and I thank you for letting her come.'

Queenie turned to embrace her daughter. 'How are you, Mum?' the girl asked.

'Not too bad considering,' murmured Queenie. 'But I'm so pleased you've come.' She immediately busied herself making some tea as she attempted to answer the host of questions that Billie had obviously been storing. It was the tenth one that proved to be fateful. 'So the police don't yet know who did it?'

'There were no actual eye witnesses,' agreed Queenie. 'But the number one suspect is apparently Frank Cootes. Especially since he disappeared a few days ago.'

'Disappeared? What d'you mean, disappeared? I've seen him not five minutes ago!'

'S-S-Seen?' stuttered Queenie. 'What, Frank Cootes! Are you sure it was him?'

'SURE IT WAS HIM?' exclaimed Billie. 'Of course I'm bloody sure it was him! I'd know that randy spiteful git anywhere. I've still got marks on my arse to prove it! I saw him walking along Great Suffolk Street as the taxi drove here.'

'But I never saw him, Auntie,' said Emma.

'No, you were looking out the other side of the cab. Frank is not the sort of man I usually take pleasure in pointing out to people.'

Queenie turned quickly to David who was already slipping into his coat. 'Don't do anything silly, David, just go to the police station that's all. If your Uncle Jim isn't there, then tell whoever is in charge. Quick, son!'

Jack Kirton's flat was exactly halfway to the police station and David gave a quick knock on the door whilst passing. His grandmother said she had not seen Jack for some hours but she believed he had returned to the club.

This placed David in a dilemma because Jack had stressed the importance of both Cootes and Max being present. Without that knowledge he could well be jumping the gun.

Now indecisive, he turned from the police station and quickly made his way to the club. He had no set plan but blindly hoped he might see Jack.

Pending the club's move, the main entrance had been padlocked for some time but there were small side-entrances to the building. The one at the end of a blind alley held the most hope. It was in this section that Jack Kirton was carrying out most of his scavenging. At first the door appeared secure but under a gentle push it moved slightly. Praying it would not creak, David eased it open. Once in, he carefully closed it behind him and paused to adjust his eyes to the gloom before tip-toeing down the dark corridor towards the staircase. Before he reached the first step, the gloom in the passage suddenly lifted as the door behind him swung open once again. Pivoting, all he could make out at first was a silhouette. On closer inspection, as the slim figure neared him he could see it held something in its hand. It was a long carving knife.

'Mum!' he hissed. 'What on earth are you doing here? More importantly, what're you doing with that bloody knife?'

'David! Blast! I didn't realise it was you! I just saw the tail end of someone entering the door. You were supposed to be at Stones End station! Why aren't you?'

'I called on Jack but he wasn't at home. I thought he might be here. You still haven't told me why you have that knife!'

'David, leave here this instant, d'you understand? For God's sake, GO!'

'Mum, why have you got that knife?' he persisted. 'If Cootes *is* here and he sees it he'll kill you. Just leave it to me and Jack, he's got it all worked—' He broke off instantly. 'Shush, what's that?' For a brief moment running footsteps could be heard followed by the slamming of a heavy outside door, then silence.

'I don't like this, Mum, something has gone very wrong. Okay, I'll leave but you're coming to the police station with me.'

'No, son,' she said, slipping the knife into her coat pocket. 'Cootes has destroyed my life and I'm going to destroy his.'

'But, Mum, you don't understand! The man's a monster! Supposing he survives your first attempt – what then? He killed Nathan Green and he was a friend, so he wouldn't think twice about killing you.' He put his arms around her. 'You're all I have, Mum,' he pleaded. 'If Cootes doesn't kill you, the law will. C'mon, let's leave it to the law then, eh?' He could see he had almost persuaded her when distant cries echoed throughout the building.

'That was Frank Cootes' voice!' she exclaimed. 'I'd know it anywhere!'

'Mum! Can you smell burning?'

She seized his hand and ran towards the staircase. At the top was a partially open door which led to an area where, judging by the boxes, Jack had been working. There was no sign of fire but the scent of burning was infinitely worse. 'I think it's upstairs,' she said, running towards the next flight. 'It must be in Max's office. My God, we've got problems if it is. There's only one staircase!'

As they reached the foot of the flight that led to the top floor, smoke was billowing down and the heat from the burning wood-panelled walls made it impassable. Screams echoed from the other side of the flames. 'I don't think the flames can have reached them yet though,' said Queenie. 'They're simply cut off. If the brigade get here they still have a chance.'

Clutching David's sleeve, she tugged him back down the

staircase. They reached the street within a minute and the large group that had already assembled opposite assured them the brigade was on its way.

'Did you tell them there were people trapped?' asked David.

'Nah,' said a one-legged, pipe-smoking old man. 'I'm the watchman from next door, I called the brigade meself. There ain't no one in there. They all moved out this morning. You shouldn't'a bin in there by rights. That's trespass, that is!'

'Look, Mum!' said David, pointing at an open door in the adjacent building belonging to Messrs Redmayne and Baxter. 'They got scaffolding all over the place. Perhaps the planks will reach across the alley to Max's windowsill? It's worth a try.'

''Ere, just a minute,' demanded the limping watchman. 'Yer can't go in there wivout my permission. I'm the watchman. I'm in charge o' those premises, I am!'

Ignoring him, the pair raced to the door. Just moving became difficult and when they finally climbed on to the flat roof, smoke shortened their breathing and their eyes streamed in face-tightening heat.

'LOOK THERE!' shouted David, pointing across the narrow alley to a small iron-framed window. The faces of Max Roff and Frank Cootes were pressed tight against the reinforced glass. Picking up a pole he yelled at them to stand clear and thrust it several times at the window frame before it finally shattered and tumbled down into the alley. As the pair gulped gratefully at the relatively fresh air, their blessings changed to curses as the sudden draught fanned the flames into an even greater inferno. Queenie chose the longest scaffolding plank she could find and slid it to the edge of the roof. At first, distant fire-bells caused her to stop in relief but the screams of the men told her there was no time to waste.

'David!' she panted. 'If we run the plank from this

parapet, it may just reach the sill. It's not very wide but it's all we have.'

David's gut feeling was that the plank was going to be a fraction short but anything was better than standing helpless whilst two men roasted just feet away. He and his mother delicately balanced the board across the top of the alley where it was seized by the clawing men who slid it on to the glass-strewn sill.

'Careful!' called Queenie. 'There's only a fraction to spare!' Securing her end as best as she could, she looked up but was appalled to see Frank and Max involved in a life and death fight to be first on the plank.

'FOR GOD'S SAKE, STOP!' she screamed. 'I CAN'T HOLD MUCH LONGER. IT'S TOO HOT!'

Frank emerged the victor as he threw Max back across the room into the billowing smoke and flames. He was quickly on to the sill, then the board, though as he knelt on it, it was obvious that he had overestimated its width and length. In a slow crawl he inched his way across the chasm.

Queenie and David both stretched towards the survivor before David's mind flashed back over the years to the balcony in Queen's Buildings. Instinctively he pulled back, dropping his hands at the very moment Frank reached out to grasp them. One second they were there, the next they were not. The imbalance caused Frank to topple to his left, although Queenie managed to seize his forearm with both her hands. For a second she managed to steady him but there was never any likelihood of salvation with Cootes' weight balanced only by hers.

'LET HIM GO, MUM! LET THE BASTARD GO!' screamed David. 'LET HIM GO OR YOU'LL GO WITH HIM!'

She tried for one second more until her feet lifted clear of the floor. During that time she stared into his eyes from inches away. Emotionless, she opened her fingers and released him and the smouldering board into a canyon of flame and smoke.

As her gaze followed him, she heard David suddenly whisper? 'My God, Mum, look!'

Climbing on to the sill opposite, clothes aflame and begging to be saved, was a barely recognisable Max. Looking down desperately through the smoke, she saw the brigade had already rolled out their tall escape ladder from the rear of a fire-engine whilst many uniformed figures were racing towards the building. Even so, the flames at Max's back told their own time.

'Try jumping, Max!' called David. 'Come on, it's not far. You can do it! You can! You can!' he encouraged as he leaned over the parapet and stretched out his arms.

Queenie found herself repeating over and over, 'He won't! He won't!'

Terror lent Max impetus but not quite enough. Two fingernails did manage to scour the opposite wall but that was as close as he came. By now, the smoke between the buildings was so thick that the watching pair hardly saw him fall. With raw eyes and scorched lungs, they turned despairingly to each other before both losing consciousness from the smoke and the serious burns each had sustained.

As Queenie came to, she was aware she was being carried. Opening her eyes she could see a fireman in a large brass helmet over a smiling shiny face and, a few steps to the rear, her son being carried by another man. The fireman winked at her 'It's alright luv,' he whispered reassuringly. 'I won the toss and got the privilege of carrying you. Not all bad being a fireman, yer know.'

'You should have given me notice,' she croaked. 'I'd have had a bath.'

He laughed as, avoiding her burns, he lay her gently in the ambulance. 'They're going to take you both to Guy's. They'll look after you well enough there. Don't worry, afore yer know where you are, you'll be right as ninepence.'

'I told 'em! Didn't I tell 'em they were trespassin' on me

premises wivout me permission?' came a familiar voice. 'Serve 'em right fer not lis'nin.'

The fireman's prediction of their recovery time proved wildly optimistic as they lay in hospital for several months. The inquest had been furnished with their written statements, though fortunately without their disclosing their real reason for being there, and when finally discharged, they were collected from their respective wards by Jim Forsythe and Grace. Gingerly walking down the hospital steps to the waiting taxi, David idly wondered if people only had cab rides after momentous occasions. In his case a society wedding and after months in hospital.

'I won't stay, I'll just see you both to your door,' offered Jim. 'I expect you three will have lots to talk about anyway.'

Queenie made a token protest but in truth she ached for the sanctuary of her own home around her before piecing her life together again. On reaching her door, Jim kissed her lightly and departed.

As the trio entered the flat, they saw a hand-delivered letter on the mat. 'It's for you, Mum,' said David, running it lightly past his nose. 'Smells nice, I must say.'

'Put it on the mantelpiece, I'll make some tea first. I'm parched,' said Queenie. It was as they sat drinking the tea that Grace apprehensively told her news.

'I've taken that hostess job, Auntie. You know, the one at Jack's Place.'

'Jack's Place!' echoed David. 'What d'you mean, Jack's Place?'

'Jack Kirton of course,' she replied. 'He's opened what was going to be Maxie's club at the Elephant and Castle. I thought you knew?'

'How could I? I've hardly been out of bed for months,' he replied bitterly.

'Yes, I'm sorry about that,' mumbled Grace. 'I should

have visited I know but—' She fiddled with a little dress ring on her finger. 'Well, I knew you'd be angry, I suppose I was afraid to come in and tell you.'

'Afraid? Why should you be afraid?' he snapped. 'I have no claim on you, you can do what you wish.'

'Well, I for one don't blame you,' said Queenie, as she poured out more tea.

'Are we allowed to know what a "hostess" does?' asked David acidly.

'I talk and dance with customers and get a percentage of whatever they spend.'

'How much time d'you spend with them?'

'As long as they want me.'

'And if they want you all night, what then?'

She made no reply though her gaze fell once more to the dress ring.

'So you're a whore?' he announced sharply. 'Whoever wants you, has you – providing they've got enough money, that is. What's the going rate? Is it worth me saving up or would I feel I'd been short-changed?'

'DAVID!' shrieked Queenie. 'Don't you *dare* talk to her like that in my house! Grace is a free agent and owes allegiance to no one. Not a minute ago you said you have no claim on her. Now you're trying to run her life.'

'So what does your gran think about it then?' he persisted as if he had never heard his mother's protests.

'She doesn't know. But if it really bothers you, I'll tell you – she wouldn't like it one bit.'

'Even if you haven't told her, she must have guessed, particularly with the hours you must keep.'

The girl flashed a quick look of desperation towards Queenie before replying, 'She doesn't know because, well because . . . I no longer live there. I've my own flat.'

'YOUR OWN!' he exploded. 'Jack Kirton's really set you up in style, hasn't he? I suppose when trade's bad he sleeps with you in case you get out of practice?'

'Jack Kirton's never laid a hand upon me, or any of the girls for that matter.'

'So he's not only the owner, he's now the perfect gentleman, is he?'

She shook her head in confusion. 'David, you do muddle me so. Look, a lot has happened since the fire. Yes, Jack has certainly changed – in fact, amazingly so. He's more self-assured now, with no outside interest other than the club. He's got rid of all of Max's gang and—'

'—and he's seen the light, got religion, taken holy orders and is hoping to turn all you whores into nuns, right?'

Queenie was on her feet in a flash and slapped two furious stinging blows across her son's face. 'It's all right, Mrs Diamond,' said Grace, rising wearily from her chair. 'I asked for it and I got it.' Then she turned to David. 'For what it's worth, Dave, Jack Kirton never beds any of the girls, for the simple reason they happen to be the wrong sex.'

'My God!' he muttered. 'Whatever sort of place is it?' He seized her arms. 'Do you know I lay in that hospital bed thinking of all the things I would say to you when you came to visit? Even when you didn't come I still hung on to the dream.' He released her arms and thrust her roughly across the room. 'And now you're a prostitute working for a queer.' He gave a short hollow laugh. 'What an idiot I was! Well, congratulations, girl, you've cured me. Now get out. And as you have your own flat, there's no reason for you ever to come here again. Goodbye.'

With tearful eyes the girl kissed the stunned Queenie goodbye and walked silently out of the flat.

Queenie stared vacantly at her son for a moment as she attempted to come to terms with even part of what she had just heard. 'I think you and I are destined not to make the best of our relationships, Davy boy,' she said with an ironic little smile. 'D'you reckon they take mothers and sons in the Foreign Legion?'

It was as she hugged him that she saw the letter again. She tore open the scented envelope and studied the letter in silence before looking thoughtfully up at her son.

'Well?' he asked curiously.

'It's from Jack Kirton,' she said. 'He wants me to work for him.'

Chapter 29

'How is David?' asked Jack. 'I really did intend to visit you both in hospital but I was so busy trying to keep to Max's schedule for opening night that I was spending twenty-four hours a day here. Once I get everything settled, perhaps he can come here with his girl friend for a meal one evening.'

'I would forget that if I were you,' advised Queenie. 'His life-long love happens to be working for you and you're not top of his Christmas card list at the moment.'

'Working for me?' said Jack in genuine puzzlement. 'Whoever . . . Oh you mean Grace! Good heavens! I had no idea there was anything between those two. I just thought she was a kid who happened to live nearby and was fun to hang around with.'

Queenie closed her eyes in mock horror. 'For my money, Grace Melia not only has the best legs in south London but possibly the best everything else. She is arguably one of the loveliest creatures God made! I think "fun to hang around with" is not quite as my son sees her. Anyway, even you must have realised that to offer her a job as hostess.'

'Yes, of course I did. Silly of me. Obviously I can see she's beautiful. It's just that I needed two or three hostesses and she came readily to mind. But I must confess I never thought of David seeing her in a romantic light.' He gave an easy relaxed laugh. 'When I think of Grace Melia, I think of a scruffy dirty-nosed eight-year-old bean pole, not some knockout creature who turns everyone's head. Still, I suppose we've all changed. Speaking of that, how's Emma? I haven't seen her since the inquest.'

'I haven't seen her either, though Miss Bardell – suppose I shouldn't call her that now she's Lady Hathaway – said she has been convalescing well in Devon and is almost fully recovered and hopes to see us soon. Emma's written to me several times and the last letter indicated a serious romance. Who knows? Perhaps I'll be a mother-in-law soon? But anyway, Jack, let's get to the point. You didn't ask me here to inquire about my family's welfare. So what do you want?'

'All cards on the table?'

'All cards most certainly on the table.'

'Good!' he replied. 'My plan is to make this the best club of its kind in London. I'm not interested in any of the other sordid little practices Max indulged in and I'm powerful enough to make sure that no one else thinks of muscling in here. This is my entire empire but it's going to be great. The food, comfort and entertainment are going to be excellent, the girls are going to be class, and everyone I have working here will be 'specially selected. Hence I've dumped every one of Max's old gang.'

'So where do I fit in? I'm assuming I'm not to be a mature hostess?'

'Don't think for a moment you're not still attractive enough,' he said flatteringly. 'But you, my dear, are probably the most dependable person I know. Therefore I'm offering you the job of assistant manager. You will be second in command to Melvyn Flynn, responsible for everything and paid accordingly. What d'you say?'

'Grace did say you had changed, Jack, but I had no idea just how much. What's brought all this on?'

'I have the one thing I've wanted all my life,' he said. 'My own empire. You have no idea how good it is to sit down and be king of all you survey. I've worked and planned for it ever since I can remember.'

'The fire helped though, Jack, didn't it? You'd have been well stumped without it. What did the coroner say caused it – dangerous wiring and kids? Bit fortunate, wasn't it?'

'I know what you're thinking and you're wrong. Just as soon as people move out of buildings kids move in, particularly down Red Cross Street. I don't suppose they did it on purpose but I told Max many times about that top floor *and* the wiring. Bloody death trap it was. Still, you of all people don't need to be told that, do you?'

'No, and neither does my Davy. We'll both carry the scars, physical and mental, till we die. But then, whoever it was did both Davy and me a favour. We each had the intention to do away with Sam's killer. If we'd been quicker in the queue I'd probably be in Holloway prison now instead of here.'

Jack shook his head firmly. 'No, you wouldn't, you've never have had it in you. If you had, you'd never have made that stupid attempt to save them on that roof.'

'They were two totally different situations,' she protested.

'Of course they weren't,' he said dismissively. 'You say you set out to kill Sam's killer? Yet you had the classic opportunity of making sure the task was done and putting yourself in the clear. All you had to do was take your time coming out of that building and sending for the brigade. Instead of which you bloody nigh saved the pair of them and got burnt to death yourselves – and for what? Are you telling me that once you pulled them to safety you'd cheerfully have cut their throats just so you could say "I done it!"?'

'I don't know how I would have done it but as it's cards on the table time, I tell you this. I would never find it hard to kill anyone for murdering my Sam because make no mistake, Jack, that's what it was. It was brutal, it was horrific, and it almost turned the mind of my poor Emma. I didn't enjoy seeing Frank Cootes fall from that plank but if there's any God at all, he had to go.'

'And Max? How did he fit into your scheme?'

'I think Max was probably the cause, though I'll never know the answer to that one. If he was, then he got his deserts. If he wasn't . . .' she shrugged. 'Then it was a sad accident for which neither Davy nor I was responsible. Either way I have the clearest of consciences concerning Maxie Roff.'

'So after all these confessions, are you taking the job or not?'

'Well, I'm not sure I care for all this "responsible for everything" bit. If you've got – what'd you call them? – hostesses, I don't fancy getting arrested for living off immoral earnings.'

'Poor Queenie, you do seem to have the wrong end of the stick, don't you? Our hostesses aren't prostitutes! What *are* you saying? They're normal young women. They may well meet someone in the course of their work whom they very much like. Happens all the time in factories, doesn't it?'

'But we're not in a factory, we're in a club, and a club that actively encourages the sexes to meet.'

'Quite. Now if one of our girls' decides she would like a nice young man to see her home, I can't see as that can be any concern of her manageress, can you?'

'Put like that, I suppose not. So who's Melvyn Flynn and when do I meet him?'

'If you agree to take the job you can meet him right now.' He reached for the telephone and dialed. 'Melvyn? She's agreed. If you'd like to meet her pop up now . . . I'll tell her . . . fine.'

Replacing the telephone he turned to Queenie. 'Be here in a minute or so, said he's heard a great deal about you and is dying to meet you. I have to go out soon so I'll leave Melvyn to explain your duties but should you have any problems, don't forget, you can see me any time. You and

Mr Diamond were very good to me when I was young and it's time I compensated you . . . Ah, here he is now.'

The door had opened to reveal a caricature of a military type. He was a tall fresh-faced upright man of some forty years. He had thick blond hair with a narrow side-parting and curly ends. A meticulously clipped moustache topped a display of teeth so white and perfect that – along with the smile – they had to be false. Below this a white shirt, cravat, flannels and ostentatiously crested blazer perfectly dressed his athletic frame. He held out a well-manicured hand and exclaimed in a sharp clipped accent, 'M'dear! The descriptions, excellent though they were, failed to do you justice.'

Though Queenie's instant gut reaction was 'What a phoney! hopefully her diplomatic 'Very kind of you Mr Flynn' concealed it.

'Melvyn, I told Mrs Diamond that you would explain her duties and that, though she will report directly to you, because of our long friendship she's free to call me any time. I'll leave you two now but all being well, Queenie, perhaps you'd care to start tomorrow morning?'

There was no doubt that she was thrown. Grace had said Jack had changed but still she had not been prepared for such a transformation. She had almost caught her breath at the potency of his perfume and why had he not seen through this poseur who still held her hand? The old-style Jack would not have given him the time of day. 'Er – yes,' she faltered, slipping her hand free from Flynn's. 'Everything else being in order, tomorrow will be fine. Thanks, Jack.'

He patted her arm and clutched Flynn's now free hand for longer than Queenie thought necessary, then left. He had barely vacated the room when she noticed an instant change in her companion. The smile had wearied and so had the owner. Even his voice was not the same.

'You do realise the offer of the open door is just a gesture?' he asked gruffly. 'Because I understand from Mr Kirton you have high standards of loyalty and I would consider it particularly disloyal if you did not consult me first. Before troubling Mr Kirton, that is.'

'Mr Flynn,' said Queenie sharply, 'I think you should realise here and now that I'm not in the habit of scuttling to *anyone* with problems, particularly at work. I would expect to deal with them myself. I assume that's what I'm paid for? If it's not, say so now, then I'll know where I stand.'

Chameleon-like, the veneer reappeared instantly. 'So sorry, m'precious. No offence, I'm sure. Just streamlining proceedings, y'know.'

'Good. Now we've got that straight, perhaps you'll tell me my duties.'

For the next ten minutes Flynn laid out the requirements but she knew he was waffling. He was trying to pick up more from her in his questioning than he could ever impart in his answers. It was Queenie who finally cut the interview short by deciding she would be better to work on a trial basis.

'Okay,' she said, rising to her feet, 'I think I've got the gist. If you're still agreeable I'll see you tomorrow at 8 a.m.?'

'Ten is more suitable. But take the keys in case you need to come to my room to wake me. There are few things to be done at eight that cannot be better accomplished at ten. Don't you think so, m'dear?'

'Early hours don't bother me, Mr Flynn. But till ten then. Goodbye.' On reaching the door she turned for a moment. 'By the way, my name is Diamond, Mrs Queenie Diamond, It's not *precious*, it's not *dear*. Neither yours nor anyone else's.'

'More's the pity,' he said condescendingly. 'A sweet young thing like you should most certainly be someone's dear. Perhaps we'd better work on it?'

Seething with indignation, Queenie fumed every step of the way home until the final flight of stairs to her flat from where she could clearly hear the voice of her daughter. In spite of her exertions she fairly skipped the last half flight whilst fumbling nervously for her key. They had heard her steps and the door was opened quickly for her.

'Emma, my darling!' she cried. 'How well you . . .' Of her daughter's physical well-being there appeared no doubt, but then pregnancy suited some girls more than others. In Emma's case she positively bloomed. They stood locked in an embrace for several minutes whilst Queenie tried to think of a question that did not end with '. . . and what the hell have you been up to?'

'Well, come on,' said Billie. 'You've obviously noticed. Let's get it over and done with before the small talk begins.'

Queenie released her daughter and closed her eyes. 'Let me alone for a minute,' she mumbled through trembling lips. 'I think I would have preferred notice of this.'

'Please, Mum, please!' cried Emma, who attempted, kitten-like, to snuggle back against her mother.

But for what seemed an eternity, Queenie remained immobile. Slowly, painfully slowly to Emma's eyes, Queenie began to move again and resumed the embrace. 'Okay, Emma, I've decided to sit down and be brave about this, so make some tea and tell me about it.'

'This sounds the right time for a devoted brother to leave,' said David. 'Because in the absence of a father, it might be me who has to wield the shot-gun otherwise!'

'No problem there, lad,' said Billie. 'If I thought for a moment he'd been that sort of bloke, I would personally have blasted his balls off!'

The culprit, a young sailor recuperating in the Convalescent Home, sounded innocent enough, and if it had been anyone else's daughter, Queenie may even have thought it romantic. But it was *her* daughter, it *wasn't* romantic, and it was time to apportion blame.

'I thought you were supposed to be looking after her?' was her opening shot at Billie.

The old music-hall star gave an exaggerated glance at her

watch. 'Not bad, not bad at all,' she replied. 'Just about fifteen seconds late. I forecasted you'd blame me within five minutes.' She looked across at her nephew. 'I must be losing some of the old magic, Davy boy, what'd you reckon?'

'Not you, Aunt.' He grinned. 'Anyway, I quite like the idea of being an uncle.'

'Well, I don't like the idea of being a grandmother!' exploded Queenie. 'At least not without a son-in-law, I don't.'

'Mother,' began Emma quietly, 'you will be getting a son-in-law and it will be the correct one. He had a relapse and had to go back into hospital, otherwise I'd probably be an honest woman by now. However, they say he should make a complete recovery and will be out in time for . . . well, the christening, I'm afraid.'

Queenie took her daughter's hands. 'Look, I'm not moralising, I assure you, but I don't want you to live like I have had to. I want my daughter and my grandchild to have a different life, a good one. If he can promise you that and he loves you and you're happy . . .' she shrugged '. . . then this granny will happily knit bootees.'

'Hey, I've just realised!' interrupted David as he turned to Billie. 'You're going to be a *great*-aunt! Isn't that impressive?'

Billie gave the tiniest of smiles and slowly shook her head. 'No, I'm not going to be a great-aunt, Davy. In any case, being a great-aunt's not particularly impressive. I know something a whole lot more impressive than that.'

All three looked up quizzically. 'I'm going to be a bloody great-grandmother!'

Though Queenie and David looked confused, Emma gave an understanding nod. 'I always suspected that. When I was a little girl, because I didn't have two grandmothers, I used to make one up. It was always you!'

Queenie gripped the sides of her chair tightly. 'Do I

understand this right?' she asked, bewildered. 'Within the space of two minutes I find I'm not only to be a grandma but now I have a mother – is that right?'

'I'm afraid that's quite right,' replied Billie. 'I would have told you from the beginning but firstly my own mother wouldn't hear of it. Secondly, because of the way I performed on the stage, it was better that I didn't get a reputation for being a mumsy type. Then slowly the thing began to feed off itself. I kept telling myself I would find a time to tell you but I always lacked courage. I wouldn't even have told you then if David hadn't asked me a direct question at such a vulnerable moment.'

'I could kill you!' exclaimed Queenie. 'All these years and you never mentioned it! You actually threw me out of home once!'

'I know, that came of not being your "proper" mum. Leastways, that's my excuse.'

'But why did you make such a play for . . .' began Queenie, before realising her children were present.

'Our dad?' cut in Emma. 'We weren't blind, you know, Mum. All four of us kids used to talk about it when we were little, didn't we, Dave?' He nodded.

'I'm afraid there was the simplest reason on earth for it. Looking back, I'm not proud of it but it's a fact nevertheless. There was something about Sam that really got to me. If I knew what it was it wouldn't have happened, but I didn't and it did. That plus the fact that deep down I was always a good-natured slut is about the only excuse I can offer. Any case, as I'm soon to be a great-grandmother I'm changing my ways. I'm now going to suppress all my sexual energy so I can be a riot in the old folks' home.'

'So who is, or was, my father?' asked Queenie.

'Well, it wasn't Lloyd George if that's what you hoped! Though he did try once. It wasn't even a wicked Sir Jasper. It was in fact a young sergeant in the Lancers, but the more I got to know him the more I realised – because of his jealousy – it wouldn't have worked. Out of sheer curiosity I did try to find him a couple of times but he vanished somewhere out in the great British Empire never to be heard of again. Sorry I can't give you a happier ending than that.'

'You certainly did the right thing there,' murmured Queenie ruefully. 'Leaving him, I mean. Fancy being jealous *and* married to you! It's like lighting a fire in a dynamite factory.'

'If you've quite finished knocking your mother,' said Billie icily, 'do you think we could now discuss your daughter?'

'Discuss?' echoed Queenie. 'Nice of you to let me in on it but it's a bit late for discussion, I'm thinking.'

'Not at all. She's going to need accommodation and he's going to need a job. I can offer both. Cedric needs a reliable man who can turn his hand to most things and we have a mews flat to go with it. I didn't want you to think the decision had been made without you, that's all.'

'But the decision *has* been made without me, surely? I take it he's agreed and she's agreed, so what else is there to say?'

'You know,' said Billie thoughtfully, 'I think I know now why I kept the secret so long. You only found out five minutes ago and already you've picked two fights with me.'

For the first time since her arrival, Queenie's face broke into a real smile. Walking across the room, she placed one arm around her daughter and the other around her mother. 'I'm pleased he's a sailor, it somehow makes it all right.'

'Don't I figure in this?' asked David. 'Because I'd like to know where I stand. Am I being led to believe that I now have a very rich grandfather? If so, tell me. After all, I would like to know exactly who I need to keep in with.'

'Well, you may be in with chances there, Davy,' replied Billie. 'Because the pair of you certainly have something in common.'

'What's that?' asked the young man curiously.

'You're both a couple of mercenary buggers! Tell you what, though, you've given me an idea. Why don't we all go back to my place for the rest of the evening to celebrate our new family members? I'll get the taxi to run you back here later.

'What d'you say, Queenie?'

She shook her head slowly. 'I'm not being a wet blanket, honestly,' she said. 'But apart from starting a new job in the morning, it's been quite a day for me one way and the other. I'd like to sit down quietly on my own and sort out my thoughts. I really would love to come but another day, eh?'

'Promise, Mum?' asked Emma.

'O' course, dear. But don't let that stop Davy going. We all know he'd love to.'

'Thanks, Mum!' he replied enthusiastically. 'Sure you don't mind? I won't be too late.'

'Not at all. Stay as long as your "grandfather" will have you. It'll be nice to enjoy a bit of peace and quiet for a change.'

They said their goodbyes and there was a particular warmth in the kiss exchanged between Queenie and Billie though, almost before the footsteps had faded down the stairs, Queenie afterwards slumped exhausted into the chair.

As she sat she wondered what Sam would have made of it all, and as she mused her eye was caught by an opened official-looking buff envelope wedged behind the mantel-piece clock. Climbing wearily from the chair, she discovered it was addressed to David. She was about to replace it when her curiosity got the better of her. Even though she was the only person in the room, she glanced guiltily about her before slipping out its contents. It was a letter from Scotland Yard inviting her son to report to Peel House Training Centre three Mondays hence.

What a day! In spite of his bitterness, she knew Sam would have been proud. If things had only turned out differently perhaps they could even have been serving at the same station. She was glad now that she'd stayed at home and was just losing herself in a doze when she thought she heard running footsteps on the staircase. Living so high, running footsteps were a rare occurrence and sometimes only caused by children playing. Yet the hour was late and these were not child's steps, nor child's sobs! As the knocker urgently crashed, she moved towards the door.

'All right, all right, I'm coming,' she said as she opened it gingerly. As she did, it was pushed wide and a sobbing, bloodstained, half-naked Grace Melia fell screaming into the room.

Chapter 30

'My God, Grace! Whatever's happened to you?' Queenie eased the girl to her feet and laid her gently on David's bed. The girl threw her arms around Queenie's neck and shuddered uncontrollably.

'C'mon, darling,' she encouraged. 'Pull yourself together, there's a love.' She patted her and began carefully to peel away the remnants of her clothing. 'Listen,' she whispered as she saw her wounds, 'I'll heat some water and clean you up. You have some nasty cuts and bruises.'

'No! Please don't leave me!' cried the girl hysterically.

'I'm not leaving you,' soothed Queenie, prising away the clutching hands. 'I'm just crossing the room to heat the kettle. I'll be back in seconds, honest.'

'Promise?' Grace begged.

'Of course, my pet.' As Queenie moved towards the sink her eyes began to take in the extent of the girl's injuries. There were several abrasions to the face and she was obviously going to develop at least one black eye. Her top lip was split and so was the base of her left ear. Deep scratches ran across the side of her rib-cage up to and across her left breast, whilst grazes and scratches abounded across her hips and thighs. With the gas ring soon roaring beneath an old iron kettle and a saucepan, Queenie was back at the girl's side.

'I'm going to put a towel beneath you because I'll need to clean you up. But first I'll put the covers over you while we wait for the water. Lift up, pet.'

Slowly, as the hysteria subsided, the girl calmed. Minutes later, with a bowl of hot soapy water, Queenie sat at the side of the bed and began the task of attending to the wounds. 'Who did this to you, Grace, a client?'

The girl did not answer but shook her head vigorously. 'Who then?' persisted Queenie. 'Because you need to go to hospital and to the police with these injuries.'

The girl opened her eyes wide in terror, 'No! No, please!' She clutched at Queenie's dress with renewed intensity. 'No, I mustn't. He said he'd kill me if I did that.'

'Who did it to you? You must tell me!'

At first the girl did not reply, but then pulling Queenie's head down, whispered, 'Melvyn Flynn did it. But you must promise to say nothing.'

'But, darling, you can't let him get away with this! He could have maimed you for life. Don't worry, I'll see he doesn't hurt you again.'

'Oh, but he won't. I'm not worried about him. He's not in a state to do anything, he's dead!'

'DEAD! Look, Grace love, I don't understand. 1 thought you just said he threatened to kill you if you told anyone? Anyway, who's killed him?' As the answer came of its own accord, she clapped her hands to her face. 'Jack Kirton? Did Jack kill him? He did, didn't he?'

The girl nodded.

'Listen to me, Grace,' said Queenie as she carefully sponged the girl's face, 'it's vital I know the whole story. Take your time but tell me exactly what happened.'

She swallowed hard and appeared to be gathering her senses before replying. 'I was at home because the club's closed on a Sunday but Flynn had sent a message for me to see him urgently. He said he had received a complaint from a client that I was cold and emotionless. He said as the place was empty he was going to teach me some passion. He locked the door but I refused to let him touch me. At first he just slapped me around a bit. I told him that I would tell

Jack when he returned. He said Jack was a queer and wouldn't give a damn. I said I wasn't just a hostess, I had been a friend of Jack's since we were kids.'

She gulped a glass of water. 'He said that Jack would never believe me because he and Jack were . . .' she faltered. 'Well you know. I don't really understand that sort of thing. I said that I would still tell Jack that he had knocked me about. That seemed to do it. He suddenly went mad and kept beating me and I honestly thought he was going to kill me. He ripped my clothes off and finally got me to the floor. He was in the middle of raping me when the door burst open and Jack rushed in.'

'Oh, my poor Grace!' said Queenie, cuddling the girl tightly. 'My poor, poor kid.'

'Jack pulled him off me and called him a traitor. Jack said he had thought that Flynn was in love with him, instead he finds him raping me. He said he was going to throw him out on the streets but Flynn said he wouldn't dare because he knew too much about Jack and how Jack killed Sam and—'

'WHAT!' gasped Queenie. 'Killed Sam? Who? Jack Kirton killed Sam?'

'That's what Flynn said. Anyway, that seemed really to send Jack mad because he flew at Flynn and kept punching and kicking him. Even when he fell behind the settee and I couldn't see any more, he was still doing it. Eventually he came over to me and told me to get dressed and forget what I had heard because he had had no choice about Sam and if I told anyone he would kill me too.

'It was difficult to dress because most of my clothes were in ribbons and I hurt so much I thought he was going to let me go but suddenly he started to cry and said that he wished we were all kids again and that we'd never grown up. He went to a cupboard and took out a bottle of scotch and started to drink. I've never seen him drink before, I'm sure he's not used to it. He insisted I drink as well but I don't like the stuff and kept pouring it under the desk. I kept asking him if I could go and eventually he passed out and I managed to get away and run here.'

'What happened to Flynn?'

'Dunno, still there, I suppose. I was too frightened to look.'

'Grace, this is so very important. Are you absolutely sure he said he "had no choice". Think very carefully now.'

'Oh, yes, I remember it very clearly. It was when he told me he would also kill me. I'm not likely to forget that in a hurry.'

'Look, Grace, you must have these wounds properly attended to and we'll have to report it to the police. Especially if someone's dead.'

'No, no! Oh, please no, don't! I'm so frightened. I was hoping to leave all this behind me and start afresh. I'll never be able to do it now, Aunt Queenie, will I?' She threw herself forward and sobbed uncontrollably on Queenie's breast.

The years suddenly fell away for the woman as she remembered soothing many a grazed knee for her in many a tumble at the park. Kissing the top of Grace's head, she whispered, 'You lie down and sleep for a while. Meantime, I'll go and see what's really happened. Perhaps Flynn wasn't as badly injured as you thought. You won't be disturbed and I promise I'll not be long. When I come back, we'll have another look at those injuries of yours and make our decision then, okay?'

The girl tearfully agreed and Queenie kissed her once more and slipped quietly out of the flat.

If anyone ever asked her about the journey through the dusk from her home to Jack's club, she could never recall it. She remembered closing her own front door then blind fury occupied the whole of her being until she found herself turning the key in the lock at Jack's Place. The Sunday cleaners had done their job well because the whole building smelt clean and fresh though there was no sign of life. She climbed the stairs to Jack's office and saw the door was closed. She paused for a moment before deciding to walk straight in.

The room was dark but a bright glow shone from the new gas fire burning cheerfully away in the centre of the wall. There was no doubt that a tremendous struggle had taken place. Apart from the overturned furniture there were still a few items of Grace's clothing scattered around the room. Lying a short distance from the back of the settee, wig slightly askewed, was Melvyn Flynn. Even to Queenie's untutored eye his neck was broken. Overseeing the whole scene was Jack Kirton. He sprawled to one side in a huge leather armchair, mouth open and arm hanging heavily to the floor. His eyes were staring and Queenie's first impression was that he was dead. However, on moving towards him, she noticed his chest heave slightly. This was followed by a long double blink.

'Jack!' she said sharply.

There was no response.

She repeated it several times before a faint flicker of recognition showed in his expression.

'Jack, it's me, Queenie. Can you hear me, Jack?'

'Grace?' he slurred. 'Wharra y'doin' here? G'wome.'

'It's not Grace, Jack, it's me, Queenie. Remember me? I'm your aunt. You do remember your Aunt Queenie – and your Uncle Sam, don't you, Jack?'

'Unnca Sam's dead. He's . . . dead.'

'How do you know he's dead, Jack? Did you kill him?'

'Killed him,' he nodded. 'Had to, y'see. Had to.' He carried on nodding several times before repeating, 'Had to.'

'Why did you have to kill him, Jack? I thought he was your friend?'

'Max an' Frank said . . . dangerous.' He laughed chokingly. 'Was bloody dangerous for them, wasn't it? Y' nearly fucked it up though, didn't cha? Y' nearly saved the fuckers. HA!' He put a finger to his lips and, shaking his head, gave a long, 'Shush!'

'But why did you kill Sam?' she persisted.

'Had to. Y'see, made me ver' important. B'sides no one'd suspect me, would they?' He gave a loud laugh and followed it with another great, 'SHUSH!'

'No, Jack,' she murmured quietly. 'You're probably right. I for one certainly didn't suspect you.'

She looked carefully around the room with the knowledge that no one was expected, until the delivery men early next morning. Picking up a bottle with her wispy blue chiffon scarf, she poured him another scotch and slid the glass invitingly towards him. 'Have a drink with me, Jack,' she murmured coldly. 'You deserve it.'

He gave a short silly laugh. 'Dunno if I should. Fink I've 'ad enough. Jus' one p'raps.' Her eyes never left him as he steadily drained the glass.

'I think you deserve a long sleep now, don't you, Jack?' she asked.

He grunted what she took for a reply. As he snuggled deeper into the chair, his head was thrown back some way to reveal a white unprotected throat. She wrapped her hand in the scarf and moved it towards an unsheathed letter opener lying invitingly on the desk. Just before she grasped it, the drunken figure gave a short guttural cough.

'Jack!' she said. 'Jack!' But this time there was no reply. Pausing to check his eyes were still closed, she resumed her quest for the blade. As she fumbled in the poor light, her hand passed over it and came to rest on a dead cigar and some matches. She froze for a moment as instinct gave way to cunning. Leaning forward quickly, she pushed the wheeled armchair close to the hissing fire. 'You know all about matches, don't you, Jack?' she muttered, before scattering a dozen of them over the hearth-rug. With a final glance at the now comatose figure, she propped the empty box against his outstretched hand. Using her scarf wrapped around one hand, she turned off the gas fire and, by its dying glow, collected the remnants of Grace's clothing and her glass before watching that sickly white throat fade into the darkness of the room.

With the vanishing of the fire's glow, she again picked up her scarf and deliberately turned on the gas tap. Then she walked calmly from the room, closing the door quietly behind her.

As she approached the entrance to her block, a loud honking of a taxi horn drew her attention. The driver, obviously briefed by her son, swung the vehicle into the kerb alongside her. 'Hullo, sweetheart!' called David from the back of the cab. 'Fancy a ride wiv a posh geezer?'

'I'd bet the posh geezer hasn't even enough money for the tip,' she replied, to the instant consternation of the driver. But it appeared that the posh geezer did indeed have sufficient for the tip. Back at the Buildings it was an enthusiastic David who joined his mother halfway up the first flight of steps.

'It was smashing, Mum, absolutely smashing!' he enthused. 'You must go soon. You'd love the old boy once you get to know him. He's quite a charmer and you'd never guess what . . .' He broke off as he saw her face clearly in the dingy staircase light for the first time. 'Mum! Whatever's happened? And what're you doing out of doors anyway? I thought you were tired.'

'You don't know how ironic that is, Dave. Tired? Yes, I should say I'm tired but I don't think sleep's going to come easy.'

He put his arm around her. 'What is it, Mum? Something's badly wrong, isn't it?'

They were five flights up when she stopped and faced him. 'Don't talk any more until we're indoors. Then sit down, be very quiet and I'll explain everything.'

As she stepped into the flat she put her finger to her lips and peeped behind the bed-curtain. Grace had hardly moved from the position she had lain in when Queenie had left. 'Come into the other room, Dave,' she whispered.

'But who's in my bed, Mum?'

Ignoring his question, she ushered him into her own bedroom and pulled the door to behind them. Slowly and deliberately, avoiding omissions, she recounted events since he had left earlier in the evening. He pounded his fists on his thighs and kept repeating: 'And I wasn't here! And I wasn't here!'

'Never mind that now. We must talk, Dave.' She slipped an arm around his shoulder. 'I've seen your letter from the police. Your dad and your uncle would have been so pleased for you. I think you should go to Miss Bard—sorry, my mother, and ask if she can put you up for the next couple of weeks. I think it would be better if you're not here when inquiries into Jack's death begin, don't you?'

'No, I don't. You did what I should have done, or at least been involved in.' He shook his head despairingly. 'How could he do that, Mum, how could he? We were like brothers!' He rose and began to pace the room. 'I'll go round there and . . .'

'YOU WON'T! You'll do nothing of the kind! Do you think I've done all this for you to go blundering in? Yes, he killed your father. Yes, he betrayed us. Yes, he was at least indirectly responsible for the state of that poor girl in the other room, but all that is squared now. Nothing, absolutely nothing, would be achieved by you storming into that place. If you'd like to do something really constructive, you might try helping that poor kid in the other room to patch up her life.'

'That "poor kid" is a woman,' said the soft voice behind her. 'Maybe not a very bright one but old enough to have deserved everything she got.'

'Grace!' exclaimed Queenie. 'I thought you were asleep.'

'Not much chance of that with you two ranting at each

other,' said the girl ruefully. 'Actually I was awake when you came in but I felt too tired to open my eyes.' She wrapped the bed cover around her. 'Dave can have his bed back now.'

David rose to his feet and opened his arms. 'No, Grace, please listen to me, you must stay. Mum's right.' He placed his hands around her wrists and pulled her towards him. 'What would you say if I asked to begin our friendship all over again? We can get to know each other, go out, do all the things that two people like us have always done. If it doesn't work then what have we lost? I'm certain of one thing. If we don't, I'll regret it for the rest of my life.'

'Good heavens, Davy!' Grace said. 'That's sweet of you but I haven't been away in the Girl Guides, you know. I've been—'

'I know what you've been and I know where you've been. But I also know why.' He shrugged. 'If I'd been born female, who's to say I would have done different? Anyway, what's past is past. Are you prepared to give it a go?'

'Prepared?' She gave the merest hint of a smile. 'Prepared – no. Want to – yes.'

'Good, then the first thing is for you to put on some of Mum's clothing, because you're coming to Guy's to get those wounds seen to, young woman.'

'But the police!' she protested. 'What will they say?'

'Who knows? You haven't been shot or stabbed so it's possible they may not even be interested. But if they are, then we'll cross that bridge when we come to it.'

Queenie had already begun to move the clothes around in her cupboard. 'Not sure if I've much that fits you, Grace, I'm afraid. But if you tuck in a jumper, pin a skirt and turn up a coat collar, you could just possibly make it to the casualty department I suppose.'

For the second time that long night, she fell exhausted into the fireside chair as the others left for the hospital. She had tried to put the potential repercussions of both Jack's and Flynn's death out of her mind but it had not worked. Yet somehow she must have slept because just before daybreak David woke her on his return. 'They think her wounds are basically superficial but they're keeping her in for a few days to be sure. You don't mind, Mum, do you?'

'What, if they keep her in hospital?'

'No! I mean, do you mind if I become serious over Grace again?' He gave a little laugh. 'Not that I've ever really been anything else.'

'I've always liked Grace very much, son. In my own youth I may have been a little too idealistic to do what she did, but since then I've experienced such grinding poverty that I'll not blame anyone for doing anything to escape it. Remember that, Davy, particularly when things aren't going well and you may find yourself speaking thoughtlessly. Look after her because she's really a good girl and it's always the women who suffer longest.'

'I'll not throw anything back at her if that's what you mean, Mum. But meanwhile, I think it's time you went to your proper bed.'

To her surprise Queenie slept well and did not stir until she heard David moving around in the next room. He opened her door with his foot and presented her with a cup of not very good tea. 'I'm off to work now, Mum. I'll go straight to hospital when I've finished so don't worry. I'll eat at a coffee stall.'

As she lay after his departure she began to assess her situation. She had never actually started work at Jack's club so she could hardly be missed. On the other hand, if anyone knew she *was* due to start – but had never arrived – awkward questions could be asked. So she decided to return to the club as if nothing had happened. Ten, Melvyn Flynn had said. Well, there was still plenty of time. She glanced at the clock and wondered at her lack of remorse.

There was a solitary policeman outside the front door of the club and after asking her business, he told her to wait whilst he inquired inside. It was some fifteen minutes before a particularly young detective emerged. Her first impression was that he was 'pretty'. She suddenly realised she must be really ageing if she had decided *any* policeman could be so classified. He asked about her connection with the club and she told him of her prospective employment. 'Well, everyone's right busy now. But I'll take your name and address and someone will call on you for a statement. Okay?'

It was mid-afternoon before the 'someone' came and it was Jim Forsythe who climbed the steps. 'One of us has to move off this manor,' he said wearily. 'I can't keep climbing these damn' stairs. I'd forgotten just how many there are.'

Although Queenie had not expected him because he was now senior man at Stones End, she was not completely surprised. She had even rehearsed her statement well enough for him to compliment her on it's clarity. After she had signed it, they relaxed and updated each other on their news, with him showing particular interest in Emma's impending motherhood.

'Still no sign of you settling down, Jim?' she asked.

'There has been the occasional lady, I must confess,' he said lazily. 'But somehow something always seemed to be lacking.' he shrugged. 'I only wish I knew what it was.'

'I should think you'll know soon enough when it strikes,' she replied. 'Anyway, let's change the subject. What's emerged so far about this particular drama?'

'Well, there's no doubt whatever that Kirton killed Flynn. But it's Kirton's death that's the mystery. He'd certainly had a great deal to drink, too much in fact, but it's strange that someone who had enough savvy to batter a man to death was incapable of lighting a well-fitted gas-fire. We tried it on several occasions and it always lit first time and easily. Yet there wasn't even a dead match to be seen. Perhaps the pathologist can help. I'm on my way to the post-mortem when I leave here. Incidentally, as you were one of the last to see Flynn alive, I'm afraid you'll need to attend the inquest. It'll be in a week or so I'd guess. Don't worry, it's only routine and I've never had a witness hanged yet.'

It was in fact two weeks before the inquest was held. By that time Grace had been discharged from hospital and David had taken a few days off work before he reported to the police training school. The pair of them sat reassuringly either side of Queenie in the drab waiting room to the Coroner's Court near London Bridge. After some thirty minutes the door opened and a stout bewhiskered constable boomed: 'MRS QUEENIE DIAMOND, THIS WAY PLEASE!' The youngsters gave her a quick squeeze of each hand as she rose from the bench and walked white-faced into the court.

An usher furnished her with a Bible and, after taking the oath, she turned expectantly to the coroner. 'You are Mrs Queenie Diamond and you live at number 25 Queen's Buildings, Collinson Street, London SE1. Is that correct?'

'Yes, sir.'

'I understand you last saw the deceased, Mr Melvyn Flynn, at around midday on Sunday the twenty-first . . .' The voice droned on and all that was required of her was to slot in the occasional 'Yes sir' and 'No sir'. After three or four minutes, he seemed to have all the yes's and no's he required and finally peeked at her over his pince-nez and smiled. 'Thank you, Mrs Diamond, you may stand down.'

She was followed in the box by Jim Forsythe, who, after giving his name and rank, said that first impressions were that the deceased turned on the gas but, owing to his inebriated state, lost consciousness before he could light a match, thereby gassing himself. However, after a post-mortem, the pathologist had come to a different conclusion which he would now explain to the court. Queenie dug her nails hard into the palm of her hands.

A portly but smart middle-aged man strode briskly to the

witness box and confirmed himself the pathologist. After laying out some notes he recited his anatomical findings as calmly if he was describing the view from a bus. Queenie soon lost most of his detailed dialogue but it was his summing up that really caught her attention.

'. . . so you see, sir,' he concluded to the coroner, 'whether the deceased did or did not turn on the gas tap is purely academic. Gas had nothing to do with his death. There was not a trace of coal gas in his lungs. He died by choking on his own vomit. With his head hanging back so far from the chair, he simply asphyxiated.'

The coroner then thanked him and preached a blessedly short, if predictable, sermon on the evils of drink before bringing in a verdict of Accidental Death.

'I don't understand,' whispered Queenie to the smiling Jim. 'What does it mean?'

He took her arm and escorted her to a quiet corner of the waiting room. 'It means, my dear Mrs Diamond, that the unaccustomed drinking made him sick. Vomit made him choke and choking killed him – finito! It's not at all unusual in drunks, especially one who's not used to drink.'

'So is that finally it?'

'That most certainly *is* it,' he assured her. 'Jack Kirton is now history, together with his less than illustrious predecessors, Frank Cootes and Maxie Roff. The serious crime book at Stones End will now hardly be ruffled until some other bloody tearaway decides to fill the vacuum. Anyway, come over the road to The Crown for a drink, I think I might have a job for you.' He turned to the two youngsters and said pointedly, 'I'm sure you two have more interesting things to do than listen to a job offer, am I right?' Grace, being the first to understand, tugged the puzzled David in the opposite direction and waved a cheery goodbye.

As they settled in the corner of the saloon bar, Queenie was the first to speak. 'Okay, what is it? I hope it's good because I'm out of work yet again.'

'How d'you like to work for me?'

'You? Where, at the station?'

'No, at my flat.'

'You want a cleaner?'

He shrugged. 'A cleaner, cook, partner, wife. The pay's lousy and the hours long but you'd get the odd bonus and you'd never be more appreciated . . . or loved,' he added with a smile.

Tears welled in her eyes as she buried her head against him. 'I don't believe this is happening to me but I'm going to take it quick before you change your mind.'

'Good!' he exclaimed as he lifted her face. 'Do you mind being kissed in a pub?'

'Only by strange men,' she replied. 'You're not a strange man, are you?' She put her arms around his neck and kissed him long and hard. 'No, you're not the least bit strange, in fact you're almost normal. Okay, mate, test's over. You can now kiss me.'

He laughed and slipped his hand into his coat pocket. 'I've got a little present for you.' He uncurled his hand to reveal a wispy blue chiffon scarf.

'I'd give you a reference any time, sweetheart. That old brass gas tap was fair spotless, I've never seen a cleaner one. Gleamed like gold it did, just like bloody gold.' He tilted his head thoughtfully. 'Just as well Jack Kirton didn't hang around long enough to see it though. He might have been so impressed you'd still be working for him!'

More Enchanting Fiction from Headline

BORN TO SERVE

Josephine Cox

'I can take him away from you any time I want.'

Her mistress's cruel taunt is deeply disturbing to Jenny. But why should Claudia be interested in a servant's sweetheart? All the same, Jenny reckons without Claudia's vicious nature; using a wily trick, she eventually seduces Frank, who, overcome with shame, leaves the household for a new life in Blackburn.

Losing her sweetheart is just the first of many disasters that leave Jenny struggling to cope alone. When Claudia gives birth to a baby girl – Frank's child – she cruelly disowns the helpless infant and relies on Jenny to care for little Katie and love her as her own.

Despite luring a kindly man into a marriage that offers comfort and security to them all, Claudia secretly indulges her corrupt desires.

Always afraid for the beloved child who has come to depend on her, Jenny is constantly called upon to show courage and fortitude to fight for all she holds dear. In her heart she yearns for Frank, believing that one day they must be reunited. When Fate takes a hand, it seems as though Jenny may see her dreams come true.

'Driven and passionate, she stirs a pot spiced with incest, wife beating . . . and murder' *The Sunday Times*

'Pulls at the heartstrings' *Today*

'Not to be missed' *Bolton Evening News*

FICTION / SAGA 0 7472 4415 4

More Compelling Fiction from Headline:

JOSEPHINE COX

JESSICA'S GIRL

In the grand tradition of Catherine Cookson

'Don't let him break you, child'

Despite her beloved mother's deathbed warning, Phoebe Mulligan has no choice but to throw herself on the mercy of her uncle, Edward. Wrenched from all she holds dear, the tragic young girl is delivered to Blackburn town, where she must live in a household terrorised by the cold, forbidding presence of her mother's brother.

Phoebe cannot understand why she is treated so harshly by Edward Dickens. She is not to know the guilty secret that lies in his past, a secret that casts its sinister shadow over his feelings for his lovely niece.

But Phoebe's spirit will not be broken. Her natural warmth and cheerfulness win her many friends and although she must endure horror and heartbreak, all the riches a woman can have come within her reach.

'Cox's driven and passionate book... stirs a pot spiced with incest, wife beating... and murder.'
The Sunday Times

Don't miss Josephine Cox's other sagas of North Country life: HER FATHER'S SINS, LET LOOSE THE TIGERS, WHISTLEDOWN WOMAN, ANGELS CRY SOMETIMES, TAKE THIS WOMAN, OUTCAST, ALLEY URCHIN, VAGABONDS and DON'T CRY ALONE all available from Headline.

FICTION/SAGA 0 7472 4112 0

More Enthralling Fiction from Headline:

HARRY BOWLING

Backstreet Child

Carrie Tanner's transport business in Salmon Lane is prospering by 1939 and she has earned the grudging respect of her business rivals, even the Galloways, father and son, who have played such a fateful role in the Tanner family's fortunes. The years have been kind to Carrie and her deep love for Joe Maitland has helped him through the darkest times of prison and his alcoholism. But the scars she bears from the long-running feud with the Galloway family are deepened by her daughter Rachel's blossoming love for Geoffrey Galloway's illegitimate son.

Personal feuds though are overshadowed by the outbreak of the Second World War, which brings the terrors of the Blitz to the Tanners' neighbours: enterprising Maurice Salter, and his three daughters; publican Terry Gordon with his guilty secret and his wife Pat, who has had her eye on Billy Sullivan since his wife and children were evacuated; Josiah Dawson, out from the Moor, and his wife, long-suffering Dolly, and simple son, Wallace.

Drawing on all their reserves of courage and humour the close-knit community is determined to survive the difficulties of poverty, rationing and nightly air raids. Even as, one by one, the men are called up, go missing in action or are killed, and homes are bombed, their extraordinary spirit shines through.

Don't miss Harry Bowling's previous Cockney sagas, THE GIRL FROM COTTON LANE, GASLIGHT IN PAGE STREET, PARAGON PLACE, IRONMONGER'S DAUGHTER, TUPPENCE TO TOOLEY STREET and CONNER STREET'S WAR, also available from Headline.

FICTION/GENERAL 0 7472 4180 5

A selection of bestsellers from Headline

THE CHANGING ROOM	Margaret Bard	£5.99	☐
BACKSTREET CHILD	Harry Bowling	£5.99	☐
A HIDDEN BEAUTY	Tessa Barclay	£5.99	☐
A HANDFUL OF HAPPINESS	Evelyn Hood	£5.99	☐
THE SCENT OF MAY	Sue Sully	£5.99	☐
HEARTSEASE	T R Wilson	£5.99	☐
NOBODY'S DARLING	Josephine Cox	£5.99	☐
A CHILD OF SECRETS	Mary Mackie	£5.99	☐
WHITECHAPEL GIRL	Gilda O'Neill	£5.99	☐
BID TIME RETURN	Donna Baker	£5.99	☐
THE LADIES OF BEVERLEY HILLS	Sharleen Cooper Cohen	£5.99	☐
THE OLD GIRL NETWORK	Catherine Alliott	£4.99	☐

All Headline books are available at your local bookshop or newsagent, or can be ordered direct from the publisher. Just tick the titles you want and fill in the form below. Prices and availability subject to change without notice.

Headline Book Publishing, Cash Sales Department, Bookpoint, 39 Milton Park, Abingdon, OXON, OX14 4TD, UK. If you have a credit card you may order by telephone – 0235 400400.

Please enclose a cheque or postal order made payable to Bookpoint Ltd to the value of the cover price and allow the following for postage and packing:
UK & BFPO: £1.00 for the first book, 50p for the second book and 30p for each additional book ordered up to a maximum charge of £3.00.
OVERSEAS & EIRE: £2.00 for the first book, £1.00 for the second book and 50p for each additional book.

Name ....

Address ....

....

....

If you would prefer to pay by credit card, please complete:
Please debit my Visa/Access/Diner's Card/American Express (delete as applicable) card no:

Signature .... Expiry Date ....